ALSO BY SARAH BIRD

HOW PERFECT IS THAT

THE FLAMENCO ACADEMY

THE YOKOTA OFFICERS CLUB

VIRGIN OF THE RODEO

THE MOMMY CLUB

THE BOYFRIEND SCHOOL

ALAMO HOUSE

The Gap Year

The Gap Year

A NOVEL

Sarah Bird

Alfred A. Knopf
NEW YORK
2011

THIS IS A BORZOI BOOK PUBLISHED BY ALFRED A. KNOPF

COPYRIGHT © 2011 BY SARAH BIRD

ALL RIGHTS RESERVED. PUBLISHED IN THE UNITED STATES
BY ALFRED A. KNOPF, A DIVISION OF RANDOM HOUSE, INC.,
NEW YORK, AND IN CANADA BY RANDOM HOUSE OF CANADA,
LIMITED, TORONTO.

WWW.AAKNOPF.COM

KNOPF, BORZOI BOOKS, AND THE COLOPHON ARE REGISTERED
TRADEMARKS OF RANDOM HOUSE, INC.

GRATEFUL ACKNOWLEDGMENT IS MADE TO RANDOM HOUSE,
INC., AND THE WYLIE AGENCY LLC FOR PERMISSION TO REPRINT
AN EXCERPT FROM "LULLABY" FROM *COLLECTED POEMS OF W. H.
AUDEN* BY W. H. AUDEN, COPYRIGHT © 1940, 1968 BY THE
ESTATE OF W. H. AUDEN.

LIBRARY OF CONGRESS CATALOGING-IN-PUBLICATION DATA
BIRD, SARAH.
THE GAP YEAR : A NOVEL / BY SARAH BIRD. — 1ST ED.
P.   CM.
ISBN 978-0-307-59279-8
1. MOTHERS AND DAUGHTERS—FICTION.   2. COLLEGE
FRESHMAN—FICTION.   I. TITLE.
PS3552.I74G36 2011
813'.54—DC22   2010051495

JACKET PHOTOGRAPH BY JOHN CLARKE
JACKET DESIGN BY BARBARA DE WILDE

MANUFACTURED IN THE UNITED STATES OF AMERICA

FIRST EDITION

The anchor or the arrow?

—QUESTION FROM A DREAM WHILE
EIGHT MONTHS PREGNANT, JULY 1989

> But in my arms till break of day
> Let the living creature lie,
> Mortal, guilty, but to me
> The entirely beautiful.

—W. H. AUDEN, "LULLABY"

To the entirely beautiful mothers
of our entirely beautiful children

The Gap Year

I once believed that I was physiologically incapable of being unhappy while submerged in water. Sunk in a bathtub up to my eyeballs, I was as free of earthly cares as a turtle sunning herself. Yet here I am, wallowing through my tenth lap, feeling prickly and unsettled rather than weightless and dolphin-sleek. Instead of soaring into silent galaxies, I am snarled up in annoyance that my right eye is stinging because these crappy goggles are leaking and that the ladies' aqua-cardio class in the shallow end is blaring "It's Raining Men" and that the flip-turning jerk I'm sharing a lane with drowns me every time he powers past and that because I didn't expose my only child to enough dirt, Aubrey will hit the germ factory that is a college dorm with a weak immune system and that she will die of spinal meningitis.

Although I am a slob and raised Aubrey with plenty of messiness, my worst enemy—Recent Studies—now tells me that I should have gone the extra step and provided actual squalor. Recent Studies says that the absolute best thing for building antibodies is close contact with livestock. If I'd only put a goat in the playpen with my baby she probably wouldn't have asthma today.

I speed up my stroke, pushing my hands beneath me like a Mississippi paddle wheeler, annoyances scattering in my mighty wake. But, persistent as a school of piranhas, the worries and regrets stay right with me and continue nibbling. They have massed for this attack because Aubrey turns eighteen tomorrow. The day before she leaves for college. Not that we'll be doing any celebrating together. She's already made it clear that she plans to spend every second until she gets on the plane with Tyler.

I force myself to ignore the "Hallelujah, it's rainin' men!" chorus and concentrate on the comforting slurp and slap of my hands cutting into the water. I tune in to the stretch of muscles and tendons pulleying in harmony. I pay conscious attention to the shifting mosaic of wobbling squares of late-afternoon sunlight sliding across the turquoise pool bottom. I plan out where I will install the wheelchair ramp after meningitis renders my only child a vegetable.

Is it too late for the goat?

Hydrotherapy is not working. I yank off the leaky goggles just in time to see that my best friend, Dori Chotzinoff, has finally emerged from the dressing room. Dori always says that her last name is pronounced like you're saying, "One shot's enough" even though, for Dori, one shot is never enough. She sashays over with her head cocked to the side, tucking her hair into the retro flowered cap with chin strap that she wears to look *Mad Men*–ish and to save her expensive dye jobs. Her vampire-pale skin is coated with a layer of sunscreen thick enough to mute her many tattoos to pastel smudges of blue and green.

I squint into the sun. "I almost gave up on you."

She gives me a little Mae West pinup pose, one hand on her cocked hip, the other pretending to puff up her hair, and says, "Sorry, Cam, had to gild the lily." Dori kneels down and waits for the guy in the lane with me heaving and whipping himself through the water with a butterfly stroke to reach us. When he's close enough to hear her, she yells out, "Excuse me, sir!"

Ignoring her, he barrels into a flip turn, and for a split second we are treated to the sight of his upturned ass with its black censor bar of Speedo. He is about to push off and blast away when Dori grabs his ankle.

The butterflier—middle-aged once you see his face—pops out of the water. "What the . . . !" He punches a button on his waterproof watch and snarls, "I'm timing my splits."

Alert as a herd of gazelle scenting danger on the Serengeti, all heads—the moms rubbing sunscreen on skinny shoulders, the just-turned-teen girls tanning on lounge chairs, the boys waiting in line at the diving board to show off for the girls—swivel in our direction.

Dori jumps in and informs Flip Turn, "We're sharing this lane."

"What is your problem?" Flip gestures to the lane next to us. "There's only one person in that lane."

Dori puts her arm over my shoulder. "Yeah, but that one person is not my BFF, Cam Lightsey."

Flip starts to argue so I lean my head on Dori's shoulder and say, "Plus, we're lesbians. Sorry." We're not. But it's fun to say. And it ends the discussion.

Flip shakes his head, dunks under the white floats of the lane rope, jerks a thumb in our direction, and announces loudly to the woman in the next lane, "They're making me move."

I grab my kickboard, hand Dori hers, and decree our favorite cardiovascular activity, "Kick and kvetch!"

As we chug past Flip, busily resetting his watch, Dori yells out for his benefit, "Hey, Cam! Sorry for breaking up your romance with Mr. Banana Hammock!"

Dori is like my grandmother Bobbi Mac. Not the piercings or tattoos or broken marriage to the lead singer in an Aerosmith tribute band, but her take-no-shit, get-the-party-started vibe. Spunk— Bobbi Mac was big on spunk, something she didn't think her own daughter, my mom, Rose, had had in sufficient quantity. Spunk is Dori's middle name. Single-handedly, she almost made being a Parkhaven outcast fun. Dori loved to laugh over which mom had "shit the biggest brick" when she dropped casual asides about her years as a member of the all-girl band Tampaxxx. "Triple-X," she'd clarify with a lascivious wink. "I guess you know why."

"So," Dori asks as we stretch out and churn the water behind us with our fluttering feet. "What are we obsessing about today?"

I share my thoughts on brain infections and barnyard animals.

"Yes? And? So? Aubrey gets a shot."

"They have a shot for meningitis?"

"Der. Cam, you're a medico."

"I'm a lactation consultant."

"Medico enough for me. You're supposed to get the shot before you ship your kid off to college. Twyla's pediatrician told me that."

At the mention of her daughter's name, the blotches Dori gets when she's trying not to cry appear like scarlet storm clouds around her overplucked eyebrows. The white sunscreen lightens them to a pretty pink. Her grip on the kickboard tightens until the spongy material dents beneath her clenched fingers and her flutter-kick turns into an exercise in grim determination that propels her ahead of me. I let her surge forward; Dori always needs a few seconds after her daughter's name comes up to put her tough-girl front back on.

Twyla moved out over a year ago to "tour" with Dori's ex and his band, and the only contact they have now is a phone call every few months in which Twyla details all the ways in which Dori was a horrible mother and ruined her life. Then tells her where to send money.

Meanwhile, the inoculation news lets me relax and I frolic through the water, happy as an otter. This carefree state lasts for a lap and a half before the real problem surfaces again and it's not meningitis. My kicking slows to a near halt.

Dori, recovered, her face again uniformly pale, waits for me to catch up, then, commenting on my look of brooding worry, demands, "What? Tyler Moldenhauer?"

At the mention of Aubrey's boyfriend's name, I moan, "A suburban white boy, redneck football hero with no plans for college. If Aubrey's first serious boyfriend had been Glenn Beck, I could not have been more surprised."

"Surprises," Dori repeats wistfully. "So many surprises."

"When did he take over Aubrey's life so completely?" I ask, even as I try to figure out when my daughter turned into a stranger. Six months ago? No, it's been longer than that. In that time, she's become like a guest forced against her will to live in my house. A guest who would happily pack up and leave and move in with said boyfriend if I pushed her even the tiniest bit. I keep waiting for this evil spell to be broken. That it will be like the flu and one morning she'll wake up smiling and help me make pancakes and tell me she'll set the table as soon as she finishes this chapter. That she'll be my little nine-year-old again, the one who saved up her allowance to make me a memory bracelet for my birthday then snuggled up next to me and told me what each bead strung onto the wire coiled around my wrist meant.

"See this?"

"The turquoise one?"

"That's for your favorite color and because you love to swim. This little microphone is for you being such a bad singer."

"I'm a bad singer!?"

"Really bad."

"This one is beautiful. Is it ivory?"

"No! Do you know where ivory comes from? Elephants! Poachers! It's just the color of ivory."

"Right. Oh, look, it's a tiny baby curled into a ball."

"That's for your job and also for me. Inside of you."

"Aubrey, I love it. I love it so much."

"So," Dori continues. "Aubrey's boyfriend is not who you would have picked out of a catalog."

"Dori, he's got her slaving away in a damn roach coach. She's supposed to leave for college in two days and she absolutely refuses to come with me to claim her trust money. That damn trust was the reason I signed off on Martin's—"

"Tsoo! Tsoo! Tsoo!" Dori pretends to spit three times in my direction to ward off the evil eye cast when I invoked the cursed name of my ex. Joking about our exes and being single mom outcasts in the suburbs is how we've survived.

"—screw job of a divorce settlement. I mean, how hard could it be to claim your college tuition? Aubrey knows I can't do it without her. We both have to be present. We could have gotten it anytime in the past two weeks, but will she take a few hours to do this one simple thing? No. She keeps putting me off."

"Maybe she doesn't want to take anything from Martin."

"Who knows? She doesn't bring him up much. Like, ever."

"Can you blame her? Given that the school board is in an uproar over evolution, being the daughter of a cardinal or bishop or grand wizard or whatever of a church that believes we all descended from a race of space travelers isn't exactly the magic ticket to becoming homecoming queen at Parkhaven High."

I glance over at Dori so that she knows I am not amused. "Believe it or not, Dori, something as ridiculous as having your husband leave you for a . . ." I stutter, trying to come up with an epithet strong enough to contain my hatred for Next and have to settle for, ". . . a nutball religion actually makes it more painful, not less."

"Oops. Sorry. Sixteen years. Too soon, huh?"

I splash Dori.

"Hey, at least you lost your husband to something kind of spiritual. Mine ditched me so he could wear scarves and tights and rat his hair up and sing 'Walk This Way.' "

I don't laugh.

"Cam, don't stress. Aubrey is a good kid. Too good, really. She is going to be fine."

Fine.

Our relationship is built on Dori telling me that Aubrey is going to be fine and me *not* telling Dori anything about how *un*fine Twyla is. Dori might actually be the only mother in Parkhaven for whom "fine" really is fine. The only one who doesn't want *super*fine. Superior. Sublime. A five-point GPA and a full ride to Harvard. I know Aubrey is going to be *fine*. Eventually. But I want so much more than *fine*. And I want it to start in two days when she leaves for Peninsula State College.

"What can I do? Drag her to the bank bodily?"

"We all know how the dragging bodily ends."

Dori is referring to the night last December when the roads turned into chutes of black ice and I tried and failed to keep Aubrey from going off with Tyler. That was the first night she didn't come home. But not the last. Ever since Black Ice Night, Aubrey and I have both known that habit, manners, and whatever residual love she still has for me are the only things keeping her under my roof. We know that Tyler Moldenhauer would welcome her with open arms anytime she wanted. So I walk on eggshells with my child and will until the second I shove her onto that plane the day after tomorrow.

Dori splashes along beside me, a living reminder that a child can simply get up and walk out your door and not come back. I turn to her and say, "God, if only I hadn't made those stupid comments about—"

"Do not say 'hat,'" Dori cuts me off. "Cam. I am warning you. You can say 'solar protection apparel.' Or you can say 'brimmed headgear.' But one more time with the damn hat and I will . . ." She circles her raised fist like Popeye warming up to clobber Bluto.

I clamp my lips into a tight seam and press my crossed index fingers against them, *X*-ing out the forbidden topic.

But as I flutter-kick away, all I can think about is Aubrey and that damn hat. That hat was where it all started four years ago. She was a skinny freshman in baggy cotton shorts and a T-shirt, heading off to the first day of band camp, when the hat made its debut. Since the name of the landlocked team playing for her landlocked high school in our landlocked state is the Pirates, the hat was a goofy tricornered number with a giant white plume curling off it.

This had caused me to greet my skinny freshman with an "Ahoy, matey, did your parrot die?"

Aubrey, who'd recently discovered how funny talking like a pirate was, answered, "Aye, me hearty. 'Twas a burial at sea."

Pirates became a running joke between us. When she was a sophomore, I once served her artichokes, arugula, and arroz con pollo for dinner, and we "arred" our way through the entire meal. Sometime during her junior year, though, she stopped laughing when I called her a scurvy bilge rat and threatened to shiver her timbers. I should have noticed and dropped the pirate teasing then.

Certainly I should have ceased and desisted long before the start of her senior year last August. Exactly one year ago today, which was when everything started to spiral out of control. If only I had stopped my stupid teasing, she might have worn the damn hat and *not* gotten heat exhaustion and *not* dropped out of band. Certainly that goofy feathered hat would have immunized her against Tyler Moldenhauer's attention. If only I hadn't persisted in making those moronic jokes. But like a hummingbird returning to an empty feeder, I kept going back for one more drop of nectar, one more shared joke.

The hat, though, that's just a theory. I get frantic sometimes wishing I knew for certain. I think that if I had the whole story, I might be able to reverse the evil spell, cure her psychic flu, and send her off to college with a happy heart. Even if having all the details gave me no power at all, I would still give anything to know what really happened to my daughter on that day one year ago.

It's the first day of my senior year. Well, unofficially, school isn't really in session yet, but the whole band has to be here a week early for "camp." The big marquee sign at the edge of the field where we march reads: AUGUST 12, 2009. 10:43 A.M. 92 DEGREES, WELCOME, BAND CAMP!!!! SCHOOL STARTS IN ONE WEEK!!! . . . WEDNESDAY, AUGUST 19!!!! SEE YOU THEN! GO, PIRATES!!!!

Rivers of sweat run down my back. It is way too hot for all those freaking exclamation points. And way, *way* too hot for Mr. Shupe, who is bellowing at me, "Clarinets, wake up!" I try to focus. "Lightsey, get your section under control! You're a senior now! Start acting like one!"

Once Shupe finishes bullying me and the section I lead, he moves on to torture the freshman trombone players. "T-bones! Did they teach you the definition of 'line' in middle school?" Their section looks like an amoeba wobbling all over the field. Mr. Shupe does not do wobbly. Mr. Shupe does crisp.

Then he tells us what he tells us at the start of every school year about how we are "Shupe's Troops" and the way they did things "in the Corps."

The Corps? Dude, you were in the Marine Corps band.

This fake military stuff makes the band boys feel like they're Green Berets. They are as delusional as Mom, who is always telling me that I am "marching, both literally and figuratively, to the beat of a different drummer" and that "being uncool at Parkhaven is the coolest thing imaginable."

Uh, right, Mom, hang on to *that* dream.

Shupe yells at the percussion section, "Drum line! It's called a line, not a squiggle! What did you all spend your summer doing? Smoking crack?"

The freshman horn players laugh so hard they lose their embouchure. Wait until they're seniors like us and have heard all of Shupe's lines often enough to recite them along with him.

I can almost remember when the first day of band was fun. When it was a thrill to be one of a hundred people all marching in perfect, straight lines. When I loved the neatness and crispness of it and felt like

I belonged. Now, though, it is like that moment when you discover that you're too old to ride the Teacups. That they're not the tiniest bit scary or fun and that even riding them as a joke, goofing on the whole thing, isn't fun anymore.

My fingers drip sweat and slide around on the keys, which doesn't really matter, because I've been faking it for the past hour anyway. My lips are barely touching the mouthpiece. The *air* is too hot to touch. Like I am really going to stick a piece of scorching metal in my mouth. I feel weirdly distant from everything. It is taking more and more energy just to ignore the monster headache squashing my head.

"Lightsey!"

Oops. At first, I think Shupe has noticed that I am fake-fingering and fake-playing, but it is worse than that.

"Where's your hat? Did you not read the three, count them, three e-mails I sent that specified that for today, and today only, everyone was required to wear their hats?"

Maybe it's the weird distant feeling, but I shout back, "Sir, yes, sir! I was unable to find said hat! Sir!"

Anyone would have known that I was messing with him with that fake marine stuff. Not Shupe. He believes that this is how the entire world *should* talk to him—like respectful recruits.

"You're a senior, Lightsey! You have to set an example! It's *Semper Fi*—"

"Not *Semper I!*" I shout along with him.

Yelling at Shupe is not worth the effort, because now not only is my head pounding insanely, but I don't seem to have the energy to even sweat anymore. I am suddenly as dry as this dusty field I've been tramping back and forth on for the past three years. Then everything gets brighter and brighter. When it starts to seem like a flash has gone off in my face, I signal to Shupe that I am stepping out to get a drink of water.

"Make it fast, Lightsey! You need to tune up your section!"

The water station is on the side between our practice field and the football team's. Since it is so hot, the football guys are practicing without pads, just the stretchy tees and shorts they wear under their uniforms, so they look like humans instead of the hulking video-game predators they resemble with their shoulder pads on.

It feels like I've been walking forever, but the big red-and-yellow Igloo cooler of water doesn't get any closer. Then everything turns bright. Really bright. The football players seem to be in a movie that has been overexposed. One player separates from the others and heads toward the water station. He looks like he is running in slow motion through a shimmery mirage. The number seven printed in black on his white jersey floats through space. His dark, shoulder-length hair rises and falls with each step. In the overexposed movie, he looks like an invading barbarian, some warrior from an ancient time.

Then the movie gets even slower and everything begins to float—players, Igloo cooler, goalposts. All the sounds—the tweets from the drum major's whistle, tuba blats, football coaches yelling—they fade farther and farther away. Then I am looking at a pure white sky. Then yummy cool darkness.

"Drink this."

Water dribbles across my cheeks and into my hair. I open my eyes and am staring at a black number seven. With some effort, I part my lips. The water funnels into my mouth and I swallow. Big mistake. It comes right back up, along with the Diet Cherry 7UP and half a bagel with strawberry cream cheese I had this morning. The barfing brings me around and I notice that I have just puked all over Tyler Moldenhauer.

Even though I've spent the past three years marching at every football game Parkhaven ever played in, I made it a point of honor to know as little as possible about the sport. But Tyler Moldenhauer is such a god at Parkhaven that he managed to penetrate even my footballo-phobic consciousness.

"Sorry."

"Why? Did you puke on me on purpose? Keep sipping. You get over-heated, you puke. Simple as that. I do it at the start of every season. Besides, I never saw anyone puke pink before. Is that a band thing or a girl thing?"

I attempt a smile, but it comes out as rubbery as I feel.

He looks up, searching for help. Someone to take me off his hands. "Your band director guy hasn't even noticed yet. Is he blind or what?"

"It's hard to see much when you've got your head shoved that far up your butt."

He laughs and his abs bounce against my ear. When he yells at Shupe—"Uh, man down over here!"—I feel the rumble through my whole body.

Shupe looks over at me, holds his hands up to the sky in irritation, yells, "O'Dell! Acevedo! Get Lightsey to the nurse's office!"

Tyler helps me up as the two girls run toward me. Everyone considers Wren and Amelia my best friends even though we've been drifting apart for a long time. When I am on my feet, he asks, "You OK?" Not wanting to release any more puke breath in his direction, I just nod.

Wren and Amelia reach us. He lets me go, but keeps his arms out, ready to catch me. "You got her?"

I say I'm fine and wave Wren and Amelia away. But when I take a step forward, my knees buckle like Bambi learning to walk. Tyler grabs me. "A little help here," he orders the girls, setting me between them. They feel like tiny pipe-cleaner people compared to Tyler. Like they would crumple if I put any weight on them. My arms around their skinny shoulders, I limp off the field.

The instant we are out of hearing range, Amelia loses it and squeals, "You had your head in Tyler Moldenhauer's lap!"

"OK," Wren blurts out, "that means that Amelia and I are now, officially, the only girls at Parkhaven who have *not* had their heads in Tyler Moldenhauer's lap. Or their faces, at any rate."

At that point, I am supposed to go, "Wren! You're so bad!" and slap at her and get all giddy and hectic. But I can't say anything. These two girls who I ate lunch with almost every day since freshman year, and sat with through endless band trips, and helped through endless crushes, seem like people I knew a long time ago. And never had that much in common with anyway except marching around in a really ridiculous hat.

Since my otter happiness has drained away, I ditch the kick-board and flip over onto my back. The big cottonwood overhead makes a green lace against the blue sky. My arms windmill backward, grabbing for water handholds to propel me forward. I focus on lengthening the glide and finally fall into an easeful rhythm.

The tweet of a lifeguard's whistle ruffles the serenity and I recognize Madison Chaffee at the other end of the whistle. "No running!" Madison orders, and two little girls, formless as baguettes in their fluorescent bikinis, giggle and slow down to a tippy-toed canter. The taller of the two has flyaway blond hair shot through with red and gold like Aubrey's. The smaller one, a sturdy coppery redhead just like Twyla was, yells out, "Sowwy!"

Though the blonde looks like Aubrey at that age and the cute redhead reminds me of Twyla, Aubrey was the one who had the speech impediment; it took years of therapy before she could manage her *R*s and *W*s.

Madison swings down off the stand. She is a streak of long tan legs, sunglasses, a glint of silver from the whistle around her neck. Madison Chaffee used to be part of a playgroup that her mother, Joyce, organized when Madison and Aubrey were in the same mothers'-morning-out preschool program. Joyce decided that we would all bring our kids to the pool on Sunday afternoons when time stretched into a Sahara without the oasis of even a tumbling class.

All the moms traded off hanging out on a blanket in the shade of the cottonwood trees, a veritable grove that used to ring the pool, while one of us stayed in the water and played Marco Polo and tossed weighted rings for our polliwogs to retrieve. I quickly came to prefer Marco Polo over the other moms' discussions of whether the Suzuki or Dalcroze method got better results with the three-year-old violinist. Mostly, though, they all just wanted to hang out with other moms who had quit their jobs and lived in a world where every social encounter their child ever had was arranged by an adult and involved getting in a car. They wanted what we all want: reassurance that they had made the right choices.

I don't know why Joyce stopped inviting Aubrey and me to the pool sessions. Maybe because I was still shell-shocked from the divorce. Maybe because my ex had left me for a cult whose theology could be summed up in its founder's wisdom: "What is, is. What ain't, ain't." With the unspoken coda "Now give me all your money." Maybe because I regularly dropped the *F*-bomb and didn't shave my legs. Luckily, though, Dori and Twyla appeared not too long after the expulsion to rescue me from total pariahhood.

Another lifeguard, a boy I vaguely recognize from Aubrey's senior class, also one of the popular kids, comes to relieve Madison. He stands at parade rest next to the guard tower, legs braced shoulder-width apart, hands folded, vigilantly watching the swimmers as Madison climbs down. Jayden? Brayden? Hayden? I imagine this boy as Aubrey's sweetheart, both of them poring over college catalogs together, shopping for extra-long jersey sheets for their respective dorm rooms, debating whether to take biology first or second semester.

As Madison stands beside the guard tower while the boy climbs up, the highlights of her résumé scroll through my mind: senior class treasurer; a math whiz; performed around the state with her select choir group; spent the first half of the summer in Nairobi on a church mission helping build a pump station; accepted at Duke.

I replay Aubrey's life. This time, I am a permanent part of Joyce Chaffee's group of Moms Who Had a Clue. I shave my legs, watch my language, and stick a violin in Aubrey's hands when she is three. Instead of spending every second with Tyler this summer microwaving breakfast burritos, she is in Africa pointing to something on a blueprint while Masai tribesmen, tall and lean as Giacometti sculptures, tilt in to catch every word spoken by their pale child savior. I hear Aubrey's angelic voice echoing off cathedral walls.

Yes. I decide that these adventures are worth putting up with the suburban moms.

I make this decision as if it were an actual possibility. As if I were swimming through a wormhole, a rip in the space-time continuum, and would find Joyce and her crew nestled on blankets in the cottonwood grove, opening Tupperware containers of Goldfish and carrot sticks, figuring out which camps to sign up for. As if I could still join them. As if Aubrey would still be standing on the edge of the pool at this very moment, tummy round and plump, hair two squirts of pigtail above the goggles strap, hands tucked into her armpits, shivering a little, bouncing as she yells, "Mom. Mom! Watch me, Mom; I'm gonna dive! Mom, are you watching?!"

A continuous loop plays in my head, focusing on me barely glancing up from my book—I had so little time to read back then—and yelling that I was watching. *Dive already and give me two seconds of peace.* I barely tore my eyes from the page—it was *The Handmaid's Tale*! Who could resist?—as Aubrey steepled her arms above her ducked head, curved her fingers, bent over until she slowly toppled into the pool. A moment later, she burst to the surface. "Did you see me? Mommy, did you see me?" Hungrier for my approval than for oxygen.

I'm certain I gave it. Probably with too much rote lavishness. Precisely the sort of knee-jerk self-esteem building that Recent Studies just revealed is the psychic equivalent of feeding your children lead-based paint chips. The overpraising and inevitable blue ribbons have left an entire generation undermotivated and overentitled. Except when they are driven, achievement-addicted anorexics.

I am deciding that, henceforth, I will praise Aubrey only if she's done something to really deserve it. That's when I notice that the single cottonwood above the pool is the only tree left. The big grove was cut down years ago. Probably around the same time that Aubrey's world stopped pivoting on my praise.

I dive underwater and swim down into silence. The whistles tweeting, children yelling, the tinny music, aggravation from Mr. Banana Hammock, my worries about Aubrey and her college money, for one second they all stop. I dive deeper, so deep that slivers of pain crack into my ears. At the bottom of the pool a Sponge-Bob SquarePants bandage floats like a wisp of yellow seaweed and I wish I had bought the Little Mermaid Band-Aids that Aubrey begged me for, instead of always cheaping out and getting whatever was on sale.

I pop to the surface, grab my kickboard, and churn through the water.

At the turn, Dori falls in next to me. "You're doing it again, aren't you?"

"Doing what?"

"Don't pretend. I recognize that expression. That's your regret expression." Dori breaks into her chanteuse mode and belts out, " 'Non, je ne regrette rien!' "

"Look, I completely agree with you and Edith Piaf. And *moi*? My own life? I really have very few regrets. It's this whole other life, Aubrey's, that I was supposed to arrange that I wish I could have a second chance at."

Dori reaches over and slugs my biceps.

"Ow!"

"Sorry, I read where you can interrupt negative thought cycles with a sharp physical stimulus."

"Well, tell your buddies back at the lab that it works." I rub my arm. Joyce Chaffee would never have given me a monkey bump. At this very moment, we—Joyce and I and the other Moms Who Had a Clue—would be discussing what kind of under-bed storage containers to buy our daughters for their dorm rooms.

Dori sees me doing it again. "You are hopeless. Okay, purge, spew, ralph up those regrets. Come on, get them out. You can't control what you can't name. What are the regrets du jour?"

The Secret Garden," I wail. "I always thought that Aubrey and I would read *The Secret Garden* together." I see us as we should have been. Aubrey is eleven. Lanky. All long, skinny legs and bony arms. Just got braces. Her bangs hang over her eyes. We are each in our own cozy armchair, silently companionable in a sun-splashed room that faces onto an actual garden. I have set a tray of tea and cookies on the coffee table. Chamomile with lots of cream and sugar for Aubrey, Earl Grey for me. Lorna Doones for us both, just like the ones I'd eaten the first time I read *The Secret Garden*.

"I missed the window of opportunity. One day I was reading *Amelia Bedelia* out loud to her, and the next she was holed up in her room devouring gigantic, fat books about a girl in love with a vampire."

"Oh, God. *Twilight*. Don't get me started. What is the appeal of that crypto-Mormon sexual-repression shit? Such crap. What else?"

"A cabin in Maine?"

"Okay . . ." Dori is dubious.

"I always thought we'd rent a cabin in Maine for two weeks every summer so that Aubrey would have memories of picking blueberries, and sailing out to a secret island in the middle of an icy blue lake."

"Somehow Aubrey never seemed like an icy-blue-lake kind of kid. God, remember our sad little single-mom campouts?"

"That last time?"

"When that family of jackwad hillbillies took the space next to us?"

"In a Winnebago!"

"Hauling a trailer of dirt bikes. Oh, that was fun. Listening to them revving up the bikes at six in the morning."

"And they used the park's barbecue grill as a stand for the television set they kept turned on all day so loud that Aubrey told us that she liked the 'nay-choo' back at our house better?" I see Aubrey, solemn, steadfast, as she makes her pronouncement about nature. Her sunburned nose is peeling; she wears a Pocahontas T-shirt.

"Stupid idea." I dismiss the whole cabin-in-Maine fantasy. "My busiest season is summer."

"Yeah, all those moms who were drunk-dialing on New Year's Eve need to learn how to breast-feed."

"And it's not as if I've ever made enough for a cabin in Maine anyway."

"So, no cabin in Maine. Boo-fucking-hoo. You get Aubrey to the bank tomorrow, even if you have to do it at gunpoint. Day after tomorrow, you shove her on a plane to Peninsula. Done and done."

"God, I wish that my only begotten child was as clear on all of this as you are." The five-o'clock masters swim class starts trickling in. "I gotta blast. Aubrey should be finished microwaving burritos for construction workers now. I'm going to call and tell her that tomorrow is nonnegotiable."

"You go on. I need to drag my fat ass through a few more laps."

I heave myself out of the pool and pad into the locker room. My wet footsteps dry on the hot cement a second after I leave them.

Heat. That was the whole problem. Aubrey was never really the same after she got heat exhaustion at band camp. I *knew* I should have insisted that she see a doctor.

S ince school has not officially started yet, the assistant principal, Miss Chaney, who wears blazers and keeps a walkie-talkie clipped to the belt of her Dockers, takes me to the nurse's office even though the nurse isn't there, gives me a cup of lukewarm blue Gatorade, then leaves. I hear her talking to the campus cop about spotting potential signs of gang activity as she walks down the empty hall.

I sip the fake-sweat drink and wonder if it is possible that I hallucinated Tyler Moldenhauer cradling my head in his lap, since, although band completely exists for football, no football player has ever acknowledged the existence of any band geek. Him doing that, helping me, is like Brad Pitt stepping out of the movie *Troy*, walking into the audience, and giving some random girl a sip of wine from his golden goblet.

I finish the Gatorade and study a chart that shows the bones of the ear. Though I actually feel fine and figure I must have just passed out from sheer boredom, I sit in the nurse's office and am deciding what my new look for senior year is going to be when Miss Chaney returns and asks, "You OK in here?"

I give her a wan look and shrug.

"Outstanding! Head on back to practice then."

The thought of going back out to that field makes me sick. Actually, physically ill. When I don't move, Chaney prompts me, "You don't need a pass. You're good to go."

As if I need her to tell me that. Me, who's worked in the attendance office for the past three years. She waits for me to jump up and run back out into the heat and dust so that Shupe can march me around. My whole being is so repelled at the thought that I can't make myself move. She's still waiting when she's called away again.

I see my life branch into two paths. One . . . I don't know where One leads. But Two, the other, the one where I go back to band practice, is certain to end up with Tyler seeing me at some point in that stupid pirate hat. And no matter what, that must never happen. I go to the nurse's computer, boot it up, log on with my attendance office aide password, and Google "heatstroke." When Miss Chaney comes back, I report to her that I am "dizzy, nauseated, weak, disoriented, and having difficulty breathing."

Her diagnosis is immediate: "Heatstroke. God, how many times do I have to warn Shupe? You require immediate transport to an emergency room. Let's get a parent or an ambulance over here, *stat!*"

Since Mom is doing her morning consults at Parkhaven Medical Center, I call Dori. Dori lives to be a bad girl. This will be right up her alley.

"Aubsie Doodle," she answers on the first ring. "What's up, buttercup?"

"Mom," I whimper as Chaney eyes me sharply. "Can you pick me up? Mom? I'm sick. *Mom.*"

As expected, Dori is rarin' to go. "Gotcha. A little cutting action, you're getting a jump on the old senioritis. Hells to the yes." Dori works so hard at being hip that half the time I don't know what she is saying. "You shouldn't be in school in the middle of summer anyway. I am so there. *Daughter.*"

"She's on her way," I whisper to Miss Chaney.

A minute later, Chaney gets a call to "inspect suspected contraband" and rushes off after warning me not to leave until she returns. I am grateful to all the stoner kids who like to spend the summer leaving baggies of grass clippings and oregano planted around the school just to start the year off with Chaney's paranoia in high gear.

When Dori shows up, I rush her out before Miss Chaney can stop us. Outside, Dori can't wait to announce, "Welcome to the dark side. Really happy I can help bust you out of Parkhaven Penal Colony. You gonna go hook up with your besties and blaze up or just chill?"

"I actually don't feel good. I just didn't want to bother my mom."

Her hectic eagerness falls away. "Oh."

Out on the field between us and visitor parking, I can see the team practicing. I step back so that the school building hides me from view and ask, "Can I wait here?" I try to sound especially weak and pitiful.

"Sure, Aubsie. I'll go get the car." She is so nice that I feel bad about not wanting to be seen with a woman who has hemoglobin-colored hair and a barbed-wire bracelet tattooed around her arm.

The instant she leaves, I peek around the corner of the building. Through the distance and the dust, a hunched-over player shoves the ball between his knees and Tyler takes it. Everyone on the field—players, coaches, the water boy—they all focus on Tyler as he dances away, pulling his arm back like a Roman javelin thrower or the tribe's best hunter, the one all the rest depend on for food. He yells orders at the others tramping aimlessly around the field. Pointing with his free arm, he hurls the ball in such a way that it spins as it flies through the heated air, landing in the hands of the exact player he had pointed to.

Dori pulls up in her Toyota RAV4. Still staring at Tyler, I get in and, for one second, Dori watches with me. What the players are doing is suddenly so obvious that I can't believe I have never seen it before. I take Dori's silence to be a sign that she is seeing what I am. I am wrong.

She clucks her tongue and goes, "Can they be any more ridiculous? All those steroid cases in their tight pants. Why don't they just drop trou, whip it out, and decide once and for all whose dick's the biggest? Just get it over with already. All that butt patting and sticking their hands under each other's asses. Football is more homoerotic than a gay pride parade in San Francisco."

Dori automatically assumes that I agree with her. I don't. For the first time I understand what has been happening right in front of me all these years. Maybe because for a few seconds I was close enough to have heard one beat, I can now see how football lets all those ordinary boys show what is in their hearts: They want to be heroes. They each want to be loved and admired for their courage and skill. They want to be the one who saves the tribe. They want to be the hunter who brings home the deer, the warrior who slays the enemy. Or, at least, they want to help the one who does. What is wrong with that?

As we drive away, I wonder what it would have been like to grow up in the polygamy part of the Mormon Church believing that the Lord wants your mom to be one of fifteen wives and that it is holy and righteous that you are going to get married off as soon as you have your first period. To believe that your way is right and that the rest of the world—the normal world—is deluded and doomed to burn in hell, and that the normal world persecutes you only because they haven't been saved. Or are reading the Bible wrong. Or are secretly jealous.

Then one day, something happens, and you see that everything you were taught to believe your entire life is wrong. You see that the whole time you were the deluded one.

In the locker room, hands still dripping, I fumble with the lock in my haste to get to my cell phone and see if Aubrey has returned any of my half-dozen increasingly shrill messages. I fish the phone out and, of course, there are no messages. I punch in her number. When, as usual, it goes straight to voice mail, I clench the phone, and my fist hovers two inches from the locker as I fight the impulse to smash it to pieces.

I calm myself and send a text message. Cursing my spastic thumbs, I type, CLA ME NOW!! HV 2 GET $$$ 2MRW!!! MST IMPT DAY OF YR FILE!!!

I peel off my wet swimsuit and am standing naked in front of the locker when a woman in a tankini with a slenderizing tummy panel spots me and squeals, "The boob whisperer!"

I wince and consider not answering. I should strike a blow for the dignity of my profession and ask her to please not refer to me or to any lactation consultant as a boob whisperer. Or even her bosom buddy. But she's already rushing over, wailing, "Oh, Cam, you are just the person I need to talk to!" She yanks a shoulder strap down, scoops her left breast out of its cup, and holds it up for my inspection.

I can't recall the woman's name, but remember her raisin-colored areola and writing "dense tissue" on her chart. A ring of raw, badly chapped skin outlines her nipples.

"Oh, sweetie," I coo. "Todd does not like whatever it is that you're doing now." Even though all the moms become Sweetie, I can almost always recall their babies' names. I see Todd and his mother together again as they were when I visited her at her house a few days after delivery and found her weeping in despair, and it comes back to me: infant with a small mouth, mom with dense breast tissue.

"It's painful, isn't it?"

"What am I doing wrong?" Her eyebrows arch together in anxious pleading. "I'm not making enough milk, am I?"

Kristin. Amazingly, out of all the thousands of names, I recall hers. If only I had that level of command in other areas of my life. Like with Aubrey.

"Kristin, no, don't stress about that. I've seen about a thousand moms a year for the past fifteen years, and do you know how many couldn't make enough milk? Four. I am not worried at all about your supply."

Kristin nods, relaxing a bit.

Always looking for the teachable moment, I ask rhetorically, "Todd is not getting a good latch, is he? And so, in spite of your more than adequate supply, he's not getting full. And he struggles when he nurses. And that tires him out. And he falls asleep. And you can't bring yourself to rouse him. But then when he wakes up he's too frantic to nurse right."

"Yes!" Relief floods Kristin's face and she looks at me as if I'm psychic. This lasts for about a second until the relief is replaced by a look of puzzled disappointment that is very familiar to me as Kristin realizes that she might not be the first woman on earth to nurse a child.

"Okay, remember what I taught you? About putting the two pieces of the puzzle together?" If we were in one of the hospitals where I consult right after delivery, I could touch her and demonstrate what I am talking about. Instead, using my own breast, I have to mime the lesson I gave her when she attended one of my classes, about pulling Todd and her breast together at the same time. "Remember, Todd has no neck muscles. You have to shove and hold. Keep the pieces together."

"I thought I was doing that."

My cell phone starts playing "Slipping Through My Fingers" by ABBA. Dori put the song on as the ringtone because I started sobbing halfway through *Mamma Mia* when Meryl Streep was singing to her bride-to-be daughter about letting her childhood slip away. Maybe it was because of the thermos of margaritas Dori and I had sneaked into the afternoon matinee, but I lost it when Meryl, wondering what had happened to all the adventures she'd planned to have with her daughter, answered herself, "Well, some of that we did, but most we didn't."

As the song plays on my phone, I tell Kristin, "I've got to get this.

Work on Todd getting a good latch. Just shove that mommy muffin as far as you can into his little mouth, okay? You have my number. Call me if things don't improve." I make myself turn away even though I see another fifteen minutes of questions in Kristin's eyes. The one thing that can pull me away from being an endless source of reassurance to my moms needing help with their children is my own child needing help.

Miraculously, I catch the call in time to answer, "Hey, punkin."

"Ee-yeah?" my daughter responds in the tone that makes her sound like an annoyed drug addict, both testy-hostile and nodding out. It is a tone she uses only with me.

"What's up." She can't even summon the energy to make it a question.

Instead of shrieking, *What do you mean, "What's up"?! What have I been screaming at you about? What have we been waiting for for the past sixteen years!*, I bank the anger that flares up at her cavalier response and invoke my inner Zen Mama.

Zen Mama is made of Teflon. Delayed-adolescence annoyance and college jitters expressed as surly crabbiness slide right off Zen Mama. Zen Mama understands that her only child's extreme bitchiness is a necessary and natural part of the separation process. Because Zen Mama has been reminded repeatedly for the past two weeks that her child is one day away from being eighteen, or "legal age," as said child prefers to call it, and can vote, drink in certain states, be drafted if she were a boy, sign a binding contract, and run her own life, Zen Mama sounds like Hal the robot as she repeats a version of the bulletin that she has been hammering into her daughter every day for the entire summer: "Aubrey, you can't put me off another minute. I've already had to get two extensions from the university, and now tomorrow is the absolute last day we can collect the money from the trust fund to pay for your first year's tuition without having to pay a huge late penalty."

"Oh, yeah. That."

It helps me to pretend that my only offspring has either just landed on Earth from a distant planet or has suffered a head injury. " 'That'? *That*, Aubrey, is your college money. *That* is your education and ticket out of here. We have been waiting for this day most of your life."

"Well, *you* have."

"*I* have? What does that mean?"

"Uh, I really gotta go. Tyler needs me to set up the coffee for tomorrow."

I squeeze my eyes shut, shift into my highest gear of über–Zen-Mamadom, and say, "Aubrey, I sense some reluctance on your part about going to college. Sweetie, if you're not ready, you know, we talked about gap-year options. Gap years are getting really popular. You can get credit for working on an organic farm in Wales. The trust will pay as long as the program is accredited. Or there's another one where you study with the monks in Tibet. If you're not ready—"

"Can we talk about this later?"

"There is nothing to talk about. You *will* come home tonight and you *will* be with me when the bank opens tomorrow morning."

"Uh, yeah, okay, I'll see."

Was it me? Did I teach her to say that? To say, "I'll see"?

"Aubrey, there is nothing to see. You have to come to the bank with me. You know this. They won't release the trust funds if you're not there to sign off. I have your letter of acceptance from Peninsula and the invoice from the bursar's office, so they can just transfer as much as you need for the first year."

"Sorry, tomorrow morning is impossible. Two new crews of framers start tomorrow, so Tyler and I are going to be slammed."

Zen Mama cracks and morphs into Prison Matron Mama. "Oh, you will be slammed, Aubrey Lightsey. If you do not get your behind home this instant, you will be most definitively slammed."

"Okay, I gotta go."

"Aubrey, baby, don't do this. Not for some guy who's working in a roach coach." I am apologizing before the last two words are out of my mouth. "Sorry, sorry, I meant catering van. Erase. Erase. Not 'roach coach'—catering van. Lunch wagon. Food truck." But it is already too late; I have spoken the forbidden words.

"I cannot keep having this conversation with you. If you insist upon belittling me and demeaning what Tyler and I are trying to do, the business that he and I are trying to build, our discussions are at an end. Your disrespect totally invalidates all the initiative and discipline and hard work and everything else you supposedly *want* me to show that I *am*, in fact, already showing."

It stuns me how anger can transform my daughter from a mono-syllabic mope into Rumpole of the Bailey. If Rumpole had a degree in counseling.

"Aubrey, please. I'm sorry. I slipped." I grovel to no avail. She hangs up. I call back and it's straight to voice mail.

I consider driving to the dump of a shack that Tyler rents with a rotating crew of dead-enders and miscreants, and dragging my daughter home by her hair. But ever since Black Ice Night I've known exactly what that would accomplish: She'd move into that shack with Tyler.

A *Jerry Springer* montage plays in my mind, featuring some blob of a skanky trailer-trash mom sitting next to her blob of an even skankier trailer-trash daughter—both of them wearing Daisy Dukes and radiating hatred toward each other—while someone in the audience stands up and, neck veins bulging, index finger stabbing toward the sullen daughter, who is rolling her eyes onstage, yells with self-righteous, Old Testament wrath, "If she were my kid, I'd lock her sorry ass up!" Or, "I'd call the police on her sorry ass!" Or, "I'd toss her mother-*bleeping duh bleepitty-bleep-bleep* sorry ass out on the mother*bleeping* street! S'what I'd do!"

I try to recall who I was when I watched these hillbilly jamborees. I have vague memories of being a puzzled, superior, teen-free mother who knew sure as gravity that she and her daughter would never go down that path. We would read *The Secret Garden* together and pick blueberries in Maine. We would never even come anywhere near that path.

And, I remind myself, we aren't anywhere near it. Not really. Aubrey's not doing drugs. She's not giving blow jobs in the boys' locker room. She's just changed beyond recognition in the past year.

Forget anthrax. The greatest chemical threat facing our country today is the hormones delivered to our daughters at puberty. Hormones that, in Aubrey's case, were not fully ignited until Tyler appeared.

If only I can get her shipped off to college.

I think of Aubrey twenty-four hundred miles away in the state of Washington, rushing to class across the Peninsula State College quad beneath towering evergreens that shelter the campus. It's drizzling. It's always drizzling there. But that was part of the appeal when we chose Peninsula at the start of her senior year, back before Tyler Moldenhauer scrambled her brain. Back then she wanted something as different from the sunbaked grids of Parkhaven as possible. She couldn't wait to leave the world of megachurches and malls. Besides, Peninsula, her dream school, was close to Forks, Washington, where all her vampire books were set.

In the shower, warm water pulses against the top of my head and I wonder again when it happened. When Aubrey went off the rails. A lightning-quick chain of associations takes me from there directly to a memory so strong and so familiar that it even brings back all the smells of the pivotal moment twenty-two years ago when my own life was decided.

The cumin scent of body odor; the hot metal-and-grease smell of the iron wheels against the rails; a citrus aroma from the Berber grandmother sitting across from me feeding sections of blood orange to the three grandchildren crammed onto the seat next to her; the fragrance of mint tea and falafel from the vendors working their way through the car; and a whiff of cedar and rosemary from the arid plains and hillsides carried on the hot, dry air that blows against my face.

Voices speaking a throaty language with volleys of glottal jerks fired back and forth rise above the clattering hubbub of an ancient train lumbering across Morocco. Back home, everyone would be plugged into their brand-new Walkmans. But here, the boom box is still king, so while one at the front of the car blares traditional, snake-charmer-sounding Moroccan music, another at the back rips loose with Whitney Houston pleading, "I wanna dance with somebody."

It is 1988. I am sitting on a wooden bench seat beside a glassless window. The aisles are crowded with men in turbans and striped djellabas. On the bench beside me is the battered backpack that I will be living out of for the next three months of hitchhiking and Eurailing around Europe, visiting as many of the places where my grandmother served during World War II as I can on this trip she financed. A reward for finishing nursing school.

I glance at the Atlas Mountains rising in the hazy distance, and translate the tan, sage, and blue of the landscape into my grand-mother's black-and-white photos. Each picture is populated with the grinning faces of Bobbi Mac's friends. All the game gals with nick-names like Pee Wee, Speedy, Slats, who called my grandmother Crazy Mac and turned World War II into the most fun sleepover ever. I'd heard their stories so often that they were like characters from a fairy tale.

I wish that I were traveling with them, with a gang. I knew about all the amputations Mac had assisted at, all the handsome young men who died, but none of that was as real as the stories of cocktails made from rubbing alcohol, dances in airplane hangars, dating gen-erals who took you to eat lobster at castles, wearing a long black slip that passed as an evening gown to a formal dance, singing silly Hawaiian songs for the troops in a grass skirt and a coconut-shell bra, arms and legs darkened with a mixture of Pond's cold cream and Hershey's cocoa powder.

On the bench across from mine, the Berber grandmother and her grandchildren stare at me as the red fruit churns in their open mouths. The grandmother wears a djellaba of a rough weave the color of mulch and a cotton head scarf dyed indigo blue. The youngest child, a scrawny girl with bright, dark eyes and a wide smile in a grimy pink caftan with a beige turtleneck underneath it, picks her nose as she chews and gapes at me. The two grandsons beside her both wear ragged T-shirts that must have made their way to North Africa via Goodwill. One features the Ghostbusters logo. The other depicts a silver hand gripping a giant silver gun beneath silver letters that spell out ROBOCOP.

I smile weakly, trying to prove that though I am an American I am a friendly person of goodwill and not a poltergeist hunter or android assassin.

The tea vendor passes and in the shiny, round surface of his silver pot, I see my twenty-one-year-old face and find it just as round and gleaming and heart-stoppingly perfect as the pot itself. In the next instant my young self traveling on that train twenty-three years ago notices that her spiral perm has grown out, leaving the top of her hair and her bangs flat as a poodle that needs to go to the groomer. That her face is greasy and she needs to put on some lip gloss. And that a really cute guy is heading toward her.

The first time I set eyes on him, Martin was swaying down the aisle of that packed train rocking across North Africa. He is thin in a haunted, poetic, punk-rock star/drug addict way that hints at secrets and reserves of worldliness. He is actually thin in a seriously ill way. He pauses beside my bench, indicates the seat next to me, asks, "Any chance?"

Without a word, I move the backpack off the seat and he all but collapses onto it.

He is surprised when I ask, "How long have you been sick?"

"Do I look that bad?"

"You don't look good."

"How do you know that this isn't the way I always look?"

"I don't think you'd be alive."

"Good point."

I ask about symptoms. He is nonchalant. He has Siddhartha *in his backpack; he is above caring about "the physical apparatus."*

I diagnose gastroenteritis and dip into the traveling pharmacy that Bobbi Mac insisted I take with me. I press tablets of Imodium into his hand and warn, "It may be amoebic dysentery. If it is you will have to go to a doctor and get a prescription for Flagyl." I make him drink the mint tea I buy from the vendor walking the aisle.

"Drink it all," I coax. "You need to rehydrate and there's lots of sugar in there to get your glucose levels back up. You know, if it is dysentery, you could always eat fresh camel dung."

"Did you just tell me to eat shit?"

"My grandmother was an army nurse in North Africa in World War Two. She had a bedouin wardman who told her that cure." I want to impress him, and my World War II army-nurse grandmother is the most impressive thing about me. "After the invasion of Sicily, they ran out of everything. Morphine, bandages, sulfa powder. So some of the boys who were the worst off, the ones who might have died, tried the camel dung, and it worked. Olive oil is also good."

"Excellent. Some camel shit with an olive-oil chaser." He puts his arm over the back of the seat. He smells like really good pot. He scoots closer, whispers in my ear, "The old lady's tattoos . . ." He nods toward the bedouin grandmother sitting on the bench seat across from us. A series of dots the color of strong green tea drip from her

bottom lip down her chin. They are faded and almost lost in wrinkles elephant-hide deep.

"They were done when she was a little girl to give her strength, power. To protect her. If her parents had wanted to enhance her attractiveness to a prospective husband, she might be tattooed along here. . . ." Martin traces his finger along an imaginary necklace across the tops of my breasts. "The designs would have all been geometric." He draws cross-my-heart marks along the necklace. "The tattoos on her hands are hints, samples of the delights to come."

We both know that we will sleep together. All that is left for me to decide is how much it will mean and how I will make it mean that.

After we drink mint tea with extra sugar, Martin fishes out his battered copy of Siddhartha. I lie and say that I love the book. One of my all-time favorites. Right up there with . . . with . . . As I know he will, Martin prompts, "The Tao Te Ching? The Gnostic Gospels? The Bhagavad Gita?"

"All of the above." I don't know what makes me stop pretending that I, too, love books about spirituality. That we "share an interest." Probably the calculation that I'd already made that we are going to be together, and figuring in how long I can act like a scholar of religious texts, then adding in that, even more than most men, he appears to like to be the one with the answers. I compute all of that and admit, "I don't know. I've never read any of them."

"So you just said that? About loving Siddhartha . . . ?"

"To impress you? Yeah. Pretty much. Did it work?"

"Absolutely. Would you be impressed if I read your favorite book to you?"

And so, reciting from memory more than from the page open in front of him, Martin tells me the story of the handsome son of the Brahman, Siddhartha, his shoulders tanned from performing sacred ablutions in the river, his forehead surrounded by the glow of his clear-thinking spirit, who left his family and all his riches to search for enlightenment.

I hear the words in my head again, in Martin's caress of a voice carried on a breeze scented with rosemary and cedar: " 'In the shade of the house, in the sunshine on the river bank by the boats, in the shade of the sallow wood and the fig tree . . .' "

If Martin had left me for another woman, I could store this memory and all the rest of them away in the past where they belong. But when he left, it felt as if he were going off to war. Next always seemed like something he *had* to do. That he hadn't left me so much as been taken away against his will.

I flip the shower lever to shut off the water and am momentarily scalded when I accidentally turn it the wrong way. I step out of the shower, briskly wrap a towel around myself, and rush back to my locker to check my phone. Maybe Aubrey called.

I hear the metal door to the locker room open and the little girls—one with copper curls like Twyla's and speech impediment like Aubrey once had—bounce in. The older one dictates to the younger girl, "You will be the baby manatee and I will be the mother manatee—"

"And we migwate to the Amazon wain fowest!"

"And we dive into the deep blue sea and there are dolphins and mermaids—"

"And faiwies!"

"Not fairies in the deep blue sea!"

The younger girl looks stricken.

"That's silly!" the older one says.

Demolished by her idol, the little redhead teeters for a second near tears. Then she laughs a child's theatrical imitation of laughter and, game once again, says, "Yeah, faiwies in the deep bwoo sea. That's siwwy!"

Happy again, the girls run off toward the vending machines.

As I scroll through all the unanswered calls I've made to Aubrey, they beep like a movie-submarine sonar, warning of the disaster of an approaching torpedo. I roll tape back to last August and try again to identify the moment that set my child on this course.

As I try to connect the dots between Tyler Moldenhauer and heatstroke, from down the white-tiled hall that leads to the vending machines, the little girls' voices echo back to me, silvery and far-away, like coins falling from a torn pocket, lost forever.

Back home, I help Pretzels to her feet so she can hobble with me and we both head for my room, where I plop down on my bed with the laptop and Google "Tyler Moldenhauer." Someone has made a fan page for him on Facebook. He hasn't posted any comments, but he is tagged in dozens of photos.

The pictures of him on the field, face hidden behind a helmet, bring back his smell, like the ocean on a cold day. I watch and rewatch a video of him zigzagging through a field of players, vanishing so quickly that they lunge after him and grab nothing but air.

But there is one photo I keep going back to. In it he has his helmet off and is laughing with his mouth wide open; his tongue is hanging out a little, and he looks like every smirking jock asshole I've ever hated.

What is wrong with me? My type is, has always been, reedy art boys. The first crushes I ever had were on Jack White and Adrien Brody. Stick-figure boys. Though that was back when Twyla and I were friends. And, come to think of it, Adrien and Jack were both more her crushes than mine. Still, I can't like Tyler Moldenhauer. A jock? Mom would flip out.

Just to get my mind off this whole ridiculous thing, I click over to my Facebook page and see that I have one friend request. Before I check who it is my heart bumps. Tyler? Already? Tyler Moldenhauer wants to be my friend? Is this one of those *Twilight* Bella/Edward things where we don't even really have to talk because just my scent alone drives him more insane than any other woman's in all his centuries of vampire existence?

I recall that my scent was bagel vomit, click on the Friend Requests icon, and see a name that I don't recognize: Alex Well, which means that "Alex Well" is some clever business that targets teens through social media. No doubt "Alex Well" has some unlimited texting offer for me, since, of course, *all* teen girls just live for unlimited texting. And lip gloss. *Earn Lip Gloss Using Our Unlimited Texting Plan!*

I don't confirm the request, but, just to see what kind of scam Facebook thinks I should be targeted for, I click on the bogus name. Expecting to be taken to a page hectic with offers and great news about a great product and giveaways if I confirm the friend request, I am surprised to end up looking at a page with nothing on it except for the dippy white cutout of a person with that curlicue hairdo against Facebook's blue-gray background. Alex Well has no friends. Not one. Nothing is filled in. Birthday, Hometown, Current City, Relationship Status, they've all been left blank. In his Info section there is no contact information, no groups he is a member of, no pages he follows. They are all blank.

The only information on his wall is a status update next to the curlicued photo that says:

11:56 A.M. AUGUST 12, 2009
Hello, Aubrey. Thank you more than I can say for coming this far. I used a fake name because I didn't know how you would respond to seeing my real name. More than anything in the world, I would like to know you. Even if it is just this. Just messages on Facebook. I can think of a thousand reasons why you wouldn't confirm this. But I hope you will. This is Martin, your dad.

I can't say how long I sit on my bed staring at those three letters. *D-A-D.* The way, when you are standing on a skyscraper and you think you might—just accidentally—jump off, I start feeling like I might—just accidentally—hit the little "Respond to Friend Request" button. So I step away from the edge and slam the laptop shut.

I lift my gaze to the teddy bears that Mom and Dad (D-A-D!) stenciled along the top of the walls before I was even born. I love thinking of them doing that together. Me still inside Mom, listening to them laughing. Maybe Dad painted a dot on Mom's nose like in those old movies when husbands thought their wives were just so cute.

So much is exploding inside of me that I feel like a bag of Orville Redenbacher's in the microwave. Too much has happened all at once. I stagnated for years with nothing happening, and now, all in one day, too much is happening.

I open the laptop, go back to Facebook, back to "Alex Well's" page. I stare at the little box next to a faceless cartoon that is now a faceless cartoon of my father, and read and reread "Respond to Friend Request" roughly a million times. Then, like she always does, Pretzels—who can't hear anything, but somehow manages to hear the refrigerator opening and the garage door going up, grumbles—and starts struggling to her feet.

This is my signal that Mom is home. I quickly sign out of Facebook. She can't know about the message. Thinking about my dad makes her so sad. And me going away to college next year is stressing her. I can tell by the way she stares at me so much more now that she's imagining being here without me. If she knew about this? Dad contacting me? It would upset her so much.

A few seconds later, she rattles the knob of my door, yells when she can't open it, "Why is this door locked!"

"Why do you never knock!"

"Open the door!"

"I'm taking a nap!"

"I need my laptop to see how many I've got registered for my class tomorrow!"

Amazingly, it appears that her Siamese twin, Dori, hasn't told her yet about picking me up from school. I crack the door a few inches, just enough to hand the laptop out. "I don't see why I can't have my own laptop. They're not *that* expensive."

"That is a discretionary item."

This is her way of saying that I have to use the money I made working as a counselor at Lark Hill. "I would except that I don't want to go to school naked, and, P.S., most mothers don't count clothes as 'discretionary' items. For your information, Parkhaven is not clothing-optional."

She gives me Hurt Look Number 85. I hate Number 85, which translates to *I am trying not to cry because I got totally screwed in the divorce and don't make enough to buy us all the stuff we need.* I am suddenly so sick of knowing what every twitch of her face means that I want to scream. I try to close the door, but she has her foot wedged into it.

"How was band camp?" she asks in her fake, ultracalm voice, which means that she wants to scream at me but she is such a superior being that she won't descend to that level. *My* level.

"Fine."

The foot does not move. "Did you reconnect with your band friends? Wren? Amelia? You haven't seen them all summer."

Great, now I am getting Anxious Look Number 113, which means *Why don't you have any friends? Exactly what is the precise nature of your loserhood?*

"Yeah."

"And?"

"They're fine."

"What did they do this summer?"

"We didn't really talk about it."

"So? Was it blazing hot out there?"

I can think of no nonsarcastic answer.

"Is Shupe still a jerk?"

"No, he had a lobotomy and he's a prince of a fellow."

Mom laughs too hard at that, rewarding me for joking with her. Then, her eyebrows all crinkled up high and happy, she waits for me to say more. I have nothing.

"Anything else happen today?"

I pick through the avalanche of unbelievable things that happened today and try to grab on to one that she can handle. There isn't one. I can't even make something up. I've been at parties—everyone drinking, smoking weed—and listened to girls step out onto the patio, then chat happily with their moms about how they're watching *True Blood* at Olivia's house and can they spend the night? Then Olivia calls her mom and asks the same thing, then they both get wasted and stay out all night. I could never have gotten away with that with Mom. She knows me too well. One word and she would have been all, "What's wrong? What's going on?" She can literally read my mind. Obviously, until today there wasn't much I cared if she read. She even bragged about it: "Aubrey and I don't have any secrets from each other."

Tone, I guess. The words aren't even that important; she just knows me so well that if I open my mouth, if I say one, single word now, it'll be, "What's wrong? What's going on?" So I can't open my mouth.

When I don't speak, she gives me the look that is under all the other looks. It is so basic it doesn't even have a number. It is just Hunger, and if I pause even long enough to translate that one, it will eat me alive.

She finally shakes her head, allows me to shut the door, and I have a few minutes of peace. I know it won't last. I know that, at that very moment, she's checking in with her twin, and the instant that Dori tells her about the "heatstroke" she'll be all over me.

Which she is. A few minutes later, she bursts back into my room with eighteen different drinks including Pedialyte, which she must have had left over from when I had measles.

"Oh, hon, why didn't you tell me? I'm so sorry that I snapped at you." She perches on the edge of the bed next to me. When she feels my forehead, her hand is cool against my skin and makes me feel like I am really sick.

"Baby, you're hot. I'm going to see if I can get you in to see Dr. Queng."

Yeah, I really want to sit in a waiting room with a big LEGO table and an American Girl video playing to see the pediatrician who set my arm when I broke it falling off the deck in Twyla's backyard. "No, Mom, I'm fine. Really."

"We can just go to emergency walk-in. I'm sure I can get them to work you in."

Mom knows every nurse in Parkhaven and they all love her so much that I always kind of get treated like a celebrity when I'm sick. Which I usually like. But not today. "Mom, how many times do I have to tell you? I'm fine. I just need to rest. I know my own body."

"OK, hon. OK." She sticks a giant glass of ice water with a bendy straw poking out into my hands and I sip while she goes into nurse mode and arranges my covers, fluffing them up so that they float back down on me all cool and neat. I love nurse mode. She folds the sheet over the light blanket so that my chin touches only soft cotton. I feel tiny and taken care of. She's about to leave, then stops and says, "Your lips look dry."

I hold up the ice water.

She puts the back of her hand on my cheek. It feels so good I have to fight the desire to nuzzle against it. So good that, for a second, I almost think I can spend the whole, entire rest of my life riding the Teacups.

E arly the next morning, Mom bursts into my room wearing her gray scrubs. She hates scrubs and says that the hospitals where she consults might be able to force her to wear them, but they can't force her to wear ones that are pink or have bunny prints. In a lot of ways, Mom is kind of badass.

Without a word, she puts her palm on my forehead. Instead of cool and nice, though, it now feels damp and gooshy, like it could melt right into my skin if she kept it there long enough. "You feel warm." Then she does her ultra-annoying thing of *telling* me how I feel. "You're not any better. I'm staying home."

"No. I'm fine, Mom." I make my voice hit the right tone: sick enough not to go to band camp but not sick enough for Dr. Queng. "Really. You go on. You've got patients waiting for you." Luckily, at that exact moment one of the many alarms Mom has set on her phone goes off.

"Shit, I'm going to be late! Call me if you start to feel worse." She rushes out, stops, tells me, "Just call me anyway, OK?"

I promise I will, and then—*score!*—I have the house and the laptop all to myself. I can think about my dad with no fear that someone will burst through the door without even knocking, demanding to know what I am doing and when I am going to unload the dishwasher.

From under the bed, I pull out the scrapbook Mom made for me of every photo she could collect of my father. She called it the Book of Palms. The name is supposed to be a joke because he has his hand up, shielding some famous person's face in most of the photos. I think there might be a Book of Palms in the Bible. I never asked. Mom likes to pretend that I've lost interest in my father. That it upset *me* to hear about him. Actually, I stopped mentioning him when I saw how much it upset *her*. By that time, though, she wasn't my only source of information. For the past few years, I've been Googling my father's Next name constantly.

I open the laptop and check my Google alerts to see if there is anything new. There isn't. There hasn't been anything on the Internet about my father for months.

"My father." I don't even know what punctuation mark to put after those two words. Lots of exclamation points!!! One lonely question mark? I need a cartoon balloon with every symbol available in it. Something that stands for stunned/terrified/pissed off/excited/depressed/happy/mad.

I go to Facebook and stare at his friend request until it starts pulsing and glowing like it is radioactive. I close the laptop, get back in bed, and pull the covers up so that just the soft cotton is touching my chin.

I drop my swim bag on the floor as soon as I enter the house. In the kitchen, Pretzels—curled up on her rug in front of the refrigerator, strategically situated so that warm air from the vent blows on her and she's in place to snap up any morsel that might fall from the heavens—doesn't budge when I enter. We adopted Pretzels when Aubrey was five and always asking when I was going to get her a sister. A *big* sister, not a little one like Sharalynn Mahan's mother brought home. A *big* sister who would come fully equipped with all her own Polly Pockets and be ready to play from day one. Aubrey was the one who noticed that our new mostly golden retriever puppy's coat was the same color as pretzels.

I get down on my hands and knees next to the sweet old girl and coo, "Hey, Pretz. Hey, girl, you need to pee?" Since she's almost totally deaf, it startles her if she's touched while sleeping. So I increase the volume of my cooing gently until she opens her filmy eyes and is transfixed by joy at the sight of my face with all its trea-sured food-bowl associations.

"Come on, sweet girl." I loop both hands around her belly and hoist her up, causing a release of one of the paint-stripping clouds of gas that is her signature move these days. The doggie door she's used for the past dozen years has started to confuse and scare her, so I slide the patio door open and she totters out.

Pretzels pokes her nose around in the grass. As I wait for her to snuffle up an odor that will remind her why she's outside, I glance around behind me at what the real estate agent had called the "great room" when she invited Martin and me to imagine the entertaining we'd be doing beneath its twelve-foot ceiling. Had I hosted even one dinner party? One?

At the moment every horizontal surface is stacked with extra-long twin sheets; towels; long underwear; two pairs of flannel pajama bottoms, one plaid, one printed with a cow-jumping-over-the-moon pattern; warm socks; turquoise mittens with a matching knit cap; a forest green rain jacket; a first-aid kit; collapsible storage boxes; a small sewing kit; three boxes of peanut-butter-cookie LUNA bars;

vitamins; Midol; Advil; Theraflu; two tubes of triple antibiotic ointment. Everything a girl leaving home for college might possibly need.

I've listened to other moms talk about their daughters having hysterical meltdowns in the middle of Bed Bath & Beyond because the store was out of the precise Tommy Hilfiger "Biscayne" comforter set they had their hearts set on and they'd already been to five other stores. I experienced no histrionics whatsoever with Aubrey because I did all the shopping by myself. By late summer, when dorm shopping kicked off, and Target filled up with mothers piloting shopping carts and holding lists followed either by a mortified young man praying for invisibility or a young woman tossing in extra hair products, Aubrey would no longer even talk to me about Peninsula. I stopped pushing on shower caddies; we had the much larger issue of Tyler Moldenhauer.

So I took over outfitting Aubrey for college without her help just as if she were going off to sleepaway camp. But instead of buying bug spray and writing her name in her shorts with a laundry marker, I procured a coffeemaker and researched surge protectors. With each washcloth I purchased, I felt as if I were greasing the skids, paving the path of least resistance. I know that if I can only drag Aubrey to the bank to get the money, the wheels of college will be in motion and they will simply carry Aubrey away from Parkhaven. I visualize putting my daughter on the plane, happily paying extra for suitcases filled with shoe organizers and bottles of hand sanitizer.

Continuing my visualization exercise, I imagine the great room empty, Aubrey's bedroom empty, my nest empty, and though it is what I most desire I am stricken with grief at the prospect. I grab my laptop and contact the source of all wisdom: Shri Googlenami. My screen saver comes up. It shows a cartoon baby assuming some favorite breast-feeding positions: the Pop and Spray, the Look-see, the Combo Sleepy with a Toe Grab, the Pounce, the Super Distract with a Twist.

I try to Google "empty nest syndrome," but my left ring finger keeps hitting the x instead of the s so it comes out "empty next syndrome." I finally, laboriously, fix two fingers and both eyes on the keyboard, type in n-e-s-t, and a jillion entries fill the screen. There are the posters who wail, "Who will I be when I'm not Jason/Caitlyn/Whitney/Brandon's mom anymore?" Or they advise, "Look on the bright side: You and your husband can have sex anytime you want. Any*where* you want!" Since there is no husband or any other sex-having candidate in the picture, that bright side is noticeably dim. And because I've had to work—fortunately at work I love—I never had the luxury of baking my entire identity into the homeroom mom cupcakes I brought to school. So that's not exactly relevant either.

Though I'm not hungry, worry and regret drive me to the kitchen for comfort. Pretzels is curled up, guarding the refrigerator. "Pretz, honey, you're gonna have to move." Pretzels grumbles; she already moved once today. "Okay, hang on." I haul her and her rug a few feet to the right and she grumbles a bit more. On the refrigerator door, held up by a daisy magnet from the Realtor who sold us this house—"We Make Your Dreams Bloom!"—is a list that reads:

REMIND AUBREY TO:

· wear flip-flops in the community showers
· get a flu shot as soon as it comes out in October
· use the white-noise machine if the dorm is too
  loud because she turns into a different person
  when she can't sleep
· never connect the red cable to the negative
  terminal when jumping a car battery

I add, "· get a meningitis shot!!"

Inside the refrigerator, tucked behind the white Styrofoam boxes of takeout that haven't aged enough yet for me to toss them without guilt, is one lone can of Diet Cherry 7UP. This causes me to burst instantly into tears because I fear that this is the last can of my child's favorite soft drink that I will ever buy. Before Aubrey began spending all her time with Tyler, I couldn't keep the stuff in the house. She even used to drink it with breakfast sometimes. In fact, now that I think about it, she had a can the morning she got heatstroke.

A week later, after she'd missed band camp entirely and set off on the first day of her senior year, there was something different about her. First of all, she'd worn a skirt. She'd never worn a skirt to school before. But it was more than that. There was something about her as she set off for the first day of her last year of high school; she was beautiful in such a defined and settled way. I saw that her beauty would age but never change again as it had when she was growing up. Had I told her how beautiful she was?

Yes, I had. I remember saying those exact words to her on the day she started her senior year.

I outline my eyes with a pencil call Smolder, then smudge most of it away. I brush on a blush called Orgasm, so that I look barely flushed. With every stroke of the lip liner pencil, every puff of blush, I imagine Tyler staring back. I realize that this is delusional, which is why it is so important that absolutely no one knows that I am trying. Not Tyler, not any of my old friends in band, not my mom.

Especially not my mom.

Thinking about her and her freakish CSI ability to analyze everything about me, from the way I am breathing to my tiniest facial twitch, makes me rub off most of the lip gloss and blush. If she knows it is all for a football player she will implode. It will be like one of those FLDS Mormon girls in the *Little House on the Prairie* dresses telling her mom she is crushed out on Snoop Dogg. Even making an effort for Parkhaven High would worry her. Which it does anyway, because, when I appear, she analyzes me for so long that I am certain she knows everything. I feel like she is X-raying me and all the bones of my skeleton are spelling out, "She likes a football player!" and "BONUS REVELATION: She's thinking about betraying you by being Facebook friends with the ex who ruined your life!"

Then I feel her passing judgment and it is like being held underwater. So when she finally says, "Wow, pretty dressed up, aren't you?" I am already sputtering for air.

"Why? Just because I'm wearing a skirt? In case you haven't noticed, it's like a thousand degrees out there and skirts are not as hot as jeans." I know she is going to bust me on my "tone." But if I don't tone her a little bit, she is like that robot annihilator in *Terminator 2*. Run him over with a semi and all his quicksilver innards just slurp back together and keep coming at you. I am already too nervous to deal with that level of unstoppability.

"Sorry. You look nice is all."

"Uh, it *is* the first day of school."

"God, bite my head off. All I said is that you look nice."

"And all *I said* was that it's the first day of school."

I cannot wait to get my own car. Not just so that I won't be the only senior who doesn't have one, but so I don't have to start every single day of my life being laser-scanned to make sure I match someone's standards. And, P.S., thanks, Mom. Way to destroy my confidence.

The entire first day of school, I feel like I am looking through a pair of binoculars turned around the wrong way so that everything is happening far, far away. All the people jamming the halls are like extras in a crowd scene as I search for Tyler's face. The teachers introducing themselves and passing out their grading policy sheets and either trying to scare us or charm us seem like someone is making them play charades and they all want to lose.

After school, I find a spot in the shade at the very edge of the field where the band marches and right next to the adjacent field where the football team practices. The team hasn't come out of the locker room yet, but most of the marching band is on the field, gathered around Mr. Shupe, who is passing out permission slips for trips.

I sit with my skirt spread out around me in a half circle and my legs swept under it. I imagine my father, hidden away behind the bleachers next to the football field spying on me and wondering . . . what? If I have any legs? Realizing that I look like the Little Mermaid, I reposition and just sort of sprawl. Tyler especially has to believe that I am a casual person with lots of options who hasn't thought twice about him. Mr. Shupe finishes handing out the forms, catches sight of me languishing on the sidelines, and waves me over, yelling, "Lightsey, double-time it! I need you to work with Johnson on field blocking!"

I don't move.

"Lightsey!"

I don't look up. After trying to get my attention two more times, Shupe gives up, orders the drum major, "Johnson, get them started on 'Joy,'" and walks over to me.

The thought of marching up and down a field with the words "Jeremiah was a bullfrog!" playing in my head makes me even more certain that, even though I don't know how to have a new one, I can never, ever, *ever* go back to my old life.

Shupe's big, puffy white sneakers appear beside me. "What's the deal, Lightsey? You're section leader. We covered for you during band camp, but we need you out there now. Do we need to talk about electing someone else?"

It is almost funny that he thinks that the threat of being replaced as section leader is going to make me leap to my feet and run for the plumed hat. "Actually," I say in a weak, whispery voice, "the doctor says . . ."

He can't hear me, so Shupe squats down in front of me like he *is* Jeremiah the bullfrog. The up-close view of the Shupe crotch helps me sound woozy. "The doctor says I can't be out in the heat yet. So I am just going to sit here in the shade and, you know, take notes on the formations and stuff."

"But it's hotter than . . ." I appreciate that he stops himself and doesn't say "balls." "It's really hot out here."

"Uh, actually, the doctor says I can be out. I'm just not supposed to march."

"But you're section leader. These jabonies"—he jerks a thumb back to the chaos that is the first week with a bunch of incoming freshmen—"need a lot of work. A *lot* of work."

"Maybe you should just go ahead and tap Wren. Or Amelia. They both know the drills as well as I do."

"What? You told me that you'd only need a week to recover."

"Well, yeah. That was the initial diagnosis. But the doctor says it's more serious than he thought at first. One more degree and there would have been permanent brain damage." Three years of working in the attendance office is paying off. I know exactly what to say and even how to say it to make a teacher start worrying about lawsuits. I squint like both the sun and his questions are making my head hurt.

Shupe bounces a little on the balls of his puffy white shoes, and I go on even whisperier, as if all the talking is wearing me out. "Actually, the doctor says that I might never regain the ability to regulate my body temperature." I slump a bit to help him imagine me with a pointer strapped to my head, blowing into a tube to control my wheelchair.

Shupe exhales and puts his hands together like he is going to ask me to pray with him. But he just looks over his shoulder at the mob scene, winces when LeKeefe Johnson yells, "Left face!" and all the returning people go left and smash into all the freshmen who have turned right. "When did they stop teaching left and right? Is that too much to ask of our educational system?" He stands up. "We could really use you out there, Lightsey."

"OK, Mr. Shupe." I pretend to try to struggle to my feet, letting my head flop as I do.

"No, no. Keep your place." He waves his hands over his head to signal LeKeefe to stop, orders me, "Get well," and runs off without even asking to see the doctor's note that I'd carefully forged using the wide variety of forms I have amassed while working in attendance. I guess that after three straight years of my not being anything—not emo, not Christian, not prep, not jock, not ghetto, not punk, not hipster, not skank, not prude, just a half-assed band geek—no one can believe I'd do anything so well defined as lie. I like my new superpower.

Out on the field, Shupe yells, "Band! Ten-*HUT!*"

LeKeefe tweets his whistle, holds his right foot up high, and orders, "Mark time! Mark . . . *AND!*" He brings his foot down, trying to get everyone to hit the first beat together. They don't. They *really* don't.

"T-bones, arc it up! Arc it up!" Mr. Shupe runs onto the field to make certain that the trombones do the choreography perfectly so that, from the stands at halftime, they will all look like very talented ants forming into triangles and figure eights.

The brass players are swinging their instruments up and down, the drummers twirling their big, padded sticks with each beat, everyone just working it as hard as they can.

Do any of them even know that they are playing "Fat Bottomed Girls" by Queen? Have they watched the YouTube video of Freddie Mercury? I did, and from that moment on, all I could ever think about when we played that song was this skinny guy in a stretchy unitard thing singing about how fat-bottomed girls make the rockin' world go round. You can't erase that image and get back into believing that you and Wren Acevedo and LeKeefe Johnson and Amelia O'Dell and all your other band friends are really, secretly cool any more than you can believe that girls of any bottom size made Mr. Mercury's rockin' world go 'round. You just can't.

The football field is still empty, but the aluminum bleachers set up next to it are filling in with the girls who Mom and Dori call the Parkhaven Princesses. They are all wearing Nike running shorts, flip-flops, and weirdly uncool T-shirts that they make look cool. And, somehow in the swampy humidity, they all have hair straight and shiny as Christmas tinsel. Flatiron hair. My whole life Mom has told me that I am "just as good as any of those Parkhaven Princesses." Which, until she mentioned it, I had never really considered, but the instant she made a point of telling me I was just as good as them, I saw that the whole question was open to debate and she was cheering me on because I was on the losing team.

I suddenly wonder why I ever hated these girls and realize that I don't. I never did. My mother does. Dori did. Or they hate whoever their version of them was in their high schools. But why should I hate them or idolize them or feel anything at all about them? They are just being who they were born to be. Exactly like I, only child of a semideranged, quasi-hippie single mom, am being who I was born to be.

Everyone on the bleachers claps when the team runs out. The players have on their video-game-predator pads and helmets. Tyler is so encased in plastic that all I can identify is his number. The only sound is a clatter when the players ram together.

In the end, it doesn't matter that I have worn a skirt. Tyler never looks my way once. Which is good. I am dressed all wrong.

I grab the Diet Cherry 7UP, dump most of the can into a glass—a giveaway from the breast-feeding conference I attended last March, inscribed with the proclamation, I AM A LACTIVIST!—dig out a half-finished bottle of merlot, pour a healthy jolt in, and hope that the chemical cherry taste and aspartame will be enough to sweeten the vinegar tang of the old wine. Since Dori isn't around to slug me on the arm, I need at least a modest buzz to disrupt my current cycle of regrets.

I take the drink and settle into my usual spot on the sofa where I've sat up more nights than I care to recall listening for the rumble of Tyler's truck. To take my mind off my fear that this will be one of the nights when Aubrey doesn't return, I listen to my messages. The first one is from Simone, who reminds me that I saw her late last week in the hospital after her delivery. The message breaks up but sounds frantic enough that I call right back.

"Thank God you called!"

When someone asks why I do the work that I do, that's what I should tell them. Those four words. "Thank God you called." How many people ever get to hear that at their jobs? Her problem is engorgement. I walk her through expressing by hand. "That should help soften the breast a little. The nipple won't be so flat and little Joaquin"—as usual I remember the baby's name—"will be able to get a good latch."

"My mother-in-law says I should use cabbage leaves."

"Great idea if you're making cabbage rolls, but there's really no evidence that they work any better than a nice cold compress. An ice pack will help with tissue swelling." I tell her that it's safe to use acetaminophen or Advil.

I know Simone will be fine, but she's still uncertain and pleads, "Could you come over tomorrow?"

"I'd love to, but my daughter's leaving for college and I've had to clear my schedule for a few days to help her tie up some loose ends." I promise to check back as soon as Aubrey is safely winging her way toward a bright and shiny future.

"College," the new mom whimpers while Joaquin cries in the background. "Will we ever make it that far?"

"Blink twice, Simone."

She laughs. Always a good sign. I give her my colleague Janis's number. "If Joaquin is not drinking like a frat boy by tomorrow, Janis can help you." I think about Janis, who I split shifts at the hospital with—late thirties, married, two sons, kind eyes, an inexplicable affection for animal prints—and am relieved that there is finally another competent lactation consultant in Parkhaven who can fill in for me.

I hang up and notice that among the many things annoying me are the misbegotten Betty Page bangs I'm trying to grow out. They've reached the sheepdog stage and are driving me crazy. I pin them back before I return the rest of the calls.

The calls—each one so absorbingly unique, yet all variations of problems I've dealt with hundreds of times before—occupy me so completely that a couple of hours slip by before I finish the last one, switch the light off, and stretch out on the couch to listen in the dark for what I want to hear most: Aubrey coming home.

As I strain to detect the muffled squeak of the front door being quietly opened, I drift into the cozy place that floats on the outskirts of actual sleep. Memory overtakes me with the vividness of a dream, and I am back with Martin in our sweet little duplex in Sycamore Heights. We are eating the dinner we've spent a couple of happy hours making together—chiles rellenos with raisins and pecans stuffed into the peppers—on the postage stamp–size deck behind our rented house. We have recently discovered that there are other white wines besides chardonnay and that they are all delicious with chiles rellenos. It is sunset. Swallows dip through the air chasing late-spring insects. The smell of newly cut grass wafts over to us. Someone across the alley is playing Lucinda Williams's new CD. We are cocooned in the simple opulence of being together.

Most mothers say that the happiest moment of their lives was when their child was born. Aubrey's birth was the most *intense* moment of my life. But happiest? My pick for pure, simple happiness would be on that deck with Martin. I will never understand how, if he'd been even a fraction as contented as I was, he could voluntarily have given up that feeling.

I jerk fully awake, force the dream-memory aside, and listen for any sound that might indicate that Aubrey has come home. But the snuffling whistles of Pretzels snoring at my feet are all that disturb the utter silence.

My mother hovered and clung more than any helicopter mom that was ever invented after her. But even she couldn't control any of the most important events in my life. She couldn't control that she died young, and she couldn't control who I fell in love with. My future was decided on that train in Morocco when I fell in love with Martin.

I pray that my daughter's future has not already been decided. That it wasn't decided twelve months ago, at the start of her senior year, when my business finally really took off and I was gone all the time and I didn't intervene when I should have. I pray that Aubrey won't pay the price for my negligence. That she will come home tonight and have the life she was meant to have.

The entire first week of school is a weird limbo zone. My old life is pretty much over, but what I am heading for is mooshy and vague. At the same time, the feeling that Tyler's face can pop out at me at any second is sharp. That and thinking about my dad getting in touch with me are these random adrenaline spikes in the endless boredom.

So I come home and, as usual since Mom's business has gotten so busy, there is nothing decent to eat. She calls, but I don't answer, and she leaves a voice mail saying there is some kind of population explosion and she will have to stay late at the hospital. Which is fine except for the lack of edibles and me being starved, since I was too nervous at lunch to eat.

I make some cinnamon toast and watch while the butter melts and the cinnamon sugar turns all bubbly under the broiler. I take it out, put both pieces on a plate, pour a glass of milk. Consume. Suck buttersugar from my fingers. Repeat.

Then, without any planning at all, I get the laptop out, go to Facebook, and, like pulling a Band-Aid off with one fast rip, I confirm my father's friend request.

I have barely begun to believe that I've actually done it when Facebook makes the bloopy sound it does to alert you that someone wants to chat.

Chat?

I hadn't considered the possibility of chat. Since I've already jumped off the cliff, though, I click on his message, and keep on falling while the first real words my father has communicated to me in sixteen years appear on the screen.

4:34 P.M. AUGUST 26, 2009
=Aubrey, hello. Thank you for confirming me.

I come so close to slamming the laptop shut and calling Mom and telling her everything. About Dad. About Tyler. Everything. But I know that if I hesitate for one second I will freeze up and this will turn into an impossibly big deal, and I'll never do it, so I just dive in and start writing whatever pops into my head.

=**How could I not after I went to your page and saw that, essentially, you'd set it up just to be friends with me?**
=**God bless Facebook! Because of my situation here, it's the only way I could contact you without being monitored.**
=**Monitored?**
=**Long story. Not what I want to talk to you about. What I want to talk to you about is YOU!**
=**OK . . .**
=**Seriously, I want to know everything about you. What music, books, movies you like. Which ones you hate. What your favorite subject is in school. Everything. Aubrey, I've missed so much. We have so much to catch up on.**
=**Oops. I hear the garage door going up. Mom's home. We share this laptop, so I have to shut this down and log out. Sorry. GTG.**

I quickly sign out, because I don't actually Got To Go. I actually have GTB, Got To Breathe. Breathing. Something that pretty much stopped the instant that chat box blooped open.

I don't know how long I spend reading and rereading what he wrote and what I wrote back, but it startles me when Mom pounds on my door, yelling, "Hey, punkalunk! There's groceries in the car. Can you at least get the ice cream and milk in? I've got to pee like a racehorse."

Thanks for the image.

I open my door. As she sprints to the bathroom, she yells back at me, "How was your day?"

"Fine."

She stops dead in her tracks and studies me. One word. One single word and she knows. I am certain that she knows about me chatting with Dad. "What happened?"

"Nothing! God! I'm sorry my life is so boring."

She laser-scans me, gathering clues.

"Groceries," I say, and rush out to the garage, to the safety beyond her force field.

I'm asleep on the couch when Pretzels, whimpering patiently by the patio door, wakes me. My first thought is, *It's Aubrey's birthday.* When I hear the sound of water rushing through the pipes in the slab beneath my feet I almost burst into tears of joy: Aubrey is home.

I help Pretzels out the patio door, then rush to the kitchen to make a Happy Birthday breakfast of Miggy Moo. While butter bubbles in the frying pan, I press a Mickey Mouse cookie cutter into a piece of bread to make a big-eared bread cutout that I slide into the pan and break an egg into. This breakfast will make up for last year, when I was gone too much and not paying enough attention. It will atone for all the dry Cheerios eaten from a Tupperware container as she was strapped into a car seat driving to day care. It will redeem all the salt and grease abominations picked up from McDonald's on the way to drop her off at school. It will counteract an entire adolescence of breakfasts that Aubrey slept through. It will welcome my daughter into her eighteenth year of life and send her off to college.

Aubrey named this creation when she was eighteen months old, back when I was a stay-at-home mom who still had a husband and time to make special breakfasts. Aubrey was with me in the kitchen, strapped into the blue plastic high chair that Martin called the Space Pod. With the intensity of a heart surgeon, she was occupied chasing bits of pear, slippery as goldfish, around the tray. When I put the Mickey Mouse cutout toast filled with egg on the high chair tray, Aubrey had gazed up at me, her mouth rounded in a perfect O of awed amazement. Then I'd painted eyes and a big smile on the egg Mickey with a bottle of ketchup and, dazzled by my magical skills, Aubrey had cooed, "Miggy Moo."

Why hadn't I made Miggy Moo for my daughter every day of her life?

"Where's my inhaler?" Aubrey bursts into the kitchen, sucking in broken, staccato breaths that pull her pale, freckled shoulders up to her ears and scoop out shadowed hollows behind her collarbones.

I squelch my desire to sing "Happy Birthday," jump up and

down, hug her, and congratulate her for coming home; I know she's short on sleep and that makes her grouchy. Plus she's told me repeatedly that she doesn't want me to do anything for her birthday. Cool as a double agent trying to act normal, I answer casually, "There's an extra inhaler in my purse."

As she dumps out a flurry of old grocery receipts, wadded-up tissues, and an assortment of nonworking pens, I analyze Aubrey's face. I check her color and listen to her breathing to gauge how serious the attack is. For a moment, all I register is her beauty. The simple, luminescent beauty of youth, the beauty of her being mine and still being under my roof. I complete my analysis and exhale. This is a serious attack of annoyance more than asthma.

Aubrey is wearing an old T-shirt of Tyler's and one of the many pairs of ridiculously overpriced Nike shorts she inexplicably squandered her Lark Hill money on during her senior year. Her hair is squashed down on one side and feathers up in a cock's comb on the other. We used to laugh at the comical forms her baby-fine hair took during the night. But it's been a long time since we laughed together about much of anything, and it certainly doesn't appear as if we'll start this morning.

Still, whether she likes it or not, I hug my baby and whisper, "Happy birthday, sweetheart."

For just a second, she relaxes into my embrace and I am certain that we have reached a turning point. That it is all going to be fine. *Really* fine. But then I add, "We'll head over to the bank right after we eat," and she stiffens and pirouettes out of my arms. At least she didn't refuse. Right after we claim the money, I'll take her to Best Buy and see what kind of laptop I can afford. A girl going away to college, a birthday girl, needs her own laptop. I'll pick up a cake while we're out. Maybe set up a farewell dinner and see if she'll invite Tyler over.

When she can't find an inhaler in my purse, she rummages through hers, pulling out three kinds of lip gloss, several tiny bottles of hand sanitizer, a white bib apron with coffee stains dribbled down the front, and more keys than most janitors carry. All held together by a chain with Tyler's senior picture in a small pewter frame in the shape of half a heart. Of course, Tyler carries the other half.

An inhaler finally rattles out. Aubrey shakes it, huffs on it a couple times, and her shoulders relax. Without a word, she brushes past me, tears my list of college reminders off the magnetic pad on the front of the fridge, and on a clean sheet writes, "Refill inhalers!!!!"

The fourth exclamation mark is overkill. Unneeded. All the fourth exclamation point communicates is Aubrey's belief that I am a loser dipshit airhead who can't be counted on to do things like keep her alive.

Being blamed for the lack of refills makes me ask, "You've sort of been going through the inhalers lately, haven't you?"

The universe that lies in my simple observation.

Though I qualify it with "sort of" and couch it as a question, Aubrey still bristles. It's never the words. Not between a mother and a daughter. It's what lies beneath the words. It's every asthma attack Aubrey has ever had. It's her having to quit the soccer team when she was eight because Dr. Queng thought that exercise triggered the attacks. It's the fact that she had her first serious attack in a long time on the day of graduation three months ago and they've continued through the summer and, judging from the one empty and one nearly empty inhaler, have skyrocketed in the past two weeks. It's that we both know that anxiety is a much worse trigger than soccer ever was. It's that we can both turn our heads and see that the great room is filled with supplies for a four-year journey she won't even talk about making. It's that I'm starting to suspect that something far more ominous than simple grumpiness and reflex resistance is at the heart of her reluctance to claim her college money.

She gives me a look that encodes an encyclopedia's worth of information and I translate every buried meaning: *Stop hovering. Stop knowing enough about me to monitor, to judge, every single, solitary breath I take.*

I go into Zen Mama state, refuse to mirror back her mood, and say with as much perk and pep as I can manage, "So, today has to be the day we collect your tuition. For the first year." No reaction. Though it's a strategic weakness, I am so desperate for signs of life from her that I ask, "Are you excited?"

Aubrey glances at me as if I'd inquired brightly, "Triple root canal today! Are you excited!?" Since Aubrey shut me out after Black Ice

Night, almost nine months ago, I have been reduced to gathering clues about her in nonverbal ways. So I step close enough that I can smell her breath. It is metallic from the inhaler. Before her expression curdles and she backs away, I inhale more of her smell and analyze it as if I were a perfume maker. I detect the odor of burned coffee and Fritos that clings to her no matter how many times she showers. I can also smell the enemy: Tyler Moldenhauer. Besides those familiar odors, though, there is a new one that I've been catching hints of for the past few weeks. Amazingly, it is the aroma of actual cooking, the last thing that might occur in the lunch wagon. I try to identify the novel odor's components—garlic, cumin, lemon, parsley, and an earthy aroma that for some inexplicable reason causes me to recall the moment I met her father on that train lumbering through Morocco.

Aubrey reaches out and flicks the clips I used to pin my sheepdog bangs out of my face. "What's this? What's going on here?"

Delighted just to be interacting, I run my fingers along the bristly hedgehog array poking out behind the clips and explain, "Oh, you know, my bangs are in that awful stage when they're too short to pull back behind my ears and just hang in my eyes."

"You look like a Chinese gymnast. I don't see why you cut bangs in the first place."

"You're serious?" I ask her, flabbergasted. "I cut them because of what you said."

"I never told you to cut bangs."

"Not in so many words."

She pretends not to remember what I'm talking about. Not to remember that moment right before we set out for her high school graduation in the middle of May when she studied me with the laser intensity that only a teenage daughter can bring to bear upon her forty-four-year-old mother, then asked, "You know who you remind me of?"

"Who?" Grateful that Aubrey had tossed me a rare conversational bone and thrilled by the unusual experience of eye contact with my daughter, I wondered who she'd name. It had been a while, but people used to tell me I reminded them of Joan Cusack. It might be because I too have a barely perceptible lisp, since both of us seem to have tongues a tiny bit too big for our mouths. Would Aubrey even know who Joan Cusack was?

"Who do I remind you of?" I prompted. I'd also heard Maggie Gyllenhaal. I knew she knew who Jake Gyllenhaal was.

"Benjamin Franklin."

"Benjamin Franklin!" I'd laughed and swatted at Aubrey, pretending the Benjamin Franklin comment was a joke. "You bitch!" Back before Tyler, when I used to know who her friends were—the sweet, gawky girls from band, the boys who hoped they were gay rather than permanent misfits; before them, Twyla—Aubrey called them all "bitch." Especially the boys.

Aubrey squinted in irritation. "Don't do that."

"Do what?" I asked, though I knew immediately what she meant: *Don't try to talk like me. Be like me.*

I had wanted to tell her that I couldn't try to be like her because I no longer knew who she was. Later that day, though, after graduation, when Tyler had yelled out, "Go, Aubrey!" so loudly that everyone in the megachurch where the ceremony was held had laughed, I'd come home and examined my forehead. Beneath the harsh overhead light in the bathroom, I saw it, the Benjamin Franklin resemblance. Where my hairline had once been thick and dark as Wolfman's, spindly, sparse hairs now barely held the line above a dome of a forehead that did indeed suddenly appear huge and shiny as any Founding Father's. I'd recently had to start wearing reading glasses, and the wire-framed numbers I'd grabbed at the grocery store after the cool leopard-print pair I'd started with had broken didn't help.

So I experimented a little. I brushed down a few strands of hair, then snipped them into the barest of feathery wisps. It was such an improvement that I snipped more. Then some more. Improvements continued right up to the moment when Aubrey barged in, blinked twice, and said, "Oh, my God. Miss Tarketti."

"What?" I play-screeched. "Miss Tarketti?!" Miss Tarketti was her second-grade teacher who wore her hair in a tight pageboy with a Mamie Eisenhower sausage roll of bangs. I squashed my new bangs down and added, "I think they're cute. I was going for a Betty Page look."

Aubrey squinted. "Who?"

"The fifties pinup girl. She's very in now."

"With who?"

"Hipsters?" I supplied.

"Uh, in case you haven't noticed, Mom, not too many 'hipsters' here in Parkhaven. Unless you're counting yourself. You probably just spaced out again and cut too much off."

Aubrey took the scissors out of my hand as if I were a mental patient. I began growing my bangs out that very moment.

"Oh, hey," I ask Aubrey now, casual, as if the thought had just that second popped into my head. "Have you gotten in touch with . . ." I pause and snap my fingers as if I can't quite recall the name of the girl assigned to be her roommate. "Sierra! Have you written Sierra back yet?"

Aubrey shakes her head, as annoyed as if bees were swarming around it. "I told you, I will."

The *Jerry Springer* audience in my head screams at me to *Whup her sorry ass! Lower the boom! Quit pussyfootin' around!*

"When? Aubrey, you're leaving tomorrow. All this girl has ever wanted to know is what your colors are so she can get a rug that coordinates. Did you even tell her that you most definitely *do* want to go in on a minifridge and a microwave?"

Inexplicably, Aubrey reacts to my innocuous questions as if I'd gone after her with a blunt object. She splays out her fingers to silence me and shrieks, "I will! I told you I will! Do you ever believe or even listen to one single thing I ever say to you?"

I know she'd rather engage me in a big, screaming argument about whether or not, in her entire eighteen years of life, I, her oppressive, paranoid mother, have ever, for one second, believed anything she's said to me than actually answer my questions, so I don't oblige her and instead invoke Zen Mama and answer in my Hal the robot voice, "Aubrey, I'm not being unreasonable here. We don't even—"

"Amethyst and turquoise."

"What?"

"Or sage and heather."

"Sage and heather what?"

"Her colors, I'm sure those are what this roommate's colors are going to be. I mean, her name *is* Sierra. And her last name *is* hyphenated. How much more über–crunchy granola can anyone get? She's probably got a nose ring and major tats and creepy white-girl dreads."

"You're reading an awful lot into a name. Sierra did take the initiative to get in touch with you. That's friendly, isn't it? She's reaching out."

"Stalkers reach out too."

"Aubrey, she's your roommate. You could be living with her for the next four years."

She starts to speak and her right nostril twitches. This is Aubrey's "tell." It unnerves me because Martin had the same giveaway twitch. If we were playing poker, I'd know that he was considering bluffing. With Audrey it means that she is hiding something. She was always a horrible liar, and I can feel now that there is something she wants to tell me. For a fraction of a second her eyes widen with panic and I am certain that she is about to reveal everything.

I lean forward, reach out, and she whirls away. "I cannot be having this conversation now. Tyler will be here any second and I have to—"

I grab her arm before she can rush off. "What do you mean, Tyler will be here any second? You don't seriously think that you're going to work today. I have canceled all my appointments except for the class I have to teach later this morning to get this done. Why are we even discussing this? You're coming to the bank with me right now. We're going to transfer the money to pay for your first year's tuition. Then we're going to pack all of this up." I wave at the college supplies. "Then we're going to put you on a plane. Tomorrow. End of discussion."

"Okay! All right! I'll go. I just can't do it right now. Tyler and I are running a business and he needs me."

"You're working at a frigging lunch wagon, and if we don't go today, right now, that is exactly what you are going to be doing for the rest of your life! Is that what you want?"

"I am not 'working at.' We rent it. We're partners. We're building something, but just because it doesn't exactly fit your perfect-daughter image, you don't want to know anything about it."

"About what? What is there to know? Seriously, tell me."

"Why? So without you knowing anything, I can listen to you tell me what a loser I am?"

"Tell you you're a loser? Aubrey, when have I ever told you you're a loser? I have bathed you in toxic levels of self-esteem your entire life. I adored every drawing you ever held up for my approval and cheered every spelling test you ever passed. Your entire childhood was nothing but a Milky Way of gold stars awarded every time you brushed your teeth or pottied. Come on. We have been waiting for this day for sixteen years. We can finally claim your get-out-of-town money. Please, sweetie. For me. Let's just keep all the options open."

She jerks her arm away. "I said I'd do it! I can go this afternoon. I'll meet you back here after the lunch rush."

"I can't believe you don't want to be at the bank as soon as the doors open. What is so hard about this?"

"Uh, honoring your commitments. Ever heard of it?"

"How about your commitment to your future?"

"Whatever."

" 'Whatever'? Did you just say 'whatever' to me?"

I stare at this surly stranger planted in the middle of my kitchen radiating disgust at me in her inevitable pair of Nike shorts and one of her redneck boyfriend's old T-shirts and wonder if she is my penance for once believing that I was a parenting genius and that puberty was a tale invented by old wives who didn't know how to accept and love their children and let them follow their own unique path to become the unique human they were intended to be. The way I, in all my enlightenment, had.

At just the moment when I want to scream, "You bitch!" and not in the chummy BFF way, I see tears, staunchly unshed, glaze her eyes. Mossy green with thick lashes, her eyes are exactly like Martin's. Exactly like the one other person I loved most in the world who also became a complete and total stranger to me.

"Aubrey, sweetie. What is it? What's going on? You can talk to me. You know you can tell me anything."

Her chin quivers. The past year of hardness and distance falls from her and she is the little girl who collected dinosaur stamps and begged me for a pink bedroom with a canopy bed. There is a second of clarity, a truce. An umbilical connection joins us and I feel her anguish as surely as if she were kicking inside me beneath my heart.

"Aubrey, what's wrong, baby? Please. Tell me. Whatever it is, we'll figure it out together."

Every day I edge six inches closer to the football field. Today I reach the midway point between the football and band fields. It's not even about Tyler. The android predator with the number seven on his jersey directing the other androids on the football field is really beside the point. Seven has become just one of 360 degrees on a compass. I could have picked any number to move toward. Just so long as it took me away from where I was, that was all that mattered.

That's also how I feel about chatting with my father. I am just going to keep edging into it. Inch by inch. He wants to know everything about me. My classes, my teachers, my friends. He was actually interested in the fact that I got Saunders, the psycho physics teacher, instead of Miss Brawley, the non–mentally ill one. He loved my Freddie Mercury insight. He even noticed that I use "hectic" a lot. I told him it is sort of my signature word except that no one else besides him has ever noticed it. He told me that his signature word used to be "churlish."

Having him to report back to makes the reversed-binocular feeling useful rather than weird. Like I am an anthropologist gathering data on the customs and culture of a strange tribe I've been dropped in the middle of.

Today is the first day since school started that isn't so humid that my hair can make you seasick with all sorts of hectic waves and loopy roller-coaster twirls. The lack of humidity is good, since I got in some flatiron action myself and my hair is almost as straight and smooth as Paige's or Madison's. Also, the Nike running shorts that I am wearing are as short and ridiculously expensive as theirs, and my T-shirt is just as unflattering and generic, and the flip-flops I got at Goodwill are just as broken-in and run-down.

Why not? It is their world I am edging into. They didn't invite me. When you visit Muslim countries aren't women supposed to cover up?

I know Mom will say that they are all clones and I am being a clone. As if all Twyla's old friends, all the emo kids, are such giant individualists in their identical skinny black jeans and hair smushed down perfectly over one eye. Or me in my inevitable pair of whatever jeans and whatever top. As if being completely and utterly anonymous is less clonish than Nike running shorts.

While I am occupied thinking of how I will word it when I tell my dad all my insights into clone levels, a guy with a video camera stations himself a few feet from my blanket. He yells to a skinny kid in cargo pants who has a mic in his hand, "That's good! Right there! Move in a little closer! We can get the whole team in the shot! OK, get Coach!"

The kid with the mic pulls Coach Hines away from practice and leads him over close to where I am sitting. I want to leave, but it would be too obvious.

The camera guy is like, "OK, rolling," and Cargo Pants is, "Hi, this is Paul Harbaugh with Pirate Video, and we're interviewing Coach Hines. So, Coach, we've got our first game against Pineridge Consolidated tonight. Are the Pirates ready?"

Coach Hines has been watching his players on the field the whole time the kid is asking his question. When he notices that the talking has stopped, he turns around and plants himself with his feet spread wide and his arms crossed across his chest. Coach Hines is a very neat person. He wears crisp, pressed khakis and made the school order him and the assistant coaches white polo shirts with their names and a little pirate embroidered on them in red. He was recruited from a small college up north and always wears a tie and blazer to games. Some older kids told me that before he came, Parkhaven's team was crap and there were no black players. Now it's about half black, and last year we went to state. Everyone expects us to go again this year.

Without really knowing what the question was, Coach Hines answers like he is on ESPN. "We've got some good athletes this year. Lot of talented athletes. Lot of seniors. Trent Dupey, returning defensive end." He talks about a "strong safety" and a "dog linebacker," how they need to focus on their defensive game. "Offensively, we've got some top players returning. Wayshon Shelf set a couple of school records last year. A very smart kid. Runs great routes."

Cargo Pants asks him a long, involved question. While he listens, Coach Hines shifts his lower jaw back and forth like a snake. Like he is going to unhinge it so he can consume Cargo Pants in one delicious pockety bite.

Coach's answer grabs my attention away from his snaky jaw. "Of course, we're depending on Tyler Moldenhauer. *Sports Desk* just listed Moldenhauer as one of the top ten quarterbacks in the tristate area. He's being heavily recruited but hasn't committed yet. A very talented player. A team leader. A prolific passer. Tyler did a great job for us last year of getting the ball where we need it to be. We just hope he stays healthy."

"Can we borrow Ty-Mo for a second, Coach?"

I tense up, wondering where I can hide, then relax when Coach gives the guy a look that asks if he is kidding and walks away without answering.

In rapid succession, Cargo Pants drags several players off the field for quick interviews. Colt O'Connor, a kid both muscular and chubby, tells Cargo that he plays tight end, that his goal this year is to "take it one game at a time," and that the one person, dead or alive, who he would most like to have dinner with is Megan Fox. When Cargo Pants asks why, Colt gives him a look like, "How gay *are* you?" and says, " 'Cause she's lookin' good, dog."

Cody Chandler, a guy with freckles and red hair, says he is a wide receiver and that he gets psyched for games by "gettin' all up in my crunk" with his teammates. That he has "Lil Wayne, 2Pac, Fiddy Cen', and, of course, my man Snoop," on his iPod. After every answer Cody, who wants to be gangsta but looks like the Lucky Charms leprechaun, asks, "Ya feel me?"

Typical wigger jock.

Cody and Colt? Why would parents give these names to babies if they didn't want to program them to be football players? I should not be puzzling over this question, because, while I am daydreaming, Tyler breaks away and jogs over, pulling his helmet off as he comes. His hair is dark with sweat. My heart hammers. I don't need to worry. Even though I am close enough that I get hit with a drop of his sweat when he shakes his head, he takes absolutely zero notice of me.

Cargo Pants is all hectic as he announces, "It's the man of the hour himself, returning all-state QB, Tyler Moldenhauer. Tyler, can you tell us a little bit about yourself?"

Tyler leans his head to the side and smiles into the camera. "What do you want to know?"

Tyler Moldenhauer has dimples.

Actually, only one. On the right side. That isn't surprising. What is is something I hadn't noticed in my postpuke delirium: Tyler Molden-hauer has country teeth. Like Miss O'Day, my third-grade teacher who told us that hers were all mottled from growing up in the country and drinking well water. Also, Tyler's teeth are crooked. Not horribly crooked, kind of cute-crooked, but crooked enough that any parents who could have afforded it would have put him in braces. My teeth were not as crooked as his are, and Mom, who *couldn't* afford it, and reminded me constantly of what it was costing her to get the inside of my mouth sliced to ribbons with metal wires, got *me* to the ortho.

"Tell us what your goals are for the team this year."

Tyler is wearing his shoulder pads over his jersey like some kind of exoskeleton. "We need to keep the same record as last year. Need to get deeper into the play-offs than we got last year. Actually, that is not a goal. That is what we are going to accomplish."

Unlike the other boys, Tyler doesn't try to sound ghetto. He picks his words carefully. He works to sound smart and well-spoken.

"Can you tell us about some of the colleges that are scouting you?"

"No."

The way Tyler says "no"—not mad, just final, not open to debate—makes me understand why everyone looks to him to tell them what to do. I wonder what my father would think of Tyler. I imagine Tyler promising him that he'd have his daughter home by curfew. My father shaking his hand in a way that made it unnecessary for him to say, "You'd better. Or else."

Cargo Pants apologizes, "Oh. Sorry."

"No problem. Look . . ." Tyler pauses, puts his hand on the boy's skinny shoulder, leans in, asks, "What did you say your name was, son?"

Son? It is such an oddly grandfatherly thing for Tyler to say to someone only slightly younger than he is. The oddest thing about it, though, is that he sounds completely natural saying it. Like it would fit perfectly if he pulled out a knife and started teaching Cargo Pants how to whittle.

"Paul. Paul Harbaugh."

"OK, Paul, here's the deal for this year. This team has all the talent in the world. Talent is not a question. We have to crank up the discipline, study our routes, and execute, and we will go to state. We will be the hammer and not the nail. End of story." He sticks his hand out. Paul fumbles with the mic, shakes it. "OK, Paul, good job on the interview. Good talking to you. I need to get back to my boys."

Tyler pats Paul Harbaugh on the back in a way that both signals the interview is over and edges him out of the way. The instant Paul leaves, Tyler steps forward toward me.

"Hey, Pink Puke, you're lookin' better. But you should definitely not be in the sun." He nods toward Shupe. "Obviously, no one's got your back. That dee bag'd just let you die out here." Still facing me, he walks backward, toward the field. "You staying hydrated?"

I raise my bottle of water.

"OK, you drink those fluids, girl. That heatstroke—"

"It was just exhaustion. Heat exhaustion."

Heat exhaustion, really? That is really what I yell at him?

"Either way. That is serious shit. People die behind that shit."

I hold the bottle up and pretend to chug it. I ignore his dimple and see only the spotted, crooked teeth. They make me believe that Tyler Moldenhauer is just an ordinary boy.

He points at me, turns, and runs back to the team.

S cared and lost, Aubrey turns from me.

"Please, sweetie. Tell me what's wrong. Whatever it is, we can—"

EEEEEEEEEEE!

The smoke alarm shrieks.

The scared child disappears and, as if the black smoke pouring off the stove and the ear-piercing shriek were occurring in some galaxy far, far away and have nothing at all to do with her and her life here on earth, Aubrey observes, "Your thing is burning."

I turn off the stove, use my shoe to bang on the smoke detector mounted on the ceiling until the alarm stops. Mickey Mouse is charcoal. Egg and Teflon fused into a blackened crust. I toss the ruined frying pan into the trash. The charred and smoking pan immediately melts a hole through the plastic can and fills the kitchen with the odor of poached polyvinyls.

I fling open the front door to wave the smoke out and hear the rumble of Tyler's truck approaching. This is a rare appearance; they usually arrange for him to pick her up a few blocks away or whatever else it takes for him to never actually set foot in this house. A topic that has been the subject of more than one fight. Among the many lame excuses Aubrey has given me for why Tyler can't come in and pick her up like a decent person is that he has some kind of social anxiety disorder and meeting new people terrifies him.

Pretzels, who's managed to sleep through the fight and the screeching alarm, is roused by either the sound of Tyler's truck or the waves of hostility pouring off me. She rises shakily from her spot on the kitchen rug, totters over to where I stand at the open door, and looses a few barks that sound like a garbage disposal chewing through a tennis ball.

An anthem more pop than country and western throbbing from the truck, Tyler barrels into the driveway, cuts the engine, and brays along with the stirring finale, "Gimme that girl lovin' up on me!"

Ah, the enormity of the cultural divide contained within the bad grammar, the folksy anti-intellectualism, the paternalistic macho swagger of the one line that a privileged suburban jock pretending to be country chooses to sing. Why couldn't Aubrey have brought home one of those vegan, tattooed boys in the skinny black jeans who love bands with arty, non sequitur names?

The song ends. Tyler presses the brim of the cap hugging his head into an even tighter semicircle, plucks the Oakley wrap-arounds off his head, and settles them over his ridiculously blue eyes.

Social anxiety, my ass.

But I say nothing. If biting my tongue and walking on eggshells is the price to free my daughter from this redneck Romeo, I will pay it.

Pretzels gives a growl more mucoid than menacing; then, her work done, she lumbers back into the kitchen and flops, exhausted, onto her rug, sighing loudly at the imposition.

Stopping only to scoop lip glosses back into her purse and snatch up her apron, Aubrey hurries past. I grab her arm. "Aubrey, I want you back here the instant lunch is over so that, as soon as I finish class, we can blast to the bank. Okay? Got it? This is nonnegotiable."

"Okay! Okay! I already told you I would. What do you want? My name signed in blood? If that's how little you trust me, why don't you . . ." She pauses, then names the thing that she's been angling for for months. "Just throw me out!" She yanks away from my grip and runs out the door like the doomed heroine of a nineteenth-century novel, like Tess of the d'Urbervilles rushing to meet Angel Clare at Stonehenge.

I yell after her, "Don't make me have to drag you out of that . . . ! That . . . ! That mobile food conveyance vehicle! Because if I have to, I will!"

Aubrey's aggrieved stomping turns into an airborne dance the moment she slips beyond my reach. She has a sanctuary and she is running to it. Wafting across what remains of the lawn I can't afford to water, her feet don't seem to touch the ground once. From her first baby steps, Aubrey had helium in her bones, springing through life like a gazelle. I never understood how such a light-footed crea-ture could have issued from my leaden body. For a fraction of a sec-ond, I allow myself to enjoy the only comfort she still offers me, her beauty. I cling to it just the way I did when she was a colicky baby howling out her jerky screams as her tongue clicked spastically in her open mouth. Babies—silky, sweet-smelling babies. They must have been a cavewoman's first luxury goods.

Tyler opens the door of his truck and gathers Aubrey into his arms, the rescuing hero. My daughter puts her arms around Tyler's neck, hiking the Nike shorts up even farther, just in case she's left anything at all to the neighbors' imaginations. The sweethearts grin into each other's faces, delirious about being the punch line of their own secret joke.

The uncontrollable "replay" button in my mind activates, and Aubrey's entire life as it would have been with a father passes before my eyes, a father who would storm out at this very second, snatch his daughter from the clutches of this marauding male, make her "put some clothes on" and go to the bank with her mother. Right this minute. That father does not materialize and Tyler hauls Aubrey into the truck.

At graduation in May, I'd overheard a mom observing Tyler's and Aubrey's mutual gorgeousness whisper to her friend, "God, imagine the children they'd have." I remember that comment and, for a fraction of a second, the regret machine stops and time freezes in the present, right now, as it actually is.

Both Tyler's and Aubrey's faces are framed by circles of white shoe polish drawn on the front windshield with their names and "Sexy Seniors!" written above the circles. Sitting in that truck, with shoe-polish halos encircling their heads, they look like Mary and Joseph. A jolt of panic squeezes my heart as I allow the fear I've been denying to surface: that the only thing missing from their Holy Family tableau is the Baby Jesus himself, standing between the haloed couple. Just an ignorant little redneck baby who would utterly destroy my daughter's life and condemn her to live in this miserable suburban wasteland forever.

God, if I'd only been able to nip this romance in the bud. If I'd even only known when it started.

I am completely and unequivocally into football territory. Paige Winslow and Madison Chaffee, sitting on the aluminum bleachers five feet away, don't notice me.

In world history last year, we studied the rise and fall of the Soviet Union. Mr. Figge explained what de-Stalinization was, how leaders like Stalin would be expunged from the country's history so completely that their faces were literally erased from photos. That's what Paige and Madison have done to me: They've de-Stalinized me. I still remember when we all played together at the pool, diving under for plastic rings, riding together on field trips to Pioneer Farm, but they don't. Friendship with me turned out to be the kind of embarrassing accident that happened when you were little, before everyone found their place in the social hierarchy.

They assume that I hate them. That I am deeply jealous and want to be them, but that since I never will be, I've channeled my envy into scorn and hatred. It is a valid assumption and generally true. But wrong in my case. I don't want to be them any more than I want to be one of Twyla's burnout buds. I don't think my life is tragic and that it would be golden if I was popular. I just think they are exactly who they were raised to be since their parents named them Paige and Madison and it is irrelevant if I hate them or want to be them.

I smile and shrug. Paige and Madison have no idea what I am shrugging about any more than I would understand them if they shrugged at me. It would just be a chance to huddle with my friends and get that delicious feeling that comes from whispering about someone who is not like you with someone who is like you. I understand. I truly do. I would like whispering with someone who is like me. But no one is.

I think it is because my sizzle doesn't match anyone else's. I want something to happen so bad that it sizzles inside of me. It never stops, but it also never fits any of the choices presented. Maybe because there is only one you are ever allowed to talk about: college.

"Which schools are you thinking about?" everyone asks, like they are taking each other's temperatures, seeing whose sizzle matches theirs. But, even when I try, I can't make myself care about colleges. About next year. Not when there is so much to pay attention to right now.

At the end of practice, the players all get in a circle, bump fists, yell, "Pirate Power!" and run to the locker room. Paige stands up on the bleachers and calls out, "Tyler! Ty-Mo! Are we studying after school today?"

Tyler turns, yells back, "Yeah, sure! I'll meet you at your car!"

The instant Tyler's back faces her, Paige bites her knuckle like she wants to eat her entire arm. Or Tyler Moldenhauer. Madison fans herself to show that she agrees that Tyler is unbearably hot.

Tyler pivots back around. Paige yanks her hand out of her mouth; he yells, "I'm starving!"

Paige answers, "I'll pick up tacos, OK?"

Before he can say anything else, Tyler's glance hits me. I hold up my water bottle and wave it at him to show that I'm drinking fluids like he told me to. He doesn't acknowledge me in any way other than a pause of half a second before he looks back at Paige and yells, "Cool!"

Half a second is exactly long enough for me to be sure that he has seen me and that he could care less.

12:12 A.M. SEPTEMBER 14, 2009

=Why did you leave us?

=Aubrey, hi. Wow, I've been waiting for that bomb. Trying to figure out what I'd say. I used to know the answer. I used to know all the answers. But I don't anymore. Not to that. Not to anything. That's a long conversation that probably can't/shouldn't be done inside a tiny chat bubble.

=Yeah. OK. GTG.

=Aubrey, don't run off. I want to answer that question. Just . . . I'd like it to be in person.

=And I'm sure that will be real soon. Aren't you, like, supposed to get excommunicated for even talking to me?

=They would not be happy about it.

=So I don't see a big in-person meeting happening anytime soon.

=Aubrey, remember this: I loved you from the first second of your life.

I loved you from the first second of your life.

Big freaking lot of good that did me.

I close the page without saying good-bye or GTG and think about unfriending him. But why? So I can join Mom in pretending that I haven't spent most of the past sixteen years thinking about him? Oh, except, unlike Mom, I would then have *two* people that I can pretend I am not thinking about. Two people who, according to her, I am supposed to hate and must erase from my consciousness.

It's impossible to make yourself *not* think about someone. Who's one of the top three figures everyone knows from Russian history? Maybe Rasputin. Maybe Catherine the Great. But, for sure, everyone knows Joseph Stalin.

De-Stalinization. Didn't even work for Stalin.

After the Water Bottle Incident, I move as far from the football practice field as I can get, all the way back to the band sidelines. Back to where T.M. will never see me again.

Shupe does see me, though, and asks, "Where are your notes, Lightsey? If you're not marching and not memorizing the new drills, I can't give you credit."

Though I already know that I am never going back, it still surprises me when I hear myself say, "That's OK, Shupey-Doo. I'm dropping band."

I am also surprised at how easy it is to walk away and leave three years behind as if they had never happened. I didn't think that I was the kind of person who could do that.

But it turns out that I am. Turns out that I am a lot of things that no one, especially not me, thought I was.

Aubrey is pregnant.

Stupid as it sounds for someone who spends every day with women who either are or just were pregnant, the thought of my daughter knocked up never crossed my mind, since I have been hammering birth control into her since she lost her baby teeth. Still, what else would explain why her sullenness has escalated so dramatically recently?

I run to Aubrey's room. It is even more freakishly neat than usual. Stark, actually, since over the course of the summer she has moved so many of her clothes to Tyler's. All her books are arranged according to when she acquired them. *Amelia Bedelia* at the very beginning and those *Twilight* books at the end. I notice that she hasn't bought the last book in the series and my pulse races even faster; this lack of interest in an unconsummated love affair is an ominous sign. I'm not a fool. I know that there has been consummation. Far too much consummation. I knew that from the first night she failed to come home.

What I want to find are signs that all this consummation has been controlled. A nice, empty pill dispenser, a diaphragm would be great. What I really *don't* want to find is a white plastic stick with a pink positive sign on it. Mostly I'm doing what I did when I sniffed at the new odors clinging to Aubrey: gathering evidence from an uncooperative witness.

Tiny bottles of hand sanitizer gleam at various spots around the room. What clothes remain in her closet all hang in the same direction. The shoes she's left behind are boxed up in perfect rows on the shelf above her clothes. Peeking down at me from a shelf beside her bed are her My Little Ponies, with their squat bodies and pastel manes, that I recall her occasionally rearranging long after most girls her age had abandoned ponies and morphed from cuddly pre-teen puppies into aloof, disdainful adolescent cats whose fondest hope was that their parents would leave their credit cards in a neat pile before signing on for an extended tour aboard a nuclear sub-marine. Listening to the other moms moan about how their daughters had mutated overnight from sweet, submissive girls into snarly tramps who hated them and wanted to wear little junior-miss stripper outfits was part of the reason I thought I was a parenting genius.

Eventually, of course, the "whatevers" and eye rolling, gasping, and utter exasperation began. I thought I'd nipped the problem in the bud by telling her, "Look, let's save us both a lot of time. Just end every statement you direct toward me with the words 'you asshole,' because that is exactly what you're saying to me."

I now look back on that time fondly because, although the "whatevs" did start, we were still connected. There would be entire weekends of truce when we would watch a complete season of *Project Runway* or shop for new tops for her together. Since Tyler Moldenhauer, however, Aubrey hasn't been connected to anyone but him.

Resting on the pillow of her neatly made bed is BeeBee, Aubrey's favorite Puffalump. BeeBee was once a Pretty Hair Purple. Pretty Hair Purple BeeBee is gray now, all the stuffing from her head has shifted into her lumpy legs, and her braids are dull, fuzzy ropes. BeeBee was a present from the last Christmas that Martin and Aubrey and I spent together sixteen years ago.

I put my nose to the bedraggled toy and a bit of wisdom I'd stumbled across in my Googling last night flits through my mind: "Your kid will always come back." *Yes, I know she'll come back*, I now want to tell that blithe poster, *but will she ever come back as a newborn with breath that smells like caramel? A four-year-old who sits in my lap through whole movies so she can bury her face in my chest at the scary parts? A ten-year-old eager to explain to me in dazzling detail why Sailor Moon must search for the fabled Moon Princess? A two-year-old who tries to say "baby" and it comes out "BeeBee"?*

A couple of poster-size collages trace her romance with Tyler through homecoming, prom, winter formal, and formals that I never even learned the names of. In the next-to-last photo, they're holding their maroon polyester graduation robes open to reveal that they're wearing nothing except bathing suits underneath. The last photo was taken at a graduation party given by their friends. Well, *his* friends, really; I didn't recognize any of the sports-capped chuckleheads or spaghetti-strapped hoochies holding up cups of beer caught in midslosh and grinning drunken grins at the camera. Tyler—wayward curls of dark hair flipping out beneath the weathered cap hugging his head, the torn-away sleeves of his snap-button Western shirt showing off arms still pumped up with football muscles—has Aubrey slung over his shoulder and is carrying her away, off toward the dark beyond the flash.

I shift to alternate-universe mode and imagine how our lives would have turned out if we'd never left Sycamore Heights, the vibrant, diverse neighborhood in the city we abandoned so that we could send our child to the best schools within driving distance of Martin's job. Would Martin and I still be together? What if I'd never gotten pregnant? Life without Aubrey is the one parallel universe I am incapable of imagining. All I know is that had we not left Sycamore Heights, Tyler Moldenhauer would never have entered the picture.

I check under the bed. Her clarinet case is shoved far off in a back corner. I pull it out and hold the instrument, stroke the keys worn smooth by her fingers. There is another box hidden so far under the bed that I have to get the broom to drag it out. I promise myself that I will take a quick peek, then slam it shut if I don't see what I'm looking for. I blur my eyes a bit so that if it is love letters, naked photos, I won't absorb any details.

I don't know why I am surprised to find the Book of Palms, a scrapbook with all the photos of her father I could gather. I run my hand over the big album. I'd pasted the title on myself using peel-off gold letters in a swirly font, hoping to underline the joke aspect of the name I'd given this volume. I wanted Aubrey to know about her father. But not to take any of it too seriously. She was such a quiet, solemn child, I didn't want her absent father to become a dark, intense issue.

I open the book and there is the first photo of his palm, frozen by the flash from a paparazzo's camera, shielding the face of a celebrity. I first saw it on a dreary, cold Monday in February fourteen years ago. I was in the checkout line at the grocery. It was sleeting outside and almost dark at six in the evening. Aubrey was four and cranky from getting her MMR vaccine and from a too-long day at day care. All the days were too long back then when I was scrambling to get my business started. Aubrey wouldn't stop fussing and whining even with black drool running down her face from the bag of Oreos I'd opened and stuck in her hands to keep her quiet. I felt achy and chilled, knew I had a cold coming on, and couldn't afford to cancel any visits with the few patients I had. All I wanted was to pay for the milk, juice, eggs, apples, and bread in my cart, go home, throw something together for dinner, unload and reload the dishwasher, pack lunches, and try to be in bed before I dropped in my tracks.

And then Aubrey threw the open package of Oreos on the floor and lunged for the box of Twix bars next to us in the checkout aisle, knocking those to the floor as well. I was on my hands and knees picking up candy bars and Oreos when I first came face-to-palm with Martin, now going by his bizarre new name, Stokely Blizzard, on the cover of the *National Enquirer,* sticking his hand out to shield the celebrity he was shepherding. The caption read, "Next! Honcho Stokely Blizzard wards off photographers as former sitcom star Lissa Doone exits a three-month stay at Ramparts, Next's! exclusive rehab clinic."

I bought the tabloid and started a photo album. Every few months I'd add another clipping. It was from them that I learned that Next sued any publication that didn't capitalize their name and include the trademarked exclamation point. That their lawyers were so ferocious they'd even battled off a lawsuit brought by Scientology that claimed Next had stolen much of their theology and most of their biggest adherents. And that "the church" christened the ultra-elite converts like Martin, who'd surrendered all their worldly possessions and enlisted for "ninety-nine lifetimes," with names that combined their mother's maiden name with their favorite meteorological phenomenon. Hence Stokely Blizzard. It was like figuring out what your porn-star name would be except with weather instead of pets.

As I'd told Dori, the fact that Next bordered on the farcical actually made losing Martin to it harder. So, no, Next would be getting no exclamation points from me.

At first the "stars" that Martin counseled and was photographed with were has-beens—pinwheel-eyed drug burnouts; sex addicts trying to look ashamed; duckbilled, eternally surprised plastic-surgery casualties. All of them caught in the act of rebuilding their careers with steel beams forged in the Next crucible.

After a few years of counseling and guarding has-beens and never-weres, Martin moved up to shielding the faces of currently working, B-minus-list actors on the make looking to move up. Or solid B-listers, maybe even a few A-minuses who were slipping off the list after a string of bombs. Actors appeared to be the ideal candidates for Next. These were people who dreamed of the chance to be whoever someone told them they needed to be. Hopefully the person doing the telling would be a director with a closetful of Oscars. But if Spielberg or Scorsese didn't materialize, Next was always there, ready to tell the world's most insecure humans precisely who they needed to be. And what Next told them all to be was a Nextarian.

Gradually the hidden faces behind Martin's palm came to belong to celebrities who were seriously worth protecting: solid box-office earners, leads in popular television series, musicians with platinum albums. Finally, he and his palm protected the faces of some of the hottest stars in the world.

As if association with celebrities that blistering could ignite any chunk of matter they came into contact with, Martin himself eventually became a paparazzi target. I knew he had arrived the day I saw someone else's palm, some other Next underling, shielding *his* face. Apparently Martin had risen high enough in Next that he required his own Swiss Guard stiff-arming the press and hiding him from view. It had been years since I'd come across a clear shot of his face.

So I collected the photos and made the Book of Palms for Aubrey, hoping that the fact that she shared genes with a father who could sell tabloids would register on some level. But mostly the palm photos confused her. By middle school, her only comment when a new one appeared was, "Weird."

By that time, she had cut her ties with the fairy-winged Twyla and told everyone that I was "a pediatric nurse." Like Dori said, Aubrey wanted to fit in, so I just stopped adding photos. Then she stopped mentioning him altogether, and, taking my cue from her, I did the same.

My mom thinks I am insane for working in the attendance office for a fourth year. But attendance is like band. It is a place to be. Also, I like what you find out when you're an aide. Such as who has an appointment every week with the orthodontist or the speech therapist. Also who has to go to AA meetings or check in with their probation officer. And, since I work fifth period, right after "B" lunch, and hand out tardy slips, I know who spends lunch getting high or having sex. It is a closed campus except for seniors with permission, so theoretically nothing like that can happen. But, as Twyla used to say, "That's why God invented bathrooms." And, in her case, Dumpsters, and prop rooms, and cars with tinted windshields. But then, Twyla was not ever what you'd call discreet.

Thinking about Twyla makes my heart hurt. I remember this one time in seventh grade when she called me up late Friday and asked if I would help her TP her house. Her *own* house. Twyla had gotten too weird for me by that time. She'd started cutting herself, and talked not about the tattoos she was planning to get, but the *sleeves* of tattoos she was planning to get. But even if we had still been friends, I wouldn't have helped her. It made me too sad to think about anyone sneaking into her own front yard and throwing toilet paper around so that it would look like her friends or, even more ridiculous, her boyfriend had wrapped her house. But Twyla went ahead and did it all by herself.

Most parents, the second they saw all that toilet paper drooping out of their trees, would have gotten their kid out of bed in the middle of the night to clean it up. Not Twyla's mom. Not Dori. She was probably proud of the streamers of toilet paper hanging down from the tall sycamore trees. Probably thought it was a bold declaration of the slob-queen housecleaning style she and my mom bonded over. As if the warped card table left out from a garage sale she'd had months ago, and the deflated husk of an ancient wading pool, and the acrylic painting she'd taped over a broken-out windowpane weren't enough clues. So the Charmin was just left there to blow in the breeze all weekend.

Sunday night, it rained.

Monday, after school, I did what I always did and waited until the very last minute to get on the bus. Then I acted all distracted, and pretended that I was trying to find something in my backpack and that I didn't see Twyla, sitting all the way in the back, waving wildly at me. I grabbed the first open seat as close to the front as I could manage. We always passed Twyla's house on the way home. That day, though, before we even reached her house, a murmur passed through the bus and kids moved over to the windows on the side that faced it.

The rain the night before had made the toilet paper clump together into lumps of gray papier-mâché. Someone—I didn't turn around to see who—yelled out, "Hey, Twyla, nice job on the wrapping!"

Everyone laughed. They all knew. Or just made the obvious guess that Twyla had wrapped her own house. I laughed with them. I had to. If I hadn't everyone would have assumed that I had helped Twyla. That I was still her friend. That night was the first time I unlatched the screen on my window and sneaked out of the house. I took the long pole with the hook on the end of it that Mom used to clean the fan in the great room with me, went over to Twyla's house, and cleared off as much of the TP as I could reach.

I get the same cringing, burning-with-shame feeling I had on the bus passing Twyla's house when I think about how I'd held up my little bottle of water and waved it at Tyler like it was some secret lover's signal. It was clear from the way he'd looked right through me that if he'd ever given me a second thought, it was, "What is the deal with that sketchy stalker girl?"

Who cared, though, really? I wanted to get out of band and he helped me do that. That's all that is important. That's all I really care about.

It's Friday. Friday is a big day for the Jims 'n' Jays crowd—the noontime equivalent of the Wake 'n' Bake morning tardies—named in honor of their lunch favorites, Slim Jims and joints. Miles Kropp, a guy I'd written lots of slips for, meandered in. We always acted like we didn't know each other, even though he'd been part of Twyla's stoner-emo-goth group since sixth grade. His eyes, rimmed in thick black liner, are rabid-bat red. He stands on the other side of the attendance counter, not saying a word.

"Do you need a tardy slip?" I finally ask.

"Hu-u-u-h?" He makes a big deal out of slurring the word and saying it real slow.

I write his name at the top of the slip, the last one on my pad, and ask, "Reason for tardiness?"

"Huh?"

"We'll just say 'personal.' "

"Yeah. Right. Cool. Per-suh-nul." He says it in a dreamy, sleepy way. "Like I'm a null person." His giggle reminds me of Twyla. So does the way he is proud of himself, just like Twyla always was when she was high and expected me to be shocked and outraged but secretly impressed and jealous.

He leaves and the office is empty. Miss Olivia hasn't gotten back from lunch yet. When she does, she'll listen to all the attendance messages, then send me out to pick up the kids whose parents have called in asking for them to be excused for doctor's appointments or to talk to the reps visiting from colleges. Today it is Hendrix and Carnegie Mellon.

I need more tardy slips and am almost out of permissions, so I go to Miss Olivia's desk. I am the only one she allows near her desk, since it contains the precious slips that she keeps under lock and key. Miss Olivia is obsessed with making sure that no student ever sneaks out of so much as one class. She still talks about a senior two years ago who'd managed to steal her pad of slips and get three of his friends out of class before she traced the stolen slips and got him suspended. For a week.

Miss Olivia's desk is covered with her massive collection of turtle knickknacks and photos. In the largest of the framed photos she is with her ex-husband and their baby daughter. Her daughter, who is in her early thirties now, has a pink bow taped to the top of her bald head. The ex has one of those eighties haircuts with no sideburns that make it look like the top of his hair isn't attached, like it is just a hair cloud floating around his head. He looks happy and proud and filled with love. Next to that one is a picture of Miss Olivia's daughter in a graduation gown with a mortarboard loosely pinned onto her big, curly hair. Miss Olivia stands beside her with the same hair. The father is not in the picture.

Not in the picture.

I guess that's where the expression comes from.

In the most recent photo, Miss Olivia is holding her asthmatic Chihuahua, Elvis, next to her face and making him wave at the camera. Her hair is thin and flat, the way it grew in after the chemo.

Since she is a giant Pirates football fan, Miss Olivia has a team photo tacked to her wall. But she especially worships Tyler and has a close-up of him pasted in the center of a red football that she cut out of construction paper. I am staring at it when a voice behind me says, "Pink Puke, so this is where you hang out."

I turn. Tyler Moldenhauer is at the counter.

Tyler Moldenhauer is at the counter.

My brain cannot absorb this information. It shorts out and refuses to send signals to my mouth to make it form words or even to my legs to order them to get me up off my butt and walk to the counter.

"I wondered where you disappeared to." He leans down and rests his head on the back of his hands, folded on top of the counter. "You work here or are you just stealing turtles?"

"What? Oh." I glance down at Miss Olivia's turtle paperweights, turtle Beanie Babies, turtle figurines, turtle paper-clip holder, and turtle mouse pad and snort something that is meant to be a laugh but comes out like I might be about to barf again.

"What are you doin'?" he drawls. While I consider and discard a thousand equally stupid responses, he hoists himself up onto the counter, swings his legs around as smoothly as an Olympic gymnast, and dismounts on my side of the counter. He leans in next to me to study Miss Olivia's turtle herd and says, "I detect a theme here."

Sadly, the nerd section of my brain unfreezes before any of the cooler parts and I jump up, babbling, "Why are you even here? The athletic faculty handles all sports absences. You can't be back here."

"I can't? Seems I am, though." He picks up a sneering turtle with a sign around its neck that reads YOU WANT IT WHEN? "This one here has got to be my favorite."

"That area is off-limits to students!" The top half of Miss Olivia's body appears at the counter. Tyler's back is to her, so she can't see who is with me. "What is he doing back there?"

Tyler doesn't turn around. He makes the grumpy turtle sniff his thumb, then fall in love with the nail. I ignore him as he puts Miss Olivia's turtle on the back of his hand and makes it hump his thumb.

"He's from the district office," I say. "He's fixing your hard drive."

His back still to Miss Olivia, Tyler drawls in a surprisingly realistic hillbilly accent, "Yes'm, your hard drive has to be recalibrated." His improv is good except that he is patting Miss Olivia's fax machine instead of her external hard drive.

"He is not from district. He is a student and he is not allowed."

Tyler turns around, "Um, I'm sorry, ma'am."

I wait for Miss Olivia to go into lockdown mode, because no one, not even her pinup boy, is allowed into her forbidden realm. I know that she will summon Miss Chaney, who will then suspend Tyler. And probably put me on probation for not dying to prevent access to the sacred excused-absence slips. But instead of turning into a shrieking lunatic, Miss Olivia bubbles out, "Tyler Moldenhauer, how can I help you? Do you need an excused absence?" She snaps at me, "Get Tyler an excused absence."

Get Tyler an excused absence?

I begin to understand why varsity players never have to come to the attendance counter. I guess administration doesn't want anyone seeing the special treatment they get.

"Stay right there, Ty-Mo," Miss Olivia orders, then chugs around to the entrance at the far end of the office that admits only the officially approved.

"OK, I'm out," Tyler says. And just like that, like a flea disappearing from one spot, he hoists himself back onto the counter and is gone before Miss Olivia circumnavigates her way around to our station.

She is huffing a little when she reappears. "Where is he? Where did he go? What did he need?" When I don't answer, she informs me, "Aubrey, that was Tyler Moldenhauer." Her voice and face are like she just said, *Aubrey, that was Jesus.*

"OK . . ." I give a vague nod, acting like I can't quite place this Tyler Moldenhauer person she speaks of.

"All-state three years in a row? Runs the forty in four-point-five? His junior year he was two thirty-two of three sixty-eight for three thousand ninety-four yards with twenty-seven TDs and only six interceptions? He's met with recruiters from six Division One colleges already, and I have excused absence requests for him to meet with two more."

Everything she tells me is obviously a giant deal on Planet Football. But it all just makes me wish that the person she is referring to didn't have all sorts of numbers attached to him. That he was just an ordinary boy who smelled like the ocean on a cold day.

U nder the Book of Palms is an assortment of Aubrey's old school papers, book reports, stories, assignments. They are festooned with stars and happy faces, thumbs-up stickers, and rainbows. Notes scribbled in the margins exclaim over what a good writer Aubrey was. I pick up an essay from sixth grade on the topic of school uniforms, written in her careful cursive.

I know that there will be many who will attack school uniforms and say they are a bad idea because they hinder a person from being an individual. I disagree and say the exact opposite. School uniforms would actually help someone be who they really are. Instead of being forced to choose a group and try to fit into it through a certain exact kind of clothes, everyone would start off on an equal—

"Are you searching Aubrey's room?"

"God, Dori, don't sneak up on me like that."

"If by 'sneak up' you mean pound on your front door, then come in and yell, 'Cam! Cam! Oh, Miss Cam Lightsey! Hello! Are you in here!,' then, getting no response whatsoever, come back here in order to start CPR or locate your corpse, then I'm sorry that I 'sneaked up' on you." Dori's sproingy curls, dyed a mauvey brown this month, quiver as she whips her head around. "You are, aren't you? You're searching Aubrey's room."

"No," I answer, and she joins me in searching Aubrey's room.

I had been friendless for more than a year when Dori showed up for back-to-school night at the start of first grade. Dori and I never would have been friends back in the city, where her tattoos and transgressions would have made her blend in rather than stand out. But, like two Americans who wouldn't have talked to each other in their homeland, Dori and I became fast friends in the alien land of Parkhaven. We bonded over being single outcasts in a place where everyone was paired up like they were boarding the Ark, and over our shared amazement that none of the other mothers had any lives—past or present—outside of being supermoms obsessed with their children and with Parkhaven Elementary.

When I met Dori, I was still smarting from being dropped by the inner circle of Parkhaven moms, and I knew the instant I saw the armband of tribal tattoos encircling her biceps and the crescent of diamond studs curling around the top of her ear that she was my soul mate. Or the closest thing to one that I was going to find at Parkhaven, where Joyce Chaffee once caused a minor sensation when she got a few magenta streaks put in her hair. Streaks that were gone a day later.

Dori happily admits that she is an "attention whore." Even when it is negative, she has to have it. Being the official Parkhaven Weirdo Mom inspired her to new heights of outrageousness. During rare playdates with other moms, Dori openly shared details of how her ex had taken up with a stripper, and how she got up every morning and balanced her Zoloft, Xanax, and Claritin with a couple of Red Bulls. There were never any second playdates. I was only too happy to let Dori take over as Parkhaven's biggest Weirdo Mom, a role I felt I'd been assigned because I had no husband or garments made of khaki.

Dori called Parkhaven her "witness protection program." She fancied herself a fugitive, hiding out from a scary ex-husband in the last place on earth where he'd come looking for her. After a few years during which the scary ex was revealed to be a rich boy living on a trust fund while he pretended to be Steven Tyler, I began to suspect that inertia more than anything was holding Dori hostage in suburbia. That and the fact that out here the attention addict was a showstopper, but back in the city she was just another former riot grrrl with tats starting to sag.

"Let's sell our blood" was one of Dori's many suggestions for how we could afford to move back to the city. She also thought we should turn tricks behind the concession stand at soccer tournaments and sell crack along with the Girl Scout cookies. But, even if we split a place in the city, the math never worked out. As part of the divorce settlement, Martin had paid off just enough of the house—sadly bought near the top of the market—so that I could barely afford the mortgage, but not enough that I'd have much left if I sold it. And even less since I was still paying off the home equity loan I'd taken out when Aubrey needed braces. Then I went even further into the hole when I broke some bones in my foot and couldn't work for three weeks. Besides, in spite of the facts that Parkhaven Elementary was far from the exemplary school its test scores had led me to believe and Aubrey never made many friends there, I hated to think about how hard it would be for my shy girl to adjust to a new place. Which is another reason why, at first, Dori was a godsend. Twyla and Aubrey became best friends for the rest of their time at Parkhaven Elementary.

The girls had sleepovers almost every weekend. They watched *Cinderella, Charlotte's Web, Beauty and the Beast, Aladdin,* and *Little Mermaid* together so many times that the VHS tapes got streaks, while Dori and I split endless bottles of Australian kangaroo wine and debated who'd gotten screwed worse in her divorce and what giant outcasts we were in Parkhaven.

Another favorite topic of discussion was the impossibility of meeting men in the suburbs. This led to us signing each other up— at first as a joke, then for real—for online dating services. We spent endless evenings culling through the candidates. Dori delighted in poking fun at the gooniest of them, the ones with hair transplants that looked like a connect-the-dots puzzle, or who bragged about "owning my own business," which we'd find out meant the guy drove a cab. We both went on dates and ended up doing unforgivable things like calling each other from bathroom stalls and whispering about dodgy odors and tasseled shoes. We both endured periods where we boldly declared that we needed "friends with benefits," and, for a few weeks, a month or two, managed to look past a guy's icky mom issues, green-ringed toilet bowls, and compulsions to correct how we drove, cut our meat, and pretty much everything else, except the one unforgivable deal breaker, how we raised our daughters.

Once I realized that the postmortems with Dori were far more satisfying than any of the actual liaisons, I took my profile down and lived vicariously through her.

Now, as I search through Aubrey's drawers, Dori asks, "Didn't we have a pact that we'd never be like our moms and read our daughters' diaries and violate their privacy?"

"I'm not violating anyone's privacy. Short of discovering a syringe, I don't care what I find." I bite my tongue, but Dori doesn't seem to take any notice of my syringe comment. I guess she believes that it doesn't apply to her, since, before she left, Twyla was abusing prescription drugs she stole from her babysitting customers, instead of shooting up or doing anything that involved syringes. I want to ask Dori if she regrets our pact, since Twyla clearly could have benefited from a few room searches.

I comfort myself with the thought that at least Aubrey never had any interest in drugs. Then I feel bad that Twyla is my At Least. All mothers have them. The child who—no matter what our own offspring is smoking or drinking or failing at—we can look at and think, *At least. At least my child is not pregnant or in prison. Or gone off to live with her drugged-out, Aerosmith-wannabe dad.* Surrounded as I am by all the Parkhaven overachievers trying to decide between Duke or Stanford, I desperately need an At Least. I just wish that it weren't Twyla.

"So what are we looking for?"

"Nothing, really. Okay, I'd love to find some proof that she's using birth control."

"You should have gotten her on the pill."

"Don't 'should' on me, Edith Piaf."

"I think my mother crushed up birth-control pills and sprinkled them on my Pablum. Oh no, wait, now I remember. She had me locked up in a chastity belt. So you think Aubrey's pregnant? Our little rule follower? No way."

Dori eliminates the possibility. Twyla was the wild one. Aubrey was the sensible one. Until Tyler came along she was the diligent student, the neat freak, the conscientious grade-grubber who was going to keep us all organized.

"Jesus. Aubrey and I should be cruising the aisles at Target, arguing about minifridges like all the other mothers and daughters."

"Well, not all."

Dori flops down on Aubrey's bed. She strokes the hardened remnants of BeeBee's purple hair. "Remember when the girls went through their fairy period?"

Instantly, Aubrey and Twyla are back in this room with us. They sit together on Aubrey's bed dressed in their fairy getups: gauzy wings from the dollar store and Goodwill prom dresses scissored into fluttery Tinker Bell creations. Twyla's copper curls are dark, almost mahogany compared with Aubrey's duckling-down blondeness. Like the two little girls in the locker room, they talk to each other with the solemn intentness that only girls of that age can bring to a conversation with a friend.

"You are the mama fairy," Twyla dictated to Aubrey. "And I'll be the baby fairy."

"And you're lost in the deep dark forest," Aubrey improvised. "And I come and find you."

"No!" Twyla shouted. Strong-willed and loud, like the little girl in the locker room she automatically vetoed any changes to her script. "I find the hidden treasure and there are jewels and rubies."

Aubrey didn't respond.

Our daughters were in sixth grade when they watched their last movie together, *Moulin Rouge*. Aubrey had liked the film all right, but Twyla, who'd recently gone as boy-crazy as any girl I'd ever seen, became obsessed. No matter what you asked her, she'd sing a lyric from *Moulin Rouge* in response. The last time Aubrey invited her to sleep over, Twyla stayed up all night watching the movie again and again while Aubrey slept. In the morning, I asked Twyla if she wanted waffles or cereal and she sang something back to me about the greatest thing you'll ever learn is just to love and be loved in return. Aubrey rolled her eyes, shook her head, and went to see what was on TV.

Another Twyla-Aubrey memory crowds in. It was early in the summer, the girls had just finished first grade, Dori and I were sitting on my rarely used front porch while the girls played inside the house. We had citronella candles burning, a bottle of kangaroo red working, and were deep into telling each other the stories of how we'd lost our virginity when Aubrey yelled out to us through a crack in the front door, "Guys! Listen, guys! Shut your eyes! Are they shut? Are you ready?" This was before she had grown out of her speech impediment, so it came out, "Aw they shut? Aw you weddy?"

After Dori and I both covered our eyes with our hands, and assured Aubrey that we couldn't see a thing. The door creaked open and the nails of our wild young rescue dog, Pretzels, clicked on the floor as she bolted out. She bumped against my legs, then swatted them with her tail as she bounded down the porch steps, rushing to check what Dori called her pee-mail.

Twyla announced, "Okay, you can look now!"

Aubrey collapsed in giggles the instant I uncovered my eyes and beheld the two little girls, Aubrey, the shy blonde, and, Twyla, the wild redhead, both done up with cartoon-sexy makeup jobs and draped in every scarf and shawl and flimsy, sheer bit of fabric that might be considered slinky in my sadly utilitarian wardrobe.

Twyla's copper ringlets bounced as she pointed a showstopping finger at Aubrey's pink boom box and commanded in her husky, baby Ethel Merman voice, "Hit it!" Aubrey, still the faithful hand-maiden, rushed to press "play" and the girls sang along with an old CD of mine, "That's the way, uh-huh, uh-huh, I like it!" They put their hands on their hair and wiggled their skinny hips back and forth. Aubrey had glittered brightly at her own audacity, delighting in how shocking and outrageous she was.

But Dori, far from being shocked and outraged, jumped up and joined right in. She dragged me onto my feet so we all could have a girls-just-want-to-have-fun bonding moment. Dori and Twyla and I bumped our butts together and tried to outthrust one another. But Aubrey's face had fallen the instant she saw that Dori, Twyla, and I were intent on outdoing her. When I'd tried to drag her into the fun, she'd gone back in the house and sat on her bed arranging her My Little Ponies by color.

Dori settles BeeBee back on the bed. "Well, at least on the untimely-pregnancy front, it's a relief that Twyla is gay."

I don't say anything; I am still a bit dubious about Twyla's lesbian-ism. Plus, I can't get "That's the way, uh-huh, uh-huh" to stop run-ning through my head. Finally, I ask, "You talked to Twyla?"

"Yeah, she called last night. For money, of course. I told her to ask her father. He's the one with the rich, ridiculously indulgent, ter-minally screwed-up parents who destroyed their son's marriage. Then she told me to forget it and that I was a bitch and had ruined her life."

"Oh, Dori." I take her hand as the scarlet patches bloom like geisha makeup beneath her skimpy eyebrows. She turns from me, scrubs the palm of her hand against her eyes. They come away clean; she's stopped wearing mascara since Twyla left. Cried it off too many times.

I open another drawer. Dori peers in and asks, "Jesus, how many pairs of identical running shorts can one human own?"

Aubrey's Nike shorts are folded neatly as a store display. Dori picks up a pair, maroon with a pink insert, and says, "I never figured Aubrey for a brand whore."

I pluck the shorts from her, tuck them back where they were—precisely placed between the powder blue with white inserts and the burnt orange pairs—and slam the drawer closed. Dori has broken the Mommy Pact: It is fine for me to criticize my kid, but woe betide she who jumps onto that dogpile. I don't snap at Dori, though; if focusing on Nike shorts for a few seconds helps, I'll give her that. Maybe at that moment she's even thinking, *At least. At least I didn't raise a brand whore.*

Dori, struck with a sudden realization, claps her palm against her chest. "God. She's not *really* pregnant, is she? I mean, seriously? Oh, shit. With Tyler Moldenhauer? The way she is now, she'd probably want to keep it. Oh, well, always room at PCC. If Kyle Dunmore and Stacy Adovada can get in, they'll put Aubrey on the faculty."

A bowling ball crushes my solar plexus. I can't draw in a breath or release the one stuck in my chest. Dori has just put names to my worst fears: pregnancy and Parkhaven Community College, where Kyle Dunmore and Stacy Adovada, everyone's favorite drug burnout and teen mom, are currently attending.

"Dori, could you please shut the fuck up?" I always liked that I could say "fuck" to Dori. Now I'm sorry that I ever gave up that word's power to shock, because I would seriously like Dori to zip it.

"Sorry. Bad joke. Really, though, you have nothing to worry about. Aubrey is not like that." She puts her hand on my arm. "Really, Cam, don't worry."

Don't worry?

Dori, mother of a daughter who left home with a stash of stolen pills, who only calls her for money, stands in front of me like a living memo, a breathing reminder of all the terrible things that happen when mothers *don't* worry.

After Twyla left, I hired Dori to help me with my classes. At first it was sort of a charity move, something to keep my friend distracted, but Dori has turned out to be surprisingly good at handling registration, getting students to pay up, invoicing hospitals for my consultations, and, generally, keeping me and the business going. She is even working on helping me "establish a Web presence."

Dori glances at her watch. "Just FYI, we've got class in twenty-five minutes."

I jump up. "Shit! How did I lose track of an entire hour? Where's my bag?"

"Chill. It's all out in the great room. I'll go pack up. You . . ." She eyes me, doing a quick triage. "Brush your hair, put on a clean top. Then we gotta hit the trail like a steaming cow patty."

I run a comb through my hair with one hand as I gather up cell phone, car keys, keys to the classroom where I teach, and purse. In the great room, Dori is stuffing my class materials into the striped canvas beach bag I haul back and forth to classes.

"Where's Britney?" she yells. Her years as a roadie girlfriend, then wife to a musician husband have left Dori with a sense of urgency about any show, even a lactation class.

"Shit, I put Britney in the laundry room. She needs to be washed. Pretzels was gnawing on her. We've gotta take Lady Gaga. Credenza. Second drawer down." Dori calls the weighted dolls I use in class Britney Spears and Lady Gaga.

Dori digs out my backup demonstration doll and jams her into the canvas bag as I shuffle my feet into the pair of sandals I locate under the couch.

"Let's turn this mother out!" Dori yells as we run for the door. "Give me your keys. I'll drive! You put on makeup!"

In spite of myself, whenever I jump into my dilapidated Chevy Malibu with Dori, an oldie plays in my head about "head out on the highway. Lookin' for adventure." It makes me feel as if I'm fifteen again and cruising with my best bud.

"Dori, slow down," I order as the succession of gas stations, Subways, liquor stores, and dry cleaners that line the road out of my subdivision, Parkhaven Country, whiz past. "I'd rather be late than dead. Besides"—I point to a sign—"school zone ahead." I flip down the visor and lean in closer to the mirror to swipe on some lipstick and mascara.

At the top of the steep hill we are descending, a football coach in royal blue stretch shorts stands blowing his whistle at some small boys—made even smaller by oversize helmets and shoulder pads—who, red faced and streaming sweat, are chugging up the incline.

"Oh, great," Dori says, "I see Child Brutality Month is in full swing."

This is another well-worn conversation. At this point I would usually jump in and suggest that Amnesty International should investigate a school system that takes children who've spent an entire summer exercising only thumbs on game controllers, wraps them in nonbreathable polyester, sticks solar-collection helmets on their little heads, shoves them into killing heat, and lets a sadist with a whistle run them around. But I don't repeat my lines. Instead, I marvel at Dori and her imperviousness to the constant, eroding drip of regret. On some level, she still thinks that we—she and I—had it all figured out. That we were the moms going our own way, unconventional but, ultimately, right.

She slows down as we approach the four-way stop at the edge of the elementary school. A moment after stopping, she mutters, "Go, asshole," and makes a face at the driver of the Jeep Cherokee across from us. The driver gestures at Dori to go ahead. She holds her hand out, impatiently indicating the empty intersection, mutters to herself, "*You* go, asshole."

He doesn't move.

"Dori, just go."

"No, he was here first. It's his turn. Oh, look, now he's giving me Little Lady Fingers."

It's true, the driver is gesturing with two fingers twitching above his steering wheel for us to go ahead.

"I hate that patronizing shit."

The cars on either side get tired of our standoff and zoom through the intersection. Then the Cherokee squeals out. As he passes, the driver flips Dori off. She gets a good look at his face and screams, "Oh my God, it's Pastor Jesus Juice from Six Flags over Jesus!" The youth minister from the nearby megachurch whom

Dori has decided is a child molester is, indeed, flipping us a giant bird.

Just as we finally cross the intersection, I shriek and flail at my pocket.

"Crap! What did I hit? Tell me it's not a kid."

"No, you're fine." I extract my buzzing phone. "Sorry. I forgot I put it on vibrate. I didn't want to miss it if Aubrey calls." I check the number, see that it's not Aubrey, and try to figure out which of my patients or students might be calling. My best guess is the dad from the young couple with preemie twins. Their case is complicated and I'm not certain I can remember all the details. I pull up a mental file on the twins. Chase and Jason? Charles and Jeremy? Chance and Jared! Six weeks premature. Nurse started them on formula at the hospital. Nipple confusion. They're losing weight. Pediatrician is pushing for formula. Mom is understandably frantic. Dad is clueless and thinks life with twins would be a breeze if his wife would just give in and do formula. He's always the one who calls, since Mom, literally, has her hands full. I put on my professional voice—calm, competent, warm—and answer.

"Hello?" I repeat when the dad doesn't respond. A scrambled fragment of his urgent answer bleeps in, then cuts out. I hold my phone aloft to try to amplify the signal, then twist around until another bar appears and yell, "I can't hear you!"

A disjointed Morse code of garbled words machine-guns my ear, then right before the connection is decisively dropped, a name jumps out of the gibberish.

Dori glances over at me. "Who was that?"

I don't answer.

Dori glances over, sees my expression. "Cam, are you all right? Talk to me. What's wrong?"

I watch Dori move her mouth, but I can't hear her anymore. We move forward along the road, but the houses, the vet clinic on the corner, the convenience store, they all pass by in silent slow motion.

"Cam!" Dori explodes. The volume comes back on and the world starts running at the correct speed again. "Who was that?"

"Martin." I let my hand holding the phone drop into my lap. "That was Martin."

6:13 P.M. OCTOBER 13, 2009

=How was school today?

=Fine, aside from the fact that it took place at Parkhaven High School.

=Any good Psycho Saunders stories from physics?

=Yeah, Matt McClune, whose big brother had Saunders last year and told him where all the crazy buttons are, said something about how many Asians have won Nobel prizes in science, and Saunders just WENT OFF! He had all these statistics about what percentage of all the engineers and chemists graduating are from Asian countries and how America can just kiss its ass good-bye in science.

=Angry white male? Get him talking about how the founding fathers meant for us all to carry AK-47s and never pay taxes.

=That's good. I'll remember that one.

=But beware, he sounds like the kind of guy who has given the same final for the past thirty years. So, one way or another, you've still got to cover the material. Here's what I find works with crazy people: Don't engage. If they—a teacher, a boss, whoever—control the board, just play their game until you're free.

=Is this the kind of stuff people pay you to tell them?

=Ha! Not impressed?

=I didn't say that. Is it?

=Not exactly. Next has its own set of rules. Sometimes they work in the real world. Mostly you have to leave the real world to make them work.

=So does that mean you don't believe them?

=More and more, no. The one rule I'm certain I don't believe anymore is the one about cutting anyone out of your life who doesn't believe.

=Aubrey? You still there?

=Yeah. Just thinking.

=About what?

=To be continued. Pretzels needs to go out. TTFN.

There is mayo on my turkey wrap when I specifically asked for no mayo. Plus the "wrap" is a cold, stale tortilla. Makes me wonder why I skipped my usual box of animal crackers eaten in the library and went off campus with Wren and Amelia to have lunch at this new place they love, Rap It Up. It has a theme going, playing loud rap music as if decibels can make up for crap food. Parkhaven could use some better lunch options. I mean, seriously? How hard can it be to put out a decent sandwich?

I can barely pull my attention away from creating the perfect lunch menu to listen to Wren and Amelia sitting across the small orange plastic table filling me in on all the band news I've missed since I dropped out.

"Did you hear that Dahlia Butler got a drama scholarship to Wellesley? A full ride."

Two words I can live the rest of my life without ever hearing again: "full ride." I can also do without "reach, match, and safety school," "early action," and "early decision." In fact, the word "college" is starting to give me hives. The anxiety level is off the charts, with everyone writing essays and filling out their FAFSA applications and retaking SATs for the eleventh time.

While Wren and Amelia debate the merits of Williams versus Bowdoin versus just going somewhere in state and which school would give them the most money, I tune out and wonder how tortillas can go stale in such a busy restaurant. I have no thoughts about or interest in any of the colleges they're analyzing and try to work out what I'd like to be eating at this moment. Hot, I am thinking, hot would be good. But not pizza. I am sick of pizza. And sick of living off the microwavables that Mom has started lugging home from Costco since her work got so busy that even if, initially, the empanada or pot pie or whatever is all right, by the time I've choked down half a dozen of the things, just reading the words "Pierce film in 3–4 places to vent" can make me start gagging.

"Aubs? Aubrey?"

"Huh? What?"

"What are your top three?"

Their eyes drill into me, waiting for an answer. "Colleges?" I ask.

Wren and Amelia blink, stunned that anyone would think there is any other topic in the entire world.

"Uh, well, I'm not totally sure." Then I remember the college I'm supposed to visit next week. "Peninsula."

"Peninsula?" Wren repeats. "Is that the one that doesn't give grades?"

"Really?" I can't remember anything about this college, not even why I ever agreed to visit. At least I'll get two days away from Parkhaven High.

"What if you want to transfer?" Amelia asks, alarm brightening her eyes, which, now that I think about it, are kind of always in a state of high anxiety. "I mean, what will they put on your transcript?"

I hold my cup up. "Do they give free refills here?" I leave Amelia blinking with worry. At the drink machine, I confidently fill the cup with Diet Dr Pepper, adding my signature squirt of Nehi Strawberry. Here is a decision I can handle.

Even though I am really late by the time I get to the attendance office, Miss Olivia is still putting her purse in a file drawer and locking it up. Unlimited tardies is the perk we give each other. Madison Chaffee's mom and dad are waiting at the counter. Unlike most parents—who are almost always harried moms come to get their kid out for allergy shots or prenatal doctor visits or meetings with their probation officers or some other reason that ranges from mundane to tragic—the Chaffees are grinning like idiots.

"Aubrey!" Mrs. Chaffee explodes. I'm surprised she remembers my name. Maybe euphoria improves a person's memory. "I'm so glad it's you. We need to tell Madison something. In person."

I look over to Miss Olivia. She nods that it is OK for me to go get Madison out of class. I take my time getting to Madison's Calculus-for-Asians-and-Kids-Whose-Parents-Put-Them-in-Kumon-Math-Tutoring-When-They-Were-Two-Because-They-Knew-That-Public-School-Math-Teachers-Suck-and-Could-Afford-to-Buy-Better-Ones Class. As I dawdle my way through the halls, I realize that I actually have nothing against Parkhaven per se. In fact, the halls, when they are empty, are quite pleasant. I like the wide, airy breezeways with little hives of learning humming behind closed doors.

Going to get Madison makes me remember how, when I was little and got called out of class, my first thought was always, *My dad's here. My dad came back for me.* I didn't even like to talk to whoever came to get me. I didn't want to give them the chance to tell me that it was just Mom waiting in the office to bring me my geography homework or an extra inhaler. Because for those few minutes, walking down an empty hall, I would just stop agreeing with the way things really were and I *did* have a dad and he was in the office waiting for me.

I guess that's what my dad did. Stopped agreeing with reality. I could do it for as long as it took me to get from my classroom to the office. He managed it for sixteen years. He must have had more mental discipline than me. Or maybe it wasn't that much of an effort to pretend that I didn't exist.

Even though Madison's class is right around the corner from the attendance office, I detour upstairs, then over to the east wing. I'd peeked at Tyler's schedule, so I know that he has English in the east wing at this very moment. I slow way, way down outside his class, enough that I can hover by the window in the rear door long enough to catch a glimpse of the back of his head. My heart seizes up the instant I see his hair cutting dark curlicues over the collar of his shirt. He is leaning back, tipping his chair on its rear legs, running a pencil through his fingers so fast that it is a ripple going over and under one finger, then the next, then back again. Like most everyone else in the class, he is ignoring the teacher. A door opens somewhere down the hall and, pulse thumping, I hurry on to the math wing.

At Madison's calculus class I hand her teacher the note. When he calls Madison's name, it is obvious from the ecstatic/relieved expression on her face that she knows immediately what this means. I'm certain it's something about college. Everything is about college. I beat her to the punch of pretending she doesn't remember me and walk briskly ahead of her.

In the office, without speaking a word, Madison's father takes a beat-up old Duke cap off his head and puts it on his daughter's. Madison bursts into tears and squeals, "I did it?"

"You did it," her father answers, beaming. "A perfect eight hundred in math. No way you're not going to be a Blue Devil now!" Then Madison and her mother hold hands and jump up and down.

After they leave, Miss Olivia beams and says, "That's a nice family."

Miss Olivia's daughter did two years at Parkhaven Community College and is selling tires at Costco now. There is so much I don't understand.

12:12 A.M. OCTOBER 20, 2009
=You there?
=Aubrey! What a nice surprise.
=Maybe. I actually really need an answer. Why did you leave us?
=OK, then I actually need to give you one. Part of it, a big part, was that I left because, if I'd stayed, I wouldn't have been a good father.
=You know, most dads aren't that great. They're not supposed to be. Not with daughters. They're just mostly supposed to be the guy in the front seat who picks you up after band practice so you can sit in the back and giggle with your friends. It's not like I ever expected any big interactions or anything. Just a dad who put oil in the car and thought about stuff like cleaning the leaves out of the rain gutters.
=Aubrey, I never would have been that dad.
=OK. Gotta study.
=Could we talk about this some more?
=No, probably not.

Get out! Martin? Martin called? I thought Next swore they would kill him in this and his next ninety-nine incarnations if he ever contacted you again. Are you sure?"

I study the number on my phone. "Well, he was breaking up. A lot."

"But he said, 'Oh, hi, hey, it's me, Martin, just checking in to see what you want to do for dinner.' "

"I think I heard his name." The longer I look at the number on my phone, the more it starts to remind me of the number of the dad of the preemie twins.

"But you recognized his voice?"

"Kind of."

What I recognized was that even though the words were garbled and mostly missing, from the first syllable that the caller spoke some switch was thrown in my reptile brain and my heart shifted into overdrive, thudding with a high-voltage mixture of surprise, fury, and hope. Since Martin's voice was the only one that had ever been able to reach that switch, I'd concluded that it was him.

"Reception was all weird and wobbly."

Dori shrugs indulgently. "Nerves. It's a big day."

"Yeah." I take the absolution she is granting me for being a pathetic dork.

"Gary has a friend who sounds really nice." Gary is a Match.com date who's turned into Dori's regular, two-nights-a-week guy.

"Thanks." Gary's friend gets brought up whenever Dori thinks that I am tragically hung up on Martin and need to move on.

By the time we reach Parkhaven Medical Center, where I hold my classes, I'm 95 percent certain that the caller *was* the preemie dad. A blast of polar air whooshes when the front doors slide open. We trundle onto the elevator and as it inches downward I do what I always do before I teach class and put everything else out of my mind—Aubrey, the preemie dad, Martin—and focus.

As usual, the basement annex is chilled to exactly the same temperature as the pathology lab next door. On summer days, I enjoy a break from the asphalt-melting heat. Today I can't seem to warm up and wish I'd brought a sweater.

Five minutes before class is supposed to start nearly all of the folding chairs Dori and I set up have been taken. At the back of the room, Dori helps a few stragglers sign in. She checks that they've registered and paid, then loads them up with handouts.

Most of the twenty-nine parents-to-be are coupled up; a lot are well-off: husbands checking iPhones, wives sporting French-manicured toenails and linen blouses fresh from the cleaner's. Some are less well-off. A couple in their late teens slump in the back row. Mom runs a tongue stud across her front teeth. Dad, in oversize jeans and a hoodie pulled up to hide most of his face, glances around, then retreats like a turtle back into the safety of his hood.

A teen mom comes in with her mother. The teen mom is slutty-beautiful with a sullen Elvis Presley sensuality. She turns away from her mother, curls herself around a phone, and starts texting. The mom glances at a young couple in the row ahead of her. They're holding hands, heads tilting together, as they study the handouts. She-Elvis's mom's face tightens and she sits up ramrod straight, as if the couple's settled, successful married state is a rebuke to her. I want to go to the mother, take her hand, and tell her that although she and her daughter believe that every bad choice the daughter has ever made in life is her fault, it's not. It's really, really not.

Everyone speaks in whispers. They all have the awkward air of people trying to avoid eye contact in a proctologist's waiting room. From the back, Dori raises her arm and shoots a big thumbs-up, signaling that everyone who's signed up is present and paid for.

"Hi, everyone. I am Cam Lightsey." I launch into my spiel and, the way they always do when I step in front of a class, all my worries disappear. I am doing what I do best on earth, the one thing I have no regrets about. After a dozen years teaching this class, I have honed and fine-tuned it like a stand-up act.

"Welcome to Breast-feeding One-oh-one." I hold my phone up. "Let's all practice cutting the cord," I say, turning my own off.

"Just by coming today, you all are giving your babies the best start in life they could possibly have." As I say them, the words come alive and so do I. I become a funnier, bawdier, warmer, wiser, all-around better version of who I am.

"I'm here because I am exactly the person I needed after my daughter was born, and there was no one like me this far from the city. Eighteen years ago, the choices in Parkhaven were, you could either go the hard-core route that insists you have to breast-feed until the junior-senior prom. Or you go with formula and your kid ends up with a dozen bodies buried in the backyard.

"I assume that you're here because, like me, neither of those paths works for you. Maybe you're here because you've heard I'm not a lactation hard-liner, but that I'll help you succeed at breast-feeding your baby. Maybe you've heard that I'm not gonna tell you you have to quit your job or divorce your husband if either one gets in the way of nursing. Or maybe you just heard that, at some time during the class—not saying when—I'll probably touch my breastesses."

The guy in the hoodie grins at his girlfriend: This is exactly what he's heard. She swipes at him playfully. The whole class relaxes.

"I didn't have the help I needed, so I flunked breast-feeding and I thought I'd failed at something as basic as peeing. I'd look at pictures of refugees living in boxes and they all had a kid plugged in. Women who'd never seen a book could breast-feed, and there I was. I could annotate a bibliography. I had gone to nursing school. But I couldn't breast-feed.

"A lot was happening in my life around the time my daughter was born. She had colic, serious, serious colic. I had postpartum depression. My husband left me for a cult religion."

I wait for the glances to skitter up and ricochet off my face, gauging the depth of this revelation. Decide if I am joking. They see that I'm not.

"Yeah, Next. It wasn't Jonestown or Heaven's Gate, but it wasn't the Unitarians either."

I don't know what it is about the truth, but telling it is like having a noisy generator cranking away in the background suddenly go silent. As always after my big overshare, the barometric pressure in the room drops and everyone listens, really listens, for the first time.

"Nothing was the way I wanted it to be with my first, my only, child. Not one thing was right. If I'd had good help, though, if I'd had me, breast-feeding could have been my one right thing. I am going to give you the information you need, or tell you who can, to make it right for you."

At first, it made me feel too exposed to talk about myself. Especially the part about losing my husband to a cult. So I tried substituting "another woman." Even "a man," but anything other than my own exact, specific, bizarre truth never connected. Never made the pressure drop the way the true, inexplicable, utterly humiliating, nonlinear randomness of life did.

"I've been a lactation consultant for fifteen years. It's a silly job. When I meet people, they either think it's some tech job or, if they do know what a lactation consultant is, the guys ask if I need an assistant. So I just say I'm a spy."

Hoodie Boy laughs out loud and a few of the other dads join him. Now we can start learning. Next to truth, humor is the most important element.

"I'm not here to rip on formula. I was formula-fed. I don't hate my mom. That's not what caused the obvious emotional scarring."

They laugh again. This is a good group.

"I'm just here to give information. I'm sure you all have researched the car seat, the crib, and the monitor. Anybody know how much formula costs?"

Lots of shrugs. No guesses. No one knows the answers to any of the truly hard questions. Cribs, monitors, Boppies, organic washcloths—hell, breast-feeding, breast-feeding classes—they're so ultimately incidental. It's too late, though, to tell any of these young parents, brimming with the most concentrated, aware love they will ever feel, that of the millions of decisions they'll have to make as parents, the only irrevocable one has already been made. It was made when they picked a person to have a child with.

"At least twenty-five dollars a can. On sale. Usually it's closer to thirty. If your baby is average and goes through ten cans a month, that's two hundred and fifty dollars. Minimum. That's a car payment every month. Here, I'm going to pass around this wheel. Check it out. Just dial in what formula costs for different time periods." I whirl the wheel. "Oh, look, three weeks and you've got an iPod."

I walk down the aisle like an evangelical preacher going out to lay on hands and pass the wheel around.

"When I first started teaching, I'd lead off with a big download about immunity and antigens and lower rates of sudden infant death and less plastic in the landfill. All very true and, eventually, I will get to some of that, but since there are whole organizations out there already telling moms they can express world peace, I figure that you're probably looking for a different approach. So I start with the shiny baubles."

The teen mom in the back row has taken control of the wheel and is checking out what each day of breast-feeding is worth, as if someone will be handing her a gift bag every time she unbuttons. I think of this girl with her sneering Presley beauty that will turn sloppy, her life ended before it can begin, all because she never escaped Parkhaven, never went to college, and I tilt off balance for a moment. More than anything, I want to speed over to Tyler's roach coach and free my daughter this very second.

Peninsula. I have to get her to Peninsula.

I yank myself back on track and return to the podium. "Hey, I saw a formula ad the other day that said, 'Now even *more* like breast milk.' You know what is *just like* breast milk?" I look around the room. "Breast milk."

A wispy blonde in pink yoga pants, the straps of her sports bra showing at the neck of her top, puts her hand up hesitantly. I know what she's going to ask just from the way she glances at her husband, seeking his permission. "Is there any . . . Does a woman have to be, you know . . ." She makes arthritic hands in front of her chest.

"No. This is not *Juggs* magazine. Size really does not matter."

Another hand goes up. It is the teen mom. Flecks of black polish dot the stubs of her chewed-off nails. A tiny bell hanging from the ring on her thumb tinkles. "My mom"—she gives her mother a die-bitch look—"told me that formula is more complete nutrition and that breast-feeding is just in right now, but that it's a fad. And my boobs'll droop if I do it."

"A fad? I'm sure that Joseph was out trying to find a convenience store open at night to buy some formula for Mary."

The mother folds her arms over her chest and I make a note to myself to schedule some extra, free visits with her daughter.

"Breast-feeding won't make your boobs droop any more than having a baby will. But it will help you lose weight like a speed freak."

I wince inwardly and search the room for any possible speed freaks. There don't seem to be any candidates, but you never know. I make a note to myself to remove "speed freak" from the routine. The last thing I want to do is alienate any mother or father trying to do right by a child.

A Latina with the bone structure of a Slavic supermodel says, "My doctor told me that I would have to pump and dump for five days after I had even one drink."

"Really? Five days? I'd like to know where the formula company sent that doctor for a cruise. No, the rule is: If it's in the head, it's in the milk. If you feel drunk, don't nurse. But nursing is not like being pregnant. You can eat sushi; you can change the cat box. Just don't eat the cat box. A drink or two is not going to hurt your baby. In fact, a beer now and again might increase your milk volume."

Two young women, whom I assume are sisters because of their identical sloping chins, give each other party-girl thumbs-ups.

"*One* beer," I emphasize. The sisters press fingers against their lips to suppress naughty-me grins.

Without raising her hand, a large woman in a tight-fitting top that makes her look roughly thirteen months pregnant starts speaking in a loud voice. "I have a whole different deal. This is my second"— she pats her stomach—"and my first one wanted to nurse all the time. Twenty-four/seven. Nonstop. My nipples were like hamburger meat."

In the front row, the husband of the woman in yoga pants glances back at Hamburger Nipples, shudders, and shakes his head to dislodge the image.

"Yeah, and your husband might want to have sex three times a day. But we don't always get what we want, and we don't let ten-pound people make the decisions." Then I tell her, tell the whole class—mostly, though, I tell myself—my mantra: "There's a reason that God gives the little people to the big people."

I start in on the lecture portion of the class with this basic fact: "Women have two breasts because all mammals have one more teat than the average litter. And it looks better in a sweater."

Clutching the weighted doll in the crook of my arm, I use Lady Gaga and my own breast to demonstrate the football hold. We cover colostrum, letdown, engorgement, and, the holy grail of breast-feeding, the good latch.

We watch a video that features a new mother having a beatific, transcendent nursing experience. I take a seat next to Dori as the infant's fuzzy head roots at his blissed-out mother's breast and I narrate. "Breast-feeding is exactly like that. Except that you're late to work, the baby was up all night with croup, your sitter just called and said she locked her keys in her car, and your two-year-old, who you're pretty sure has head lice, is in the bathroom trying to flush the cheese grater down the toilet. Other than that, it's all serenity and bliss."

A few seconds later I remember that I forgot the trust agreement for Aubrey's tuition. I whisper to Dori, "I've got to zip back to the house and pick up the papers we'll need at the bank. Could you finish up the class? I'll come back for you, then we'll pick Aubrey up from here. Okay?"

"Sure."

I pause the video to tell the class I have to leave early. "But don't worry about breast-feeding. Like everything else we do as parents, we will have a million opportunities to screw it all up and another million opportunities to make it right. If I can't help, I know someone who can. So you don't need to worry about nursing."

I want to add that it's everything that happens after nursing that they need to worry about. But new parents don't need to know that. They'll have plenty of time to discover what horrors lie ahead. Like the College Tour.

H ey, college girl! Rise and shine. The big day is here."

Mom is in a superhigh, excited, bubbly mood. It is like being woken up by a Japanese game-show contestant. I slide my phone open, check the time. "It's four thirty. Our flight isn't until nine."

"We need to leave a little early to beat traffic into the city."

"Mom, it's Sunday. There is no traffic."

"Well, we have to allow time to get our bags through security."

"Only because you refuse to check a suitcase."

"Aubrey, that would add thirty dollars to the trip. Both ways. We can go out and have a nice dinner for that. Come on; security is going to be a nightmare."

Getting through security at the airport *is* a nightmare. Mostly because Mom makes me wear the ultrajumbo, puffy, rainproof parka that she insisted on buying. I guess she thinks that the I'm-heading-to-the-Yukon-to-do-the-Iditarod look is in. I want to apologize to everyone in line behind us when she spaces out and doesn't get her old waffle-stomper boots unlaced and off her feet before it is her turn to go through the scanner. Then the vast array of clinking bracelets she thinks are so cool and hip set off the metal detector, and there is another delay when she gets herded off into the Plexiglas cubicle and wanded.

When we finally get all dressed and ready for the dog sleds again, she goes, "Do you see why I insisted that we leave early? Getting through security is such a nightmare." And I want to point out, "Don't nightmares only happen when you're asleep?" But I don't say anything because she *is* in a superhigh, excited, bubbly mood and even I can't tear the wings off that butterfly.

As for me, I am in a superlow, *un*excited, dangerously undercaffeinated, sleep-deprived mood. Mom and I had a screaming fight last night in which I essentially begged her not to make me go on this tour. Her final big ultimate argument was that the tickets were nonrefundable. The fact that my whole entire life was going to be decided based on a couple of airline tickets caused my Inner Bitch to spring to life. My Inner Bitch will protect me from being stampeded into whatever version of life Mom has planned out for me. Inner Bitch is going to go on the tour with us.

On the plane, I immediately put my earbuds in and ignore the music while I remember the way Tyler's voice had rumbled through me. I must have gone to sleep, because when Mom pokes me I feel as crabby and imposed upon as if she'd thrown on the light in the middle of the night. She is making it very hard for me to keep Inner Bitch restrained. I yank the earbuds out. "What?"

"The pilot just said that the Grand Canyon is coming up on our right."

Instead of rolling my eyes or gasping like I want to, I just peaceably nod, and try to put the earbuds back in. But she stops me to rhapsodize about how beautiful the clouds are when viewed from up above. "Don't they look like enchanted castles of feathers?"

"I guess."

"You don't seem very excited."

"This is not the first time I've seen clouds."

"But it's the first time you've seen them on the way to visit your dream school."

"When did Peninsula become my dream school?"

She is genuinely surprised. "Aubrey, we spent your entire junior year sifting through all those catalogs and going to all those College Nights."

College Nights.

Eating subpar cookies and listening to kids ask suck-ass questions. That's when it started to sink in that I was running like a hamster on a treadmill just so I could prove what a very special, very speedy hamster I was and be allowed to spend a fortune for the privilege of running on an even faster treadmill. I guess Mom hadn't noticed that all College Nights had ended up doing was making me very, very tired.

"You're acting like you don't remember any of this. That we didn't jointly decide that Peninsula sounded like the only college that would really let you find your own path."

"I'm tired," I say. Then, before she has a chance to broadcast one of her Embrace Life lectures, I jam the earbuds back in, shut my eyes, and think about how much easier it would be to be an Asian kid. If you are Asian, the deal with your parents is clear from day one: "You have to be exactly like me except better or I will hate you and the whole community will hate you. Even all the ancestors will hate you."

There is none of this "find your own path" bullshit. Asian parents are right up front: "Be a grade-getting android. Crush everyone around you in academics, music—as long as it's classical—and forget about sports, friends, and sex. Be valedictorian or here's the sword to commit hara-kiri." Clear. Simple. Honest.

It is misting when we get off the plane six hours later in Seattle. We pick up our rental car, a Dodge Microdot, maybe a Toyota Flea, some ridiculously tiny clown car that my mother has gotten a deal on, and head south. For the entire hour-long drive, she issues bulletins about how gorgeous everything is. Even though she's pretty much claimed every admiration molecule available, how can I argue with giant evergreens, misty rain, and this soft light that makes all the colors so deep and saturated that looking at a petunia hurts your eyes?

At Peninsula, the visiting seniors and their parents are herded into a big, open meeting hall that is decorated with carvings of salmon and whales and has an immense totem pole planted right in the middle like we are going to spend four years learning how to chew deer hide to make our moccasins all nice and soft.

The president welcomes us. He is African American. I look around the room. If a bomb went off, there wouldn't be a Phish fan left alive. Almost everyone is not just white, but phosphorescent, Scandinavian white. Seems the only way they can get a black person to come to Peninsula is to make him president of the college.

Which doesn't stop him from going on about "Peninsula's commitment to diversity." Since there aren't any actual races to get diverse about, the next speakers are from the Ps & Qs, Peninsula's queer alliance, the Transgendered Students United, then the Feminist Majority. If I was actually interested, I would mostly want to hear about majors and teachers, but instead I get schooled about Peninsula's zero tolerance for pretty much anything that would hurt anyone's super-evolved feelings.

Then we all march in a big group across the quad and into the campus dining hall.

"Can you believe this?" Mom asks, loading up her tray with heirloom tomatoes and baby arugula grown in the student-tended organic garden. The vegetables are displayed behind lights like they are Broadway stars. "You would pay a fortune for produce like this at Whole Foods."

My mom's celebrity vegetation euphoria makes me crave a cheeseburger, and I go outside where a grill has been set up for sad outcast carnivores like me. I decide that the diversity group I'd organize would be dedicated to bacon. I imagine saying this to Tyler. Imagine him laughing.

Back inside, Mom waves at me in her insane way that causes every single person in the entire cafeteria to stare. She is sitting with the woman who stood in line in front of us when we bought our dinner tickets. Naturally, Mom bonded instantly with her.

"Aubrey, this is Julie and her daughter, Tinsley." I nod, but Tinsley, who is wearing a lilac jacket identical to the one her mom has on, sticks her hand out and I have to shake it.

"Tinsley plays clarinet too!" Mom announces in her hectic, separated-at-birth way.

I nod and try very hard to keep Inner Bitch under control. "OK. I don't. Play clarinet. Haven't really since last year."

"Aubrey got heatstroke—"

"Heat *exhaustion*. And it wasn't that bad."

"—from not wearing her hat at the beginning of the year and is sitting out for a little while. She'll hate my saying this, but she's been first chair for the past two years."

Mom, did you forget to tell them about how you couldn't potty-train me until I was three? And, seriously, they're going to want to know all about the ringworm episode in second grade.

"Actually," Tinsley says, light flickering across the silver ball stud in her tongue, "I play in my boyfriend's band."

Of course you do. And your boyfriend is Win Butler and his band is Arcade Fire.

"And I am seriously done with the clarinet." I stuff my mouth with cheeseburger while everyone else picks at their yellow beets and snow peas. My mom looks away. Great. Now she is hurt because her playdate isn't working out. I wonder at what point she'll stop thinking that any random girl sort of near my age is my soul-mate-waiting-to-happen? Like the whole Paige/Madison thing worked out so well for me. To say nothing of Twyla. How about if I went out and set up a dinner for *her* with the first middle-aged woman I ran into at Walmart, then sat back beaming, waiting for the instant, lifelong friendship to start?

My mom goes to the dessert carousel and returns with a plate loaded with sweets. "Can you believe this? They're all vegan."

I stab a piece of cake and take a bite. "Yeah, it's amazing that just by taking out eggs and butter and sugar and pretty much everything else that makes cake cake, they can create a product with the exact texture and taste of a pink sponge. Super yum." I smile a big fake smile as I chew. If nothing else, I've given Tinsley permission not to be a suck-up. I figure she is finding this process as excruciating as I am. I am wrong.

Tinsley takes a delicate bite of the cake and mutters, "Actually, Mama and I have been vegan for almost three years." Her eyes meet her mother's. "We always were vegetarian. Then, three years ago, Mama witnessed to me about the suffering of dairy cows and egg-laying chickens. We prayed over it and I just knew I could not be part of that cycle of unconsciousness any longer."

Mmm, thanks, Mom. How do you do it? A tongue-studded, Christian, vegan suck-up. You know me too well.

As we leave the dining hall, my mom informs me that she has signed me up to spend the night in the dorm.

"Without asking me?"

"I'm sorry, I noticed that the deadline was coming up, so I just went ahead and signed you up. I meant to tell you."

"So I'm supposed to what? Spend the night with some random person? Gee, I hope it's a transgendered Mennonite who only eats pine needles." *Did I say that out loud?* Inner Bitch has arrived to protect me.

"It's a great opportunity to get a real feel for the Peninsula community."

"Oh, I'm getting a 'real feel.' "

"Aubrey, please. Come on."

"What? I'm supposed to be Riverdancing at the prospect of spending the night with some stranger? Who, I'm really sure, is going to be just as thrilled as I am about getting some high school kid dumped on her. Or him." *Thank you, Inner Bitch. You get off some good lines.*

"Aubrey, they would not put you in a boy's room."

"Why not? Wouldn't it be sexist or antifeminist or gender-specific or something like that?"

"Aubrey, you're being—" *A bitch? Bingo.*

"God, Mom, you love this place so much, why don't you just buy one of those caps with the weird dog-ear flaps and go here yourself?"

"There is no need for that tone or that attitude. This trip is for you. I took off work. Canceled classes—"

"Fine! OK, I'm an ungrateful bitch. I'll spend the night in the dorm."

"No, never mind. We'll just tour the dorms tomorrow."

Mom is quiet for a long time and I almost apologize and muzzle Inner Bitch, but before I can, she jumps in and starts telling me about all the different kinds of dorms there are. "They have all these learning communities. The art students have a wing. And the science kids. I read online about how one semester all the drama students picked someone from Shakespeare and stayed in character for the entire term."

Mom goes on about "quiet dorms" and "substance-free dorms." But she isn't doing her usual superexcited sell job, so I don't have to push back so hard.

"Yeah, Mom, we'll check them all out tomorrow."

We stay at a Red Roof Inn near the campus. As we pull into the parking lot, Mom gets a little smile on her face and I know that she is remembering how when I was little motels were this gigantic treat for me. Since we've never had cable, motels meant I could gorge on Nickelodeon and the Disney Channel.

In the room, I crawl into bed with the laptop and Mom throws the blackout curtains open. "Oh, my God, this view! I can't get enough of this view! Want to get something delivered?"

I try to sound neutral when I say, "Fine." The second after I say it, though, I remember that she always tells me that "fine" really stands for Effed-up, Insecure, Neurotic, and I can't remember what the *e* is supposed to mean. Evil? Evasive?

"Too bad they don't have room service." She leafs through some flyers on the nightstand. "What sounds good? Pizza? Thai food? Oh, look, there's a place that delivers sushi. You choose."

"Mom, we just ate."

"All I had was a salad. And you hardly touched your burger. Come on, we're on vacation. Let's live a little. What about sushi? Sushi was always your favorite."

Yeah, when I was in middle school, and it was mostly always Twyla's favorite. Macaroni and cheese was my favorite.

She picks up the remote and starts flipping around the channels. "Oh, hey, Aubrey, look, *Mystery Science Theater*. They're doing *Hercules*."

Mystery Science used to be a staple of our Friday-night dates. I remember when she rented the one playing now, a fifties epic set in ancient Rome. We baked brownies with expensive Belgian chocolate, she drank her kangaroo wine, we snuggled up together under a quilt and laughed at the snarky comments the narrators made about how cheesy Steve Reeves was all shaved and oiled up and flashing his six-pack in a minitoga, and I thought she was the funniest, coolest mom in the entire world. For one second, I wish that brownies and a movie with Mom were still the most fun I could imagine having.

"I thought they were supposed to have free Wi-Fi in all the rooms," I say the third time my connection gets dropped.

"Maybe if you sat closer to the patio doors."

"Maybe if it wasn't pouring rain, I could sit *on* the patio. But it *is* pouring rain and it appears it will always be pouring rain."

"It's not 'pouring rain.' The English would call this kind of weather 'soft.' And besides, that is one of the things you liked about Peninsula. A completely different climate."

The word "whatever" forms in my brain without my willing it to. I can tell from her expression that Mom reads it like a thought bubble above my head.

She makes it almost five minutes without saying anything, then starts sighing, and finally announces, "I'm PMSing madly."

I force myself not to respond to her unbelievably irritating comment. Mom has this idea that our periods are synced up the way some study she read a couple of decades ago says happens to sorority girls. What she is actually saying is that I am a moody, irrational bitch, but that it is OK because she is getting her period too and understands and excuses me.

I remember something from my human development class sophomore year about how, at first, babies don't understand that their foot or their hand belongs to them and isn't just another part of the alien world they've been dumped into. Before they figure out where they stop and the world begins, they also think that their mother's bodies are part of their bodies.

They need to add a section to that chapter about how some mothers never get past the developmental stage of thinking that their daughter's body is actually theirs.

I shut the laptop and say as pleasantly as I can, "I think I'll try downstairs."

"Good idea," my mom bursts out. "They might still have cookies left. They're supposed to put cookies out in the afternoon."

"Yeah, OK. Cool. I'll bring some back."

"Chocolate chip!" she yells after me.

The instant I get into the motel stairwell, I plop down, open the laptop, and play and replay Tyler's interview. Especially the part where he calls the kid with the microphone "son."

I feel like a sad Justin Bieber fan. And even though I am, in a pathetically literal, emo-poetry sort of way, between floors, for the only time that whole horrible day, while I listen to Tyler's voice, I feel like I am exactly where I belong.

I run back into the house to get the trust agreement. In the short time I've been gone, the house has stopped being mine. When I step into the great room, it's as if I'd just walked in for the first time with the Realtor, lifted my face to the high windows far above me, put my hand on my pregnant belly, and fallen in love with the weightless feeling of a room with a ceiling I couldn't have touched standing on a chair.

The great room.

I traded Aubrey's life, the life she should have had in the city with a swirling tribe of creative, diverse friends who had creative, diverse moms, for this. For a great room. The great room and the allegedly great schools had convinced me to talk Martin into moving. If we'd stayed in our tiny duplex in Sycamore Heights, I'd told him, not only would we not have had a great room; she wouldn't have had a big yard with soft grass where she could run barefoot with friends. Or a safe, quiet street for her to ride her bike on. But the real problem, I'd said, was that Sycamore Heights Elementary was a disaster, with the worst reading scores in the district.

"What do you think?" I'd asked Martin the first time he'd set foot in this cathedral-ceilinged room. I'd already previewed dozens of houses and narrowed the choices down to two. That was two too many for Martin. Still, I'd managed to drag him out to have a look.

He'd glanced around, his expression stunned, distracted, and answered, "Good. Seems good. I guess."

To which I had wanted to scream, *Could you be any less involved? Like it or not, buddy, we're having a child.*

But since the Realtor in her navy blue knit jacket with gold buttons was hovering beside us, all I'd said was, "The schools are excellent." I hoped Martin would see the same picture in his mind I had in mine of Sycamore Heights Elementary. The rust stains beneath the rain gutters and splintery play equipment the parents had put together themselves and set on a field of hard dirt. Parkhaven Elementary was brand-new and had ·a safety-engineered playscape nestled on giant, spongy, head-injury-preventing mats made from recycled tires.

Martin was not convinced.

"We can be at Gwock's in twenty minutes." I named our favorite Mexican dive. We loved their margaritas and guacamole. "What's twenty minutes? A couple of songs on the radio? An NPR commentary?"

Martin had nodded and said nothing. He didn't want to move. He didn't want to have a baby. He didn't even want to admit to not wanting those things. He wanted to read the Gnostic Gospels and Edgar Cayce and the Bhagavad Gita and *The Tibetan Book of the Dead.* Which had become much less charming than it was on a train traveling through Morocco with all the time in the world to take a detour up to Spain and stay for weeks in a cheap hotel getting high and making love.

After we'd viewed the house in Parkhaven, our dinky duplex in Sycamore Heights felt like a cave, a claustrophobic, airless den. "Where will we put a crib?" I'd moaned. "A high chair? A swing?"

"Do we need all those things? Right away?"

"We will, and I can't move with an infant. We need a settled place to bring our baby home to."

Martin had nodded, still not convinced. But, at the time, high on hormones, I was sure enough for both of us. "Look," I'd argued, "house prices are skyrocketing. If nothing else, this will be a great investment, and if we don't like it, we'll sell, make a nice profit, and move back to the city."

We bought the house. We moved out of Sycamore Heights and into Parkhaven.

The drive was never twenty minutes. Traffic seemed to double every few months. Plus, after Aubrey was born and the colic kicked in, twenty minutes was all the time in an entire day that I had to myself. Twenty minutes was either a shower and brushing my teeth or reading one-half of a magazine. I had dreamed of being one of those moms who slung her baby into a piece of kente cloth, then headed out for the early show. Instead, I became a pack animal. It was a sherpa-level effort just to gather up the diapers, wipes, change of clothes, bottles, formula, ice packs for the bottles and formula, sunscreen, diaper rash ointment. Then, the few times that I could muster the energy and organization to get us out the door and put up with Aubrey—who never really made peace with the car seat—

howling through the car ride, I'd arrive to discover that I'd forgotten my purse. Or the one pacifier that would soothe her. Or something. Always something.

After the colic siege ended, Aubrey and I did manage a few trips into the city so that she could clamber around on the oversize hamster tubes at the children's museum and throw stale bread to the ducks in the lake, but we came as visitors. The city no longer felt like mine, and it had never been Aubrey's.

Those arduous, early months when I failed at everything—trips into the city, nursing, marriage—were one of the reasons I became a lactation consultant. Therapists would say it was my compulsion to reenact this drama in order to "get it right," master it, make it turn out the way it should have. Maybe. But no matter how many classes I teach I still end up divorced and living in Sprawlandia.

It takes me a few minutes of searching through my hopeful stockpile of off-to-college items to remember that I had squirreled the trust documents away in a special spot on my bookshelf between *The Womanly Art of Breastfeeding* and a journal with an article I intend to read about inducing lactation in the female transsexual. I grab the papers, check the reassuring words at the top—"Irrevocable Trust Agreement"—carefully fold the packet into my purse, and run back to the car.

I take a shortcut to the hospital that leads me through a neighborhood I haven't entered for years. Before I can even consciously recall why, I remember that, in fact, I *have* done all I could for Aubrey's immune system: As Recent Studies advise, I *did* let her play with livestock.

It was Aubrey's first-grade field trip to Pioneer Farm. Aubrey had asked me so many times when I was going to be a room mother, or bring cupcakes, or read to the class like all the other moms, that I'd signed up to drive. I couldn't exactly explain to Aubrey about how some moms had to work while others just got to stay at home and worry about which spinning class to take.

It turned out that Madison Chaffee was one of the three little girls—Paige and Kelsey were already strapped in the back—assigned to ride with us. This, the neighborhood I'm driving through now, is Madison's neighborhood. That field trip started to go wrong when Joyce came out of her Tara-columned house in her dry-cleaned jeans and a celery-colored sweater, with expensive highlights gleaming in her hair. It was the first time Joyce and I had been face-to-face since Aubrey and I were dropped from her pool-mom gatherings.

"Cam! How have you been?" Joyce had greeted me with a high-pitched effusiveness that made me remember that she'd been a sorority girl.

When Joyce went to set up Madison's booster seat, it was bad enough that one of the back doors on the old Corolla I drove at that time was broken and that I had to redirect Joyce to the functioning one. But did that side of the car *have* to have a stalagmite of bird shit crusted on top? After loading her daughter up with enough Fruit Gushers and Goldfish to cross the Kalahari, Joyce had pointed to the other two girls already strapped in the backseat and told me, "You can just drop Paige and Kelsey off back here after the field trip."

But not Aubrey? I wanted to ask. *You're having a playdate and not inviting my little girl?*

The pain of that rejection was exponentially stunning: It was the pain I knew Aubrey would feel when the other three girls skipped off to a playdate that did not include her, multiplied by not only my own rejection as a fit Parkhaven mother, but by every slight I had ever endured in my own life. The experience showed me that the instant she gives birth, all the defenses a person has built up in her entire adult life are stripped away.

Consequently, Joyce's unkindness, and the $115 I was losing by not teaching my usual Tuesday-morning class, were what I was dwelling on while Aubrey fed a pink piglet from a bottle. I wasn't really paying attention to any of it. Not the smell of wet hay. Not that the piglet had a spot of gray over his right eye. Or how the sunlight shining through his ears gave them a salmon-colored glow. Not how the hood of her pink parka trimmed in fake white fur had fallen down, and staticky strawberry blonde hair floated around her face in the dry winter air. Or how her lips were chapped to a perfect, tender red, and tiny, saw-toothed ridges of white enamel glinted in the space left where her two front baby teeth once were. Or even how Aubrey shrieked with delight as the piglet power-sucked down the milk, almost tugging the bottle from her hand.

And then, without a single connecting thought, I switch from regret–time traveling to creating alternate universes. In this new and improved version of "Piglet," I am actually fully present at that field trip. Instead of toggling from imagining Joyce Chaffee with a meat cleaver buried in her thoughtless, behighlighted head to wondering how I am going to pay my property taxes on what I make as a lactation consultant, I am focused entirely on Aubrey as she feeds that baby pig. This time around I savor her joy like crème brûlée and notice that for just one second, piglet and girl, their eyes shut in contented slits, wear identical expressions of bliss. In this version of Childhood Done Right, Aubrey has two straight-arrow parents like Madison and Paige and Kelsey do, instead of a crazed single mom driving around in the Bird Shit Mobile encouraging women to flash their boobs in public, and a father who has joined a cult. Aubrey is the girl all the moms want for playdates.

I speed out of Joyce Chaffee's neighborhood, check my phone, and see that I forgot to turn it back on. When I power it back up, the phone plays cheerful notes, alerting me that I have a message. I hit the "voice mail" button, praying it will be Aubrey but expecting the freaked-out preemie dad.

After some electronic sputtering, I hear the message, clear as a bell: "Cam. Sorry, reception is impossible. I've finally got a signal, but I don't know how long it will last, so I'll cut to the chase. I hope that you're back from your trip to Europe, because I need to warn you that there might be . . . I'm not saying there will be, but there might be a problem with the trust. So you and Aubrey should probably get over to the bank as soon as—"

Scattered words blip in and out, then nothing.

The next day, after getting dragged to a couple of classes meant to show how open and cool all the professors are, sitting next to my mom who won't stop beaming at all this open coolness, I snap and Inner Bitch reemerges. The thought of spending four more minutes in this place, much less four years, freaks me out so much that I can't breathe. Literally. I get such a bad asthma attack that Mom wants to take me to the hospital until I get enough breath to tell her to calm the eff down.

She and Dori have pretty much made it that I have to drop the *F*-bomb to get taken seriously. Still, Mom lets me spend the rest of the day at the motel and she has a great time going to all the sample classes.

Too much of the asthma medicine combined with my usual too much thinking keeps me awake most of the night so that I am a total crab by the time we drive to the airport.

Mom, meanwhile, continues with her one-woman-show monologue all fakethusiastically, like an old-pro actress playing to a bad audience, until she finally gives up and asks, "Can we just start over today? Is that possible? I was up most of the night trying to figure out what I am doing wrong, and I remembered how your grandmother used to drive me crazy.

"I hated everything about her. I hated the way she chewed, and put on lipstick. I hated the way she smelled. I hated it when she stared at me like she was looking in the mirror and wasn't sure about her hair or the outfit she was wearing."

I don't say anything, but I hate that my mom assumes that my mood and entire being are totally determined by her. I also hate the way she chews. I hate the way she puts on lipstick. And I really hate it when she stares at me the way she is right now, like she is looking in the mirror and isn't sure about her hair or the outfit she is wearing.

"Anyway, I know that it's all part of the separation process. I guess that the closer you are, the more it hurts. With you and me. The single mother/daughter, it's even more intense. Maybe I wanted too much closeness because I didn't have that with my mother. My mother, your grandmother Rose, and I, we were never . . . We were always such very, *very* different people. And then she was sick so much of the time when I was growing up. Maybe I was closer to Bobbi Mac, your great-grandmother, because I never had to go through the whole separation process with her. God, I wish you could have known her."

She starts to get sniffly, the way she always does when she brings up the legendary Bobbi Mac. Fortunately, she reins herself in and goes on. "For a while I thought that, maybe, your father's family might, you know, fill in."

This is another story I know too well. I pray that she won't retell the sad tale of her schlepping me to visit Dad's family back when I was too young to remember and how his super-Catholic parents were all grief-stricken about their son joining this weirdo cult and for some bizarre reason they blamed her for not being able to hold on to her man. As if she'd driven him to leave us.

Thinking about grandparents who never really wanted to know their own grandchild makes me wonder how bad it must have been for Dad to have had them as parents.

By the time I tune back into my mom, she is telling her favorite story, the one about meeting my father on the train in Morocco and seeing strange tribal people and eating strange tribal food.

"That's all that I want for you, sweetie." Her voice has that icky wobble that means she just might start bawling in the hopes that her tears will melt my callous-bitch heart. "I just want you to have adventures. Adventures like my grandmother had. Even the adventures that all kids used to have when we'd go out the front door first thing in the morning and not come home till after dark and our parents didn't know where we were. We were with our friends, riding bikes, building forts, getting sunburns, mosquito bites, breaking our arms. I hate it that you never had a friend whose house you could walk to. That no kid has ever knocked on our door and asked if you could come out and play."

"Sorry I'm such a pathetic loser."

"No! No, that's not what I mean. It's not your fault. It's Parkhaven. It's always been Parkhaven. I thought it would be kid paradise. Then, once we were stuck there, I realized that, yeah, there are lots of kids, but they are all in Mommy and Me or select soccer or Space Camp. Or something. I was stunned. Honest to God, you could see more children on Wall Street than you could out playing in our neighborhood. Anyway, this is your chance to start your life."

I want to thank her for negating my entire childhood and pretty much everything that made me me, but that would definitely have made her cry.

"To meet new people," she adds.

Meet new middle-class white people with parents who never got over being hippies.

"To have adventures."

Have your adventures.

"Aubrey, don't shut me out. Please, I love you more than anyone on this earth. I want to know you. I want to know what's in your beautiful brain."

Yeah, right. Just so long as it happens to be exactly what is in your *brain.*

"Please, can't we talk?"

"Sure, Mom." Then, because I have been, I say, "I'm sorry I've been so churlish."

At the word "churlish," Dad's signature word, she whips her head in my direction so fast it's like she just got an electric shock. Dad must have still been using the word when they met. She studies me until I get scared and have to say, "Uh, Mom, the road," because we're driving on the shoulder.

Her reaction pretty much confirms my suspicion that if I utter one wrong word, she will know everything. I also see really clearly how upset the slightest mention of my father would make her.

We drive in silence for a long time and the car fills up with her sadness. I stare out at a drizzly, gray world that looks like the inside of an oyster and try to think of something to talk about to comfort her, to get her bubbly mood back, even if it was fake. But honestly I can't think of one thing to say.

G et the fuck out!" Dori squeals when I tell her that Martin called. Really called. That it really was him.

We're sitting in the parking lot of Parkhaven Medical Center while I figure out what to do. "He said he hoped I was back from my trip to Europe."

"Was he kidding? Does he know that the only trip you've taken in the last ten years was the College Tour from Hell?"

"It wasn't that bad."

" 'Trip to Europe'? Does Martin have a really bad sense of humor?"

"Actually, he had a good sense of humor. Before Next. Forget Martin's sense of humor; he said there might be a problem at the bank."

"Call him! Call him! Call him!"

I try. Several times, but don't get through.

Dori gasps in wonderment. "You just heard from the love of your life for the first time in sixteen years."

"Dori, calm down, okay? This is not an episode of *Gossip Girl*, and who said he was the love of my life?"

"You. On more than one occasion."

"Had there been drinking beforehand?"

"There is always drinking beforehand with us. Um gee!" she bursts out, her abbreviation for the abbreviation "OMG." "Do you remember that article I e-mailed you?"

"Dori, you e-mail me roughly half a dozen articles a day. I don't always have time to catch up on *Cosmo*'s 'Seventy-five Crazy-Hot Sex Moves.' "

"No, the one about rekindled romances."

"Dori, please."

"Seriously, this researcher wrote about why Classmates-dot-com and Facebook and all these sites where you reconnect with old sweethearts are causing this epidemic of divorces. A person's first big love gets stored in the brain in the exact same place as crack cocaine does and just even seeing the old flame's picture on Facebook can, like, reactivate the addiction. So are you all rekindled?"

"Dori, no kindling. No crack. Okay? I have got to focus."

"No, really. This is all true. The researcher did a whole study on it and found out that the most amazing thing is that these couples who get back together, you know, leave their wives and husbands of thirty years for their first big love, have incredibly successful relationships with the first love. I mean, it's a delusion, but a delusion that totally works in the real world. So are you blown away? You seem blown away."

"Dori, you're not following the plot here: There is a very real possibility that something has happened to my daughter's college fund."

"You don't know that. Maybe he was just checking to make sure you got the money."

"He said there was a problem."

"Where was he calling from?"

"He didn't say. Sounded like he was driving. I heard traffic."

I hit Aubrey's number. For roughly the thousandth time, her voice mail picks up and I scream at the phone, "Answer, damn you!"

Dori states the obvious: "Call Tyler the Defiler."

I hesitate. Not just because Tyler is the last person on earth I want to talk to, but because when, under great duress, I did manage to extract his number, Aubrey made me swear that I would use it only under very precise circumstances. Like if I were bound and gagged in the trunk of a kidnapper's car. For the past six months, Aubrey has done everything in her power to keep Tyler and me as far apart as possible.

I dial his number and, of course, it's straight to voice mail. I put his message on speakerphone for Dori to hear, and slump back as I wait for whatever cocky, football-hero attempt at lame humor will follow. I predict white-boy ghetto wannabe, "wigger," as Aubrey so charmingly calls such poseurs. Instead, we hear a polite young man tell us, "Hello, you have reached the number of Ty-Aub Enterprises."

Dori pops her eyes, mouths, *Ty-Aub Enterprises?*

"Please leave a number and one of us will return your call as soon as possible."

I press the phone to my mouth. "Tyler, this is Aubrey's mother. I need her to call me right now! Immediately. There might be a problem at the bank. So, seriously, when you get this have her call me. *Stat.*"

I hang up. " 'Ty-Aub Enterprises'? That delusional asshole has upgraded his goddamn roach coach to 'enterprises.' God, I hate that cocky little bastard." I calm down, turn to Dori. "So, you up for coming with me to drag Aubrey to the bank?"

"Absolutely."

"Thanks for being on my side."

"Is there any other?"

We drive in silence as I beeline along the fastest route to the roach coach. A horn honks when I cut a pickup off. I wiggle through a yellow light, then floor it, blasting down the road, swerving from lane to lane, passing nothing but an endless loop of Best Buy–Ross–Home Depot–Joe's Crab Shack–TJMaxx–Best Buys.

A person looks at his or her surroundings in completely different ways depending upon whether they are temporary or permanent. Parkhaven, for the eighteen years we've lived here, has been softened for me by the gauzy scrim of impermanence. It was just the place Aubrey and I had to be to get her an education good enough that she'd never have to live in a place with no sidewalks, where no one knew their neighbors, and all physical activity started with loading children into a minivan. With that scrim now in danger of being ripped away, with Aubrey's college escape plan threatened, Parkhaven's awfulness hits me in a whole new way and I speed up even more.

"Uh, just FYI," Dori says, gripping the sides of her seat. "That light? The one you just barreled through? It was red. A deep, dark, hemorrhaging, corpuscle red."

I recognize in a distant, abstract way that if Dori Chotzinoff is scared, I should slow down, but I am too intent on my mission. I nod without taking my mind off passing a dump truck overloaded with gravel.

Pebbles are ricocheting off my windshield when Dori asks, "So?"

Even though I know exactly what she means, I say, "So what?"

"Oh, come on. Any tingles?"

"Dori, please, this really is not the time."

That's what I say, but I am remembering the split second after Martin said, "Cam." Before the more orderly parts of my brain had processed what was going on, there were, in fact, nothing *but* tingles. Massive, heart-stopping tingles. Colossally irritating, humiliating tingles that I will never acknowledge.

I blast past the truck. It is several miles before I warn Dori, "Look, when—if—*if* he calls back, there will be lying."

"God, of course. Will it be of the I-am-surrounded-by-hot-hunky-lovers-lining-up-to-kill-for-what-you-tossed-away variety or the my-life-without-you-has-been-an-impeccable-dream version?"

"The impeccable-dream one."

"Great. In that case, Aubrey is all packed and ready and eager to go to college and she has a major picked out and her roommate has already invited her to spend Thanksgiving with her family on Cape Cod."

"Yeah, the Cape Cod version. Sign me up for that one."

cram my backpack under the attendance counter. There is already a swarm of students waiting on the other side.

"You're late," Miss Olivia teases. "Should I write you up?"

I shrug. "Go ahead."

"How was the big college tour?"

"Fine." *I.e., effed-up, insecure, neurotic, and evil. Highly evil.*

And then I am besieged by kids shoving notes at me from their orthodontists, pediatricians, marriage counselors. I don't care. I am supposed to care, supposed to check, but I don't. They could hand me a note cut out of letters from the newspaper telling me where to drop the ransom money and I'd write them out an excused absence slip. If Peninsula or, really, any college is what I'm supposed to be working toward, caring about, then I seriously, *seriously* do not care.

When Twyla's old emo-stoner friend Miles Kropp, the chronic Jims 'n' Jays guy, shows up with his eyes flaming red, he no longer seems like a giggling ass. He suddenly seems like the only person in my whole universe who has the tiniest clue. He's figured out that Parkhaven High requires anesthesia. All the synonyms that Twyla was so fond of for getting messed up scroll through my brain, because, for the first time ever, I am overwhelmed by the desire to "toke up till I woke up." I want to ask Miles to take me to his car and get me stoned, blazed, blitzed, toasted, tore up from the floor up, wrecked, high, ripped, buzzed, and then I can't remember any more. Wasted? Wasted might be one of Dori's.

Tacked under the counter is Miss Olivia's latest list of all the students who aren't allowed any more excused tardies. Miles Kropp is at the top of her list.

Miss Olivia has her headset on and is listening to messages using her supersleuth powers to decide whether the person calling in is a parent or a conniving student she must hunt down and punish. Possibly kill. As fast as I can, I write Miles a slip, shove it at him, and whisper, "Next time they'll suspend you."

The wheels turning very, very slowly, he finally nods in understanding and is about to leave when Miss Olivia rips her headphones off.

"Aubrey, what are you doing? That's Miles Kropp! Kropp is on the list. Aren't you reading your list? No more excused tardies for Kropp."

I grab a note off the pile in front of me and wave it at Miss Olivia. "He has a note from his doctor. See?"

Miles manages to fire just enough synapses to snatch up the slip and disappear. Miss Olivia, who is not a fan of standing or, really, moving her body in any way, rolls her chair toward me. "Let me have a look at that." She sticks her hand out. "It's probably forged."

My doom wheels closer and I am oddly elated to discover that even then I don't care. I wonder how many lines I'd have to cross to get suspended. "Suspended." Why has that word ever held any terror for me? Suspended. Suspended animation. *Not* having to decide where to go to college and what to major in and, essentially, plan out the rest of my entire life. Just to completely freeze everything. Like Sleeping Beauty. Only not at Parkhaven High. Anywhere but Parkhaven. It sounds like the most blissful state I can imagine. I *want* to be suspended.

Miss Olivia abruptly stops dead in her tracks and looks up at someone behind me. A voice asks, "Hey, Pink Puke, how was Penn State? Awesome team. They recruiting you? Hold out for a car."

As I turn around, Miss Olivia babbles at me, "He asked where you were. I told him Penn something and he knew right away what I was talking about. Didn't you, Ty?" She giggles. Miss Olivia giggles.

The sun is angling in through the glass doors behind Tyler and sending beams of light shooting out around his head in a haloed, He Is Risen way so cheesy even *I* can't take my pathetic fan-girl crush seriously anymore. A handsome, sexy quarterback? Could I be a bigger cliché? And it is so clear from the way he is acting that this happens all the time. It happens so much, in fact, that, like a celebrity, he's learned to handle it gracefully. To be nice to the Little People.

I have to laugh at myself.

Tyler thinks I am laughing at his recruiting joke and the Dimple appears. OK, now *he* is being a gigantic cliché. It is so ridiculous that it feels like we are in some bad comedy sketch together and I have no choice but to treat it that way.

He drapes his hand over the counter for me to shake and says in this skeevy Rico Suave voice, "Tyler Moldenhauer. Pleased to make your acquaintance."

We joke-shake and he hangs on to my hand while gazing into my eyes and giving me the Dimple. Talk about cheesy. I cannot *not* call him on it. I bat my eyelashes in a flirty pickup way as corny as his soulful gazing and Dimple-dimpling and ask in my best Southern-belle accent, "Why, suh, are you one of the Savannah Moldenhauers or are you a Buh-mingham Moldenhauer?"

Tyler gets that I have busted him and drops my hand and the whole Señor Suavecito act. He leans down, rests his head on his hands, and points a finger at the official name tag pinned to my chest that Miss Olivia makes all the aides wear. Mine reads **AUBREY J. LIGHTSEY.** Tyler flicks the edge of the plastic tag. "So is that what you like to be called?"

He understands. He gets an entire life of defending a name I never liked to start off with. Correcting people, saying, "No, it's *Aub*rey, not *Aud*rey." Then they call me Audrey anyway. Or the real smarties ask me if I know that Aubrey is a boy's name.

"Actually," I answer with no more thought than I'd give to my next breath, "my friends call me A.J." No one in my entire life has ever called me A.J.

"What's the *J* stand for?"

"That's classified."

"A to the J, I miss you. Why don't you ever come to practice anymore?"

"I quit band."

"You don't go to games, do you?"

"Only if I have a clarinet in my mouth, and that is never going to happen again. Not in this lifetime."

"Ty," Miss Olivia breaks in with the false intimacy of a fan who would call Britney Spears "Brit." "What do you need? You know Coach already has you automatically excused from fifth period."

"No, I'm good, Miss Olivia." He shoots her an extra helping of cheese complete with the Dimple and some kind of crinkling twinkling of the eyes that makes me wince and Miss Olivia wheeze like her asthmatic Chihuahua. "I just want to say hey to our girl here. See how the big college tour went. So how'd it go, A.J.?"

"It went."

He nods as if I've just given the correct answer to the hardest question on the test. I know I am supposed to ask him about the schools he's interested in and where he's applied and what his first choices are. But I don't care. Even if it is Tyler Moldenhauer, I can't make myself care. So I say nothing. The moment gets awkward; he taps his fist on the counter and leaves.

The instant he is gone, Miss Olivia, her face bright and shiny as a kid on Christmas morning, asks, "A.J.?"

It is me and Tyler she wants to unwrap. To tear through the crinkly paper and pull us out and exclaim, "Oh, my God! Oh, my God! Oh, my God!"

But even if there is nothing inside the package—or maybe especially *because* there is nothing inside—it is my package, to unwrap when I want.

So, dry as toast, I answer, "Yes, Olivia, A.J. In the future, I'd like to be called A.J."

There's the exit," Dori says, pointing to a giant sign welcoming us to the future home of Heritage Acres. Miles of subdivided lots stretch into the distance, prime lunch-wagon territory, since the construction workers would have to drive so far just to get out of the place. We follow the trail of newly framed houses and the sound of air hammers firing nails.

The one other time I ever drove out here was a month ago, the middle of July, when, for the third time in a row, Aubrey had stood me up for a date to go shopping for the stuff she needed to take to college, and I was determined that, by God, we would buy a dust ruffle together. So, righteously pissed off, I'd made my way to the lunch wagon, then taken a place in line hidden behind a couple of construction workers. Weather-beaten men with hands rough as tree bark, they'd joked with Aubrey as she took their orders. They made her laugh. I tried to recall the last time she'd laughed in my presence. Filling the orders, pushing food wrapped in white paper out the window, she was engaged, expressive. She was a person I didn't recognize.

She's happy. This is where she's happy.

That thought was immediately eradicated by the memory of an old black-and-white photo I'd seen once of Chinese coolies racked out on planks as they took their leisure at an opium den. They had looked happy too.

When the guys in front of me had stepped aside, and the smell of frying onions, bad coffee, and fermenting ketchup wafted out of the order window on a blast of oven-hot air. Aubrey pivoted, saw me, and her happiness curdled. She leaned down and hissed, "What are *you* doing here?"

Tyler, his back to us at the grill, had yelled, "A to the J, was that hold the jalapeños? Or extra jalapeños on the Mexi-burger?"

The steam and heat had twisted his dark hair into heavy curls that flopped across his forehead. Without the ball cap, wearing a white apron streaked with orange chili grease, he was harder to hate. Aubrey whispered in his ear. He jerked his head up, smiled, and pivoted, sticking his large, scarred hand out the order window. His class ring caught the sunlight. The only people I ever knew who wore high school rings were proud that they'd graduated from high school; they never went on to collect college rings. That made me remember that Tyler Moldenhauer was the opium trapping my daughter in this hellish den.

Before I could shake his hand, Aubrey leaned in and told me that she couldn't leave and I could buy whatever I wanted without her; she, *they*, had customers. And they did. Half a dozen hungry men jostled behind me. That day, for Aubrey's sake, I didn't make a scene. Today I am going to make a scene.

"There it is." Dori spots the catering truck before I do, a dingy rolling metal box with PETE'S EATS written above the order windows and a line of workers waiting outside. "Pete's Eats? Who's Pete?"

"I'm not sure that there is a Pete. It's sort of a franchise. Tyler rents the truck. Something like that. Aubrey hasn't exactly shared all the details with me."

"Probably because 'Pete' is exploiting them."

"That is a distinct possibility." I park behind a flatbed truck loaded with planks of engineered wood flooring. The planks are the same blond-colored woodlike product that's in my house. I know how light and airy and elegant the floors will be after the installers have finished and tiptoed out in their stocking feet. I know how scratched up and cheap and shoddy those floors will look after a few weeks. Even when you go crazy and insist that everyone who enters the house put on slippers like the Japanese do. I know how the floors will delaminate around the doors and windows and anyplace where even a drop of water hits them. I know that, unlike real wood that can be walked on for centuries, then sanded back to newness, once this stuff gets scratched, it can only be ripped out and replaced. And if you can't afford to do that, you just have to live with it.

I start to get out and Dori opens her door as well. I tell her that it might be better if I go alone.

"Good point. Don't want to look like we're ganging up on her. I'll be in the car. Just wave if you need backup."

"Thanks, Dori. Really. Thanks."

She waves my gratitude aside. "Eh, you'd do the same for me."

As I approach the wagon from the side, I plan out what I am going to say. Mentally, I dial in a calm yet forceful tone as I rehearse how I will tell Aubrey that there is a problem at the bank and we have to go. Right this very second.

Aubrey will, of course, be embarrassed by my very presence. She'll lean down and hiss through the window, "I'm working. We have customers."

Tyler will pause in his microwaving activities and ask her what the problem is. Then he'll stand beside her, maybe wrap his arm protectively around her, a united front against the threat that is me.

I don't care how big a scene I have to make to get her to come with me. I don't care if I make her so mad that she seethes like a bad nuclear reactor rod. As long as I can get her into the car and to the bank, she can melt right through the burgundy plush upholstery. If a little China Syndrome is the price I have to pay to collect what Martin owes us, and get her the hell away from Tyler Moldenhauer and out of Parkhaven, then I will gladly pay it. Martin owes us both so much more, but if college tuition is all we'll ever get, I'm going to make damn sure we collect every cent we have coming.

At the lunch wagon, I duck behind a guy I assume is a carpet layer from the knee pads he has strapped on over a pair of jeans flocked with fuzzy beige carpet fibers. I don't want to lose the advantage of surprise. Through the order window, I catch glimpses of Aubrey's slender torso. Everything from the shoulders up and midthighs down is obscured. I always hated that, the way her crotch was practically at eye level with every goon who ordered a burrito. It gave me the creeps, like seeing her in one of those places in Amsterdam where the girls waited behind picture windows.

Girding for battle, I pump both my fear for Aubrey's future and the adrenaline overload released when I was ambushed by Martin's voice into the edgy pugnacity this showdown will require. By the time the carpet layer steps out of the way, I am ready to dive through the window and drag Aubrey out by the throat.

Except that it's not my daughter's face that leans down into the order window and asks, "Know what you want, hon?" Though she has the body of a teenager, the woman asking for my order has to be forty at least. A hard forty. A forty who could be selling corn dogs in a carnival midway.

"Is Aubrey here?" I stand on my tiptoes and crane into the order window to see if Aubrey or Tyler is hiding inside. The only other person, though, is another carny-looking individual, a younger woman in a tank top that shows off ropy muscles bright with gaudy tattoos, stretching up to pull a tower of Styrofoam cups off a high shelf.

The young woman turns, catches my frantic investigation, and regards me with a hostile gaze that I classify as lesbian hatred for a straight suburban breeder. A crown-of-thorns tattoo encircles her neck. "Something we can help you with?" she asks suspiciously, as if I might be about to whip out a subpoena.

"I'm looking for Aubrey Lightsey. Or Tyler? Tyler Moldenhauer?"

The two women exchange looks. Crown of Thorns answers, "You mean that chick and her boyfriend used to have this wagon?"

"Used to?"

The older woman speaks up. "Oh, yeah, they gave notice to Pete. What? Week ago? Ten days? They're gone."

I am standing at pickup/dropoff, reading *The Scarlet Letter* for the essay that is due in English on nature imagery, and I am sweating because we're having a weird late fall heat wave. Mostly, though, I am holding a book in front of my face so that I can act like I am not aware that I am the only senior at Parkhaven who does not own a car. Usually I take the bus, but Mom arranges her schedule so she can pick me up on Mondays and drop me off at Mrs. Cherniak's. I babysit for Mrs. Cherniak when she goes to continuing-ed classes so that she can keep her nurse anesthetist license current for when her kids are in school and she goes back to work gassing plastic surgery patients. She doesn't want to work, but they need the money. "College fund," she explained to me. College, school, they control our whole, entire lives.

Since the *Guinness Book of World Records* is nowhere in sight, I know Mom won't be on time, so I sit down on a bench next to a chubby freshman wearing a yellow T-shirt with a piñata on it and the words I'D HIT THAT. Then I dive back into *Scarlet Letter*. I actually like *Scarlet Letter*. A lot. Maybe because it is practically the only book I've ever read for school that has a female heroine who is just a plain-vanilla WASP and not hiding from the Nazis or dealing with getting her feet bound or some other ethnic dilemma that I honor and everything but is not exactly real pertinent to my own personal life. Mostly, though, I like the way love was back then. Important. Important enough to be cast out forever for. To die for. To risk your immortal soul for. Love, marriage, family, your kids, nowadays they're all disposable. Just something you can walk away from the second a better idea comes along.

I block out the buses lined up like elephants at the water hole and the kids running for them with heavy packs pummeling their backs, and get deep into my Hester and Dimmesdale. They are meeting in the forest, sitting beside a brook, and I am imagining Dimmesdale with his shirt off pressing his flaming cheek to the scarlet letter heaving on Hester's bosom. I have Hester unlacing her bodice a little when, in the outermost rim of my peripheral vision, I notice some jerk in a gargantuan truck with a bumper like he is going to be clearing cows off a railroad track cut to the head of the pickup line and start honking. Then yelling. Which makes the people behind him start honking for him to move. He ignores the honking.

I am tuning the jerk out and feeling really sorry for whoever his poor kid is when the chubby freshman nudges me and says, "I think Ty-Mo means you."

I look up. Tyler has leaned over and is yelling out the passenger window of the truck, "A.J.! Yo! Hey, A.J., you wanna ride?!"

In the suavest of moves, I glance over both shoulders, then, seeing no one standing behind me, stab a finger into my chest where Hester would have had her big *A* and mouth, *Me?*

He waves me over as the honking from the minivan moms rises to an angry crescendo. Before the honking can get any louder or any more people start turning in my direction, I run over and hop into Tyler Moldenhauer's truck. Once I slam the door shut, I say with my trademark flair for the obvious, "You're not at practice."

He points to his ankle, wrapped in an Ace bandage. A pair of crutches is jammed in the space behind the seat. "Sprained it."

"How'd you sprain it?"

"Being an asshole."

"Yeah, but what did you do that was different?"

Without taking his eyes from the road, he points a finger at me, says, "Good one," and whips a U-turn that fishtails us into the traffic going the other way.

It is stupendous being up high with windows all around. I wonder what I've ever had against trucks, then remember that it is Mom who hates trucks. Or, at least, the people who drive trucks. As for me, I never want to ride in a teeny-tiny, claustrophobic car again.

As we head away from school, I spot Mom pulling into the end of the pickup line. The only thought that crosses my mind is, *I hope she doesn't see me.*

"Where we going, Aubrey Josephine?"

I smile at the joke name, at him trying to guess what the *J* stands for. For a second I think about Mrs. Cherniak, all showered and dressed up, excited about seeing her nurse buddies, about getting the classes she needs to take out of the way. Kyle, six, and Jessica, four, waiting for me to come and play "Dance Dance Revolution" with them on their Wii. On the refrigerator, a twenty-dollar bill under a magnet with the Papa John's delivery number on it.

Then I answer, "The quarry."

G one? Gone where?" My fingers clutch at the inner rim of the order window as if I'm preparing to leap into the food trailer.

The younger woman with the noose of thorns around her neck steps forward, snarls, "Why do you need to know?"

"I'm her mother, for Christ's sake. She's supposed to meet me today so we can go to the bank and get the money my asshole ex left for her college education."

The older woman waves the younger one aside in the peremptory fashion that only a mother can get away with and I see that the younger woman is her daughter, not her lover. Mention of the ass-hole ex seems to have forged a common bond, because the mother's tone is been-there sympathetic when she leans down on her elbows so that her eyes are level with mine and says, "Darlin', I wish I knew more to tell you, but I don't. I know she's not anywhere around here, though. Pete makes everyone sign one of those noncompete deals."

"Ten days?" I mumble, too stunned to form a coherent question.

"Least that. Pete demands two weeks' notice or he keeps your deposit. But we just finished switching everything over yesterday and she gave us the keys last night."

I try to wedge this new piece into the puzzle, but it won't go. All I keep thinking is, *Does this mean it is more or less likely that she's pregnant?*

"Did you check the bank?" the woman asks. "Maybe she thinks you're meeting her there."

Her daughter leans in. "Mom and I are always getting our wires crossed like that. She'll think she said, 'Meet me at the Safeway,' but she really said Albertsons. So I'm over there twiddling my thumbs for an hour."

"You weren't there for an hour, and what's so hard about keeping your phone turned on? Darlin', are you okay?"

I realize that she's asking me and mutter that I'm fine.

"It's gonna get better," she tells me.

Recognizing that I am talking to a woman who's spent her whole life waiting for it to get better, I try to pull myself together and move out of the way of her customers. Instead, I hear myself saying, "Today's her birthday. She turned eighteen today."

The mother puts her hand on top of mine and sounds exactly like me talking to one of my mothers when she says, "Oh, sweetie, they always know exactly how to hurt you the most, don't they?"

I nod numbly and back away.

"Good luck," she calls out to me.

Back at the car, Dori's response to this new development is "What the fuck?" Then she brightens. "Maybe the woman's right. Maybe Aubrey got confused and is waiting for you at the bank right now."

"Anything is possible, but why would she? She knows that the trust stipulates that we both have to be present for her to make the withdrawal for the first year's tuition. As many times as I've hammered that into her, she *should* know that. What if she is pregnant? She could be God knows where, doing God knows what right now."

"You mean an abortion?"

"I don't know what I mean. I'm in shock. Why isn't she here?"

"Cam, really, Aubrey is the sensible one. She's going to be fine."

"Fine? Like Twyla's fine?" I regret the words before they're out of my mouth. "Dor, I'm sorry. I'm so sorry. I'm a bitch. I don't know why I said that."

"No prob. You're under a lot of pressure."

I nod.

"And you *are* a bitch. So, we have to find her. What now? Coach Tighty Whitie?"

"No. There is no way on earth I am ever going to speak to that asshole again." Coach Tighty Whitie is Coach Hines, the football coach Tyler lived with until graduation. As I understood it from what sketchy information I could gather from my limited Parkhaven High mom contacts, Tyler had been "recruited" from another school district by Hines. Hines let Tyler live with his family so that he'd have an official address within Parkhaven High boundaries.

Early in the summer I'd gone to Hines's house trying to find Aubrey. When I introduced myself, he'd made a sour face at the mention of Aubrey's name. While I explained my mission, Coach Hines had shifted his jaw back and forth like his dentures were bothering him, except that he didn't wear dentures. Probably a tooth grinder. He was the type. He told me in his self-righteous way that he had "severed all ties with Tyler Moldenhauer." Except that he'd pronounced "severed" like the adjective "severe." Which described him pretty well. He'd probably "severed" a lot of people in his life.

"Hines already told me everything he knows, which was nothing."

"I guess this means . . ."

"What other choice do I have?"

"Animal House it is."

Animal House is what Dori had dubbed the shack that Tyler has been renting with some of his football-player buddies since graduation. We'd located it after my visit with Hines, when the one thing he'd told me then was that Tyler had moved "out past El Dorado Estates somewhere."

Drawing on Dori's extensive training in reconnaissance acquired during her years as a groupie, we had taken her Toyota RAV4 and done a drive-by. That's when we discovered that El Dorado Estates was located on a farm-to-market road just off the interstate and that the Golden Estates consisted of a few acres of mobile homes permanently immobilized on blocks curtained behind sheets of flimsy wooden lattice. A few miles farther down the country road that had once been surrounded by nothing but acres of sorghum and alfalfa, we had spotted Tyler's truck parked in front of a shotgun shack.

Headbanger music had boomed out of the house. A couple of football players who looked like they'd been carved on Easter Island sat transfixed on a broken-down brown Herculon tweed couch, the blue light of the TV they stared into flickering across their faces. One other light was on in the house. I had edged the car forward so we could peek into that window.

"Are they playing Monopoly?" Dori asked when we caught a glimpse of Aubrey and Tyler seated at the kitchen table beneath a wagon-wheel chandelier.

"That's what it looks like."

"What do you want to do?" Dori had asked.

"Hmm." I pretended to ponder the question. "I guess I could either have a screaming fight with her, drag her out by her hair, shove her into the car that I've removed the inner door handles from like a serial killer so she won't immediately bolt, or just accept that she's safe and go home."

That day Dori and I had gone home. Today, I am determined, will be different. I am going to go completely Jerry Springer on her "sorry ass!" Even if bodily force is required, I will drag my daughter to the bank with me.

Once we're on the highway, Dori turns the radio on, hitting "seek" until something comes on that's loud enough and mindless enough to derail the worry loop that's twisting my expression.

Slow ride! Take it easy!

"Oh, Foghat, can you do no wrong?" Dori asks, cranking the volume, then screaming along, " 'Slow ride! Take it easy!' "

I turn the volume up even louder and scream with her, " 'Slow ride! Take it easy!' "

Dori throws in a "Woot!" and, for a split second, it's almost like we're having fun.

We exit onto the farm-to-market road and follow it past the crusty rash of El Dorado Estates trailers. A few miles on, we find the shot-gun shack again. Tyler's truck is nowhere in sight. We pull off onto the shoulder, the car tipping a bit where the road slopes into the drainage ditch running alongside it.

We cross the yard that has been reduced to a few patches of abused grass making a last stand on the hard-packed, cracked dirt. With the toe of her sandal, Dori taps a rusty Road Runner–and–Coyote whirligig and makes it spin so that Coyote is forever, futilely, chasing Roadrunner, and says, "I see the boys have decorated."

I climb the concrete steps up to the front door and knock, dreading having to face whatever bullet-headed throwback answers and the white-trash extravaganza that is sure to ensue. But there is no response. I knock again, harder.

Dori leaves me on the porch and walks around, trying to find a window not covered from the inside by blinds. When she does, she stands on tiptoe, shades her eyes, peeks in, and yells back to me, "Check this out!"

I take her place at the window and stare into a living room that is completely empty except for a few scattered crushed beer cans and a poster of "Chopper Babes" drooping from one tack.

A "Chopper Babes" poster? That is where they have all led, all the lies that started in earnest when? Sometime last November? What would I have done if I'd known that this was where they were heading? What would I *not* have done?

I face Dori. "Okay, I am officially worried now."

A ll right! The quarry. That is the correct answer, Aubrey Jean."

We keep the windows rolled down and our seat belts unbuckled. He looks over at the tornado of hair whipping around my face and I know that he likes it that I don't roll up my window or hold my hair in a ponytail clutched at the side of my face. He hits the gas and we leave the cramped little cars and minivans behind.

We drive far out into the country. When we get to the quarry, no one else is there. Before it was abandoned, the quarry supplied the granite for all the state buildings constructed around the turn of the century. Since then it has filled up with rainwater supposedly a hundred feet deep. The water is clean, but the quarry has a dirty reputation. It is where the wild kids hang out to drink, do drugs, have sex. I don't know about water depth or drugs. I have never been to the quarry before.

"Great idea to come here on a weekday, Aubrey Janine," Tyler says, parking at the edge of the cliff that is one wall of the quarry. "We have the place all to ourselves." He hops out of the truck, careful to land on his good foot, and has his shirt off before he hits the ground.

Swimming. Of course, I should have realized that swimming would be involved.

Already unbuckling his belt, he looks back at me still sitting in the truck and asks, "Shirts or skin?"

I don't know what he means, but neither one sounds good. I know it is already too late to introduce "parasol and bloomers by the side of the water" as an option. I take off my shoes and T-shirt since I am wearing an exercise bra that covers up more than a bikini top would. The Nike shorts are definitely not coming off. Outside the truck window, Tyler makes a big oval of his arms above his head as he tugs off his T-shirt. His jeans drop. He leaves his underpants on. Boxer briefs. Gray. He hops to the long rope hanging from an immense cypress tree at our backs and grabs onto it. "Come on, Lightsey! Let's see some hustle, girl!"

I climb out of the truck in time to catch a glimpse of him pushing off from the edge of the cliff with his good foot. He swings far out above the quarry. At the top of the arc, he lets go of the rope. Arms thrown out wide, face tilted up to the sun, water forty feet down, nothing behind him but sky, Tyler hangs in the air for one impossibly long moment.

Suspended.

The water in its granite tub far below is almost black.

Tyler flips in midair, makes a wedge of his hands, and, without even a splash, slides into the dark water clean as a knife. I peer over the edge, down the sheer face, and wait for him to reappear. In my mind, I see him popping back up to the surface, slinging a high Mohawk of water into the air as he whips his hair out of his eyes.

But he doesn't pop back up.

"Tyler?" My voice echoes off the stone cliff. There is no answer. "Tyler!"

I will his head to burst up. It doesn't. I imagine him trapped underwater, his arm driven into a crack in the stone, leg tangled in a sunken tree, eyes bulging, hair floating around his head like ink swirled into water as he fights to come up. Maybe the water only looks a hundred feet deep. Maybe it is actually shallow and he dove into stone and is paralyzed, his head lolling forward on his spine like a wilted tulip.

I am afraid of deep water, more afraid of heights. Getting up on a stool to change a lightbulb makes me swoony. I don't jump off cliffs. I had planned to crawl down, slowly picking my way along the path looping almost to the far side of the quarry before reaching the water. Tyler will be dead by the time I get down. I think about living the rest of my life as the girl who was with Tyler Moldenhauer at the quarry when he died and did nothing, and I jump.

W hat now?" I ask Dori as we drive away from Chopper Babe Palace.

"The bank?"

"What good would that do? Aubrey and I both have to be there."

"Well, who knows? Maybe they can tell you if there are any extraordinary circumstances clauses or something. Or you can get them to just transfer the money straight to Peninsula. I don't know. Do you have a better idea?"

"Besides beating Tyler Moldenhauer like a circus mule? Not really."

Which is how I end up in a line at the bank while Dori takes my car to zip over to PETCO and pick up the gourmet cat food that her grumpy, obese cats, Three-Way and Green Beer, insist upon.

When, at last, I actually get to speak to a teller she looks maybe thirteen. I thrust the irrevocable trust document at her and explain that I know I can't withdraw any money without my daughter being present, but I just have a few questions.

The teller's long, silky brown hair is pulled back in a ponytail. She's wearing a gray empire-waist dress with a tiny white cardigan pulled over it. Her smooth skin wrinkles as she studies the trust agreement. "You'll have to speak with an officer of the bank. If you'll just have a seat in our waiting area, someone will be with you as soon—"

"No," I interrupt. "You don't understand. I'm not cashing out or anything. I just need to know—"

"If you could just step over to the waiting area," she repeats, already holding her hand out for the deposit slip the man behind me is passing her over my shoulder. He eddies around me and I am edged out of line.

In the waiting area, I mechanically drink bad coffee until I realize that I'm sending myself into tachycardia and my heart is beating like a hummingbird's. This causes me to recall that I hate coffee and never drink the stuff. After a long wait, I'm ushered into an actual office inhabited by an actual grown-up wearing a reassuring blue shirt with white cuffs and collar. He looks familiar, but it's not until he leans across his desk, and sticks his hand out for me to shake that I remember him. "Brad Chaffee."

Perfect. Of course. Of course I would get Joyce Chaffee's husband. Luckily, it doesn't appear that he remembers me. "What can I help you with today?"

I hand over the trust agreement. "Actually, as I tried to explain earlier, I just have a few questions."

"Okay, let's see what we've got here." He spreads the trust out on the desk. Turning it toward me like a car salesman, he produces a Cross pen, touches Aubrey's name, and says, "And the beneficiary?" He glances up, looks around.

"Aubrey's not here. Again, just fact-finding. I know I can't get any money unless she's here."

"And the grantor is . . ." He searches the document, finds Martin's new, famous name, takes another look to make certain he's reading correctly, and asks, "Stokely Blizzard?"

The first time Martin used his new Next name was when he had the trust drawn up sixteen years ago.

"*The* Stokely Blizzard who's . . ." He rumples his eyebrows in my direction, prompting me to fill in the blank if his suspicion is correct and not wanting to insult me if it's wrong. "With all those pictures with . . . ?" He holds his hand out as if to block the lens of an intrusive paparazzo. Next has been in the news quite a bit lately, what with Singapore banning Nextarians from entering the country and an IRS investigation into their status as a church.

I give Brad a nod tight with censure, warning him to back off the celebrity chicken-hawking and be professional. "Could you check on this account? I'd like to see if there might be a way to just direct-deposit it as tuition payment. Or, really, all I want to do is find out what the options are, since Aubrey is. . . unavailable."

"I can do that for you." Brad swivels to face the computer screen. "Let's take a look." His fingers skitter over the keyboard. He works the mouse with needless flourishes, as if to emphasize the heroic measures he is taking on my behalf. "Come on, come on," he urges his computer, circling his hand in a hurry-up gesture.

While he waits, he asks, "Where is Aubrey going this fall?"

I am flustered that, apparently, Brad Chaffee *does* remember me.

But, of course, any boob-whispering single mom *would* be a Parkhaven gossip staple.

"Uh, Peninsula. That's what the trust is for. And Madison? Duke, right?"

"Yeah. She'll be closer to her mother out there."

"Joyce? Joyce is . . ."

What? Going to college with Madison? Sharing a dorm room?

"She moved out to Chapel Hill. After the divorce last winter. Joyce has family there. We made sure Madison got into Duke before we filed."

"Oh. I hadn't heard. I'm sorry."

"Yeah, well, you know. These things happen." Brad is a little too cavalier: Joyce must have been the dumpee. I search his desk and spot a photo of Brad and a petite, dark-haired woman who looks young enough to be one of Madison's friends. They're both wearing running shorts that show off their matching long, muscular legs. Numbers are pinned to their tank tops. Gleaming with sweat, they hang on to each other and grin, having obviously just clocked a couple of personal bests.

"All right," Brad announces, beaming at his monitor. "That's the page I was looking for. Just have to access that account now." He places his finger beneath a number on the document, types it in, hits "enter." A few seconds later Brad's smile fades and he hunches forward, squinting at the screen with his head poked out between hunched shoulders like a vulture.

"What?"

He ignores me.

"Brad, what is it?"

Brad straightens back up, swivels around to face me, states, "The available distribution has already been made."

"In what sense do you mean 'made,' Brad? Because no distribution is possible since I wasn't here."

This is a mistake and it will be cleared up; Brad has confused me with some other boob-whispering ex-wife of a cult bigwig.

Brad resumes his vulture study of whatever carcass he's seeing on the screen. "No, our records show that all available funds were distributed to Aubrey this morning."

I hit wrong. The air and sense are knocked out of me and I sink under. The water that fills my mouth tastes like it came from a tin cup, cold, clean, metallic. I will drown. My body will drift all the way to the bottom of the dark quarry to rest on top of Tyler's. I fear even more that he is not dead and will see that I have made a fool of myself. Again.

And then Tyler is dragging me back up through the water. I soar to the surface, where he yells, "Breathe, A.J.! Breathe!"

I can't obey. My mouth is open, but no air pulls into my lungs. As I flail about, panicked, Tyler holds us both up, treading water. The water is a hundred feet deep. The shore is too far away. I am going to die. I hope my face won't contort in agony as I drown. I hope that Tyler will carry an image of me dying with a serene, yet ultimately incredibly hot, beauty.

Tyler hugs me tight, stares into my eyes until I stop struggling, and orders, "Aubrey, chill. I've got you." He sounds the way he did when he called that kid "Son."

I stop struggling and let myself be held aloft by the strong, steady surge of his legs scissoring together. The air is still knocked out of me, though, and I can't fill my lungs. His tone is casual, like he's making a suggestion, when he says, "Breathe."

I cough, sputter. When I can tread water, he lets me go.

"Seriously, Puke, you have got to regulate your fluids. First not enough. Now too much. Props for the jump, though. Not that many girls jump."

In a mousy, embarrassed voice, I say, "I thought you were going to drown. Or that you were down there paralyzed."

"Paralyzed?" He almost laughs, then doesn't. "You jumped to save me?" He stares hard, checking whether I am joking. When he sees that I'm not, he says, "No one ever tried to save me before," in a suspicious way.

I feel my hair plastered to my skull like Wednesday from the Addams Family, take a big breath, and dive under to wash it back off my face. Tyler plunges under and soars past me, going deeper and deeper. He goes so deep that his tan skin turns pale and blue. I follow him until he stops and we face each other with our hair swirling around our heads and patchwork squares of light wobbling across our faces. He puffs his cheeks out and flutters his hands under his jaw, imitating a blowfish. I stretch my arms out and wriggle in S shapes, curvy as an eel, then clamp Tyler's face between my powerful moray eel jaw hands.

He acts like my jaw hands have forced all the air out of his puffer fish lungs. He blows bubbles into my face, then grimaces, squeezing his eyes together, challenging me to try to stay under longer than him. My lungs are on fire, but I mime a yawn, look at the watch I pretend I am wearing, tap my fingers on my chin like I'm bored. I am stretching out for a nap when he shakes his fist in my face, then blasts off toward the surface. I am a fraction of a second behind him.

With the first breath I suck in, I yell, "Loser!"

"I don't think so!" Tyler inhales a lung-busting gulp of air. I do the same, then we plunge back down. Tyler flips backward in elegant circles, going farther and farther down. Then he stops, crosses his arms over his chest, and tilts his head up at me, cocky as a rapper in a battle who's just spit out some deadly rhymes, challenging me to top him. I dive farther down, do some body popping and a goofy, jokey robot, then freeze with my arms crossed over my chest, throwing pretend gang signs with both hands. We go back down again and again, breakdancing and having rap battles and seeing who can stay under the longest.

I always win because I can hold my breath forever, since I know how to move on the outside and stay silent and still on the inside.

1:13 A.M. NOVEMBER 2, 2009

=Is it a happy or a sad thing to feel like you just had the best day you will ever have in your entire life?

=For me, Aubrey, reading this, it is a very happy thing.

=Does it matter if there will never be another one as good?

=There will be.

=How do you know?

=You will. More than you can count. It's late. Why aren't you asleep?

=Good question. G'night.

=Sweet dreams.

=Sweet dreams to you, Dad.

I haven't dabbled in drugs much since one unfortunate incident involving marijuana that should have been labeled "crack weed." I suddenly have the same feeling that I had after smoking the crack weed: The world around me dissolves into wavy lines and recedes at a panic-inducing velocity. Though a roaring in my ears prevents me from hearing exactly what Brad is saying, I'm getting the picture and state it as clearly as I can: "Aubrey took the money? All the first-year money?"

Brad nods.

"That is not possible. The trust specifies that I, the guardian of record, have to be present. I was not present. My daughter doesn't even have a copy of the trust agreement. You could not have given her the money. Or if you did, it was illegal and your bank is criminally liable."

Brad is as calm as a yoga instructor as he murmurs, "Situations like these involving divorce and estrangement from the child are difficult, I know. It can be hard for everyone to get on the same page."

Oh, shit. Brad is giving me Zen Banker.

" 'Page'! There is no 'page' to be on! I have the page! All the pages!" I hold the trust agreement up.

"Our records indicate . . ." Brad swivels away from me to study his monitor with the weary demeanor of a man who is tired of dealing with crazy, screaming bitches. Was Joyce a crazy, screaming bitch beneath her perfect highlights? Or did it make it easier for Brad to leave to pretend that she was? ". . . that we received a fully executed codicil to the original agreement that altered the terms of distribution with the principal trustee mandating that the beneficiary be given full and complete access to all funds designated in Section—"

"You gave the money to Aubrey? You didn't send it to Peninsula State College?"

"That appears to be the case."

"You just gave a child a year's worth of college tuition?"

Brad scans the form on his computer. "Our records indicate that Aubrey's birthday is today and she turned eighteen—"

"Oh, God! Her birthday. *That's* what she was waiting for. Fucking 'legal age.' How much?"

Brad had taken his hand off the mouse at "fucking," and I already feel him distancing himself. "I'm going to need to check on a few things before we—" He means he's going to talk to lawyers.

"Something in the vicinity of thirty thousand dollars, I guess." The way Brad's eyes flicker back to the screen confirms how close I am. "Fuck! Fuck! Fuck! Fucking Tyler Modenhauer, he put her up to this!"

I am now screeching like a howler monkey, which causes Brad to go to his ultimate Zen Banker level and start scribbling down the phone numbers of "someone in corporate" who might be "better able to assist" me. Then he uses the word "defund" and I come close to losing it altogether until I remember that I'm in a bank and that Brad, no doubt, has a button under his desk he can push and I'll be eating industrial carpet with a security guard's knee on the back of my neck if I don't calm down.

I stumble outside into the parking lot. It takes me a second to remember what my car looks like. Dori is waiting for me in it with all the windows rolled down, texting madly, when I collapse into the passenger seat.

"Cam, what? You do not look good."

I stare at her.

"Say something. You're white. Greenish white. You want to lie down in the backseat? Come on, put your head between your legs. God, you're trembling."

Dori forces my head down. As I lean over, hyperventilating car rug fibers, I see, under the seat, a yellow Peeps bunny looking back at me. I try to recall what Easter he dates from and calculate that he must be a minimum of ten years old. And still as fresh as the day I tucked him into a nest of shredded green cellophane grass in Aubrey's basket.

I sit back up.

"You haven't eaten anything all day. Have a bite of my wrap."

I take the wrap and gnaw on rubbery tortilla and whatever vegan abomination she had them fill it with. My guess is nonegg tofu egg salad. Or tile grout.

"Is this," I ask, holding up the wrap, "supposed to balance out smoking, drinking, drugs, and your powdered-sugar-doughnut binges?"

"Oh, good, you're feeling well enough to bitch me out." She snatches the wrap out of my hand. "Crisis over." She eats and waits for the story.

I hold out for roughly thirty seconds. "She got it. They gave it to her."

Dori's mouth drops open and I am treated to the sight of half-mulched vegan egg salad. "The bank gave it to her? I thought you had to be present to sign off."

"Martin, that psychotic, lying asshole, added a codicil to the trust so that Aubrey could get the money without me. Something that, apparently, is possible the second she turns eighteen. The entire first-year tuition is gone."

Heat waves shimmer off the parking lot pavement, but I am chilled to my bones. "What the hell has my life been about for the past sixteen years? I exiled myself here so she could get a good education, go to college, and have a wonderful, fabulous, exciting, fulfilling life."

"You don't know that. Aubrey is a sensible girl. Beside, worse comes to worst, it's just the first year."

"You don't understand. This whole codicil thing means that Martin must have had contact with her."

"Yes. And?"

"And any contact nullifies the trust agreement. It gives Next the right to defund the entire trust."

" 'Defund.' Is that even a word?"

"Brad Chaffee used it. He and Joyce broke up."

"No! Ken and Barbie split up? Is he gay? Please tell me that Brad Chaffee is gay."

"It's gone. It's all gone. I cannotcannotcannot believe this."

"Maybe Next won't find out."

I squint, which gives Dori time to remember that article I showed her about Next hacking into the IRS system.

"Hmm. Probably not. Cam. Cammy, no, don't cry. Oh, shit, yeah, cry."

"What do I do now? What *can* I do? Please, will someone please tell me what I am supposed to do right now? I have no idea on earth where my daughter is. I no longer know any of her friends. And even if I could track her down, then what do I do? Stand outside a locked door and scream at her? Call the police to drag her home? At which point they ask how old she is and hang up when I say eighteen."

"Preaching to the choir," Dori agrees.

I'd been on the extension when, after Dori's ex had told her that he didn't know where Twyla was, Dori had called in a missing person report. The officer's first question was, "How old is the missing person?" When Dori answered eighteen, the woman on the other end delivered a speech that she had obviously given a thousand times about "law enforcement guidelines" requiring that if the missing person is an adult there has to be "concrete, solid" evidence that he or she is in grave physical danger or will harm himself or others before a police report can be taken. The woman had ended the conversation with these words of wisdom: "Adults are free to roam about as they please."

"So much for my delusion of easing her into college with dust ruffles and comforters. What kind of a fantasyland of denial was I living in? Even if I could get the money, I'd have had to drug her to get her on a plane for Peninsula."

"That would have made for an interesting freshman orientation."

"You know who has that money? Right now?"

Dori nods.

"That redneck, football-playing, swaggering, entitled . . ." As with Next, there are not words foul enough. "How could Martin have done it? How could he have let her have all that money? I can't stand it that they've been conspiring behind my back. I wonder how long that's been going on."

"And, of course, there's still the possibility that she's—"

"Don't. Don't say the *P*-word. Please, not at this exact moment. I just cannot deal."

"Not a problem. You know me. No deal is good deal."

"So," Dori asks, "cocktails?"

Apparently my shift as a mother is officially over and whatever higher purpose I might have deluded myself into believing my life in Parkhaven had no longer exists. At this point, a downward spiral into alcohol with maybe a little drug sidebar looks like my next logical move.

"Why not?"

I kick myself for not being more vigilant back when all this started. Shaniqua, the star of all Aubrey's November lies. How could I have fallen for Shaniqua?

Tyler and I went to the quarry yesterday and again today.

I tell Mom that I have a new friend, Shaniqua, and I am going to her house every day after school. To work on a physics project. Study for a Spanish test. Swim in her pool. I tell her that Shaniqua's father is an obstetrician and her mother is a lawyer. As expected, Mom is so thrilled that I have not only a friend, but an *African American* friend, that she doesn't ask any questions. Like what Shaniqua's last name or phone number is. Or where she lives. Or how, exactly, I met the Huxtables.

Here are the things Tyler and I do *not* talk about: College. Football. Our "plans for the future." His dad. My dad. His mom. My mom. Why he lives with Coach Hines. How weird it is that he is hanging out with me.

Here are the things Tyler and I *do* talk about: Whether you can double-punch on old VW Beetles in Slug-a-Bug or just on convertibles. Whether *Mister Rogers* or *Sesame Street* was better. The best way to pull a Band-Aid off. Whopper or Big Mac? Worst sore throat you ever had. Worst sunburn. Best way to keep fireflies alive in a jar. Whether my feet with the creepy middle toe freakishly longer than the big toe are grosser than his feet with the disgusting permanently yellow big toenail.

Here are the things Tyler and I do at the quarry: play.

No one would believe that that is all we do. That Tyler Moldenhauer would take a girl, an ordinary girl no one remembers knowing, to the quarry and just play like a couple of kids. We jump off the cliff holding hands and hang in the air, suspended in sunlight. We dive under and float in the metallic water, suspended among the glittering bits that sparkle around us like we are swimming through the Milky Way.

Halloween was last Saturday. I try to remember how many years it was hot when I trick-or-treated and how many times I wore a parka over my costume. It seems about fifty-fifty that the weather will hold. I don't want the warm weather to ever end. I want to stay suspended with Tyler forever.

S ince I don't have the energy or money for anything other than the first convenience store we pass, we pick up a suitcase of Milwaukee's Best, which meets my very exacting standards of being available, alcoholic, and cheap, and head to my house. I fill a cooler with ice, plant the beer in it, and Dori, Pretz, and I install ourselves on the front porch.

Something about the day's combo platter of shocks has left me boneless. Semicoagulated in a rocking chair with my feet planted on either side of the cooler, by the time I've drained my first Beast in one long glug, I am wondering why I don't do this more often. Just sit out on my own goddamn front porch and take the world in.

Next to the great room and the theoretically great schools, the porch—sweeping across the front of the house, raised up above the street by seven broad, concrete steps—was this house's biggest selling point. As the Realtor showed Martin and me around, I imagined Aubrey and her little friends—sweet, pigtailed girls—coloring on the porch, cooled on a hot summer day by breezes rolling up the sloping yard, while I served lemonade to their mothers. I bought two rockers and a glider and figured I'd keep adding seating once our porch became the spot where everyone gathered on lazy evenings to share kindly gossip and watch the kids chase fireflies through the endless summer nights.

Who was I channeling? Aunt Bee?

We moved in and I found out that, although, yes, there were kids galore, none of them ever had a single unscheduled moment. On summer evenings and every other second they weren't in school, they were getting tutored or coached or enriched. None of them walked or rode bikes the five blocks to the blue-ribbon elementary school. The only social interaction I enjoyed on my porch was catching glimpses of kids strapped into minivans while they waited for the garage door to go up before they disappeared inside. This was mostly because, though the appearance of a stranger made antennae bristle as if a red ant had wandered into our black ant colony, every parent in Parkhaven Country believed they were one unguarded moment away from seeing their offspring on the back of a milk carton.

I pass a beer to Dori and methodically start in on my second.

"On the bright side," Dori says, "you can sell the house now."

I give a little snort to indicate how impossible that is.

"No, seriously. What's stopping you? You sell the McMansion, get some adorable, tiny little place. Maybe not actually *in* the city, but close to signs of intelligent life. Why not?"

For a lovely ten, maybe twenty seconds, selling the house seems like an actual possibility. All it takes, however, to remind me why that is impossible is to lift my butt cheeks off the rocker. Which I do when I reach for *cerveza tres*. Just this slight change in my viewing angle allows me to look up and down the street and see seven For Sale signs planted in seven yards. Three of them are being circled by the foreclosure vultures. Every time there's another round of layoffs at the computer-chip factory or the price of gas goes up and those commutes into the city become more expensive, another sign appears.

Dori leans forward, follows my gaze, and sees what I see. "Oh, yeah. Forgot about that little detail."

After a malt-enriched meditative moment, I muse, "I read this book about a British expedition in 1845 to explore the Northwest Passage. Or, actually, not a book so much as a book review. In any case, this expedition sailed into the Canadian Arctic looking for the Northwest Passage from the Atlantic to the Pacific. They couldn't find it. But the captain was a stubborn, classic male-answer-syndrome guy who would never admit he was wrong, so he refused to let them turn back. Winter set in. By the time the captain admitted he might possibly have been the teensiest bit wrong, massive planks of ice had frozen their boat in place and escape was impossible. All the men died hideous deaths—starvation, exposure, scurvy. They found corpses with black tongues, which showed that a lot of them had succumbed to lead poisoning. There were knife marks on some of the bones. Which meant cannibalism."

"What's the title? I need a fun summer beach read."

"I'm like that expedition. I waited too long. I am frozen in place."

Dori stands. "Well, much as I'd love to stick around and tenderize, then eat you, Gary's waiting and I need to pick up a few things. If you know what I mean."

She bumps her eyebrows up and down. I do not need the hubba-hubba signal to know that what she means is that she and her beau are going to stick a variety of preordained items into each other's orifices. What she really means is that she is a wild, lascivious lady of untrammeled wants and desires who cannot be tamed into suburban beigeness. Since she's mentioned it before, I know that one of the things she will be picking up is lactose-free whipping cream, because dairy does unmentionable things to Gary's bowels. I would never tell Dori this, but no matter how many ball gags and gel-filled dildos might be involved, once your partner is apprising you of his or her digestive inconveniences, you've moved out of untrammeled territory.

"Are you going to be all right?" Dori asks, pulling the keys to her Toyota RAV4 parked in the driveway from her pocket.

"Is there an alternative?"

"I'll stay if you want me to."

"No, go. I'm just going to sit here, get drunk, and wait for the phone to ring."

Dori leans down, gives me a hug, and, for a couple of seconds, I cling to her. She whispers in my ear, "You raised a great kid, Cam. She was great before this happened. She'll be great when it's all over. She is going to have a great life. A great big, wonderful, happy life."

"Thanks. Twyla too." I reseal our covenant of denial and wishful thinking by adding the obligatory, "They're just on their own time-tables."

On Thursday the first cold front of the year blows in. At the quarry a chilly wind pebbles the surface of the water. We jump in anyway. And play until our lips turn blue. We drive home with the heater on full blast. The windows steam up from the cold air outside and our wet clothes inside.

It is obvious by now that Tyler is not attracted to me and that is fine. Most likely he is gay and squelching rumors by taking a girl out to the quarry. A girl that none of his friends will ever talk to. I don't care. Our suspended moments are better than any of the so-called sexual encounters I've had where I did things that I made myself believe I wanted to do. Then worried whether I was doing them the right way and whether my body was good enough. My whole life Mom has drilled into me that sex is all natural and beautiful and nothing to be ashamed of.

Playing with Tyler at the quarry feels the way she always told me that sex was supposed to feel.

ori's departure stirs Pretzels. She hobbles to the edge of the high porch and sniffs, her black nose twitching as she picks up the scent of a squirrel she can no longer see. Some ancestral synapse is triggered by the smell; she growls her muted, grumbling growl and her legs twitch.

"Steps, girl! Steps!" I yell, remembering Black Ice Night. I jump up and lead Pretzels to the stairs at the middle of the porch. Once she's positioned in front of them, I hoist up her arthritic hindquarters, and as she puts one trembling front paw down, then another, I help her down to what remains of the grass. She settles onto a sunny patch and pokes her nose into the breeze.

I return to the porch and watch my sweet old girl. She drops her big head onto her front paws and discovers a black-and-white mockingbird feather lying in the grass beside her. After chewing on it for a bit, she picks it up, waves it around in the air as if she's conducting a tiny orchestra, lets it fall, rediscovers it a moment later, snaps the feather up, and starts conducting all over again.

With Dori gone, I am free to play my favorite game, Time Travel. I return to my last Christmas with Martin and replay the way it really happened: Two-year-old Aubrey unwrapped BeeBee and hugged her to her chest. I hugged Martin to mine and pleaded to know what I had to do to keep our marriage together. He told me, "Join Next and raise our daughter as a Nextarian."

Aided by my fourth Milwaukee's Best, I rewrite that history into an alternate reality in which, instead of my informing my husband that he had gone totally fucking insane and that my child would be raised in his science-fiction pyramid scheme of a cult over my dead body, and him then walking out of our lives, I say, "Hallelujah, sign me up, baby!" And Martin, Aubrey, and I live happily ever after in this and the next ninety-nine incarnations.

In the Beer Five alternate version of reality, I respond by finding the most bloodthirsty hellhound of a divorce lawyer ever created in the cyborg attorney lab, so that when Martin comes to the table flanked by a couple of Next's legal pit bulls, and announces that he has signed over all his worldly assets and basically indentured himself for all eternity, in exchange for "the church's extraordinary generosity" in putting a big chunk down on the Parkhaven house and setting up an irrevocable trust that will fund Aubrey's college tuition, provided he never has any contact, whatsoever, with either of us again, my goons would have taken Martin to the mat. Or at the very least written a document that couldn't be codiciled into irrelevance.

The Beer Six version of history, oddly, takes me back to an unusually clear-eyed replaying of events pretty much exactly as they happened. I got pregnant. We bought this house. I began my suburban exile. I quit my nursing job in my sixth month. Martin was miserable at his job in the city, where programming, a skill he'd developed as a hobby, an intriguing mental challenge to supplement his interest in systems of logic, had become his whole life, the thing he could do that made money.

Then "some guy" at work told him about Next. From the beginning, Martin was open about his interest and committed to getting me involved with him. At that point, I knew nothing about Next except that a few starlets with more silicon than gray matter were ardent followers. But I could see that Martin was benefiting from it. At first in ways that I actually liked. Though he was home less and less, when he was here there was more and more of him. Just as my belly was swelling, Martin began filling his body in a way he never had before. He'd always *been* tall, but for the first time he *seemed* tall. And he'd always had a deep voice, but before Next he'd modulated it, swallowing his words so that I'd have to lean in close to hear what he said. His timidity had forced me to make more and more of the decisions—like having a child and buying this house—for both of us.

After a few months of Next, though, Martin the Soft-spoken was transformed into a Rush Limbaugh clone. Suddenly his every utterance was delivered in a bone-rattling bellow with a majesty and volume that reverberated off the high ceiling of the great room. His new assurance made everything he said sound obvious and irrefutable, like he was explaining gravity and I was an idiot if I didn't agree.

Which is why, when I was eight months pregnant and he said, "Cam, the best thing you could do for yourself and our child is to go to the Hub and take the basic Next course," I agreed. "The Hub" was the converted nursing home that "the congregation" met in for classes and exorbitantly expensive "counseling sessions." It was where Martin had taken to spending all his lunch hours and most evenings except for the few when I put my foot down and made him stay home and do something like assemble the crib, whereupon he'd act like a teenager who'd been grounded. So I thought, *Why not?* I tried to look upon it as something we could do together, a shared interest like salsa-dancing lessons or a wine-tasting class.

The course turned out to be two parts assertiveness training combined with one part three-year-old's birthday party. We had staring contests in which the first to blink was the loser. We played Simon Says and took turns ordering other class members to "Go stand on the chair!" "Jump up and down!" "Go drink out of the aquarium!" The entire time our trainer kept yelling that if Next technology was not causing us to be filled with "bright surges of energy" and "connecting with our own power source," we should leave. Walk out. Right that very moment. Then the class, champing like hounds on the hunt, waited for the backsliders among us to reveal themselves. It was a canny crowd-control intimidation tactic. Each time you didn't have enough gumption to declare yourself an infidel by walking out, you were, essentially, doubling down on Next; you were publicly announcing, "I believe."

For our final challenge, the trainer took away all our money and commanded us to go out into the city and use our newly honed mastery over time, space, and the unenlightened boobs of the non-Next world to get something for free.

I drove to the nearest convenience store; bought an Almond Joy with the five-dollar bill I'd slipped into my bra; went to the library; discovered that all material about Next was kept under lock and key, since adherents considered it their sacred duty to steal or destroy anything negative about the church; gave the librarian my driver's license to hold while I perused what books and articles they'd been able to replace; researched Next; concluded that it was one Spanish Inquisition away from being the most dangerous group ever to pass itself off as a religion and that I had to save Martin and our unborn child from its patent idiocy.

When Martin came home that night—late as usual because he'd had to attend "muster" at the Hub—I expressed the belief that he was being brainwashed by a dangerous nutball cult and demanded that he quit. Now. For me. For our child. For us.

"Cam, how do I make you open your eyes?" he'd asked, his own eyes glittering the way they always did after a session at the Hub. He spoke quickly, with a hint of mania. By that time, even his smell had changed. It was sharper, almost acrid. "I want my life to be a masterpiece. I want *your* life to be a masterpiece. I want the life we create together with the child we have created together to be a masterpiece. Next has the tech to give us that."

"Martin, Next is a scam. A giant, snake-oil-drenched scam."

With all ten fingers, Martin pointed to his eyes and demanded, "Is *this* a scam?"

"Martin, your vision was never that bad to start with."

"But bad enough that I needed glasses when I drove. I ran Opt Tech and look." He indicated his glasses-free face. "Do I wear glasses anymore when I drive?"

"No, but that doesn't prove to me that you no longer need them. In fact, I might be endangering my life and the life of our unborn child every time I get in a car with you."

He shook his head at that, more sad than angry. "There is something worse than not being able to see, Cam. Imagining that you can see when you are totally blind."

"Oh, my aching ass. Did you really just say that?" I laughed. Laughing was a mistake.

"You dismiss Next at your own peril," Martin intoned in the Old Testament voice he'd developed. "And the peril of our entire planet. I know this for an absolute, indisputable fact: The only way we will survive as a species is if we all learn and implement Next tech as expeditiously as possible."

"Martin, please, I need you. Our child needs you. Come back to us. Quit Next."

"If I had a kidney disease would you beg me to stop doing dialysis?"

"You don't have a kidney disease."

"I might as well. Without Next I'd be just as useless to you, to myself, and to our child."

We argued until dawn. I dragged out all the articles about Next that I'd Xeroxed, along with warnings about tactics cults use to brainwash converts and separate them from their families. Martin tossed back brainwashed-cult rantings that separated us more and more.

In very short order, we became a virulently hostile interfaith couple, Martin turning from me to protect the bright jewel that was the beliefs I ridiculed. Me hanging on, clinging to the hope that the instant his child was placed in his arms, Martin would come back to us.

I was pregnant through one of the hottest summers on record. At night, I stopped sleeping. During the day, I sat on our porch and pretended to work on the online course I was taking to upgrade my nursing diploma to a bachelor's-in-nursing degree. But every time my eyes hit terms like "concepts of management" or "collaboration with an interdisciplinary team," they glazed over. My grandmother Bobbi Mac had died that spring, and all I wanted was to be with her and her nurse buddies in North Africa. With Pee Wee, Speedy, Slats, but especially I wanted to be with Crazy Mac. I wanted nursing to be having a gang of friends who put on talent contests and watched out for one another. Mostly, though, I wanted to walk into a room where a person was hurting and make it better. Right away. Not after "collaborating with an interdisciplinary team."

I might have stuck it out with nursing if I hadn't been pregnant. Or not in despair. Or not lonelier than I'd ever been, trapped out in the suburbs where the one person I knew had turned into a stranger. But I *was* pregnant, lonely, and in despair, so instead of studying, I sat on the porch and rocked, like I am rocking now, while Martin spent his days in the city working at a job he hated and his evenings at a place he loved more than me, and I watched our new suburban lawn parch and turn to straw.

Right after the delivery, when Martin and I were alone in my hospital room for the first time since two became three, he picked up our child, and the love that flooded his face was so undeniable that I knew the spell had been broken: Martin had been returned to me. To us.

He cooed to our child, bounced her gently, sniffed her head. We decided to call her Aubrey after a song that Martin used to sing to me because it was about a "not so very ordinary girl or name." Aubrey's eyes flickered beneath blue lids closed tight against a painfully overlit world as he stroked her head. I thought we were going to be all right.

But Aubrey had colic and screamed eighteen hours a day. Martin begged me to allow him to take her to "a practitioner" at the Hub. "We do astonishing work with gastro issues," he said, but all I noticed was that he said "we" when he talked about Next, and I couldn't recall the last time he'd used "we" when he talked about us.

Martin spent more and more time at the Hub. In addition to sleeping, I stopped eating and having rational thoughts.

When I sobbed through Aubrey's twelve-month well-baby visit, the pediatrician sent me to a psychiatrist who put me on Lexapro. Clearly, I was too far gone for Lexa-amateur. Martin promised that if I swallowed the same fistfuls of Next-produced vitamins and supplements that he did, I would have no need for the "lobotomy in a bottle" dispensed by psychiatrists. I suggested that he was a deranged lunatic who should either stop actively torturing me or get the hell out of my life.

Martin begged me to try to understand. He bared his soul. He wept. We had desperate, amazing sex that I thought signaled a new beginning, but was actually a long good-bye. By Aubrey's second birthday, Martin was in the process of turning over all his worldly possessions to Next. At the divorce hearing, I learned that it was an extraordinary concession on "the church's" part to let Martin hold out enough money to put a big chunk down on the house and set up the college trust fund. Of course, Next made Martin promise in return that he would have no further contact with Aubrey or me. And if he ever did, that would lead automatically to the forfeiture of the trust. And, for the next sixteen years, there had been no contact.

It is obvious now, though, that he and Aubrey had been in contact. Just one more of the apparently limitless things my daughter did last year that I knew nothing about.

Friday is cold enough that Tyler wears his corduroy jacket and we don't jump in the water. We take chunks of limestone and scrape powdery outlines of each other into the flat slabs of black granite at the top of the quarry. We do a crime scene story, each of us changing positions and taking turns outlining the other.

We start with our dead bodies. Corpse outlines. Then we draw our victims' bloody fight. We keep adding scenes, backing the story up in time. The last scene we draw, which is really the first, where it all starts, is a kiss. I lie down on my side first and Tyler draws around me, being especially careful to trace my profile as I lean forward, head tilted up. Then he lies down. I trace around his back, his butt. I reposition his head and trace his profile. Limestone powder dusts his jacket, his jeans, his chin. My fingers touch his lips as I outline them. In the drawing our lips meet.

We step back and look at the whole story wobbling across the uneven surfaces. I try to figure out which one of us made it into a lovers' quarrel but can't. It is like the Ouija board, where the answer just magically comes out of two hands touching. Maybe he was imagining that he was outlining a guy. That's fine. I had my own imaginings.

Tyler takes the back route home, a narrow, twisty road that used to be lined with farms and small ranches but is now deserted. We are deep in the country when he points to a road with weeds growing up through the cracks that has an old rusty mailbox beside it and says, "I used to live down a road like that one."

"You did?" I try not to sound too interested. He never talks about growing up and I don't want to scare him away from telling me stuff.

He glances in the rearview as if the only way he is ever going to look at that mailbox is if it is far behind him. He watches until it is lost in the darkness, until he has a safe head start on it; then he says, "Yeah," in a way that makes me know that that is all he is going to say.

We slide onto the freeway. He turns on his player. Carrie Underwood. In a million years, I never would have imagined that I'd be driving around in a pickup truck with a gay football player who likes Carrie

Underwood. And that it would be more fun than anything else I have ever done in my life.

I try to sound casual as I lift one of the crutches stowed behind us and go, "You're not using these anymore."

"I never really needed them that much. I kind of strung this out a little." He pauses. "But Coach says I have to come back to practice Monday, though, or he won't play me in the game next Friday. So—"

I rush to save us both from embarrassment. "No problem. It's cool. It was fun. Maybe we'll hang out again sometime."

"Sometime? Uh, yeah. Like at practice Monday. I mean, if you want to."

"Really?"

"Yeah, 'really.' Why not?"

"I don't know. Guess I thought that what happens at the quarry would stay at the quarry."

"Why would you think that?"

"I don't know. I just did. The quarry . . . You know. It's the quarry."

"Yeah. I wish my whole life could be the quarry. Just simple like that. Like we could all be some primitive tribe that existed at the quarry hunting and gathering and shit."

"I know. Like you either kill the rabbit and eat or you starve. That day. Just that day. Not like, 'Oh, I have to figure out a whole strategy for eating for the rest of my entire life. And I'd better be hunting at only the most exclusive hunting spots or the whole tribe will think I'm a big fat loser.' "

"That's exactly it. Puke, you're amazing. You are exactly who I thought you'd be right from the beginning."

"What? What's that supposed to mean?"

"I guess it means I'm psychic."

Tyler won't tell me anything more about who he thought I'd be, just nods, happy about being psychic or right or whatever, then stares out at the landscape like he is trying to figure out how to turn it all into one big quarry.

Tyler has been dropping me off at the corner for the past week so that I can tell Mom that I walked home from Shaniqua's house. He stops a block from my house and, before I get out, asks, "So? Monday? Practice?"

I have my hand on the door handle. I want to be simple. I want to be the one simple thing in his life, but I can't *not* ask. "Not that it matters one way or another. I mean, I seriously don't care. But, just for curiosity, why are you hanging out with me?"

He faces me, turns the engine off. "I don't know. You're fun. I liked it when you busted me for macking on you."

"You mean when you were all, 'Hey, baby, I'm Tyler Moldenhauer,' that time at the attendance counter?"

"Yeah. You treated me like such a creeper. That cracked me up. In fact, the first thing I ever heard you say cracked me up."

"You mean, after I puked on you?"

"Oh, that was hilarious too. No doubt. But, no, before that. The first time I noticed you I was like, What is different in this picture? Oh right, one girl doesn't have a giant feather protruding from the side of her head. Then that band director dude—"

"Shupe."

"Yeah, that dee bag. Such a jarhead wannabe. He is yelling at you that 'it's Semper Fi!' and you come back at him in this total Parris Island DI voice, 'Not Semper I, *sir*!' That cracked me up. And he completely did not get it. No one on the team got it. I got it."

"So I didn't have to puke on you to get you to notice me?"

"Hells to the no." He goes into his skeevy playboy act. "I had my eye on you, girl."

I play-flirt back at him, purring, "Mmm. Tell me more, my fine playa manwhore." It is exactly like being with Javier, the gay kid who was my only real friend last summer at Lark Hill. We loved to pretend in front of the other counselors that I had a giant crush on him and no idea that he was gay. It was fun to mess with them, to have some designated representative come over to me and whisper, "We're worried about you, Aubrey. You do know that Javier is gay, don't you?" Then I'd pretend to be shocked and in mad love denial and say, "Gay? No! My Javier is not gay! He's just *theatrical*!"

I play-slap at Tyler, just like I used to do with Javier, and he jokes back, "How could I resist. You were like the palest person I had ever seen. What did you do all summer? Sleep in a coffin? I thought you were an albino. And that was *so* sexy."

"You did *not* just call me an albino!" I windmill a flurry of bunny pats onto his chest. It is like slapping a saddle.

He raises his hands in front of his chest and I slap at those. "I just had to see those white-rat red eyes up close. Find out what lab you escaped from."

I accelerate my attack. He squeezes his eyes shut and squeals. It seems irrelevant whether he is gay or not and I kiss him.

Tyler's eyes spring open. For a fraction of a second, I think he is going to kiss me back. But he doesn't and I want to blurt out that I know he is gay and I didn't expect him to kiss me and let's just pretend I didn't do that.

He drops his arms. "You are a nice person, A to the J."

"Nice! That is such an insult. Nice is the most boring thing anyone can be."

"No, believe me. Nice is not an insult."

"Well, I'm not that nice."

"Yeah, you are. You're so nice that you don't even know how nice you are, which is why I better make you leave right now."

I walk home in a state that ping-pongs between ecstasy and utter humiliation. Inside the house Mom ambushes me and asks, "Why don't you bring Shaniqua over here sometime?"

"Oh, she has to babysit. She's got two little sisters who fight all the time. And a brother who's got dyslexia."

"Bring them all over. Give me a time. I won't schedule any consultations and I'll help her watch the little ones."

"Mom, you always do this."

"Do what?"

"Try to take my friends over."

I see the same question going through her mind that is going through mine: *What friends?* Knowing that she would never actually say the words, I escape before she can figure out another way to grill me.

I am all the way in my room, closing the door, when she yells out, "Peninsula sent you something! It's from the housing office!" Her voice startles me. I'd already forgotten that she was there. And I haven't thought once about Peninsula since our trip. I pretend I didn't hear her, shut and lock the door, and go back to remembering how Tyler's lips felt on mine.

Thinking of how Martin and Aubrey have been plotting behind my back does me in. I dig out Aubrey's pink boom box from elementary school, find her favorite CD—the sound track from *Toy Story 2*—select "When She Loved Me," hit "play," then "repeat." I am gravid with grief and this song is the Pitocin I need to deliver. As Sarah McLachlan sings in her aching mezzo-soprano, "When somebody loved me . . ." I bury my face in Aubrey's pillow just the way I imagined I'd do after she'd left for college to build a bright future and I was missing her. Except that now she's gone from my life and there is no college, no building of a bright future, to comfort me.

She is just gone and my "next" seems empty indeed.

The first time I heard "When She Loved Me," Aubrey was sitting on my lap because movies on big screens scared and overwhelmed her. She tolerated the frantic action adventures of all the boy toys—Woody, Buzz Lightyear, Mr. Potato Head—but she came to life when Jessie the Yodeling Cowgirl doll appeared on-screen. I felt her grow lighter on my lap as she strained toward the screen, drawn into the tale of how Jessie the doll had once been loved by a little girl, Emily. As the years passed, though, Emily grew up, dolls were replaced by nail polish, and Jessie, crumpled and lonely beneath Emily's bed, was forgotten. I'd thought it was adorable when, after the movie, Aubrey had rushed from the car to her room, found Bee-Bee, whom she'd been neglecting, and spent the next hour brushing the Puffalump's purple hair, fastening it with tiny plastic barrettes, talking to the doll the entire time.

I was so certain that I would remember every adorable thing that she'd said that day that I didn't write it down. And now I can't recall a single word.

When somebody loved me.

Jessie the Yodeling Cowgirl's song washes over me, the lyrics like a horoscope, a fortune cookie I opened years ago and should have paid more attention to. I agree wholeheartedly with Jessie as she sings about how everything was beautiful when Emily loved her and she had the power to dry her tears. When Jessie the doll sings that every hour she spent with Emily lives within her heart, but that now she is left alone, waiting for the day when Emily would say again that she would always love her, it is my song.

Feeling deeply, satisfyingly sorry for myself is a luxury that I've had no time to indulge for the past sixteen years. I am snuggling in to enjoy it when I suddenly switch from grieving about Aubrey abandoning me to remembering when my own mother had the power to dry my tears. When had I abandoned her? When she became ill? When I hit puberty? When my grandmother appeared with her more vibrant version of life? If my mother hadn't died, would we both have ridden out adolescence until the day when I returned and said that I would always love her?

When Jessie sings about how she stayed the same, but Emily began to drift away, "she," the one drifting away, becomes Martin. But I am still Jessie and everyone I have ever loved has drifted away and a cartoon movie about discarded toys has become the template of my entire life and I am just going to blubber about it for a while.

I gather Aubrey's pillow—still smelling like her special "volumizing" conditioner—BeeBee, and Pretzels into my arms and hug them to me. As I am noticing that one part of my bouquet of loss needs a bath and a visit to the vet to get her teeth cleaned, thin shafts of reflected light stream in from the window and play across the wall.

I release pillow, pooch, and Puffalump, and peek outside to trace the source of this heavenly host–esque illumination just as an extraordinary and extraordinarily silent vehicle pulls up to the front curb. The car is silver, stately, and opulent. It looks as out of place on this street as a brontosaurus. Though I've never actually seen one, I identify this car immediately: a Bentley. I am equally certain that I know only one person on earth who might be driving such a vehicle: Martin.

The practice field is a different place beneath a gray sky with a freezing wind knifing across it. I try to time it so that I'll appear on the field right as practice finishes, but I am early. The players wear long-sleeved, stretchy shirts under their uniforms. Most wear gloves. Tyler's hands are bare.

The metal bleacher under my butt feels like a plank of ice as I sit there waiting for some version of the moment when Ashton Kutcher jumps out and everyone cackles about me getting *Punk'd*. Madison, Paige, and the rest of them are all huddled beneath a blanket together at the other end of the bleachers, hoods of their North Face jackets pulled up like a row of little monks.

The players run up and down the field. They slam into one another. They grunt. Their hard plastic pads clack together. They weave around the field even more like ants than the band kids, all trying to pick up the scent of a trail. It is random chaos, a minor distraction from watching Tyler.

Coach Hines whistles, yells, "All right, y'all huddle up, now! Huddle up!"

They end their meeting with everyone piling hands together, do a tick-tock-the-game-is-locked, clap, and head for the locker room.

Madison yells to Tyler in a singsongy, babyish voice, "Ty-Mo, I already finished your assignment in English. Wanna come to Paige's house and I can print it out?"

I think of Madison's perfect 800 on the SAT math section. I guess math geniuses don't always sound smart.

Tyler pulls his helmet off. His hair is flattened against his head with sweat. He shakes it out and shoots Madison the Dimple. He doesn't even look my way.

Did I imagine the person he was at the quarry? Did I hallucinate him asking me to come here?

The team manager hands him a towel and takes his helmet. He wipes his face and walks toward the bleachers. By the time he reaches us, he still hasn't looked at me once and I've concluded that he's a psychopath who set this all up just for the fun of torturing me.

"Madison, thanks, you're a sweetheart. But I'm good. I think my girl A.J.'s got me covered." He tilts his chin my way. "Paige, Madison, you all know A.J., don't you?"

There is a fraction of a second's pause. Enough time for me to study Paige Winslow's and Madison Chaffee's faces to see if they are in on the joke. They aren't. Instead they deal gracefully with whatever reversal of the laws of physics has allowed me to enter their gravitational field.

The team manager takes Tyler's used towel.

"Madison, you want to give A.J. my homework?"

Madison nods her head, probably to help the process of me going from utterly invisible to being a fully formed object capable of stimulating the rods and cones in her retina. "Not a prob."

When Tyler leaves for the locker room, the girls turn away from me. Not in a mean way. Just a sort of been-there way. No doubt they figure that I am some epic skeeze bag who is doing things to Tyler that require the limberness of a Ukranian gymnast and the morals of a bonobo monkey. That there have been others like me before and there will be others like me after.

Madison pulls some papers out of her zip-up notebook and brings them to me. I want to tell her that I am as baffled as she is and that, no doubt, Tyler will return to their planet very soon. But she seems so genuinely friendly when she says, "Don't write too neat. That's a giveaway," that I just nod and take the papers.

Some might say that Tyler Moldenhauer is just using me to be his gay cover-up. But so what? I'm just using Tyler Moldenhauer too. To be happy.

Which character do you think is the most important in *Animal Farm?*"

Tyler, lying on his back on the red vinyl padding of his weight bench, ignores the question. We've gotten into a groove over the past week. I refused to straight-up *do* his homework for him like Madison and the other girls before me had, so we do it together during his after-practice workouts. He explained that, with all the workouts Coach demanded on top of the program he'd designed for himself, he could either spend time with me or do homework. And he'd rather spend time with me.

Which is why I am with him in Coach Hines's garage. All the times I've come over, I've never actually been inside the house. Or seen Coach Hines. Or his wife. I hear his giant dogs barking a lot but I haven't even seen them. Tyler lives in the garage. It's his choice. He has a room inside Coach's gigantic house, but he likes it better in the garage. On his own. Coach likes it better too.

Most of the space on the polished concrete floor is taken up with weight equipment. A single bed with an orange sleeping bag flung across it is pushed up against the far wall. Clothes, mostly shirts and jeans, hang in dry cleaner's bags from nails hammered into the walls. It is surprisingly neat for a garage where a football player lives.

I want to know why Tyler is living with Coach, but the answer to that question involves his mom and dad and lots of other unsimple issues that he obviously wants to avoid. Like why he is really hanging out with me.

I know that it isn't homework. There are so many girls who'd do it for him that I can't even seriously consider that he is interested in me only for that. Besides which, Coach Hines has a list of "tutors," fan girls willing to do homework for any player who can't recruit his own volunteers. Tyler's choosing me to do his work for him is a strange honor in his world.

"So which character do you think is most important in *Animal Farm?*" I repeat, trying to remember whether I'd read *Animal Farm* in seventh or eighth grade. I do recall, though, that, even then, the study questions had been about the political allusions and the dangers of groupthink, not which character was "most important."

As Tyler considers *Animal Farm*, he is gritting his teeth, quivering, and hoisting barbells up and down. I wonder if his face looks like that—almost a grimace, lost in what his body is doing—when he makes love. What it would look like making love to me.

"And ten!" The clang of the barbells as Tyler sets them down on the holder above his head jolts me out of my ridiculous daydream. I refuse to be that girl with an impossible crush on a gay guy.

Tyler is wearing a gray sweatshirt with the arms cut out. He sits up. Sweat streams down his face. He sticks his hands under the sweatshirt and lifts it to wipe off his face. His abs belong on a movie screen. Maybe I *would* be that girl.

"OK, most important character in *Animal Farm*? I'd have to say the horse."

"Boxer? Yeah, I can see that. He is certainly the one willing to sacrifice the most for the good of the group."

"There's no *i* in teamwork." He grins, picks up a dumbbell, and starts doing curls. His biceps swell up, then flatten like a speeded-up film of a python swallowing a pig.

As he works out, I read him the next question: " 'Is *Animal Farm* set in (a) wartime Germany, (b) a desert island, (c) a farm?' "

"Is that a trick question?"

"No, just incredibly stupid."

"Uh, I'm going to solve the puzzle, Pat: (c) farm."

"Farm it is! Bringing your total today to seventeen dollars! Next question: 'In the end, the pigs become like (a) robots, (b) humans, (c) dogs.' Is this a joke?"

"No, it's just 'keep the jocks in school as long as they're winning games and keep collecting the money from the state for every day all the morons show up.' You know how it works."

I do. In spite of Miss Olivia's personal obsession with tracking down a few kids here and there who ditch, the whole attendance office is mostly about proving how many kids *are* in school so that Parkhaven High can get paid by the state. Or else that the kids who are absent are at doctors' offices or something else that is excused and the state will pay for. That and crowd control. Attendance is also mostly about crowd control.

Tyler finishes ten reps, then pauses, waiting for the next question. Without thinking, I ask, "Here's a question with no wrong answer. Seriously, you'll get an A for whatever you say."

He starts in on the next set. Watching his muscles bulge up and down, he nods my way. "Shoot."

"Are you attracted to me? In any way? I mean, is there any bi possibility? And, seriously, it really is not an issue if you're not."

Tyler stops and holds the weight half up for so long that his arm starts quivering and I deeply regret my question.

"Forget that I asked that. I love hanging out with you. And it's way less complicated that you're not. You know. Interested. In me. That way." I have to physically press my finger against my lips to make myself stop babbling.

Tyler puts the weight down, pulls up his sweatshirt to wipe his face, and flashes his perfect abs again. This time, though, he keeps his head lowered, buried in the sweatshirt. His back and shoulders quiver, trembling a little bit. Alarm shoots through me, and I don't know what to do. I would give anything not to have opened my big, fat mouth. Not to have made his being gay such a gigantic issue.

"God, Ty," I say, my voice squealy from embarrassment. "I was only kidding." I play-slap at him. "Come on, girlfriend."

He still doesn't answer.

"Tyler, it's fine. I am cool with all forms of alternative sexuality."

He lifts his head then, and I see that the trembling is from laughing. "All forms, huh?" He looks at me like a dad whose little kid has just said something cute.

"Well, you know. Not bestiality."

"Damn! And I was just about to introduce you to my girlfriend, Bossie."

He sees that I am embarrassed.

"Hey, Aubrey Julie, come on. I was just kidding. I like that you're the way you are. That's why I want it to be different with us."

" 'Different'? Different how?"

He reaches out, almost touches me, stops himself, and picks up a weight instead.

"Just different, OK? Forget it. More workout. Less talk."

The weight in his hand is heavier than any I've ever seen him use before. He props his forearm on his knee and lifts. As his chest beneath the gray fleece rises to meet his fist, his whole body trembles from the effort. I don't know if it is from the effort of lifting the heavy weight or the effort of keeping something out of his mind that he doesn't want to think about.

Not now," I whimper to myself as the Bentley slows to a stop. Not with Aubrey God knows where and my life at the point of greatest disarray it has sunk to since he left. In the dream scenario, Martin would have driven past while Aubrey and I and our hunky, successful, sensitive, insanely smitten boyfriends were romping on the front lawn together, joyous at sharing the perfection of our lives. Maybe we'd be playing badminton or some other sport that would allow the sun to illuminate our radiant complexions and stream through our golden hair and spotlight the obvious adoration of our menfolk. It would be a scenario that would leave Martin withered with envy and stupefied by the full extent of his idiocy in throwing away such paradise and the angels who dwelt within.

Not this. Not Aubrey gone and me looking like Courtney Love after a bad bender. I lick my finger and rub as much smeared mascara from under my eyes as I can. I don't have time to do more: I have to get to the porch before Martin does and preempt any possibility of him getting a peek inside at the warehouse of untouched college supplies. He has no right to any image of my life that I don't choose him to have. And I choose the Cape Cod version.

On the porch, I take a breath and brace myself for Martin to step from the car. But, instead of Martin, Martin's father emerges. A second later, he disappears and Martin, sixteen years older, is there in his place. Where Martin had once absorbed light—dark hair, dark olivey skin, dark thoughts—this middle-aged man reflects it. I see now that the shielding palm in the more recent photos had also hidden hair that has thinned and turned the color of ash. A pair of silver-rimmed glasses now magnify his eyes, giving Martin, in the instant he sees me again for the first time in sixteen years, the goggling, bewildered look of a newborn.

Is he wondering why my mother has replaced me?

He's wearing a suit that must have once been expensive. Perhaps it's the same one he'd worn in the photos I'd seen of him palling around with Oscar winners and dodging paparazzi. Now, though, the rumpled, bagged-out suit has a Dust Bowl–soup line look, as if he's slept in it for the past few weeks. He removes the glasses, tucks one stem into the collar opening of his shirt, and smiles up at me. A trio of lines strain around the edges of his eyes. More net his forehead. His lips, once almost girlishly plump, are less generous, more sharply etched.

"You're looking good, Cam."

"You're kind of beat to shit," I call back down to him.

The thought that these are the first words we've exchanged face-to-face in sixteen years runs like the steady crawl beneath a chaotic disaster story.

"You're wearing glasses," I point out, really saying, *What about Opt Tech, Mr. Master of the Universe?*

"I am." His answer rejects my hidden sneer. He opens the trunk of the Bentley, removes a tire iron, and holds it out to me as if it were an olive branch. "Wanna hit me in the face?"

"Is that an attempt to defuse the situation?"

Arm raised, head dipped in thought, Martin hangs for a second on the upraised trunk lid. In that instant of hesitation he is transformed. Like fabric that shows iridescent from certain angles, the Martin I met on a train twenty-two years ago peeks through and again I see the young man who was seeking answers. I see the bump of glossy hair he was always pushing out of his eyes. Like Abe Lincoln, the haunted ectomorph, Martin's wrists, hands, Adam's apple were all too large for his gangly frame. There still is the juicy bottom lip that I wanted to kiss immediately.

Martin tosses the tire iron, the attempt at levity, back in the trunk, slams it shut, straightens up, and the iridescence disappears. He points toward the house. "You never fixed that leak." I glance at the dribbling faucet with a beard of black fungus staining the brick beneath it.

"I had a lazy husband."

"Must have been a loser." He saunters toward the porch.

"Oh, he was."

His walk—cocky, shoulders rolling—is something else that came along with Next. I'd fallen in love with his old walk, his old voice. They were tentative, uncertain. The way Martin mumbled acknowledged that the world was a place of doubt and nuance that could not be battered into line with bluster and positive thinking. After Next that hesitant young man with his boyish awkwardness disappeared. I waited and waited for him to return, for the android stranger who'd claimed his body to release him back to me. But it didn't happen then, and, aside from that iridescent flash a moment ago, it clearly isn't going to happen now.

He stops to pet Pretzels. I'm hoping she'll give him the tennis-ball-in-the-garbage-disposal growl. Maybe a feeble attempt at a bite. But the traitor wags her tail and follows Martin to the porch. When he sees her struggling to climb the stairs, he stops to lift her hindquarters and help her up. As he draws closer, I see that his white dress shirt is speckled with smears of ketchup and mustard, a spritz of soy sauce.

Before he sets foot on the porch, before he can get the first shot in, I go on the offensive. "You changed the trust. You changed it without consulting me."

"That's one of the reasons I'm here. I thought I needed to address that enturbulation in person."

"Could you not talk to me like that?"

"Like what?"

"Like with those bogus words made up by . . ." I can't bring myself to say, "Next." Next is the name of the other woman who stole my husband. But that isn't right. No metaphor is exactly right, except maybe the one involving body snatching; it was confusing when he left that his body was not either dead or in the possession of another woman. And it is confusing now that the body of the man I loved more than any on earth—though now with a few wrinkles, a loud voice, and a strutting walk, yet still, essentially, the same body—stands before me.

"No, you're right. Sorry. I'm trying to talk like a normal person again, but I lose track of what words come from what world."

I think of Dori's article about rekindled romance. There is clearly no rekindling going on here; still, Martin's voice, even the altered Next voice, is worming into someplace in my brain beyond my conscious control and making synapses I'd thought were long dead sputter back to frantic life, and that annoys the shit out of me.

"You gave a girl you haven't seen in sixteen years thirty thousand dollars. What kind of a pea-brained numbskull does a thing like that?"

"A panicked pea-brained numbskull. I panicked. Aubrey called and said there was an emergency. She needed to pay her tuition immediately and you were out of the country."

"What?"

"Clearly you were not out of the country."

"Jesus. Did it ever occur to you to check with me?"

"I wanted to, but. . ."

I watch as he decides what to tell me. Aubrey inherited Martin's dark lashes and the soulful shape of his eyes, tugged down a bit on the outer corners like Paul McCartney's. Her nose, with its teardrop-shaped nostrils, is his in miniature. These similarities confuse me.

He shakes his head, overwhelmed at the impossibility of making me understand. Another similarity with Aubrey. "Cam, so much was happening. Things got crazy. I had to act fast."

"You didn't have time to make one phone call?"

"Yes, actually, at that moment, I literally did not have time to make one phone call."

"So? What? You amend the trust, then just hop in the old Bentley and cruise on down? That's a two-thousand-mile drive."

"Yeah. I've been on the road nonstop since I faxed in the codicil. And, just for the record, the car belongs to the church."

I note that, although adrenaline, shock, and anger are keeping my mind fairly coherent, the beer has worked its malty magic on my legs. Refusing to falter in front of Martin, I ease back down onto the rattan rocker. Martin takes a seat on the glider, the same glider that he assembled from a kit we bought together at Home Depot. It creaks beneath his weight. I hope he doesn't notice how new and unworn it is. I hope he imagines Aubrey and me gliding through sixteen summers of happy, firefly-lit evenings and mourns for all that he missed.

As he settles in, his shoulders slump the tiniest bit, and just that minute shift causes the hidden iridescence to emerge, transforming him back into the Martin I lost, and I remember the last time he was in this house.

He'd already moved out by that time, but still came over to take care of Aubrey. I'd given up on nursing and, after my own bad experience with breast-feeding, had decided that Parkhaven needed a decent lactation consultant. So while I put in the hours at the hospital I needed to become certified, Martin babysat.

It was two days before Christmas. I was late getting home that night because the consultant I was training with was working with a baby girl who had developed jaundice and was too sleepy to nurse and a mom brainwashed into believing that nursing was some kind of sacred experience that would be ruined if she jiggled her breast enough to wake up Sleeping Beauty.

I'd splurged on a big tree, hoping that Aubrey would remember the smell of pine, shiny bulbs, and silver tinsel rather than a haggard mother who cried a lot more than she did. But even the biggest tree I could afford looked ridiculous dwarfed beneath the high ceiling of the great room. Martin didn't hear me come in that night. He was sitting slumped as he is now, in the darkness with his back to me, watching the automatic lights fade from blue to yellow to green to red. Along with so much else, he'd stopped slumping once he'd pumped himself up with Next theology. A box of ornaments sat opened beside him.

When we lived in Sycamore Heights, we used to collect ornaments all year long. Mostly as souvenirs from trips we took together. A Statue of Liberty from a visit to New York spent eating the kind of Italian food it was impossible to find down here and seeing every play we could get half-price tickets to; red satin lanterns with yellow fringe from Chinatown in San Francisco; a tiny ristra of red-lacquered chile peppers from a visit to Santa Fe. At Christmas, we hung them on whatever spindly Charlie Brown tree we put up. Those pretend trees confirmed our belief that we were pretend adults. We rode old, fat-tired bikes everywhere and picked jobs by how casually they allowed Martin to dress and how few hours I could put in as a nurse and still make a living. That Martin could wear cargo shorts and a T-shirt to his software-writing job balanced out the ridiculous hours he had to work. Wardrobe and flexible hours were more important to us than things like earning potential and insurance. The things that I should have been paying attention to.

On that last Christmas, I'd stood at the door and watched Martin for a moment, slumped in the chair, and he was Martin again, the Martin I'd fallen in love with, fully occupying the body I'd fallen in love with. He was the Martin I could have a conversation with about the mom I'd just been helping at the hospital whose baby had jaundice. Then I remembered that that Martin was gone and I armored myself once more. I walked in and my tone was crisp, unapologetic, when I said, "Sorry I'm late."

I was in front of him before he could turn away. In the stained-glass illumination cast by the colored lights, I saw that he was holding the first ornament we'd ever collected, a drink coaster made of cedar and inlaid with ivory we'd bought in Morocco not long after we met on the train, and that his face was streaked with tears.

Martin put the ornament down and lifted his arms up to me. I held him and he cried into my neck. He pulled my scrubs off and put his mouth and tongue on all the places that he knew pleased me the most. He pushed into me, but even as we surged together, he went farther and farther away. I felt the sliver of connection between us being hammered to nothing and grew frantic. I took him into my body, but he withdrew more and more of himself from me, from our life together, until, finally, he surrendered. His erection obstinate and unconvinced between us, Martin wiped his face dry, whispered, "I can't," and left.

The last time I saw him before the divorce proceedings was on Christmas Day, when we gave Aubrey Pretty Hair Purple Puffa-lump. And now, sixteen years later, he is back. At any rate a body is back similar enough to the one I fell in love with that, despite my howling rage and ardent desire to be beyond caring, its presence agitates me more than the presence of any other male body has in the past sixteen years.

D*ifferent with us.*

    I don't know what that means. Tyler didn't answer my question about whether he is attracted to me. I've always scoffed at stories of women marrying men who came out as gay after four kids and thirty years of marriage. I didn't think that kind of thing happened anymore. Now I understand exactly how it could happen. How the wife would almost be happy for it to happen.

He likes hanging out with me.

    Whatever the real reason, I am sure about that much. For the past week we have gone everywhere together. In the mornings before class, we go to the Starbucks in the grocery store across from school and get coffee drinks with whipped cream, then sit with Tyler's friends and eat our drinks with a spoon. Serious winter has started and the girls wear their North Face jackets now every day. Just like the Nike shorts, they all have the same style but in different colors.

    In the evenings, after school, we hang out at Paige's watching movies in the media room, playing "Guitar Hero," and drinking beer from the refrigerator her parents keep stocked just for us.

    Tyler and I do the things that me and the other band kids made fun of and that we pretended we had no interest in. We pretended there weren't any cliques, that there wasn't a ruling elite. We pretended we believed what my mom and, probably, all of their moms too said: that school is so diverse now that the kids in Computer Club, or the emo kids running the literary magazine, or the choir queers or drama dweebs were really the cool ones. And in a happy, pretty, gentle, glowing-rainbow way, it is true that all the groups *are* cool. But it is even more true that only one of them is golden.

    I can never tell my mom any of this. She would say, "No one interesting is ever popular in high school." Or, "All the stars in high school end up selling cars or being housewives and mourning their glory days. It's just sad." And that would be the end of the discussion. Except to maybe add that Parkhaven is a wasteland and life will be totally different and totally wonderful the instant I leave.

She would never understand how much fun I am having being Tyler's pretend girlfriend. I make a big point of hanging all over him when we are together. He seems to like that. When we are alone, though, it is completely hands-off. There is no way my mom could ever understand any of this. Especially since I don't.

Y ou got an extra one of those?" Martin reaches between my legs and grabs a beer, his gaze falling on the empty cans scattered about.

There would not be this many empty cans of Milwaukee's Best scattered about in the Cape Cod dream life I want Martin to believe I am leading.

I sit up and explain, "Some friends . . . several friends, a whole gang actually, were over earlier to celebrate the, you know, going away to college. Some of Aubrey's friends. She just left with them actually." Too late I remember when Aubrey discovered the word "actually," and how often it signaled she was about to stretch the truth.

I add, "To spend the night. Play board games. She has this whole group that gets a kick out of retro stuff. Playing Twister. Things like that."

Martin nods at this image of me serving Twister-playing minors unlimited beers.

"Their parents were with them. Just a few of the parents—the many parents—that I'm close to. Whole big, rollicking gang."

He holds the can up—"To rollicking"—uses the tail of his shirt to wipe off the top of the can, pops the top, drains half the beer in one gulp. A dramatically un-Next thing to do.

I wish I had bought classier beer. Certainly bottles. Then I chastise myself. *I am not the one who should be feeling apologetic.* I go back on the offensive. "I thought Nextafarians didn't drink."

" 'With our thoughts we make the world.' "

"What is that supposed to mean? How does that pertain to anything? Seriously, one more word of Next bullshit and this conversation will involve lawyers."

"I thought you liked Prince Gautama. That was from *Siddhartha.*"

In a blinding moment of clarity, I see how insane it is that Martin, who is wearing a pajama suit with a shirt that looks like a sampler platter of condiments, is sitting on my front porch enjoying a cold one. "What the hell are you doing here?"

He gives the one answer that could have made any difference: "I fucked up."

At that moment I understand how Elaine, a nurse I go to lunch with whenever our shifts synchronize, felt when her ex-husband, father of her two boys, had come out as a woman mistakenly assigned to a man's body. A woman with a deep affection for bustiers and mall-rat hair.

If Martin had dropped his jeans and revealed a garter belt and fundamentally rearranged plumbing, I could not be more surprised than I am at hearing him say that he made a mistake. Being right, being ultimately and forever correct, was the cornerstone he'd built his Next identity on.

"Not that I really had any other option, but the second, the instant, I sent in that codicil allowing Aubrey to claim the money on her own, I knew I'd made a huge mistake."

"No kidding. You invalidated the trust. You know that, don't you? You flushed not just the first year, but Aubrey's entire college fund down the drain."

"It was flushed anyway. It would have been flushed the second I left, and, Cam, I was leaving. That much was certain. I tried to stay in so Aubrey could get all four years of the tuition money. I mean, Jesus, I wanted to get at least that much out of the past sixteen years. But I could barely hang on long enough for her to claim that first year. I don't know how much she's told you about our communication—"

I shrug as if of course my daughter and I have such a close, loving relationship that we tell each other everything. Because I raised her right. Without Next.

"Well then, you know about us messaging on Facebook. It was the safest way to get in touch with her. We chatted for months. It was . . . I can't describe how powerful it was. I lived for those little chat bubbles. Those little fragments, glimpses, of my daughter. Then, right after Thanksgiving, they stopped."

And Tyler started.

"By that time," Martin continues, "I felt like a spy, a POW, in Next. I had to force myself through every day, every moment. All I wanted was to make it until they paid out for her first year. But then time came for tuitions to be paid, and no withdrawals were made, so I started sending her messages every day telling her, 'Get the money. Get the money.' But she completely ignored me. I got no response whatsoever. Why are you smiling?"

"Oh, nothing. Then?"

"Then I was done. I couldn't hang on a second longer. I sent her my cell number knowing that once she used it, you and Aubrey had a day, maybe two before Next ID'd the call, realized I'd had contact with my daughter, canceled the trust, and put their bloodhounds on my trail. So I sent the message, took the Bentley, and started running. I figured either she'd call and I'd get her to claim the money or I'd track her down and take her to the bank myself. I was on the road when she called, stopped at a Kinko's, got the bank to fax the codicil to me there, signed it, and sent it in. After that, there was no going back to Hub HQ."

Hub HQ is where Martin has lived for most of the past sixteen years, ever since he was promoted to their Celebrity Corps, the elite inner circle assigned to deal with Next's highest-profile adherents. Located outside Los Angeles, Hub HQ had once been the palatial manse of a robber baron. Its last owner, some music mogul who attributed all of his success to Next, had bequeathed it to "the church." Its 56 bedrooms and 61 bathrooms and 19 sitting rooms perched on 127 acres high above the Pacific seemed the kind of place that might have a dungeon or torture chamber.

"All I could take was the Bentley and this suit." He plucks at the dirty shirt, glances down, catches a whiff of himself. "Whew. Sorry, don't sit downwind of me. Anyway, since I don't have a dime to my name, I had to move through this kind of underground railway for Next heretics. Made it kind of hard to do a lengthy consult with you. I'm sorry."

I'm stunned: He really is out. And, from the almost normal, mostly non-Nextian way he's talking and acting, he's been separating for a while.

"But it's fine, right?" he says, waving at the empties. "You're having a farewell-leaving-for-college party? She got the money and used it to pay her first-year tuition?"

"Of course she used the money to pay her tuition. But if she wasn't such a sensible girl, who knows what she might have done? A less sensible girl might be in Mexico with her boyfriend right now. He might have made her spend that money on drugs. Or made her buy him a new truck. Or . . . or . . ."

Or diapers.

His cell phone buzzes. He checks the number and his Next armor snaps back into place. "I've got to take this."

He walks down the porch steps out onto the dry grass, barking Next-type phrases. "You are aware of the dossiers that I compiled. They've all been downloaded to a safe account out-of-network." Like baboons, Nextarians are always trying to back one another down. "If anyone from SkyPat shows up, those dossiers will be compromised. Trust me on this. I *will* initiate. Do you read me? I *will* initiate."

I think he's telling them that he's got dirt he'll spread on all the celebrities who've confessed their secrets to him if they come after him. I briefly wonder if he would have ever been tough like that with Aubrey. Would she have ever dared to lie straight to his face about her "friend" Shaniqua?

Listening to Martin boom out this secret clubhouse lingo as he tramples across the crispy remnants of my lawn brings back the insoluble puzzle of how such a smart man could have fallen for such bunk. Or the real puzzle of how such a smart woman could have lost her man to it.

M y bra is vibrating where I'd tucked my cell into it. I know it's Tyler. This is the signal we'd arranged for him to let me know that he is waiting at the end of the block so we can go hang out at his place. When I first asked him to pick me up there instead of coming to my house, he'd said, "What? Are you ashamed of me?"

Only Tyler Moldenhauer could say this as a complete and absolute joke: No girl at Parkhaven High has ever been ashamed of bringing Tyler Moldenhauer home.

"No, my mom's . . . She's different."

"Strict?"

"Yeah. Strict." My mom is the complete opposite of strict, but I don't want to go into that.

"That's why you're the way you are."

"What way am I?"

"Sweet."

" 'Sweet.' 'Nice.' Tyler, you make me sound like a cross between vanilla pudding and a kitten."

"You are. To me you are."

"I'm not. I'm really not."

"OK, you're a giant jizbag ho. That better?" He never stops smiling.

"I wish you texted. If my mom's there, I don't want her hearing my phone ring."

"Text? With these?" He held up his hands. They were as scarred and rough and almost as hard as old bricks. The little finger on his left hand stuck out at a forty-five-degree angle from where it was broken and not set right. The top of his middle right finger was missing entirely. It was hard to imagine how someone could lose the top of a finger playing football. Like his teeth, his hands are different from anyone else's at Parkhaven. "Texting is too much like homework and you know I don't do homework. Just put it on vibrate and stick your phone right there."

When he touched my breast, he was the public Tyler Moldenhauer, the player who could have any girl he wanted. Who could have me. But he'd pulled his hand away, clamped it on the steering wheel. I guess he didn't want to get my hopes up. Lead me on or something.

"That's cool," I said, silencing my phone and sliding it into my bra. "Vibrate is cool. Just call, hang up, and I'll come."

And now he is calling. I head for the door. My mom intercepts me. "Aubrey? Are you going out? You have school tomorrow."

"Yeah. Shaniqua and I need to work on our project."

While I am trying to remember if I told her it was a project for physics or Spanish, she stations herself in front of the door, folds her arms across her chest, and says, "Aubrey, there is not a single person, male or female, at your school named Shaniqua."

"What? You looked through the entire directory?"

"Only because Madison's mom mentioned that you've been seeing Tyler Moldenhauer."

"Madison's mom? When did you talk to her? I thought you hated her and all the Parkhaven moms."

"I don't hate Joyce. I don't hate anyone. We're just not . . . Aubrey, are you dating Tyler Moldenhauer, and why haven't you told me?"

"Dating? No one *dates* anyone anymore."

"OK, hanging out, chilling, hooking up."

"Ew." I cannot control a full-face grimace at how excruciatingly wrong, factually and every other way, hearing her say "hooking up" is.

"OK, sorry if I'm not up on all the latest slang. How about this: You lied to me. All those 'study dates' with 'Shaniqua'? Complete and utter lies. Lying is unacceptable. Our entire relationship is based on trust, and if I can't trust you . . ."

She inserts the Trust Tape. The volume is louder than usual this time, other than that it is the same old message. As it plays, all I can focus on is that the thought of Tyler meeting my mom makes me ill. At the moment, she is wearing a pair of ancient navy blue mesh running shorts and a T-shirt with the Virgin of Guadalupe on it, which is supposed to make some kind of statement. She is barefoot and carrying a glass of wine and has the reading glasses she started wearing last winter perched on her nose. She was proud of having "scored" them at the dollar store. They have a leopard-print pattern that she thinks makes them cool.

"Aubrey! Are you even listening to me? Say something."

"This is so ridiculously unfair! Why do you have to know every single thing I do every second of the day! I am not two years old. I'm not going to choke on a hot dog or stick a fork in an outlet. You do realize that I'm going to be gone in a few months, don't you? You won't be able to micromanage every second of every day when I'm on my own. What then, huh? I'm almost eighteen. Legal age. Then I'll be able to vote and sign a contract and, if I was a guy, I could be drafted. You know, run my own life."

"And who is supposed to finance this life you'll be running all on your own?"

"I have money saved."

"You did until you started squandering it on identical pairs of obscenely overpriced shorts."

"See!? That is exactly what I'm talking about! God! I cannot wait until I don't have someone keeping track of every cent I spend and passing judgment on every single goddamn thing I do!"

"Aubrey, I am not passing judgment on you."

"Bullshit. That is all you ever do! That is all you've ever done!"

"Aubrey, calm down."

"Me calm down? *You* calm down."

"OK, I'm calm. Look, all I want to do is meet this guy you're spending so much time with. That is not some kind of bizarre request."

The overhead light shines off her freakishly large forehead until it starts pulsing like something out of *Babylon 5*. There is no way I can explain why she must never meet Tyler. Why Tyler and I are not and never will be a *Meet the Parents* kind of thing. It just can never happen.

Desperate, I recall how, for as long as I can remember, she's been telling me that she does not want to be the kind of mother her mother was. The memory even comes with its own sound track, a song she used to sing about how your children are not really your children, and how I am an arrow and she is only there to shoot me into the future. That song used to scare me when I was little. I didn't want to be an arrow and I really didn't want to be shot into the future. Back then being separated from her was the scariest thing I could imagine. Much scarier than dying. Yet that song comes in very handy right now, when I do want to shoot out of the house.

"Mom, you're being exactly how you said your mother always was. You're trying to smother me."

"I am not trying to smother you. This is totally different," she yells in a defensive way that means she is no longer certain that she is right.

"You always said you want me to find my own path and now you're literally blocking my path." Without trying or even knowing why, I start crying.

"God, Aubrey, all I said was that I want to meet this young man."

I suddenly believe that my mother *has* smothered and oppressed and micromanaged me my entire life. That I *have* never known one second of freedom. She tries to stop me when I run out the door, but I push past her. I am still crying when I get into the truck. Tyler hugs me. But just a friendly besties hug. Nothing more. Never anything more.

As he strides across my desiccated front lawn, phone pressed to his right ear, Martin tilts his head toward his left shoulder, the thumb and forefinger of that hand plucking at his sideburn. He made that same gesture the first time he listened to me on the train in Morocco. Seeing it now is like a smell, a song, that plunges you directly back into a perfectly preserved moment. I am young again, nearly as young as Aubrey, and Martin and I are lovers and he smells like bread and sunshine and I want to keep touching him until my fingerprints wear off. And suddenly it is not a memory. It is happening that very second. I start to understand what Dori was telling me about crack cocaine, and order my ridiculous brain to behave.

Down the street some jerk starts a leaf blower and the utterly unique Martin of my youth disappears. Left behind is a generic middle-aged man with a receding hairline in a rumpled suit strutting around my front yard like Kaiser Wilhelm. The leaf blower roars, blocking out Martin's bombastic voice.

He snaps his phone shut, strides down the sloping yard to the Bentley, and leans into the open window. A second later, the back door opens and a man in his late forties steps out. I squint to see if it's a movie star. But Martin's passenger is just some skinny guy with an alcoholic's pooch of a gut and a weathered face that looks as if he might have spent time living on the street. Martin fishes a set of car keys out of his pocket, dangles them in one hand as he holds his other hand out. The guy reaches around under the back of his shirt and withdraws an envelope from the waistband of his pants. At the same moment the man slaps the envelope into Martin's hand, Martin drops the keys onto his outstretched palm.

The leaf blower stops. The man gets into the driver's seat, points a finger at Martin, says, "Okay, then," in a phlegmy rumble, and starts the car.

In the Next voice, Martin booms, "One last thing." He tosses his cell phone in the open window. "Wherever you're headed, and I really don't want to know, make a lot of calls."

"Will do."

The car glides away as silently as it arrived. Martin climbs up the hill, up the porch steps, flops back down on the glider, pops another beer, sucks it down, opens the envelope, takes a slender portion from the stack of bills therein, holds them up—"Every cent I now have in the world"—folds them into his shirt pocket, then hands the rest to me. The limp bills are still sweaty and warm.

"You just sold a car that doesn't belong to you."

"Didn't exactly get blue-book on it, but under the circumstances . . ."

"I assume that the car is on its way to a buyer who doesn't care about things like title and insurance."

"I didn't go into specifics."

"How do you even know someone like that?"

"Oh, Cam, the variety of human beings I have been required to deal with over the past sixteen years would astonish you. It takes a lot of very dirty people to keep a religion looking clean."

"Next isn't going to be very happy about car theft."

"That will actually be fairly far down on a long list of things that church management is not happy about. And 'theft'? After sixteen years of unpaid labor? I'd say they owe me a *fleet* of Bentleys."

Martin retakes his spot on the glider, grabs another beer, and we sit in silence, working our way through the suitcase like it is a job. We watch the owners of the houses around us come home from work. Their vehicles return, metal garage doors clang open, car or truck disappears. The rooftops meld into a darkening silhouette against the navy blue sky. When the black crown of the surrounding rooftops blends entirely into the night, first the streetlights, then my paranoid neighbors' crime lights come on. They illuminate my house and all the surrounding houses like a movie set.

"So," I ask, "why did you really give Aubrey the money?"

Martin looks down at his hands. His right nostril twitches. It unnerves me that he and Aubrey have the same "tell." As with Aubrey, it means that he wants to say something, but that it is hard and he worries about how I will take it. And that, quite possibly, he'll tell a lie instead. Except that after Next, he stopped lying. How can a person who is always right tell a lie, since everything out of his mouth has to be true?

He snorts, holds his beer can up to toast me. "Oh, Cam, you could always see right through me, couldn't you?"

"No. I could never do that."

"Well, it's true that I did want to get Aubrey as much money as possible as fast as I could before I left Next, but also . . ." He drops the searing laser gaze he'd learned in Next and stares at the beer in his hand as if he were trying to remember what its function is, and mumbles something I can't hear. His voice has softened back to the one I knew before Next entered his life and turned him into a blowhard asshole.

"What? I didn't catch that. What did you say?"

He looks back up at me. "I said I gave my daughter the money because I wanted her to like me."

The barometric pressure seems to drop just as it does in my classroom when I tell the truth, and all I can say is, "Oh."

"Yeah, 'oh.' We'd been communicating on Facebook for a few months. I really felt as if we were starting to know each other. Then right around Thanksgiving, it stopped. She wouldn't answer any of my messages. Wouldn't explain what was going on. We were really connecting, then it was just over. I was out. It made me frantic. You're laughing at me again."

"Sorry, I am so *not* laughing at you. This is a with-you-not-at-you laugh, believe me. I'm trying not to say, 'Welcome to my world,' but welcome to my world."

For one moment we are parents together and I get a glimpse of how nice it would have been to have an ally.

Martin leans back, pushes the hair that has fallen forward out of his face. He used to be vain about his beautiful, curly hair, using more products than I ever did, arranging it just so before we went out, obsessing about which stylist cut it best. Now that it's thin on top and what curls remain have turned the color of dry garden mulch, he no longer seems to care. Which, in many ways, is more attractive than the overtended curls were.

"Happy Aubrey's birthday," he says. He holds his can up. I tap mine against it.

We watch nighthawks dart jagged patterns around the crime lights as they chase insects. Martin finishes his beer, places the can carefully on the porch, slaps his palms against the top of his thighs like a farmer about to get up and go finish the plowing, and asks, "You want to tell me where Aubrey is?"

B oundaries. After Mom finds out that there *is* no Shaniqua, but that there *is* a Tyler and that she *isn't* going to meet him, she suddenly tries to be strict and is all about boundaries. And consequences.

Oddly, though, it is as if her actual physical mass decreases in direct proportion to her volume, so that the more she yells, the smaller she becomes. It is the reversed-binocular thing. The bigger a presence she tries to be in my life, the farther away she recedes. She has now become so distant that she could have been a Polly Pocket. A tiny doll who believes that boundaries and consequences and threats are as powerful as one minute with Tyler.

She tells me how she worries about me all the time. How everything she does is for me. How she moved to Parkhaven for me.

I say, "I never asked you to make me your whole, entire life."

That knocks the wind out of her so completely that she stops screaming and threatening and her chin quivers and I feel like total dog shit.

10:43 P.M. NOVEMBER 18, 2009

=Hey, you're back. Fantastic. I've missed hearing from you.

=Sorry, Mom keeps taking the laptop away.

=Any reason?

=I'm sure she thinks there is but, no, not really. OK, I actually, really need you to tell me why you left Mom and me.

=Whew, Aubrey, that's a biggie.

=Uh, no kidding. Try being the one who got left.

=It's so complicated. It's taken me 16 years to even start to figure that out.

=Yeah, fine, but in those 16 years, I was a kid growing up, and everyone was always telling me, "It's not your fault. You had nothing to do with it." And, surprise! Kind of a bitch to grow up thinking you are completely not a factor in your own father's life.

=Aubrey, sweetheart. I can't begin to tell you how hard it was for me to leave you and how much I've thought about you over the years.

=OK. I'm gonna go feed Pretz now. Or something.

=Wait. Wait. You're right. You deserve to know as much as I know. Where do I start? I was born scared. Maybe it's that simple. Your grandparents didn't do anything or not do anything to make me that way. I just was. I have always been scared.

=Like worried about everything all the time and can't sleep, then worried about not sleeping?

=You too?

=Yeah. Thanks for the genes. Keep going.

=It was like walking through life on stilts. Everyone else had their feet planted safely on the ground and I was teetering around way up high, terrified, certain that I was going to come clattering down to earth at any second.

=And you're going around thinking that that's just the way it is.

=Oh, sweetheart, I hope that's not how it is for you.

=A little. Not so much anymore. I've kind of figured out how to get my feet on the ground. Deal with the teeters or whatever. Keep going.

=When I was a kid, I believed that everyone around me was just a lot braver than I was. I didn't know back then that no one else was up on stilts. I thought that my mother was screaming inside when she turned off my Archies cartoons and told me to go outside and play. I thought she was like me and could only breathe when she was watching TV and that she was training me to be tough too. So I went outside and watched and waited for the birds to mass on the clothesline and peck me to death or for zombies to rise from the flower beds.

=Or for home invaders to swarm in your bedroom window. Or for your mother to lose it and drive right off the flyover on the way to school.

=Yeah. Today they would have poured every pill in the medicine chest down me, but back then I got sent to the nice lady who asked me to draw pictures of a house, then tell her why I put my father and mother and little brother in one window and me off alone in a different window.

=I should have gone to that lady.

=Why, Aubrey?

=Also, "complicated." GTG.

Cam?" Martin asks again. "Are you going to tell me where Aubrey is?"

I guess Martin can read my tells as well as I can read his. The Cape Cod/badminton scenario was never going to work. "I was hoping you might know."

"You really don't know where she is?"

Martin's alarm offends me. It pretends that this is the only, the first, the worst, of all the crises I've faced alone over the past sixteen years. Maybe it is the worst, but it is far from the first.

"You're the one who funded her disappearance."

" 'Disappearance'?" He actually has the audacity to jump from his seat, to spring into action as if this, *this* were the decisive moment. "I knew something was not right." The glider jerks spastically behind him.

" 'Disappearance' is too strong a word."

"What's going on? Why are you sitting there? What do we need to do?"

We. Two humans united to protect the one they created. For sixteen years I ached to be a plural.

"Is she not returning your calls either?" he asks.

I don't answer. What right does he have to know one single thing about Aubrey and me?

He answers his own question. "Of course not. And the boyfriend? Tyler? He's not answering either, I assume."

Tyler? He knows about Tyler?

"And her friends? His friends?"

I stare at him with annoyance rapidly accelerating toward the homicidal.

"I'm sorry. That was stupid. I'm sure you've called them. And checked the food truck. It's probably not even worth calling Peninsula to see if she's registered."

My temples throb from the hostile, bitter, sardonic responses I bite back. I am both furious that he has such an unearned connection with Aubrey, yet hanging on to the hope that he might be the connection to pull her back to me. So, for Aubrey, I summon Zen Mama and admit what I've known for a long time: "She doesn't want to go to college."

"She has to go to college." He states it as an indisputable fact, just the way he had after we came home from looking at this house and I showed him the lousy test scores from Sycamore Heights Elementary. And the insane tuition rates at the private schools. Only then had he finally agreed that we should move because "our child has to go to the best school." These two moments are an equation that balances perfectly. In both halves, he is a father who loves his daughter more than anyone else on earth. Loves her more than me. More than himself. It is the intervening years that make no sense.

"We'll locate her and I'll talk to her." He announces this with a finality that makes me want to weep.

"Oh, Martin, where have you been for the past sixteen years?"

"Going into the past sixteen years is not going to help Aubrey today. What do we do right now? At *this* moment in time?"

"God, still with the recycled Buddhism. Okay, Martin, you tell me what we do at *this* moment in time. Because at *this* moment in time, if she has one friend I could call and pump for information I don't know who it is. At *this* moment in time, even if I could get Aubrey to actually take one of my calls, what do I say to her? At *this* moment in time, do I take something away from her? I haven't had anything she wants since I took the laptop away. Do I threaten her? With what? Kicking her out of the house when she's got a loser boyfriend who's dying for her to move in with him?"

The glider wobbles as he sits back down. "What can I do? How do I help our daughter?"

"How about not abandon us when *our* daughter was two years old? How about be here when *our* daughter got septicemia and I had to drip melted Popsicles into her mouth for a week so she wouldn't die of dehydration? How about be the person with a deep voice who would take the phone and tell *our* daughter that this discussion is over and to get her little butt home right now? How about be the person who drank beer instead of Diet Coke and didn't worry about eating fries and hamburgers? Who didn't resonate and twang to every tiny mood swing, whose periods weren't synchronized with hers so you're both PMSing at the exact same hysterical time? Huh, could you do that? Could you help *our* daughter that way?"

"Every feeling you have is legitimate and justified—"

"Like I need you to tell me that."

"And we should spend a few months exploring every one of—"

"You should spend a few months staked out spread-eagled on a fire-ant hill with honey dripped on your balls." Saying this cheers me up in a way that the six-pack-plus has not. It makes me giddy to blurt out whatever comes into my mind. It lightens me so much, in fact, that I celebrate by popping another top and tossing in, "You are such a colossal fraud."

"You're right. You are absolutely right."

Again, for a second, I have a gender-change level of discombobulation at hearing Martin making such an un-Nextian admission. One of Next's favorite indictments that Martin used to hurl at me was that my "downfall" was that I was "invested in being right." I denied it and tried to expunge the very concepts of right and wrong from my thinking. But I seize upon it now like a vegetarian backsliding with a bucket of KFC.

"Oh, I know that I am right. I am right and you are wrong and everything wrong with our daughter is your fault." Staking a position. Ascribing blame. Gluttony, lust, greed, this is all the most delicious sins rolled into one.

Martin nods in solemn agreement. "A lot of truth there. Possibly the whole truth. It was stupid of me not to question her more. But when she called that first time . . . Hearing her grown-up voice . . ." He shakes his head at the memory. "God, Cam, it was exactly like talking to you. Her voice. It's your voice. It was powerful. Hearing the voice of someone you love so much after all those years. It was like . . ."

He stops, but I know exactly what that was like. I guess this is what would be called a Pyrrhic victory. At almost any time in the past sixteen years, hearing him admit how much the sound of my voice, even channeled through our daughter, still affected him would have felt like winning. Today, it's close to irrelevant.

Pretzels whines, reminding me that her dinner is late. I start to get up, but my legs don't want to cooperate. Martin is at my side, steadying me. "I don't drink," I say. "I haven't become a sad alcoholic divorcée."

"I know that."

"I haven't drunk this much beer since high school."

"I know, Cam. Here, let me help you." He takes my arm and helps me to the bedroom we once shared, stopping at the door to let me career the rest of the way by myself.

"Can you feed . . . ?" I wave toward Pretzels, then collapse on the bed.

"Sure," he agrees.

I give a noncommittal grunt. He shuts the door. The last thought I have before passing out is: *Aubrey?*

At Paige's house, we watch Tyler's favorite movie, *Never Back Down*, about a football star who moves to a new school and becomes a champion freestyle fighter. Colt O'Connor, the tight end who says that the person he'd most like to have dinner with would be Megan Fox, is there too, since he and Paige are kind of together now. So are Madison and Cody Chandler, the leprechaun ghetto wannabe.

That whole group hasn't accepted me so much as they put up with me because of Tyler. I don't feel any more or less out of place with them than I do anywhere else. Being with Tyler is its own space. Whenever I am with him I am exactly where I am supposed to be. Plus, I like thinking about the mad sex that they imagine Tyler and I are having.

We are all flopped around on Paige's long leather sectional couch like puppies in a litter, lying on top of one another, legs hanging over the back of the couch, half our bodies sliding over onto the floor. Tyler is semispooning me from behind but not really touching me. Then the star executes a flying kick to someone's face, Cody bellows, "Oh no, you dinnit!" and Tyler laughs in a way that presses his crotch firmly against my butt.

He is hard. Like, industrial-strength hard.

Is it because of the freestyle fighter in the movie who has an amazing body? Or me?

"Hey, Ty-Mo!" Paige's father comes in and we all sit up. Mr. Winslow is a project manager on big construction sites. He and Madison's father are in a group that trains for marathons together. I gather that all the marathon training is causing trouble at Madison's house. Madison's eyes are always red like she's been crying and I heard her say something about staying at her father's place, like maybe he's not living at home anymore.

Tyler stretches like he is working the kinks out of his back, casually grabs a pillow, and drops it onto his lap. Mr. Winslow is holding a platter of chicken wings in one hand. He balls the other into a fist and holds it out to Tyler, who obligingly bumps it, then takes a wing.

"What's shakin' with the recruiters?"

"Not much."

"Not what I hear. I hear those scouts have been out there watching you since preseason scrimmage."

"There's been some interest."

"Yeah, like they're flying you all over. So what are you thinking? Southeastern State?"

"Southeastern's a good school."

"Goddamn effing *great* school's what it is."

"So you're a Timber Wolf?"

Mr. Winslow holds his hand up like a paw and growls like what I assume is a timber wolf.

Tyler tips his forefinger toward Mr. Winslow. "Go, Wolves."

"The athletic director was a Pike with me. I'll put in a good word for you. Not that you need it, but can't hurt."

Tyler nods. "Can't hurt."

Mr. Winslow puts the platter down. "I'm going to send him an e-mail right now."

"Cool."

After he leaves Cody says, "You didn't tell me you were going with Southeastern."

Tyler tosses the untouched wing back on the platter. "Southeastern can suck my dick."

When he takes me home, Tyler asks me to stop coming to practices. He says he wants to keep us completely separate from football. *Us.* The word sings through my brain.

I like to think that Tyler doesn't want to talk about college because it means we'll be separated. It is what I like to think, but I know that is not the real reason. Maybe, like me, he doesn't even know the real reason.

Before he lets me out, I glance down at his crotch and get my answer: It was not the freestyle fighter in the movie. It *was* me.

I not only stop going to practices, but I make a point of never even asking about the games.

Simple. Like the quarry.

N ear dawn, I sit up in bed, heart hammering like I've been reanimated, and grab for my phone praying that Aubrey has left a message. Nothing. The reanimation motif turns out to be apt, since, in the bathroom mirror, I behold the Bride of Frankenstein. My hair is frizzed into a corona arching above my head, and mascara remnants raccoon my eyes. I cup my hand under the running faucet, sluice water down my parched throat, then jump in the shower.

In the great room, Martin, covered by my afghan throw, pajama suit in a heap on the floor, is asleep on the couch. Everyone, even your own child, is a stranger when they sleep, strange in their quiet unguardedness. But Martin is more than that. For a second, I don't recognize him at all, this young man who is no longer young. His hand drapes off the edge of the couch and rests on Pretzels's head. He's made a bed for her beside the couch. A blanket is carefully folded and arranged in the large doggie-bed basket she sleeps in, replacing the pillow that's usually there. Martin noticed what I hadn't: that the cushion I've been making my sweet girl sleep on has been smooshed flat, offering not the tiniest bit of fluffiness to cushion her old bones.

Noticing the soft bed he made for Pretzels derails me long enough for that stupid crack cocaine/rekindling effect to hijack me: I want to lie down next to Martin. Badly. I'm like a shipwreck victim who's been lost at sea for days, weeks, years, and Martin looks like dry land.

Didn't Dori tell me that an incredibly high number of divorced couples sleep together after the breakup? How many? Eighty, maybe ninety percent? At that moment, watching Martin, his bottom lip still plump, there is kindling. Which is why I'm embarrassed when his eyes open and he sees me staring at him.

Groggy, not quite awake, he nods at the phone in my hand. "Any word?"

The instant he speaks, all kindling ceases. Plus, when he sits up and tucks the afghan under his armpits like a granny getting out of the shower, it is clear that he's kind of let himself go. A bizarrely proprietorial tweak of annoyance stabs me, as if I'd lent someone my car and they returned it sixteen years later with the fender crumpled. He used to have some seriously admirable shoulders, broad and with a lovely upholstering of muscle. Now they are bonier and slump forward a little like an office worker's. Someone who's spent too much time in front of a computer.

"No word," I answer, and an awkward silence falls. Minus the beer, I never would have let him in my house. The beer and the total fucking collapse of my life.

"Hope you don't mind me crashing here. No car. Exhaustion."

"No, actually you could prove useful." *Prove useful?* I am trying a little too hard to sound unkindled and all business. "I need a male voice. Someone who can sound like a hard-ass. You can do that, right?"

"Does the pope shit in the woods?" Martin answers in his snappiest tone. It makes me remember how, once he was really awake in the morning, he was always at his peppiest. He adds, "Maggot!" and I almost smile.

There had been entire days back at Sycamore Heights when we hadn't called each other anything but maggot.

I wave my hand in the direction of the condiment-print shirt. "Did anyone on the underground railroad happen to give you any clothes?"

"You don't like the suit? I was trying to dress up."

"That is dressed up? Dressed up is you in all those pictures with movie stars."

"Yeah, that. Stylists. I haven't actually dressed myself for years. Anyone who has achieved Public Face status has to pass inspection before they leave Hub HQ. They gave me the clothes. I put them on. Someone did my hair. All that shit."

"So you don't have any normal clothes?"

"I could wash the shirt."

"You know, I think I might possibly have some of your old things stuffed away somewhere."

Yeah, like under my bed in a flat, plastic bin, wrapped up so that the tiniest hint of the smell of the man you were sixteen years ago still lingers.

"I think, maybe, I might have saved an old pair of jeans to mow the lawn in. Or something. I'll go check."

Though I stomp on the Levi's and white shirt that I pull out from under my bed, they still look clean and crisp on Martin when he emerges from the bathroom, freshly showered, water dripping from the tips of his wet-darkened, curling hair. The way he used to look when we went out.

"I'll drive," I say, wincing as soon as the words are out. *Of course I'll drive. Why wouldn't I drive?* Once again, I'm trying too hard to appear unkindled.

I head to Coach Tighty Whitie Hines's house. When we pull up in front of a massive construction of red brick with columns lining the front porch, Martin asks, "A high school football coach lives here?" A lamppost out front with an ever-flickering electric lantern twitches away. "Looks like a nineteenth-century English orphanage. How can a high school football coach afford this?"

"With the bonuses he gets from the booster club, he makes more than the superintendent of schools." As we walk to the front door, I ask, "You ready for this?"

"Cam, I was on the team that got Next tax exemption from the IRS. Then all those years managing some of the most complicated egos on the planet? Yeah, I think I am ready for a high school coach."

The instant we ring the bell, dogs start barking. Coach Hines commands, "Baron! Big Shot! *Silencio!*" and the dogs bark even louder. Coach Hines opens the door. Shoving a pair of slavering rottweilers behind him with his leg, he edges out onto the porch and slams the door shut.

Coach Tighty Whitie's casual weekend wear is a crisp pair of khakis, a pressed madras plaid shirt, and shined lace-up shoes. As usual, he makes me feel slovenly.

Martin has his hand extended and is invading the coach's personal space before Hines has the door fully closed behind him. "Coach Hines, I'm Aubrey Lightsey's dad."

The same sour look crinkles Hines's freshly shaved face when Aubrey's name is mentioned as it did when I first visited. The expression might be pain, though, since Martin is pulverizing the coach's meat paw of a hand in a grip of crushing manliness.

As soon as his hand is released, Coach folds his arms over his chest. "I told her"—he nods at me; I am "her"—"I have severed all contact with Tyler Moldenhauer."

Martin squints almost imperceptibly at the mispronunciation of "severed." Anyone else would think that Martin was just an unusually "interested" sort. I know that he is assessing Hines with his Next-trained androidlike scrutiny.

"Tyler Moldenhauer hasn't lived in our home since school ended. I have no legal responsibility for Tyler Moldenhauer and/or his actions."

I vaguely recall some rumors about how none of Hines's three children have any contact with him. I can understand why. His flintiness doesn't offer much that could sustain life.

"Coach," Martin jumps in, "we understand that completely. She"—head nod my way, exasperated tone—"told me that already."

Coach tips the tiniest of go-on nods in response to Martin's jab at meddling, overprotective mothers.

"Anyway, I know you as a man of honor, a man dedicating his life to modeling young men. . . ." Before Coach has a chance to work up a wrinkle of skepticism at such blatant ass kissing, Martin asks out of nowhere, "Say, what did you play? Middle linebacker?"

From the way that Hines draws his shoulders back, stands up a bit straighter, I have to conclude that Martin's assumption is a compliment of some sort. A conclusion that is confirmed when Hines drops his gaze and answers modestly, "Well, I started out there but ended up defensive end. Played a few seasons at Beckwith A and I before—"

"What?" Martin interrupts eagerly. "ACL tear?"

I'm impressed. Hines does favor his right leg, a stance that could, indeed, hint at a torn anterior cruciate ligament.

The coach nods modestly like a former astronaut admitting how he had to miss the moon landing because he had a cold.

"They still honor your scholarship?"

"Pretty much. Had to start going to class, though."

The two men laugh. If I didn't know that he wasn't, I'd have taken Martin for exactly what Hines does, a former jock who considered the concept of going to classes laughable. Hines not only drops his arms, he asks, "What can I help you with?"

"We'd really like to track down this Moldenhauer character."

"This" Moldenhauer character. With one demonstrative adjective Martin has put himself squarely in Hines's camp. Masterful.

Hines asks, "Did he steal from you?"

Steal?

Martin locks Coach's gaze in his with the creepy Next laser stare that, in this context, seems like plain old alpha-dog male intimidation and says in a confiding tone, "I think you know what we're talking about here."

Tighty Whitie acts as if Martin has read his heart. "You do not have to tell me about Tyler Moldenhauer. God, that boy was promising. Most promising player I have ever worked with. I put my heart and soul into that boy and . . . You know how many schools were out here recruiting him? Southeastern was going to let him start. A freshman! Mitch Winslow, one of our biggest supporters, called the athletic director there and vouched for him personally. They guaranteed him a spot. Guaranteed! You know how many kids get that? This many . . ." The meat paw forms a goose egg.

In normal circumstances, I would be extremely annoyed to listen to Martin being treated like the go-to parent. The circumstances aren't normal. I'm thrilled that Martin is opening Hines up like a tube of Ben-Gay.

"He turns his back on that? Walks away? After I put myself on the line getting his reels to those colleges, getting the recruiters to come down here, spending God knows how many weekends of my free time?"

Martin amens each of his grievances with knowing head nods of boundless sympathy. "I hear you, Coach. You give time, you give help—most of all . . . most of all you give trust."

"I opened my home to that boy. I took him in and treated him like family."

"You open your home up," Martin echoes. "You treat him like family."

"Then he just leaves. Walks out without so much as a bye or a leave to Mrs. Hines either. I guess that's what hurts the most. The way he was to Mrs. Hines, who was nothing but good and gracious to him. He got special treatment. We went out of our way to help him, and this is the thanks we get?"

"This is the thanks." Martin shakes his head in mournful sympathy. "I hear you, Coach. Boy, do I hear you."

"That truck? Bought it with money he made working construction at Mitch Winslow's company."

"Where's the gratitude?"

Coach shakes his head with sad resignation. "Raising always shows, doesn't it?"

Raising?

"It does, Coach. That it does." After many *tsks* of solemn commiseration, Martin concludes, "Well, then, I think we understand each other."

"I think we do."

I try to reconstruct when this understanding emerged.

"I've been holding some mail that came to the house after he left. Couple of pieces of correspondence in there might interest you."

"Mind if we have a look? We will be sure he gets it."

"Oh, I know you will." Hines's confiding tone makes me realize that, most likely, he has assumed that Martin is the enraged father of a pregnant daughter.

"Wait right here." Hines leaves us on the porch and fights his way past the barking, scrabbling dogs.

I start to say something to Martin, but, without changing his aggrieved expression, he bobs his head the tiniest bit toward the camera mounted above the porch. I wonder again at all the things Martin has learned over the past sixteen years.

Hines returns. The instant that Tyler's mail is in Martin's hands, I ask the coach, "Why did you ask if he'd stolen from us? Did he steal from you?"

"I'm not at liberty to discuss the ins and outs of this whole deal, but let me just put it this way: Tyler Moldenhauer is not who everyone thinks he is."

So Tyler isn't gay and he clearly is attracted to me. Why hasn't he made a move?

Maybe some really bad STD? Herpes? HIV? And, also, what is going to be different with us?

My favorite theory, though, on why he hasn't ripped my clothes off is Unspeakable Sexual Desires. That the instant he lets himself lose control, he is going to be begging me to spank him or tie him up or he'll plead with me to put on a badger costume.

I can't gather any more evidence, though, since there is a giant game coming up Friday, regional play-offs, day after Thanksgiving, and he needs to get his head into it, so he isn't going to see me for the next week.

This gives me time to consider other theories, like an abstinence pledge of some kind. If that is what it is, I decide that when he asks me to accept Jesus Christ as my lord and savior, I am going to say yes.

I think about our wedding night. A lot.

He calls me up late Friday night after regionals and, like we always do, we talk about anything other than football. We have the dopey kind of conversations that my mom always rolled her eyes about when we overheard girls curled around their cells, twiddling their hair with their free hand, and saying things like "I don't know, what about you?" And "No, you. You hang up first."

"How was your T-giving?" he asks.

"Gruesome."

"No, seriously."

"Seriously. My mom's friend Dori came over and they played old eighties songs and danced while they basted."

"Sounds fun. What did they make? Turkey? Stuffing? Yams with little marshmallows? Those baby onion things?"

"Pearl onions? Yeah, we had all the usual, typical stuff."

"What's wrong with that?"

"Nothing, except why do people get so worked up over turkey when the best thing you can say about it is that it's moist? Who wants to eat moist meat?"

"I'll get a list to you."

I think that might be a sex joke but I'm not sure, so I just say, "You weren't here."

"I will be. Soon as the season's over, you're gonna get so sick of me."

"So the season's not over yet."

"Not quite."

That's when I know the Pirates won and are going to be in the state quarterfinals. Then, like he always does when football comes up, Tyler immediately changes the subject and asks, "Did you go to sleepaway camp when you were little?"

"Wow, that was a random segue."

"These guys on the drive home were talking about sleepaway camp. Made me wonder if you'd ever gone."

"Yeah, this one summer when I was ten I went to, like, YMCA camp, because it's supercheap. I was the only girl who gained weight. I actually liked the food, since it was so much better than my mom's."

"So did your mom write your name in all your clothes?"

"Obsessively."

From there, he gets me to talking about how I gashed my head open in third grade on the jungle gym and how no one would hold my hand for Red Rover in first grade when I had a wart on my thumb and about the Christmas that I got BeeBee Pretty Hair Purple Puffalump.

"Is that the Christmas your dad left?"

"How did you remember that?"

Then, the way he always does, he asks me all about myself, my childhood, what I remember about my father.

"To me," I say, "he was like a rocket-ship ride to the moon. I can't say if this is a true memory, since I was two, but I remember how, when he'd pick me up, it was different from when my mom would. Everything would turn streaky with speed blurs as he lifted me up to him and his face would get bigger and bigger. There always seemed to be a light behind his head, which is what made it like a rocket-ship ride to the moon. But seriously, Tyler, tell me about you."

"I know about me. I want to know about you."

"Tyler! You always do this. You always make me talk about myself. I feel like some giant egomaniac. Tell me about when you were little."

He considers for a long time. "Different kind of deal."

"Tell me anyway. I want to know all about you. God, I bet you were such a cute little boy. Those big ears."

"Big ears?!"

"Oh, yeah, big ol' cute Furby ears. So tell me."

"What do you want to know?"

"Everything. Something. If you don't tell me something about when you were little, I'm going to hang up."

"Well, you know . . ." There is a silence that gets longer and longer. He is sad when he finally says, "Not a rocket-ship ride to the moon." He hears himself sounding sad and this makes him mad. "OK?"

I'd never heard him even close to mad before and it makes me wish I hadn't forced him to talk about something he didn't want to talk about. I am scared he'll hang up and never talk to me again. I am scared my life will go back to exactly the way it was before him. So I tell him, "I had a dream about you."

"You did? What kind of dream?"

"One of *those* kinds of dreams."

"Tell me."

"No!"

"A.J., you cannot say that, then *not* tell me."

"You have your secrets, I have mine," I say, making both our secrets equal. Nothing to get mad about.

Finally, he gives up trying to make me tell him my dream, holds up his iPod to the phone, and plays a song he says reminds him of me. I think it's a Rascal Flatts song or something even more mainstream and uncool.

I am just glad that he's changed the subject, because I never would have told him that I dreamed about us sleeping in the same bed and waking up together. And then sleeping and waking up together again the next night. And the night after that. And that sex, with badger costumes or spanking or whatever, sex of any kind, wasn't even the biggest part.

And I never, ever, ever would have told him that I wasn't asleep when I dreamed it.

Tyler and I go to Holiday Formal. I decorated his locker; then, the night of the formal, he decorates me with a hanger from the booster club. The long silver-and-black ribbons strewn with tiny gold footballs and helmets cover half the front of my dress. They are beautiful floating against the slinky, wine-colored fabric of the formal I'd scored at Ross for $19.99 that, in the dark, looks like real silk.

Tyler somehow even managed to find a tiny clarinet and has that pinned to the hanger as well. Or maybe whichever Pirate Pal he'd ordered it from came up with that touch on her own. I'm becoming kind of an idol to the quiet, ordinary girls who populate the booster club. A commoner like them, except that the glass slipper fit my foot. At the formal, they watch from the sidelines. Tyler splays his large, tan hands across my pale, bare back like he owns me. Like we are lovers.

I wonder what they think he is whispering in my ear when he massages the muscles along my spine and jokes, "Shit, girl, you are ripped. How did you get so scary-mad ripped? What can you bench?"

Laser lights strafe across the dark gym, which now, in addition to sweat, smells like Captain Morgan rum and Dolce & Gabbana Light Blue. The deejay plays the song that tells everyone to get "low, low, low." Groups of girls dance with one another, hiking their strapless dresses back up every time they finish getting "low, low, low." The deejay commands us to put our hands up and the gym looks like it is filled with born-again Christians.

A slow dance comes on. Lights strafe us with a pattern that is like giant snowflakes falling across our faces, our shoulders, spilling over onto the floor. Tyler puts his hands on my hips, looks down at me, and we sway to the music. The floor around us clears. A photographer crouches down and takes photos from several angles. Tyler whispers, "Smile."

It all makes me remember the Halloween when I was four and really, really, really wanted to be a princess. I can't recall if I'd actually expressed this desire in words, but I was certain that I had communicated it through the entirety of my being. I was equally certain that my mom understood, since she told me all the time that I could be anything I wanted to be.

But that Halloween, I guess, my mom really didn't have a lot of time or money or mental molecules to spend coming up with a costume. Which is why, when she picked me up from day care, she had a costume in a bag from the grocery store.

It was on the backseat next to where I was strapped into my booster seat and I immediately tore into the package, my chubby fingers aching for the touch of the fluttering pink princess dress I was certain would be inside. Instead I pulled out a Wonder Woman costume.

I trick-or-treated that year in a red plastic cape like Superman and a gold belt like a professional wrestler. I had only just figured out that I was a girl and then she dressed me like a boy. That confused me. I wanted to be a princess. I wanted everything I wore and touched and ate to be pink. I didn't want to leap and punch and fight crime and save someone. I wanted to float through life serene as a billowy cloud. I wanted to be pretty.

I put my head against Tyler's chest and he wraps his arms around me and I float across the floor serene as a billowy cloud.

I glare at Coach Hines. "What do you mean, Tyler Moldenhauer is not who I think he is?"

He purses his lips in a way that's meant to be thoughtful but is just prissy. "Where that boy came from, I wouldn't put anything past him."

"Where did he come from?"

Maybe the dogs hear the high pitch of anxiety that suddenly spikes into my voice, because they go crazy, barking and hurling themselves against the closed door.

"I am not at liberty to discuss that. I've got to—"

"Martin." I try to prompt Martin to do something, but Hines is already wedging himself back into the crack he opens in the door.

"No. Wait. You can't go. You have to tell us. You have to—"

But the dogs lunge frantically at the opening, insane with the desire to break free and crush my trachea in their massive jaws. Coach slips inside and slams the door shut.

While he yells at the dogs on the other side—"*Silencio,* Big Shot! Baron! Where's your manners!"—I start to punch the doorbell, but Martin touches my hand gently. "Don't bother. We've gotten more than he wanted to give. He's Walled In." I wince at the Nextspeak, but can't argue with his analysis.

In the car, Martin reads through the thick pile of letters and packages while I try to find my way out of a neighborhood of cul-de-sacs where all the street names start with Park—Parkview, Park Terrace, Park Ridge, Park Drive.

" 'Raising'?" I ask. "What does 'raising' mean?"

Martin, absorbed in the letters, says, "I don't know. What's Tyler's family like?"

I don't answer.

He looks up from the stack of mail. "Cam? What's this kid's family like? You met his family, right?"

"He transferred in from another district. Don't look at me like that, Martin. You have absolutely no right to look at me like that."

"Cam, I am not looking at you like anything."

"You're judging me. You're wondering 'How could she have let this happen?'"

"No. I'm not."

"'How could she not know anything about this person my daughter was spending all of her time with?' As if they were both sitting on the porch swing courting or something and I just willfully *chose* not to know anything about him. Like I was in the house getting high or something. Do you realize what my life has been like since you left? How I have had to hustle every minute of every day just to keep us afloat?"

"Cam, I honestly don't doubt anything you've done."

"How exactly are you supposed to *force* your way into someone's life? Like I said, I have nothing she wants anymore. Not even, or especially not, my love."

"She wants that, Cam. She'll always want that."

"You don't know. You don't know a goddamn thing about her."

"I know she had a wonderful mother."

"Fuck you, Martin. Just fuck you. And fuck Park Pebbles Cove." I circle the cul-de-sac I've accidentally turned into. "Where the hell are we?" I ask him automatically. Martin has a freakish sense of direction and was always able to answer that question no matter how lost I thought we were.

"Take a right, then another right at Park Vista."

I follow his directions out of the neighborhood.

"You think I should have been able to control her. That you could have. Don't you?"

"Cam, here's what I think. I think that I have no right to think anything, and that I am lucky you have allowed me to be here at all, and that some of the answers to our questions might be in one of these letters."

He holds up the one he's reading. "This guy *was* heavily recruited. So far, they're all from college football coaches encouraging Tyler to"—he skims the letter in his hand—"'seriously consider' blah-blah and to 'remember what we talked about.' Wonder what these guys were 'talking about' that they don't want to put in writing? I'm sure the NCAA would be interested too. Must be a hell of a player. I wonder why he didn't answer any of them."

"Martin, you sound like Coach Tighty Whitie back there. I could care less why this bonehead jock football player gave up his chance to bang college cheerleaders. That is not my concern. Aubrey is my one and only concern."

"We don't disagree."

"God, I hate that expression. 'Don't disagree.' You agree, okay? Could you just say you agree?"

"I agree."

I could use a little less agreeability at this moment. A screaming brawl would take my mind off the question it circles back to so many times that I can't hold it in any longer, and I ask, "Do you think he's dangerous?"

"I think we need to find out. Oh, this is interesting." He holds up a grease-smudged carbon of a form filled in by hand.

"What is that?"

"Looks like an invoice with a balance-due date of . . ." He studies the scrawls more closely. "Hmm, this *is* interesting. Today."

"Oh, spectacular. How much?"

He puts on the glasses Next was supposed to keep him from needing and studies the faint bluish scrawls at the bottom of the form. "I can't make it out. But whatever the actual sum is, it's a five-figure number."

"Great, so that's where our daughter's college money went."

Our daughter. The words are out before I have time to edit them. I hope Martin won't notice, but a minute turn of his head lets me know that he caught the unintended plural possessive.

"We don't know that. It's just a bill."

"Does it say what for?"

"The carbon is too faint to read—"

"Who uses carbon copies anymore?"

"—but the name of the business is Worthy Restorations. 'Randy Worthy, Prop.' Proprietor, I guess."

"Restorations? Is that little criminal using our daughter's college money to buy Old Masters or something?"

"Restorations? Okay, houses are restored, cars are restored, computer drives are restored."

"Oh, God. I saw this *Nightline* about this whole crime syndicate that bought used computers from Goodwill, then got these data-recovery people to mine credit card numbers and Social Security numbers off the hard drives, then sent them to the Soviet mafia."

Martin beams at me.

"What?"

"Nothing. You're just such a good mother."

"I am?"

"You are."

Martin delivers this bulletin with the explaining-gravity certainty that I learned to hate and distrust. Still, I want this one pronouncement to be true so badly that I have to clamp my jaws closed to keep from whimpering, "Really?" To keep myself from presenting all the evidence of my bad motherhood—the lax discipline, the breakfasts in the car, my complete and utter failure to also be a father—for him to rebut. Instead, I give a crisp nod toward the form and ask, "Is there a phone number?"

The smile fades and Martin studies the carbon copy. "There's no phone number, just an address on North Fifty-four out past Layton."

"We should talk to Randy Prop, don't you think?"

"Oh, we are most definitely going to talk to Randy, and sooner rather than later." Martin glances at me the instant the words are out of his mouth and says, "Sorry, soon. Just soon. So, we should probably head for Layton."

I say, "We don't disagree." We laugh. Mostly at how ridiculous it is that we can still make each other laugh.

I make a U-turn and head for North Fifty-four.

We've been sitting in his truck a block down from my house for at least an hour, maybe more, since all the windows are frosted with our condensed breath, when Tyler tells me, "Get ready for it all to end."

I stop breathing, give him popped-open disaster eyes, and he adds quickly, "No, not that. Not us. State semifinals are next Friday."

"The last game of the season, right? Unless you win?" I squint as if I'm not exactly sure. I am; I've been checking the schedule.

"Oh, it will be the last game. No question about that. Lincoln Consolidated?" He names the powerhouse team they are playing. "They will kick the snot out of us. After that, no more football. No more Ty-Mo."

"You're quitting football?"

"Uh-uh. Not quitting. That job will be over."

I want to ask about college. Won't he have to play in college? But I don't want to speak the C-word. I want to sit in his truck and look out at a world that our breath together has made into a soft, gauzy place where the ugly crime lights now make everything shimmer with a golden radiance.

Tyler murmurs into the top of my head, "You probably need to go in. Your mom's gonna worry."

"Mmm." I snuggle in tighter, thinking what a challenging but ultimately good idea it is that we are saving ourselves for marriage. He peels me off his body. "I should go in with you and meet her, your mom."

"No. Don't. She hates meeting people. She has, like, this really bad social anxiety."

"She doesn't sound like a social-anxiety person. I mean, isn't she out there teaching classes on . . ." He circles his hands around his chest to indicate breast-feeding.

"Oh, yeah, she's fine out of the house. That's not really a problem. But she hates—*hates*—having people come into her house. She feels all invaded and shit. It's a phobia."

"What about Dori?"

God, does he ever forget anything? "Dori's the exception."

He helps me out of the truck. As he is getting back in, he pauses and says, "I think it's time for us to talk. No, don't look like that. It's good. Well, not good, but . . . Just don't look like that, OK? I'll call as soon as the game is over. The second it all ends."

I watch until long after his taillights disappear before I go into the house. It is stiflingly hot.

"Are you *trying* to get sick?" Mom asks the instant I am in the door.

The shift from Tyler to her is so jarring that my brain actually hurts. She jerks the giant dogsled parka she bought me for the trip to Peninsula out of the hall closet. "Why don't you wear your jacket?"

"Uh, because it's hideous?"

"Well, it would have been nice of you to tell me that before I spent almost two hundred dollars on it."

"I didn't ask you to."

"Right. I was supposed to just let you get soaked and frozen at Peninsula. Wear the damn jacket, Aubrey."

"I'm not going to wear that jacket. Ever."

She flaps her lips like a horse. A very annoyed horse.

"Mom, I don't really get that cold."

"Aubrey, your lips are blue as we speak. And now you'll probably get bronchitis like you do every year. Then that will turn into a sinus infection. And I'll have to miss work. And you're resistant to everything now except those designer antibiotics that cost a fortune."

"Sorry to be such a bother."

That gets me Hurt Look Number 85, which is the one about how my father screwed her in the divorce and that's why we have no money. Of course, that look is based on the reality that my being born is pretty much the whole cause of the divorce. The thing that drove her husband to what she has always told me is his psycho religion. Not that I've heard his side of that story.

She yells at me that there are going to be some new rules around here from now on. The first one is that I have to come straight home after school every day or she will ground me.

After she lists a bunch of other rules like calling and checking in, I say, "Sure. Not a problem," and walk away. By the time I've closed my bedroom door I can't recall any of the new rules because I'm concentrating so hard on figuring out exactly what Tyler meant, and to do that I have to remember every word he spoke.

I twine through the web of roads that have woven Parkhaven and all the once-separate little towns surrounding the city into a metropolis with the prefix Greater.

Martin opens an envelope and pulls out a form. "Hey, his high school transcript." He studies the computer printout. "Hmm. Looks like they mercy-graduated our young Mr. Moldenhauer."

"Perfect. He's stupid. Stupid *and* a criminal. This just gets better and better. How long have you and Aubrey been in touch?"

"About a year."

"Weren't you worried about Next finding out?"

"I used a fake name."

"She's been communicating with you for a year and never said one word to me?"

"I kept asking her to tell you."

"You 'asked' her to tell me."

"Cam, what was I supposed to do? I was in no position to make demands. All I wanted was to know her. Let her know me."

I weave through a clogged intersection, then say, "It's like bigamy."

"Bigamy?"

"This double life my own daughter kept from me, it's like finding out your husband has another family. A whole other double life."

"Not that this is your favorite subject, but for the past sixteen years most of what I did every day was listen to the double, triple, quadruple lives that people, mostly famous people, live. People you would never expect."

"Movie stars? I *would* expect movie stars to have multiple lives. I mean, wasn't that really your job? Keeping the less savory ones hidden from view?"

"Not really. In my mind, not at all. But I'm not up to diving back into all that. Aubrey, all I care about now is Aubrey. All I ever should have cared about was Aubrey."

"So what did you two talk about?"

"Her classes. Her crazy physics teacher."

"Psycho Saunders? She told you about Psycho Saunders?"

"Yeah."

"What else?"

"She wanted to know why I left."

"What did you tell her?"

"Not enough. It was hard. How do you fit an answer you've been trying to figure out yourself for sixteen years into a chat bubble? Mostly I just wanted her to know that I was wrong. That I regretted leaving and that it wasn't fair to her. Or to you." He shakes his head. "God, I was an asshole."

" 'Was'?" I give him the barest peek at a smile.

"Oh, no doubt, I am still an asshole. But at least now I'm an asshole who knows that he is."

I still can't believe how completely the Next version of Martin has disappeared, and keep poking around to find out where the cracks in this facade are. "So what did make you give up all that delicious certainty?"

He leans his head to one side and plucks at the sideburn there with his thumb and middle finger. "Like I said, disillusionments. They just kept mounting. It's been coming on for years. Years while I told myself that the tenets were good and I just had to accept that flawed humans were carrying them out."

"Plus it was nice driving around in a Bentley, squiring movie stars to premieres, being the crown prince or heir apparent or whatever you were. Never having anyone tell you your shit stinks."

"You have no idea. When I first got involved, it was as if my whole life I'd been trying to sing with a choir I couldn't get in tune with. I was always the one who was off-key, out of pitch. The one who was ruining the music. With Next it was utter harmony for the first time in my life."

"I thought we had some pretty goddamn harmonious moments."

"God. Yes. I met you, Cam, and life became livable. For years. And if it had just been you and me forever . . . Who knows? Maybe I could have limped through the entire rest of my life with you propping me up."

I have no recollection of me propping Martin up.

"But with a child? That changed everything. I had to be worthy of being a father."

I turn my head away so that Martin, who is truly baring his soul, will not see me roll my eyes. It's pointless to bring up the contradiction of how one becomes worthy of being a father by not being one. I just listen as he goes on about how seductive Next was at first. How they showered him with attention, treating his every utterance as either deeply profound or uproariously hilarious.

"I think the Moonies call that 'love bombing.' When they lure a new recruit in, then lavish him with attention and affection."

"Right. The Children of God had 'Flirty Fishing' to show God's love and win converts. Nothing like plain old sex to put a man on the path to righteousness. Next called their version of all this The Bath. For some of us, being right is so much sexier than sex."

So there it was. What I'd always known—and Martin had always denied—had propelled him into Next. A part of me wants to gloat and crow and kick this man while he's down for every second that my child did not have a father. But why? Because I've won an argument I had sixteen years ago? How could any of this have been a surprise when the first thing Martin did after we met was read me the story of a young man searching for enlightenment?

Outside, the space between the businesses lining the road grows and goes from a scatter of strip malls to a fast-food joint here and there to isolated guys selling fruit and pottery out of the backs of their pickups.

Even the pottery guys are gone and the country has opened up by the time Martin asks, "Isn't that the lure of all religions? Don't they all promise to give you the answers? Let you in on the big mystery?"

"I guess," I say. "That and control the pussy."

"Cam, Cam, Cam. You were always a good one for keeping it real. How could I not know that that is what I needed more than anything in my life?"

The Bath. I see why Next calls it that, because a gush of warm delight floods through me at Martin's admission. And I see why The Bath is dangerous: A person could drown in such a pool of approbation.

I dry off and crisply demand, "So what was it? What made you give up this life of getting your ass smooched?"

"One moment? You want one moment? There wasn't *one* moment. There was an accumulation over years, then a tipping point. Aubrey mentioned that you showed her the . . ." He holds his hand out, palm up.

"Yeah, I made an album so she'd know her father existed."

"All right. Well, the last time was with . . . The star doesn't even matter. Two Oscars. Four marriages. Hair plugs like a trail on an old map. Was a great actor before he turned himself into a franchise. Anyway, it was the premiere of his latest action-hero blockbuster, *Tsunami: Wave Bye-Bye,* and he brought his youngest child with him, this beautiful little girl. Five at the time. As usual, the instant he appeared, the photographers were crawling all over him. I instinctively picked up his daughter. She buried her head in my shoulder. I put my hand out to shield her. Just like always. But this time I stopped and thought, 'What the hell am I doing? I'm protecting *this* little girl?' That was it. It was as clear as night and day. I could never again do for someone else's child what I hadn't done for my own."

This story is genetically engineered to melt my heart. Which it does. "Plus, you saw that Next was a load of horseshit and you were an idiot for ever falling for it."

"You really need me to say it?"

"Only if it's true."

"Plus, I saw that Next was a load of horseshit and I was an idiot for ever falling for it."

The barometric pressure in the car lightens and I am almost happy. Then I remember that he wasn't there when Aubrey needed him to protect her the most—he wasn't there last winter on Black Ice Night.

Three days later, Friday, I wait for Tyler to finish the game and call me. I stand in the front hall, looking out the little barred window in the door. Mom has set the heat down so low that my breath freezes on the glass. Outside, light shimmers off the ice that has turned the street black and shiny.

I check my phone for about the hundredth time to make sure it is turned on and I haven't missed his call. It is 9:43. Tyler needs to call. Soon. I have to sneak out before Mom gets home. She's really been intense with all her new rules. Her evening classes end at nine, but usually she'll stay and talk and, essentially, hold private consultations for anyone with a question. She actually really cares about her students and their babies. It is why she is such a guru or diva or something.

I strain to hear the sound of the garage door going up. If I zip out at the first clang, I can be out of the house before she comes in. I'll have to wait outside in the freezing cold until Tyler comes, but if I don't leave before she gets home, Mom will trap me. For the last few days, I've felt like she is getting ready to lose it.

I turn from the door and send Tyler a text telling him to hurry. Just as I hit "Send," the front door flies open and there is my mom. "Aubrey, sweetheart, you're home. Way to obey the new rules." She unwraps the muffler wound around her neck. Her nose and cheeks are red from the cold.

"Why didn't you come in through the garage?" I ask, panicking.

She holds up the opener. "Dead batteries. God, it's freezing out there. The roads are really getting dangerous." Her hair is up in a ponytail. My mom has this magical belief that putting your hair in a ponytail is the same as washing it.

One strap of her tote bag slips off her shoulder and all her stuff spills out onto the foyer. The rubber tit with blue veins and red milk ducts bounces away; clear nipple guards go sproinging all over; the boob apron, heavy as the one the dentist puts on for X-rays, lands with the nipples facing up.

I stoop down to help her gather the paraphernalia up. I stuff her dolls back in the bag. Those dolls with their heavy bottoms were so real, I craved them when I was little and it was a giant treat when she let me play with them.

"Did you bring my plants in like I asked you to?"

Before I can answer, she goes on, "And while you're out there, can you turn the faucet in the backyard on so it'll drip and not freeze? I'll go get the one in front. No, never mind. That one never stops dripping."

I am heading out the door with her when the phone in my bra vibrates. Tyler. I stop. "Uh, I'll get the plants in when I get back. I've got to go"—I hold up my cell—"help Tyler with his college applications." Anything to do with college grants instant immunity.

"Aubrey, you are not going out now. There's black ice on the roads. It's late. It's too—"

"Mom, I have to. Deadlines for his top-three reach schools are, like, tomorrow."

"Invite him in. You've been sneaking around seeing this boy for months—"

"Mom! We are not 'sneaking around.' We study together. Period. End of story. Since when do you have to investigate everyone I study with?"

"I'm not going to *investigate* him. And be honest, Aubrey. He's a lot more than someone you study with."

"That's your opinion."

"Aubrey, you've got on mascara. You flatironed your hair. Don't try to tell me he is just some study buddy. You're wearing . . ." She sniffs me. She is always sniffing me. It makes me paranoid that I stink. "Is that my Jo Malone?"

I move toward the door. "He's waiting."

She grabs my arm. Hard. "Look . . ."

It drives me crazy how she says "look" all the time, like she's Barack Obama. Every grown-up I know who voted for him starts all their sentences with, "Look," to clue you in that they are going to be calm and reasonable even though they think you are a raving loon.

But she quickly gives up on calm and reasonable and orders me,

"OK, that's it. That is it. You are not going anywhere. If I have to sit on you, you are not leaving this house. This is no longer up for discussion." She blocks the door, crosses her arms.

The thought of not seeing Tyler makes me frantic. She has to be moved. She has to get out of my way. I shove her aside and rush out. The wind is so cold and strong that it punches me in the chest and knocks the breath out of me, like jumping into the quarry did. I run down the porch stairs.

To my amazement, she follows me. I am already at the edge of our yard when she grabs my hair and stops me dead. "What are you doing?!" I scream at her. "Let go of my hair!"

"This is over, Aubrey. This sneaking around. This disrespect. This lying to me. You are staying home tonight! End of story!"

"Is this the way your mother smothered you?"

"Don't even try. You are so *unsmothered* it's not funny." She lets go of my hair.

"That's because you've never *had* to smother me! I have never done one single thing to make you worry or doubt me! I still haven't!"

I try to walk away, but she grabs my arm and yanks me toward her. "Get back in this house!"

I put my hands on her shoulders and physically halt her. "No!"

"Yes!" She clamps onto my wrists and starts dragging me back. "Get inside the house this instant!"

I refuse to be dragged. Light flashes from the window of the house across the street where the neighbor pulls back the blind to see what is going on.

I shove her away. A second later, she has her hands all over me, wrapping around me, pulling me down, drowning me. I wrench away, stand back, and raise my hand up above my head like the Statue of Liberty. I am going to hit her. We both know it. I stop only because, on the porch behind us, Pretzels barks a hideous, strangled bark.

Almost deaf, almost blind, she struggles to see into the darkness. She stands on the side of the porch, away from the stairs, barking, searching, ready to save us. Mom and I both realize that, no matter what, Pretzels is coming to rescue us.

"Pretzels, no!" Mom screams.

Using memory more than muscle, Pretz jumps off the porch. With only old bones to absorb the shock, she hits hard and crumples onto the ground, yelping piteously as she lands. My mom runs back, kneels beside Pretzels.

"Aubrey, come help! We've got to get her to the vet!"

Mom hoists her up around the middle. When I see Pretzels struggle to her feet and stand, I run from them.

I would have run even if she hadn't gotten up.

M artin has taken over the driving. I try to recall how long it's been since I sat in the passenger seat while a man drove. I narrow the time frame down to A Long Time.

We're passing through a field of what I know to be sorghum because Martin once identified this crop for me. At the edge of the field is a stretch of bare earth that has been molded into humps and hollows, crisscrossed by trails. A kid on a motocross bike bursts over a low hill and gets enough air to shimmy his back wheel before landing.

Martin slows down as we enter a small town. Most of the businesses are boarded up. "We're almost out of gas," he says, dropping his speed even more. He always used to do this on trips, practically crawl through small towns, reading out the names of businesses, the wisdom posted outside of churches, the funny team names being boosted on the Dairy Queen marquees. He loved cafés, diners, drugstores with lunch counters.

We pass a couple of sleek new gas stations with a dozen bays out front, but, as I knew he would, Martin heads for a battered, two-pump establishment. I always liked that he preferred the local, the homegrown.

We park next to an ancient gas pump. Martin points to the door on an outside wall of the station with RESTROOM painted on it. "You need to?"

"No, I'm fine." Much as I like the local, the homegrown, when it comes to restrooms I prefer the corporate, the national.

"We'll hit the DQ on the way out of town." It was what we always used to do on trips. How we accommodated his thirst for the authentic and my microbladder.

He hops out, flips the lock on the pump nozzle into place so that the gas flows automatically, goes into the station, and, for one second, I think, *This is how it would have been for the past sixteen years. Someone else, not always me, would have, even occasionally, driven, pumped the gas, worried about our child.*

When he returns, Martin is carrying a white plastic shopping bag.

In the car he extracts a package of pork rinds, another of CornNuts, holds them up, and asks, "Which one?"

My face wrinkles in disgust. "Martin, I hate pork rinds *and* Corn-Nuts." I'm glad I stop myself from adding, *You know that,* because he whips out a jumbo bag of honey roasted peanuts and crows, "Gotcha!"

I smile and take the peanuts, always my favorite of the gas station foods. "You are such a jerk."

Martin tears the package of CornNuts open with his teeth. Their smell fills the car, takes me back to other trips. He shakes out a handful, puts a CornNuts-crammed fist to his lips, tips his head back, and taps them into his mouth.

With the first filling-cracking crunch, I wince. "How can you eat those things?" The words are out of my mouth before I realize that this is a question a girlfriend, a wife, someone concerned about the state of a man's dental work would ask.

"Only way possible . . ." Martin answers, pausing to back out of the station, then slide into traffic. He nods at the shopping bag. "You mind?"

I fish out a can of the obnoxious red soda he always favored on road trips. "God, you don't still drink those?" I hand it to him, and keep the Diet Sprite that was always my road bev.

"You're right: It's *red* with pork rinds, *white* with CornNuts. Pass me the Diet Sprite."

I hug the drink to my chest and pivot away, protecting it from his joking grasp. "I don't think so." I fill my mouth with sweet peanuts and sweet bubbles, chew them into a carbonated mush, and watch the small town turn back into sorghum fields.

There is no DQ and Martin asks if he should turn back and find someplace with a good restroom. I tell him I can wait.

Gradually, the fields of grain are replaced by high, spindly pines that shadow the lonely road. Time rolls past so easily that Martin startles me when he says, "We're almost there."

We pass a tire repair shack and a barbecue joint. Farther on, I point to what appears to be an abandoned trailer park on the road ahead. Old trailers and RVs lie abandoned beneath the tall pines next to the rusting hulks of ancient cars. "Is that the place?"

Martin leans forward, squints, and reads off the hand-painted sign: " 'Worthy Restorations. Randy Worthy, Prop.' Well, I guess we can eliminate any high-tech Soviet-Mafia identity-theft ring."

"Yeah, that and probably indoor plumbing." I wish I'd hit the restroom when I had the chance. "This is like something out of *Deliverance*."

Martin bumps off the highway onto a dirt road and stops for a moment. The high-pitched shriek of metal being cut reaches us. Martin considers the sound and the piles of car frames and comes up with "Chop shop?"

He's joking, but in a way that shows that his antennae are tuned to the same frequencies of danger and menace as mine.

We follow the saw's whine back to a large portable building with big barn doors at either end. Parked outside are half a dozen old Airstream trailers in various stages of repair. One is finished and shines in the sun, polished to a blinding glare.

"Well," Martin says as he parks. "We know now what Randy Worthy, Prop., restores."

"Please, sweet Jesus, do not tell me that that lunkhead jock got our daughter to spend her college money on a roach coach."

Again. "Our" daughter.

The sliding doors at either end of the workshop are open. Where stalls would have been are stacks of quilted metal siding, small tires, stainless-steel sinks, slabs of foam, propane tanks. Some of the parts are gleaming new; most are crusted with rust and grease. Empty liter bottles of Mountain Dew perch everywhere. Presiding over this empire of debris is a wiry guy wearing a khaki shirt with the sleeves ripped off to reveal stringy, tattooed biceps. He's hunched over, intent upon slicing a thick metal rod. A carrot-colored beard divided into two braids pokes out like a snake's tongue from beneath his welder's mask. As he cuts the rod in two, bits of metal and sparks flash from the teeth of the grinder in his hand and ricochet off the helmet with its gun turret of an eye shield. ZZ Top—"Lawd, take me downtown! I'm just looking for some tush!"—plays over the screech.

I think two thoughts: *Outlaw biker* and *Leave. Leave now.* I grab Martin's arm to tug him away; it's time to get law enforcement involved.

But Martin is already yelling, "Yo! Hey, Randy! Hello!" and ambling into the guy's limited field of vision. I'm glad Martin's wearing jeans. No telling what might happen if this guy were to see a suit.

"Mr. Worthy! Sir! Sir!" He waves his arm and steps closer. The guy still doesn't hear him and bends forward to finish the cut. His shirt presses against the waistband of his work pants and a distinct hump appears close to the base of his spine.

"A gun!" I yell at Martin, but my warning is lost in the shriek of the blade. I point, drawing Martin's attention to the hump, and back away, waving frantically for Martin to do the same. He doesn't. He nods, gives me a stay-calm hand bounce, and keeps moving forward. It seems that the alpha-dog intimidation tactics are not just bluff. Sometime in the last sixteen years, Martin has become a badass.

The guy finally sees him and, in one fluid sequence, stops the grinder, flips the mask away from his face, and grabs for the gun in his waistband.

Martin extends his hands out in a wide I-come-in-peace gesture, and chuckles. "Whoa, dude. Hey, Randy, dude, sorry." His words echo in the sudden silence.

The guy's eyes dart from me to Martin several times. They dart a lot. Too much. I combine that with his twitchy, emaciated state and add another entry to his résumé: *meth head.*

Next must have also helped Martin become a shape-shifter, because he sounds completely relaxed, like this stranger's oldest friend playing a prank on him when he chuckles. "My bad, Randy. Didn't mean to startle you. I'd never walk into a man's workshop unannounced like this, except I don't have a number for you."

If we get out of here alive, I am definitely calling the police. This person could not be in Aubrey's world unless she is in serious, serious danger. Similar to the serious, serious danger I feel that Martin and I are now in. As with Coach Hines, though, Martin is able to play Randy so perfectly that the guy takes his hand from the gun and eases into whatever permanently wary state passes for his version of relaxed.

"You here to pick up the . . ." Randy points out toward another portable building. "The little Bambi? I guess you didn't get my message? That Hensley Arrow hitch didn't come in. They promised me. Swore up and down. I know I said I'd have it done today, but—"

"No, that's cool. We're just fans of your work. Really like what you did for a buddy of mine."

"Yeah." He tenses back up. "Who'd that be?"

"Tyler. Tyler Moldenhauer?"

"You know Bronk?"

Bronk?

"How d'ya know Bronk?"

"Football."

"Oh. You a coach?"

"Well, assistant."

"Yeah?"

"Just wondering where we can find him."

Randy's twitchy eyes narrow. He steps back a bit, the better to keep both of us under surveillance. "If you don't know where he is, then you haven't seen what I did for him, have you now, cuz they just picked it up."

"When?"

"This morning. Look, I do not know where Bronk come up with that money. That is not my responsibility. Knowing his people, though . . ."

His people?

"Coulda been anywhere. But I do not know, and furthermore, I do not care. That was a custom job, and custom jobs don't come with any ninety-day warranty. I got a strict no-refund policy on custom. He knew that. That was made clear up front."

"No, no, hell, no, man." Martin eases into the full cracker. "We ain't lookin' to recover. Not from you. We just need to locate Bronk. Talk to him."

"You the coach he was living with?"

Martin nods.

"Look, I sympathize. I dealt with his people way back to before whenever they all got run off, but this is not my responsibility. Once a customer takes delivery—"

"No, we get that, bro. We're just, you know—"

"Was there a girl with him?" I demand brusquely. I've had it with the jovial folksiness.

"Ma'am, you're gonna have to step back and take all this up with Bronk. And I'm gonna have to ask you to leave. Now. You're trespassing." He flips the visor of his helmet back down to signal that the conversation is over. It clangs into place, covering his face, he switches the grinder on, and sparks shoot out as it slices into the metal rod.

He knows where my daughter is, and he's not going to tell me? I don't think so.

I stride up to Randy and yell into his caged face, "Where did they go?"

Randy straightens up. The grinder in his hand is one inch from my belly. His finger is tense on the trigger. He wouldn't need the gun. If he let his finger on the grinder "slip," it would slice effortlessly through my abdominal artery.

Every muscle fiber in a body that looks to have been trained in biker bars and prison yards twitches. He releases the triggers, flips the visor back, orders Martin, "Get your woman out my face."

Martin steps forward, reaching for me. "Cam, I—"

"That's close enough."

Martin freezes.

Randy presses the blade of the grinder against my stomach.

"Randy, man. Let's put the grinder down, man."

I stare into the slit in the helmet, into Randy's eyes. The thin wisp of foggy color circling his dilated pupil disappears in a total eclipse as he stares back. I look into empty blackness for one, two, three seconds, then yank the entire helmet off his head. My face is close enough to his to smell the robot odor of metal, grease, and speed that is feeding on his muscles and teeth. "Either tell me where my daughter is or kill me."

"Crazy bitch." He drops the grinder. "I don't know."

"What's your best guess?"

"Fuck am I supposed to know? You are trespassing and need to get the hell off my property."

"Where? Come on, Randy. I'm just a mom looking for my kid. That's all."

As he studies me, I see that Randy is not a meth addict; he's a skinny guy with bad teeth and a twitchy temperament made worse by drinking too much Mountain Dew. "Honest to God, lady, I don't know. But if I was to guess, I'd say where all them do the food trailer mod go."

"Where's that, Randy?"

"Sycamore Heights."

A ubrey, what's wrong?"

"Drive, OK? Just drive."

The truck fishtails on the dark ice as Tyler swings it around. He steers into the skid and the truck straightens out. Within minutes we are on the highway.

"You OK? Is it your mom? We should go back. Talk to her. Maybe if she met me, she'd like me. Moms like me. They always do."

"Tyler, what's wrong? You sound strange."

The light from the tall poles overhead strobes across Tyler's face. A gash, black in the shadowed light, splits his lower lip. "What happened?"

He touches his lip. "This, yeah, sorry, I sound even more like a drooling idiot than usual."

"No, no . . ." I reach out. Tyler takes my hand, kisses the palm, pressing my hand against his lips until they leave a smear of blood there.

"I made it. I survived. It's over. For the rest of my life, I never have to go onto a field again where every behemoth out there has permission to do shit like this to me." He touches the cut on his lip.

"Then I'm supposed to turn around and shake that asshole's hand? After he head-butts me behind the ref's back? When I've got my helmet off? I'm supposed to pretend it's a game?"

His tone of thorough disgust even more than his words makes me realize "You don't like football."

"I fucking hate fucking football. You know they got linemen in high school now weigh over three hundred pounds? That's like getting hit by Sasquatch. There are guys out there paralyzed from taking hits like that."

"You . . . you hate football? Why have you been playing all these years?"

"I didn't always hate it. At first I loved it. Then it turned into what I had to do to get out of where I was. It turned into a job. A job I was good at. I was good at being Ty-Mo. But I am done."

The oncoming headlights cut his profile out of the darkness. The lights flash past, but he keeps his eyes on me as he says, "So it's over. No more football. No more football hero. Are you still . . . ?"

He doesn't finish. Instead, he pulls off into the breakdown lane, stops the truck, faces me. The cars coming up from behind splash waves of light across our faces, then leave us in darkness. When I kiss him his blood tastes metallic, like new pennies. I kiss his cheek, his jaw, the unhurt part of his lower lip.

I put my mouth on his neck, my tongue at the hollow beneath it. His breath funnels along my face, my neck. He kisses me so hard that the metallic taste fills my mouth. I think of all the fat books I used to read about a girl in love with a vampire. How she drove him into a frenzy. But I am the one driven into frenzy.

He pulls away. "Whoa. Whoa. Time-out. I promised myself it would not be like this."

"No, Tyler. It's all right." I reach for his face, a moon going behind the clouds.

"Don't, A.J. Don't let me mess this up. You have to know what you're getting into first."

"I know. I know everything I need to know."

"No, you don't." He starts the engine, drives for several minutes before he says, "Call your mom. Tell her you're fine, but you won't be home tonight. Tell her that your football-hero boyfriend is going to show you who he really is."

Boyfriend.

My mom implodes and orders me to come home immediately or she will call the police and have them bring me home.

I imagine the spinning blue lights of a cop car ricocheting around the cab of the truck. Tyler and me standing by the side of the road, a highway patrolman with a flashlight beaming a cone of light onto my driver's license. I imagine the life I've known ending. I imagine all that, then I tell my mom in a loud, peppy voice for Tyler to hear, "Yeah, that's fine. See you later then."

Mom starts crying and begs me, "Please, Aubrey, please don't make me call the police, because I will. If you force me to do this, I will."

I say, "Yeah, Mom, love you too. Bye."

As I turn my phone off, I feel like Hester Prynne going into the wild, dark forest with Reverend Dimmesdale, throwing away everything for love. Love. I haven't let myself even think that word until now.

I love Tyler Moldenhauer.

I loved Tyler Moldenhauer from the second I woke up in his arms. I would have loved him even if he'd never spoken to me again. I just never would have admitted it. Maybe at some twentieth high school reunion, if he'd gotten fat and bald, I would have gotten up the courage to tell him, "I know you don't remember me. Aubrey? Aubrey Lightsey? The girl who threw up on you? Pink Puke? Anyway, I had the biggest crush on you all those years ago." Maybe he'd be flattered. Maybe we'd laugh. Maybe he'd remember me. Maybe he wouldn't.

Still, without really understanding why he'd chosen me, fearing he'll be reabsorbed into his golden kingdom at any second, knowing that my heart is going to be broken and I am a complete idiot, I admit that I love Tyler Moldenhauer, and my DNA twists—all its helixes, double and single—around this rewriting of my essential code.

"What did your mom say? Should we go back?"

"It's fine." I slide over next to him. He puts his arm around me and I nestle there. "Don't go back."

As we drive into the night, the headlights of the oncoming cars flash on and off across our faces like a time-lapse film of the sun rising and setting every few seconds, as if time is speeding up so fast that when this one night is over, years, decades, centuries will have passed.

We are out from beneath the shadows of the tall pines before Martin notices and pulls over.

"Cam, are you all right? Cam?"

"I'm fine. Let's go. We've got to keep moving. Get to Sycamore Heights. Find out what the hell is—"

"Camille, you're shaking."

Camille.

I was Camille on the train in Morocco and for the happy years when we lived in Sycamore Heights. During the colic siege, the Next siege, I cut my hair short so I wouldn't have to deal with it, and somehow my name ended up getting snipped off as well. I guess that after Next neither one of us had the breath or tenderness for even one extra syllable.

"I'm fine. Let's drive."

He opens his arms. Am I supposed to tumble into them?

He undoes his seat belt, undoes mine. I stiffen as he pulls me into his arms like a firefighter dragging a person out of a car that is about to explode. "Camille." He summons back the person who used to fit in his arms.

"That guy back there. He is my nightmare. He is the embodiment of all my worst nightmares of what Aubrey . . . Someone like that should never have touched her world. Should never have . . . never have . . ."

As I babble, he strokes my hair and murmurs, "It's okay. We'll figure it out. It'll be fine."

"No, fine is no longer a possibility. Fine would have been me putting my only child on a plane today and sending her off to college, where she and her roommate could have decided whether to stack the beds into bunks for more room or leave them separate. Fine would have been her calling me while she's walking to her anthro class. Fine would have even been me and Pretzels, curled up on her bed with her baby pictures, me crying myself to sleep. This . . . this . . ." I wave my hand at all of it: the snake-bearded hillbilly, the stolen money, the lies. "This is most definitively not fine."

I'm the one who sounds like a speed freak as I rant on. "His 'people'? What did that mean, 'his people'? Oh, God, why would Aubrey know someone like that?"

"Apparently he restored a trailer for them."

"For *him*. Tyler Moldenhauer stole our daughter's college money."

"At least it's not drugs or guns."

" 'Bronk'? What kind of a name is 'Bronk'?"

We both know that it is not the name of a kid heading to college or the name of the boyfriend of a girl who is. Martin's breath warms the top of my head. It feels luxurious, like getting your hair washed at a salon. I want to close my eyes and lean back, but the words keep pouring out of me.

"I thought I could control her by taking the laptop away. No, no, wait, here's how stupid I was. I thought I could control her with Christmas cookies. Here's what an in-tune mother I was: I forced Aubrey to make and decorate cookies with me last Christmas. *Forced.* Five different kinds. As if I could lure her back into childhood with sweets. As if pressing hatching with a fork into peanut-butter cookies would transform her into the toddler I taught to name all the colors. Or that in the middle of sifting powdered sugar onto lemon bars the schoolgirl who sang Beatles songs with me would reappear."

Martin rests his cheek on the top of my head.

"How did I not know that all those little girls Aubrey once was were already gone?" I straighten back up. "We should go."

Martin starts the engine. "Sycamore Heights?"

"Unless you have a better idea. Dude."

Martin snorts a thin laugh and pulls back onto the highway.

A t an all-night truck stop, I go into the bathroom with Tyler. The mirror is a greasy sheet of polished metal bolted to the wall. Tyler sits on the edge of the sink. I clean the cut on his lip, wash off the blood dried on his chin, his neck. He closes his eyes while I do this.

A waitress brings tall plastic menus and automatically pours coffee, since it is either late-late-night or early-early-morning breakfast time. Tyler lets me order for both of us. We eat big, fluffy omelets, split a stack of pancakes, and drink too much crummy coffee just because we like sitting across from each other so much. We dawdle so long that I think Tyler has abandoned whatever urgent mission we'd originally set out on until he says, "You ready?" as if I was the one who'd been stalling.

There are only a few semis on the main highway. After a while, we turn off onto a road that shoots through the few scattered small towns. For a while there are one or two lights on in the towns we speed through. Then all the lights and all the towns disappear and it is completely dark. I turn on the radio. I think it will be funny to listen to crazy preachers and talk-show hosts ranting about "the puppet king, Obama, whose soul is owned by the Chicago Zionist Jewish machine."

Occasionally, I can catch glimpses of tall pine trees. Since neither of us has said anything for a long time, I ask, "Where will all these babies that the government is going to force us to abort come from after Obama makes us all gay marry?"

Tyler is concentrating so hard on the empty road ahead that a few seconds pass before he gives a weak, delayed-reaction chuckle, never taking his eyes from the hole cut out of the darkness by his headlights.

All that I can make out are dead weeds growing up through the cracks in the buckled asphalt, but Tyler sees something that makes him slow down and squint at the left side of the road. He switches off the radio, as if silence will help his vision.

At a spot that doesn't seem any more overgrown with scrub brush and spindly trees than any other, he says, "This is it," and turns off onto a road that isn't even single-lane, and has ruts running down it like a riverbed. Branches swat at the windshield and shriek as they scrape both sides of the truck.

Tyler doesn't seem to notice the scraping sound that gets louder and louder the farther in we go. The road goes uphill and the engine groans. Tyler puts the truck into four-wheel drive. We come to a sagging gate held shut with a piece of chain and a rusty padlock. The instant the headlights flicker across the gate, Tyler stomps on the gas and we rocket forward. Pebbles spit out from beneath the back tires. He rams the gate so hard that the lock pops off, flies up, and lands with a hard *thunk* on the front windshield. It startles me and I shriek like a little mouse.

By the time he stops and we get out, the sun is beginning to crack a few thin streaks of a dismal gray dawn into the new day. The ground is rocky and uneven; the air is so still and dry and cold that I can blow out a stream of frozen breath so far I lose sight of it in the dim light.

I shiver. Tyler takes off his brown corduroy jacket and puts it on over my hoodie. I protest, but he doesn't seem to hear me.

We watch in silence as the slowly rising sun, like the lights coming up on the first act of a play, gradually reveals the wreckage of an old, low-lying farmhouse. When he finally speaks, Tyler's voice is different. Twangier. More country. A little mean. "So, what do you think of the old family estate? Should I have Madison and Paige and the whole gang out?"

"Is this where you grew up?"

"This is where my mom dumped me."

I take his hand. It is dead cold. "We don't have to be here."

"Oh, we have to be here." His hand trembles. He yanks it back, jams it into the pocket of his jeans, nods to a smaller shack beside the bigger one. "That's where they put the *mojados*. The wets."

The building is a converted chicken coop. The gray boards are bowed and popping away from rusted nails. Beside it is the hulk of a windmill. The blades are crumpled and the head is hanging down like a daisy with a broken stem.

I take his arm. "Let's get in the truck. Turn the heat on."

Tyler doesn't move. "The thing I remember most about her is her laugh. She had this smoker's laugh. Shit rattling around in her lungs. Everywhere she went she had her smokes in one hand and a drink in the other. Know what she named me? Bronco. How sorry is that? Someone name a sweet, clean, newborn baby Bronco? Would you even name a dog Bronco? Ditched that sorry name soon as I could."

He lets me lead him away like someone in shock leaving the scene of an accident. At the truck, he fumbles for the keys in his pocket, drops them on the rocky ground. I pick them up. "I'll drive, OK?"

The branches scraping the sides of the truck seem even louder going out. It takes all my concentration and nerve to navigate the big truck over the ravines in the narrow road. Tyler doesn't seem to notice or care that his truck is being destroyed.

Neither one of us speaks for a long time after we emerge and get back on a decent road. I don't know what to say and finally ask, "So that wasn't your mom's place?"

"No. She lived in some piece-of-crap trailer one of her 'boyfriends' gave her. Mighta been my father. Who cares? That was my grand-parents' place."

"Where'd your mom go?"

He shrugs. "My grandparents acted like she was dead. But who knows what that means, since my grandparents thought that any-one who wasn't an android working machine was a waste of good oxy-gen. With them you were either working until you dropped or dead asleep just long enough so you could get back up and work until you dropped again. They had me bucking hay out the back of a flatbed truck by . . . Shit, I couldn't have been more than five. My age. Another little detail nobody bothered to keep track of. I'm going to shift you out of four-wheel."

He reaches down next to my feet, moves the shifter. The growl of the engine softens and the ride smooths out. I want to be back on a big highway with lots of traffic and lots of lights. I blow through a couple of small towns that are not much more than a few boarded-up shops with gas stations at either end.

A truck with wheels the size of satellite dishes zooms past us. Bumper stickers on the back proclaim IF YOU CAN READ THIS, THANK A TEACHER. IF YOU CAN READ THIS IN ENGLISH, THANK A SOLDIER and MY OTHER RIDE IS YOUR MOM.

I reach across the seat and take his hand. Even with the heater on full blast, his fingers are still icy.

"What happened to . . . ?"

"My grandparents? Died, I guess. They weren't never . . ." He drops my hand, splays his fingers in frustration, corrects himself: "They *were* never prosecuted." The mean country twang fades more and more the farther we drive. "County just let them go back home and die."

"What happened? After?"

"CPS put me in this group home. For the first time in my life I was getting fed regular, didn't have to work like a slave. Had toilet paper, soap, sheets on the bed, screens on the windows. And you want to know the really messed-up part? I missed them. I missed those heartless, ignorant peckerwoods. Missed my skank of a mother. I'd hear someone with shit rattling around in their lungs when they laughed and my heart would hurt, I missed her so bad. I woulda gone right back to my grandparents if they'd let me. How fucked up is that?"

"It's what you knew. They were all you ever knew."

"Hey, even a dog learns to keep away from someone whups up on him."

"They whipped you?"

"See? I love it that you even ask that question. Where I come from, you'd be a fool to ask that question." He laughs; it's almost a real laugh. "You'd get the shit kicked out of you for asking such a dumb-ass question."

He looks out the window and speaks only to give me directions. We are back on the highway before I can take a full breath. Farther on, out of nowhere, Tyler asks, "What do you call that kind of ice cream with chocolate, vanilla, and strawberry all in one box?"

"Neopolitan?"

"Yeah, neopolitan. There was this little black kid in the home had a face like that. Regular chocolate skin, pink scar tissue, and white where the color was permanently gone. Sweet kid. Smart too. His mother threw a pan of boiling water in his face."

"Jesus."

"He was my buddy. Idolized me because I gave him my granola bar at breakfast and also knocked the shit out of anyone bothered him. I enjoyed doing both. That's what kind of psycho thug I was. So here's

Neopolitan with his face half melted off, and you know who he cried for at night? His mother. He begged to go back to her. He loved her. He thought she loved him. For real. Neopolitan taught me the most important thing anyone ever taught me: A mother, father, that's random. That doesn't have to be who you are."

I stare out the window but am too distracted to notice the area we're driving through until Martin says, "We're almost there." We wind through the familiar streets that lead into Sycamore Heights' small commercial area.

The parking lot of the tiny grocery store where I'd once bought soy milk and rotisserie chickens is now occupied by a carnival midway assortment of food trailers. A festive street-fair vibe pervades, young and old strolling about eating food off sticks and out of cones.

Martin and I plow through the happy crowd. I run to the first trailer. It has a Dumpster-size pink cupcake perched on top, advertising its product. We cut to the front of the line and peer in. It is manned by a pair of cute hipster girls in black-and-white-striped tights, ruffled skirts, and Chuck Taylors. In the next, Kim Chi Wah Wah: Korean BBQ Tacos, an Asian man sears thin strips of meat while his wife takes orders at the window.

I race next door, where a middle-aged woman pours stripes of crayon colors onto a snowball of fluffy shaved ice. Across the street, we investigate Frankly Speaking: Purveyors of All Things Pork and find a frat-type guy selling hot dogs. Inside the KeBabulous! wagon a Middle Eastern couple skewers chunks of grilled beef and pepper.

I dodge mothers leading packs of children, bob and weave through coveys of tween girls giggling and trading bites, sprint past couples holding hands, studying menus posted on the sides of trailers. We gape into the windows of the final few trailers, breathe in the fragrance of sugar and vanilla that they exhale.

Aubrey is not inside any of them.

I stop in the middle of the closed street while what amounts to a block party eddies around me. A mother and her high school–age daughter, both of them whippet-thin, the kind that would share each other's clothes, pass by, heading for the cupcake trailer.

"Snow Cap or Red Velvet?" the mother asks.

"You get one, I'll get the other, and we'll split," her daughter answers.

I hate them both. Intensely.

Martin plows through the crowd, reaches me. "She's not here."

"Now what?"

Martin guides me away from the mob. "Cam, you haven't eaten all day. I'll grab some food and meet you at that park around the corner on our old street and we'll reconfigure."

Starved, out of ideas, and grateful to him for offering to brave the throng, I agree.

I could find my way to our old street a few blocks away with my eyes closed. The instant I turn onto it, the tumult falls away and I am back in my lost paradise. Our street, lined with tall sycamores so old their crowns have grown together to form a canopy that shades the road, gave the entire development its name. On either side of the road are one- and two-bedroom bungalows built after the war for the vets who came home but didn't use the GI Bill to go to college. Instead, they worked in the ladder factory that used to be nearby or got jobs as plumbers, painters, electricians.

The street is spruced up far beyond what it was the last time I visited several years back. The faded gray asbestos shingles that had covered most of the houses when we lived here have been removed by the new hipster owners and the houses are painted bright, imaginative colors: Periwinkle with lime green and pimiento accents. Mustard with cobalt blue trim. Seeing all the rebellious colors makes my eyes ache. I can almost not look at the tiny duplex where Martin and I lived, where we drank wine at sunset in the backyard, and decorated joke Christmas trees with souvenirs of our happiness. The place where Aubrey was conceived. The new owners have converted it into a single house with one porch and painted it soft lavender with chocolate trim.

I sit in the little park at the end of the street and my heart constricts with a pang of melancholic longing as I imagine how I could have pushed Aubrey in her stroller to this park to meet the children of my friends for playdates. How they all would have grown up together and she'd have been part of a jolly swarm of girls eating cones of pink shaved ice together right now.

Martin arrives, deposits several bags on the table, and we dig in. "Oh, my God," he says after his first bite of a taco piled with Korean barbecue, napa cabbage, cilantro, and tomato. He holds it out to me. "You have got to try this."

The taco is a revelation. "I don't think I'll ever be able to eat a taco without kimchi on it again."

"Finish it," Martin says. "I'm moving on to bachelorette number two." He pulls out a crepe stuffed with a mixture of caramelized onions, goat cheese, roast chicken, and tarragon, splits it, and slides half over to me. It is heavenly.

I find it hard to hate a man who brings you exactly what you didn't even know you craved. Food so good that it is impossible to worry while you eat it. Martin takes a bite of the crepe, puts it down, rolls his eyes back in his head, raises his fists up next to his ears, rotates them, and makes purring, lip-smacking mews of pleasure. The Happy Happy Yum Yum Dance. Aubrey would perform it while sitting in the blue space pod of a high chair if Martin or I spooned some especially tasty blob of mushed something into her mouth.

Exactly one other person on earth carries in his memory this image of Aubrey's moments of immaculate delight.

My phone rings. I grab it and hear the last voice on Earth that I expected to hear.

Tyler changes the radio station; when he hits twangy, old-time country music, he twists the dial hard to get away from it. I want to say something about what he's told me, but I can't think of a comment big enough or wise enough or humane enough. He stops on an oldies station and a band sings about *walking on sunshine.* It is one of the songs Mom and Dori danced to on Thanksgiving.

Tyler's voice is almost normal when he says, "OK, enough of my sad shit."

I turn the radio down before the singer can ask again, *And don't it feel good?* And Tyler goes on.

"Sports were good. Sports saved me. They bused us to school from the home. Since I'd never been in a classroom before and was dumb as a stump—didn't know my letters, numbers, colors, nothing—they just put me in kindergarten. I towered over the other kids. Towered. Which made me feel weird until sports came along a year or so later. And then I ruled. Whatever they had going—baseball, football, basketball—I owned it.

"From day one, I was bigger and faster than any other kid on the field. Being outside? Not having to do chores? Not getting your ass chewed or whaled on? Playing? Just playing? I'd never just played before in my life. And I was warm and clean and getting fed. I was waiting to wake up and find out it was a dream and I'd have to go split kindling or dig postholes."

"So what happened?"

"I got too big. They had an age limit, so after a few years they kicked me out of the home, and the coach at my school, Coach Randall, took me in."

"He adopted you?"

Tyler snorts a laugh. "Not hardly. He knew where I'd come from. No, state paid him. Foster-care deal."

Tyler is silent as he remembers, then shakes his head at the memories. "Coach had three daughters. Youngest was getting ready to go off to college, so he says, 'I always wanted me a boy.' Just exactly like you'd say, 'I always wanted me a cocker spaniel.' No, actually, more like you'd say, 'I always wanted me a hound to hunt.' Because he didn't want any old boy; he wanted a boy who could play football and he'd take all the credit.

"Coach spent a lot of time with me. Why not? I made him look like a genius. He said I was 'coachable.' Gave himself all the credit. Like he'd produced this great player. Bullshit. The day that asshole laid eyes on me I could have given him lessons in the one thing that football is all about: taking punishment.

"I won every game I ever played for him and I was happy doing it. Happy running the bleachers. Happy pushing a training sled back and forth across his backyard. Happy eating pancakes with him and his wife in the morning. Happy eating lasagna with them at night. The only thing he did that was really wrong was he started introducing me as his son. That was wrong. It made me believe that if I worked hard enough, if I won enough games for him . . ."

Tyler won't say what he'd believed, but I know.

"That's what an ignorant piece of white trash I was."

"Don't say that. Don't. I was that way about my dad too. I thought that if I did everything right, he'd come back. I'd have a father. And I had a good life. I wasn't surrounded by monsters like—"

"Aubrey, it's fine. I'm not telling you any of this shit so you'll hate the people I came up with. Or feel sorry for me. Or any of that. I'm only telling you so you'll know. So one person on earth will really know who I am. Then you can decide if you even want to be that person."

"I do. I already know I do."

"You don't, though. You don't know. You can't. See, that's the thing; until that last game, no one could know. This is the first day of my life since I left that shack back there that I can let anyone know. So you don't know. Like you don't know what happened with Coach Randall."

"What? What happened?"

"He took me back to the pound."

"The coach?"

"Yeah. Cute puppy turned into a big, old smelly dog. Hey, here's some shit women never have to deal with: what happens when a boy can look a man straight in the eye."

"You mean . . . ?"

"Yes, literally look him in the eye. It's a caveman thing. No, even farther back than that. More like a wolf pack thing. Coach woke up one morning, I was looking him in the eye, and he could not deal."

"Where was his wife this whole time?"

"Oh, Mrs. Coach? She was pretty much off scrapbooking every shit her daughters ever took. I remember this one time? They all went on a scrapbooking cruise. Yeah. What that all about? You're, like, taking pictures of each other taking pictures so you can come home and put them in an album with a bunch of stickers and stamps around them and remember when you took the picture?

"No, even hiding everything I could about who I really was, I was way too much real life for Mrs. Coach. She had scrapbooking and I was her husband's hobby. So when he came to me with a bunch of bullshit about his wife's migraines and how her doctor ordered her to cut all the stress out of her life or she'd have a stroke, I knew exactly what was happening. I was out of there that night."

"Is that when you came to Parkhaven?"

"Not hardly. Lots of stops before Parkhaven. They sent me to some old cow and her husband who was a long-distance trucker, so I never saw him. They kept kids for the money. Straight up. The more she took in and the less she spent on us, the more she got to keep for herself. She already had seven when I got there. Big woman. Really big. Took her half an hour to get her blubber up and off the broke-down couch she lived on. Like the queen in a hive of termites, she had all us drones bringing her food."

"Ew."

"It wasn't that bad. She left me alone. They put me in this middle school with a fairly kick-ass football team. One practice and I owned the place. Seriously. Coach—Coach Whitaker this time—was wetting his pants, calling to make sure I had all my permission slips signed and a way to get to practice and the games. He ended up driving me himself. Buying me extra food so I'd 'stay strong.' "

"How long were you there?"

"Few years."

"Tyler, how old are you?"

"Honestly? I don't know exactly."

"Didn't you need a birth certificate to start school?"

"See? I love the way you think. Way my grandparents tell it, my mom had me in a gas station. Dried me off with the hand dryer, then went out and got high. Not exactly a prime record-keeping situation."

I think of how natural it was when Tyler called the kid who'd interviewed him "son." Tyler seems older because he is older. And college? I also start to understand why he doesn't want to talk about college. I think of him always saying, when we're in a new restaurant like last night and the waitress hands him a menu, "I'll have what she's having." I think about him never texting. About how when we do his homework together he always arranges it so that he never has to read. I know he can read, just probably not well enough for college.

"Have I completely freaked you out?"

"No, Tyler, I'm . . ." What? Every word I think of—honored? grateful? humbled?—they all sound like fake, college-application-essay words.

I am silent for too long and Tyler jumps in. "Don't stress. That was weird. Too weird. Sorry. I shouldn't have . . . Just shouldn't have. Ridiculous, huh?" He pretends it is all a joke and says in this fake game-show-announcer voice, "A. J. Lightsey, come on down! You signed on for the golden-boy, football-hero boyfriend, and surprise! Guess what? You've won a redneck hick who doesn't know who his father is and whose mom is either dead or a meth whore!"

"No, Tyler, that's not it at all. . . ." I have too much to say to say anything.

Tyler apologizes again, and the silence stretches out until it is broken when I run over a few lane markers and some cans clatter around the bed of the truck.

"I should have cleaned those empties out." The Tyler of just a few moments ago has disappeared. He sounds confident again, in command. The perfect boy to be a star quarterback. He sounds the way he did when we first met. The way he always does at school when he is hiding who he really is, and I know that this will be the way he will speak to me from now on. If he ever speaks to me again.

On the highway ahead, a giant red arrow above a sign that reads **SINGLES $19.95. DOUBLES $21.95**, points to a few cabins tucked back into the woods. I turn off into the parking lot, pull up to the office, switch off the engine. Before I get out, I tell Tyler, "I never wanted a golden-boy, football-hero boyfriend. I wanted you. Just you."

Who was that?" Martin asks the instant I hang up without having said a word.

"Tyler." The one-sided conversation was over so fast, I'm not certain it really happened. "He was whispering. He told me not to worry and that he's going to get Aubrey to call as soon as he can. Probably be a couple of hours at the earliest, though."

Martin lifts his eyebrows, stands, asks, "Shaved ice or cupcake? We've obviously got time for dessert now."

I put my order in for a cupcake, watch him lope away, and do not let myself remember other times at this park.

"Hey, Danielle!" A mother yelling to her friend as she enters the park catches my attention. She is carrying an infant hidden in a padded sling. A long-legged child of about four dressed in a POTTY LIKE A ROCK STAR T-shirt and tiny black skinny jeans is hiked up on her hip. Another mom and her daughter, also around four, wave to the newcomers from the swings.

The mother lugging two children lumbers toward her friend and I recall reading about how much advocates of attachment parenting hate strollers. The latest thinking in that group is that the good mother would not think of exiling her child to such a conveyance.

The women release the older children and they streak off to the swings while their moms settle in on a bench, talking like words are oxygen and they are drowning. The mother with the sling shifts the infant hidden within its padded folds, opens her blouse, and lets the baby nurse. This scene would be impossible to imagine in Parkhaven, where, if a mother *does* dare to breast-feed in public, there are dirty looks, followed by letters to the editor about public indecency, and then an effort to get a law passed to ban such "displays."

"You really love it here, don't you?" Martin places a sinful mound of a cupcake on the table in front of me. Dark chocolate. My favorite. He tips his head to the side to catch a sunset-colored drop melting off the side of his cone of shaved ice, asks, "Did you ever think of moving back?"

I study his face to see if he is being willfully obtuse. "Oh, no, never. It was so much more fun being a single mother in a place where that guaranteed social pariah–hood."

"I knew that. Stupid question. Sorry."

"And that helps me how, your apology?"

He stops slurping on the fluffed ice and stares at me, his lips tinted orange. "It doesn't. I just wanted you to know that I am sorry."

Then he goes directly back to slurping slurps of such blithe obliviousness that I demand, "What? You think you apologize and sixteen years disappear? Martin, you're not some televangelist who blubbers on TV and tells everyone how sorry he is for sleeping with whores and Boy Scouts and Shetland ponies and all is forgiven."

"I didn't ever think I was. And I didn't realize you knew about the ponies."

Without a word, Martin hands me the shaved ice and I slide the cupcake toward him. We always did this, shared bites. *You get one, I'll get the other, and we'll split.*

He holds the cupcake up, asking if I want the rest. I shake my head, he finishes it, and says, "Move back to Sycamore Heights."

"Right." The shaved ice is cold and sweet.

"No, seriously."

I gasp at the condescension of his ridiculous oversimplification; he is as bad as Dori.

"Why not? No doubt you're underwater in Parkhaven. You either take some lowball offer on the house or just mail the keys back to the bank. Jingle mail. Happens all the time now. Then move. There's enough from the car sale—"

"Car *theft*. Yeah, that's a great idea. Next traces that money back to me—"

"Next will never come after you. Or me. Or Aubrey. I have guaranteed that." He speaks with Next's laser-lock intensity. "Nobody as high up as me has ever defected. I've counseled every major celebrity in their stable. They know that the papers and talk shows will be lining up to interview me if I ever go public. I could seriously mess with them and half a dozen of the biggest careers in Hollywood. They will never risk that. Never."

"Okay, let's just say that that's true. I now have a college fund to replace in case you haven't noticed."

He leans forward, excited, hooked on his own idea. "Right, right, sure. But try this: You give the house back and, since the trust is now gone, you have nothing on the books and the financial aid rolls in. You rent in Sycamore Heights or buy the cheapest place you can get into."

"It's a teensy, tiny bit more complicated than that."

"Cam, I know your thoughts on my work, but this is a big part of what I was doing for all those years. Helping people visualize what they want, and then actualizing that. I've strategized entire Oscar-winning careers."

" 'Oscar-winning careers.' " I snort. "Yeah, that's what I need help with."

Martin ignores my sneering. "What you want is insanely easy. And, P.S., the housing bubble has burst, so we could not be having this discussion at a better time. Especially since you're buying, not selling.

"Look." He directs my attention to the For Sale sign in front of a house down the street. "They've still got the asbestos siding on it. You think those owners aren't scared? Wouldn't take a lowball offer? Seriously, Camille, if it would make you happy, you could have that house. Just go with me for a moment and visualize yourself back here. Beats worrying about a situation we can do absolutely nothing about at the moment, doesn't it? I mean, all we can do now is wait for Aubrey to call."

Though I intend to resist, a vision of me in the neighborhood I never should have left, where I should have raised Aubrey, where Martin and I were happy, fills my head. All these years, it was the dream I had left behind. The dream I hadn't even really analyzed because it was so impossible. But now, sitting here with the hot cash in my shaved ice–chilled hands, I consider the idea. The "good school" concerns that had imprisoned me in Parkhaven are over. I could actually get many more clients in the city than in Parkhaven. And it's not as if I'd have many emotional connections to uproot.

A realization hits me: I could do it. I could actually move.

For a motel cabin by the side of the highway, the room isn't horrible. The windows rattle when an eighteen-wheeler passes, the carpet is done in a pattern like pepperoni pizza, and the paintings—a mill on a stream, a pelican in front of a beach sunset—are bolted to the wall. But it is clean and there are no gross smells.

Tyler goes in. I hesitate at the door and wonder what I have done. He takes my hand, rubs it between his. "You sure about this?"

No.

"You can change your mind."

I step in and shut the door behind us. Tyler closes the curtains, blocking the view of the giant red arrow sign outside that is shooting right at us, and the room gets dark. He adjusts the thermostat on the wall heater until it switches on and the coils heat up and glow orange like a fireplace.

We stand in front of it without touching. Tyler puts his arms out. I look at his fingers, knowing now that, like his teeth, his hands were ruined when he was very young.

He opens his jacket and rolls me into it so that I am between him and the heater. He says, "Heat sandwich."

The coils ping in the silence. I wish I had a week, a month, to figure out what to say. But I don't, so I say the first stupid thing that pops into my head: "I think you're brave."

"Brave? What's brave about being a complete and total fraud? About never, not for one day, not to one person, telling the truth about who you really are?"

I tilt away so that I can look up into his face. "That is so wrong. Think about all the guys who hang out at Paige's. Cody. Colt. All of them. They got it all, the whole eighteen-course banquet handed to them on a platter. All they had to do was pick up a silver spoon and start eating. You, you . . ." I try to figure out how to say this. "It's like you had to grow the wheat and harvest it and grind it and bake it into bread. Like you had to earn your place at the table by building the whole damn table."

"Did I grow the trees?"

Tyler's joking, but I'm serious when I answer, "You absolutely grew the trees."

"Did I chop them down and mill them?"

"Yes! You chopped them down and milled them and set the table and . . . everything, Tyler. Everything most kids get handed, all the stuff parents are supposed to do, you had to do it all yourself."

"Thanks, A.J. That's sweet of you to say."

"Tyler, no. It's not sweet. I'm not saying this right, but, listen, could a single one of those guys—Cody, Colt, any of them—could they have survived in the world you came from? Could they have made it through a single day with your grandfather? With the Termite Queen?"

A reluctant smile creeps over his face as he imagines one of the guys in flip-flops and Oakley sunglasses bucking bales of hay off the back of a flatbed.

"Is anything you've ever done on the football field a lie?"

"You mean, aside from the fact that I stopped giving a shit about it years ago?"

"Which makes what you did even more amazing."

"Hot," he says, stepping away from the wall heater. He tosses his jacket over a chair, tugs off his boots, sprawls out on the bed, pats his right shoulder. "Come here. Right here."

I am woozy with wanting to lie down next to him, but still have to say, "I just want you to understand how much this means to me, your telling me the truth about yourself."

"There's more," he says. "But I've been good long enough." He sits up, takes my hand, pulls me down onto his chest.

I've been with two guys before—Damon Shapiro, a trumpet player and fellow counselor at band camp, and Raj Rodke, the really handsome, really spoiled son of two doctors from India. With both of them, sex had been something I was supposed to like. The "normal, healthy human need" my mom was always talking about. Also I was supposed to know what to do. With Damon and Raj, I felt like I was getting graded and not passing. Those boys had learned everything they knew from watching porn on the Internet. So, in their heads, the girl was supposed to be hairless as a newt, with beach-ball tits bouncing up and down, groaning and begging for harder, faster.

With Tyler, it is like being at the quarry. We enter suspended animation together. It is clear that he has had a lot of practice with real human girls. He knows what bodies can do and how to make them do it so well that that part seems to happen all on its own. There aren't any words like "Less teeth." He isn't imagining that I am a Japanese girl in pigtails and knee socks down on her hands and knees. He is not imagining anyone except me.

After the second time, he buries his head in my neck and, for a moment, I think that he is crying. Before I can be sure, though, his mouth is on my neck and I can't tell if the wetness is his tongue or tears. But I know that he is sad and will always be sad. I wrap him in my arms and kiss the top of his head and say what my mother always said. I say that it is all right, that everything will be fine.

I don't know when we fall asleep or how much later it is when I wake up. Tyler is heading to the bathroom when I open my eyes. There is a hitch when he walks, a bounce from the arches of his feet that swings upward to his broad shoulders. He is the only person I've ever seen who looks better, more relaxed, without clothes.

He pees with the door open. For a boy with nothing but secrets in his past, he has none in the present. He pushes open a curtain on the small window beside the toilet.

"Oh, shit, Aubrey Julie, you have got to see this. Close your eyes! Close your eyes!" He rushes back into the room, makes me shut my eyes, then I hear the scrape of rings rattling along the metal rod as he opens the curtains.

"OK, you can open them now."

I do and there is so much beauty framed within the cheap aluminum sides of the motel window that I gasp. The giant red arrow, lighted now and blinking, shoots through a sky that vibrates with colors shimmering and bouncing like the aurora borealis. Compared to this every other sunset I've ever seen seems painted on. These colors—swimming-pool aqua, pomegranate ruby, neon green—go all the way through like stained glass.

"Do you like the sunset I ordered for you?" Tyler stands to the side of the window, the stained-glass colors reflecting across his face and chest.

"I love it. I want to swim in it." I reach up and sweep my arms out as if I could breaststroke into the pools of colored light.

He jumps back into bed. It creaks and rattles when he lands. I rest my head on his chest and we watch the colors fade to deep, shadowy tones that make the room feel snug. Like we are alone together in a submarine on the bottom of the ocean with a view of a world that has been hidden from me until this moment.

I magine that that house is yours," Martin prompts, excited, genuinely excited about making me happy. "What colors would you
paint that house?"

I study the gray siding and imagine the colors I would choose. A
few seconds later, I freeze, unable to conjure up any combination
fantastic enough to enter into the bohemian competition playing
out up and down the street. I'd need more time, a *lot* more time, to
pick the palette that would, essentially, express to the world who I
am. I am not ready for that level of public declaration.

"Martin, seriously, it's not that simple. I wanted to be in Sycamore
Heights when Aubrey was little."

"Why?"

"Why? Why do you think?" I point to the two women chatting
next to the swings while their children play. My voice wobbles when
I express the irretrievable. "I could have been part of a community.
I could have been around people, women, mothers I had something
in common with. Mothers who felt the same way I did."

The instant I put my longing into words, I see myself in the circle
of my old Sycamore Heights friends, surrounded by the comforting
animal smell of users of crystal deodorant, their hair in spikes,
dreadlocks, the rockabilly girls in cowboy shirts with the sleeves torn
off, interesting shoes, Doc Martens, Converse high tops, the kind of
shoes no one in Parkhaven ever wears, all of us nursing infants
wrapped in organic cotton receiving blankets, suckling babies in tie-
dyed onesies, breast-feeding sturdy toddlers. I'd have been part of a
milk sisterhood, a circle of constant, supportive friends, a happy
tribe as we watched our children, who were also the closest of
friends, grow up together.

I brace myself for Martin to tell me how this is possible. I can't
wait to ask him how, precisely, with all his Next superpowers, he will
travel through time and give me back the childhood Aubrey should
have had.

I turn away and notice that the nursing mother has finished feeding her infant. She buttons her blouse and her "baby" sits up. As he

clambers from the sling, I see that this child has to be close to three years old. The instant he climbs down, the older child scales his mother. Mom never stops talking to her friend as she sweeps the sling aside and lets the four-year-old in the POTTY LIKE A ROCK STAR T-shirt plug in.

This tableau of perfect Sycamore Heights motherhood causes me to recall all the random communications—phone calls, e-mails—I'd had with my amigas over the years since I left the 'hood.

That loose group of former friends had morphed into a Sycamore Heights Listserv that eventually evolved into a Facebook page. By the time chats with my old mom friends had faded into mass postings, maybe only those with grievances were writing. But at some point it seemed that they all had divided up into teams and staked out positions on pacifiers, circumcision, sugar, war toys, the family bed, cloth diapers, television, strollers. Women who had never competed in their lives, whose last sport had been Red Rover, chose sides. Stands were taken with an inbred Hatfield/McCoy blood feud intensity. Ultimately, even the sacred of sacreds, breast-feeding, became a hot button when a new team emerged proclaiming that nursing was a deeply antifeminist act, a plot to keep women trapped at home.

Friendships were cremated in the flame wars that erupted around that one.

I replay Aubrey's life now if we had lived here and wonder how my daughter with her early, inexplicable passion for all things pink and princess would have done in this hothouse of political correctness. Even in Parkhaven, Dori had chided me about raising a little Barbie doll.

Dori, my fellow exile. For the first time, now that it is an actual possibility, I imagine myself living in this neighborhood, a neighborhood filled with Dori clones. A neighborhood where—judging from recent postings that I'd not taken seriously until this moment—if you weren't tattooed up like the Illustrated Man and blogging about the many ways your husband/lover/whoever was begging you for anal sex, you would probably be far weirder than a little armpit-hair ranching had made me in Parkhaven.

Though I am damned if I will reveal it to Martin, I suddenly feel more like an exile than ever. A homesick exile from some Middle Eastern country who has just recalled that her lost paradise was run by the Taliban. I don't know what Martin reads in my face, but he says, "You're a true rebel, Camille."

Camille. Again, he summons up the self I had to leave behind.

"It's what I loved about you. You always knew exactly who you were and what you wanted."

"You're kidding, right?"

Martin, genuinely caught off guard, blinks. "Cam, don't you remember how Amy and Gianna and that whole Sycamore Heights group used to call you Cammando?"

"They made up nicknames for everyone."

"Yeah. Nicknames that stuck because they were so perfect."

"Me? Cammando?"

"Absolutely. How could you forget that? You made up your mind what you wanted and you went after it."

"I did?"

"Sure. A baby. Good schools. Getting certified. You were the *wo-man* with a plan."

"We made those decisions together."

"Back then? Make a decision? That was my Downfall."

Downfall. A tiny pinprick to the brain. Next worms its way in by giving free sessions with their Breathalyzer contraption in which they identify the mark's "Downfall," the thing that's wrong with the person's life, then promise to cure it.

"Not you, though," he continues. "Knowing who you were was always such a given to you. You were my anchor and I held on as long as I could."

"Held on? Martin, what was you setting us up in Parkhaven except you letting go? You planting me someplace where you could leave me behind?"

"Real estate would never have changed what happened to us. What I had to do."

" 'Had to do'?" I don't bother restraining the acid in my tone. I put hydrochloric quotation marks around his words.

"Okay, should the name of this production be *Let's Help Our Daughter* or should it be *All the Ways Martin Fucked Cam Over*?"

"I'm voting for *Martin Could Be the Biggest Asshole in the Universe*." Going beyond sarcasm straight to out-and-out insult is delicious, like wriggling out of a pair of Spanx. Martin seems to take no notice. He's more Zen than Zen Mama. I can see now why Aubrey hated my mask of implacable calm.

"I know that you, that we, want her to go to college, but why? What is our root desire for her?"

"Oh, gosh, I don't know. Maybe that she won't end up scrubbing out toilets at Applebee's. Is that a good 'root desire'?"

"Lot of baristas with college degrees. Probably even a few toilet scrubbers. No, what is your dream for her?"

I almost say "adventures," but remember how Aubrey chastised me for that and turn the question on him: "What's yours?"

Without hesitating, Martin says, "I hope she will have what we ha . . . had."

The drag before he says "had" was Martin catching himself almost saying "have." That is Martin almost letting it slip that I am as changeable a fabric for him as he is for me. That within my double-faceted weave the iridescent person I was when we first met will always wait, will always sparkle. That is when I realize that I have the same gift he does: We can give each other back our youth. This is the crack cocaine that Dori was talking about, and I am stunned to realize that Martin might be smoking it too.

My phone rings. I check it, tell Martin, "It's her."

Martin tips his head back and slaps his hand on his chest with relief, then steps away from the table, out of earshot.

"Aubrey?"

"I'm fine. Don't worry. I'm sorry I couldn't call. But I'm fine so—"

"You are not fine! You stole your college money."

"That was my money."

I am livid at her unapologetic entitlement. "That money was not yours. That money was for college."

"It was for my future."

"A future that you have allowed that . . . that . . ." No reason to hold back anymore. "That slimy jerkwad creep to steal."

"You do not know the first thing about Tyler. He is not who you think he is."

"So Coach Hines told us."

"Coach Hines? *He's* the jerkwad. Mom, you really, seriously don't know what you're talking about."

"So tell me."

"I can't right now, but Tyler did not steal anything. This was completely my idea. I had to talk him into it. Renting a trailer this summer was my idea. We made money and learned how to run a business. Then, later, we learned how to cook real food."

Those odors I'd smelled on her. I was right.

"A roach coach! That is what you threw all of your college money away on!"

"We also had to pay a year's lease on the space in advance to negotiate a good price. We had to buy all our equipment. We had to put down utility deposits. It's expensive to open a business."

"Business? A freaking roach coach is not a business."

"See? Just the way you keep saying that. Roach coach. Roach coach. Roach coach. That shows that you do not know what you're talking about."

I am almost too mad to think about the heavenly crepe with caramelized onions and chicken that I just ate. Or the mind-expanding tacos. Or the throngs of people shoving big dollars through small windows. I am certainly nowhere close to admitting, even to myself, that I don't know what I'm talking about.

I start to speak, but Aubrey cuts me off. "That is exactly why I could never have told you about the plan. You would never have let me do this. You would have forced me go to Peninsula."

"It didn't have to be Peninsula. Aubrey, you never even talked to me about any of this. Told me how you felt."

"What was the point? So you could make fun of it like you've always made fun of the only places where I remotely fit in?"

"I have never made fun of—"

"Band! Attendance office! The lunch wagon! Shit, you and Dori made fun of me for keeping my room neat."

"For God's sake, Aubrey, I made a couple of lame jokes about your band hat."

"I'm sorry if I've been a big disappointment and that I'm not off singing in cathedrals or mapping the human genome or any of those other things you think I should be doing. I'm sorry that it turns out that this is what I'm good at. What I like."

"You don't know what you like. That's what college is for."

"For a lot of kids, maybe most, yeah. For me, if I had let you force me into going to Peninsula—which you somehow would have if I'd started talking to you about it—I would have hated it and flunked out and that money would be gone and I would have nothing."

It's disconcerting to hear Aubrey talk about me as some kind of unstoppable force in her life when it has been over a year since she even seemed able to hear me.

"This is so not what I had in mind for you. You do realize that, if I made this a legal matter, the law would be on my side."

Then, with an unsettling calm, she says, "Yeah, it probably would."

Maybe she'd take my threat more to heart if I'd actually called the police that first time she disappeared. Or maybe we'd have just devolved into a *Jerry Springer*–ready mother-daughter duo radiating hatred at each other.

I read once that it takes fourteen miles for an oil tanker to change course. The same change for mothers and daughters must take a nearly equal number of years. But in all those miles and years there does come one precise moment, one discrete point in an infinite vastness, when you start heading in an entirely new direction. I know that, for better or for worse, Aubrey and I have hit that moment when instead of arguing with me, fighting to convince me to accept what she wants, she states in a steady, even way that doesn't ask for my permission or seem ready to bristle when I don't offer it, "Mom, I have to go. We have to get ready for the opening."

"Where, Aubrey? Tell me where you are. I need to see you. Make sure you're all right."

"I'd really rather not say. I'll invite you when we've got the kinks smoothed out. But I'm too nervous now and you take my strength away. I have to go. Sorry."

She hangs up. Before I even have a chance to be hurt by Aubrey telling me I take her strength away, the phone rings again.

"Mrs. Lightsey." It's Tyler. He's whispering. "Come to Town Square. But, you know, just for a look. Don't let her see you, okay?"

"Thank you, Tyler."

"I know that the money was for college. Not what we used it for. We're going to pay you back. With interest."

I'm not sure why, at that moment, I look over at Martin, who has wandered off and is studying our old house and the cartoon-colored bungalows around it. Probably because of treacherous, atavistic brain wiring of the sort that made cavewomen look to their mates, the upper-body-strength ones, when a saber-toothed tiger approached, I think of him working Coach Hines and Randy. Whatever the reason, I'm strangely confident when I say, "Oh, there is no question about that, Tyler Moldenhauer. You will pay back every single cent."

A s the sunset fades and the sky goes black, I flip over onto my stomach, prop my head on my hands like a third grader at story time, and ask Tyler to tell me, one more time, my favorite bedtime story. The one that answers the question, "Why me?"

"You're beautiful, you're smart, and you have a soul."

"Madison is beautiful, and she got into Duke."

"Right. And the soul part?"

We laugh. We are pretty much laughing at everything.

"I also like that you never wore brand names."

"But I did. I started wearing brand names for you."

"Yeah, I noticed those Nike shorts and I liked that too. That's hard work, fitting in. I knew you were doing it for me."

"How did you know that?" I play-slap at him like I used to when it was the only way I had to touch him.

"I knew. Plus you totally had the booty for them."

"Really?"

"Oh. Really."

He slides his hand down and pats my butt. I guess I have to thank Shupe and all that marching for something, because my butt is as springy as a bag of Gummi Bears. He strokes my hair; his fingers catch it, pull it into a fan, then let it fall slowly.

"What did you mean when you said that you wanted it to be different with us?"

"Different in every way."

The rumble as he answers, my chest against his, makes me think of the girl I was with my head against his heart that first time and how long ago that seems. A lifetime ago.

"Different in the important ways."

"But how? Different from what?"

"You do not want to hear any more of Tyler Moldenhauer's loser redneck stories."

"Don't say that. Don't talk about yourself like that."

The wall heater clicks as it switches on. Out on the highway a car passes with a stereo playing so loud the bass pulses through us. "You know those vampire books that all the girls are reading now?"

"Oh, yeah, right. *Twilight*? Or something like that."

"That's how I always felt. I felt like a vampire."

"You want to drink my blood," I joke, tilting my head to offer my neck to Tyler, wanting his mouth there.

"Well, that goes without saying. But it's the other part. That the vampires have lived forever and they're older than everyone else and will always be older. That's how I always felt. I mean, I was older. But it was more than that. I always had to pretend to be ignorant. Especially about girls."

"Girls? You were pretending about girls? God, you're a good pretender."

He traps me in his arms, rolls over on top of me, his hair making a curtain that encloses both of us, moves against my crotch so that I can feel him. "Yeah, I may have to start pretending again right now."

I brush his hair back from his face and hook it behind his ears. Him talking about us together is as good as sex. Better. "No, really, tell me. About vampires. About us being different."

He flops back onto the pillow. "You know, all that locker-room shit that starts, like, in grade school or something?"

"Uh, not really."

"At first, it's just guys bragging or lying about touching some girl's tit, scoring a hand job. Shit like that. But it made me feel about a thousand years old. I always wished I could be like them, wanting sex so much, wanting to touch a girl, just touch one, but you were so scared that you had to either lie or laugh about it with a bunch of dumb a-holes even more clueless than you were."

"But you weren't."

"Clueless? Way I grew up? Foster care? Ah, no. Jesus, hand jobs? I blew past hand jobs in kindergarten. Those group homes they toss kids into?" He makes a face, starts to say something, stops. "Someone should go to prison just for what they let happen there; forget the shit they personally do themselves."

"What? What did they do to you?" I think about things I'd heard on the news. About the things that happen to kids in foster care. I think about Tyler as a little boy with no one watching out for him.

He studies me, makes a decision. "No, not that part. I don't want you to ever know that part. Being with you. Like how we were at the quarry? It's like none of that ever happened. It's like everything was the way it was supposed to be. Like I was a regular kid who'd had a mom who told him if he wasn't home at this exact time she'd blister his behind for him if he was two minutes late. Then he'd go home and there'd be sheets on the bed and she'd hold up two things for dinner and ask him if he wanted chicken pot pie or steak fingers. And he'd pick the steak fingers. Then she'd make him eat peas with it. Help him with his spelling words. Make him turn the TV off, brush his teeth. All that shit. All of it."

"I'll make you eat peas."

"I knew that you would."

"Really? How did you know?"

"I just knew. Right from the beginning I knew."

Town Square is Parkhaven's cheesy attempt at a downtown. The last time I visited here was almost ten years ago. Back then it had been an empty block with a few saplings no one had even bothered to remove the nursery tags from, surrounded on three sides by vacant stores abandoned after the tourists that they'd planned to sell fudge, T-shirts, and wind chimes to failed to materialize. There was a swing, but Aubrey and I were always alone playing on it and that had depressed me so much that I made a point of avoiding Town Square. A fact that Aubrey was well aware of.

As Martin and I approach, it is clear that Town Square is not quite so dire any longer. It certainly isn't deserted. Signs of life abound. The scrubby trees have grown into broad-leafed oaks shading the park where a pack of boys in droopy shorts and thick-soled tennis shoes perform skateboard tricks on the sidewalks. Moms sit around on benches while their offspring romp on safety-engineered play equipment. Businesses have opened on the streets around the park: a card shop, a coffee shop with a display case of cookies and muffins in the window, an antique store, a Thai restaurant, a shop advertising custom tilework, and a clothes store with a rack of summer dresses marked for clearance displayed on the sidewalk.

The block at the far end of the park is still vacant except for an overgrowth of weeds and one single, solitary vintage Airstream trailer. Even shaded by the tall oaks, the polished aluminum pill bug's mirror finish shines like a huge, segmented silver bead. In spite of the new life around Town Square, the trailer is still too shiny, too hip for Parkhaven. A Grand Opening banner flaps bravely above the trailer. A few twinkle lights twined over the trailer's humped arc try for a festive touch. After the genuine gaiety of the street-fair atmosphere in Sycamore Heights, they seem forced and unconvincing.

We park out of sight and sneak in on foot for a closer look. Never taking his eyes off the trailer, Martin points to our right like the leader of a reconnaissance patrol silently signaling to his men, and we tack off at an angle that will keep us out of Aubrey's sight lines.

We hide behind the racks of sale items outside the clothes store for a long time while Martin watches a form that I know to be Aubrey, moving about inside the trailer. Within the shiny frame of the silver window she moves with efficient grace, doing things I never taught her to do, off on a field trip I never signed a permission slip for.

Martin is mesmerized, grinning as he watches his daughter for the first time in sixteen years. He doesn't seem to notice that there is no one, not one single customer, outside the trailer.

snuggle up next to Tyler and we watch the last wisps of the sunset like a happy old couple tuning in their favorite show. Finally, the darkness outside pulls us from our secret underwater world, back to the surface, back into the room. That and Tyler's stomach growling.

I switch on the bedside lamp. Tyler slugs his gut as if to knock the growl out. But it just keeps growling. "OK, Aubrey Jean, two problems. We haven't eaten since last night, and you have to call your mom. I'm gonna go out and solve the first one."

He gets out of bed. I notice his crotch and say, "I can't believe I ever thought you were gay."

He looks down at himself, laughs. "What do you think now?"

"Not. Not gay. I also thought you might be a secret Christian with an abstinence pledge."

"All true. I am a secret gay Christian." He pulls his jeans on.

"My other theory was that you might want me to spank you or put on an animal costume."

"Girl, you are a freak." He grabs his keys off the nightstand and grips them between his lips. They jingle as he hops from one foot to the other, tugging on his boots. Not bothering with a shirt, he throws on his jacket, points to me as he opens the door. "Call your mom."

"She'll just scream and tell me I have to come home."

He points again and gives me a stern look, the way a strict father would. I hold up my phone in surrender.

"Call her. Then get out the hairbrush and antlers and be ready for me when I get back."

After he leaves, I sit on the bed hugging my knees for a long time. My lips are tender, sore and soft from being kissed. My hair smells like him and like the smell we made together. When I shower, I wish I could save every drop of water that streams away. That I could distill it and bottle the essence to have forever.

Then I call my mom.

Tyler comes back holding a red-and-white pizza box with drinks in thirty-two-ounce cups and a bouquet of flowers balanced on top. He gives me the flowers. They are your average grocery-store bouquet, chrysanthemums, carnations dyed blue, leathery ferns. They are more beautiful than the aurora borealis sunset.

He holds the box out to me like a snooty waiter as he kicks the door closed with his foot. "Mademoiselle ordered the Grease and Dough Lovers Special." He is happier than I've ever seen him. Bringing me pizza, taking care of me, makes him happy.

He notices my face. "What's wrong?"

I put my nose next to a droopy daisy and pretend that it has a smell. "My mom."

He puts the box and drinks down. "What?"

"I think she's serious. If I don't come home, she's seriously going to call the cops."

"Shit. I thought we'd get to sleep together tonight. You know, sleep."

"Yeah, me too. I guess we'd better leave. This would mess up your scholarships, wouldn't it? Scare off the recruiters if they hear?"

Tyler snorts and smiles with one side of his mouth. "Yeah, I'm really worried about recruiters and scholarships."

"You don't care?"

"Me?" He taps his chest, looks behind himself, acts like I'm talking to someone else. "A.J., I told you, I am done. So this? Going back? This is totally your decision. But I like that your mom's freaked out and ready to call the cops. She's protecting you. That's the way it's supposed to be."

"Can you eat and drive?"

"Can't hardly digest without a steering wheel in my hand."

I slide my legs out from under the covers. My feet touching the dirty carpet brings me back to earth and I sag. Thinking of returning to Parkhaven, to school, to my mom makes me more tired than I have ever been in my life.

"We'll have other nights together. We'll have years together."

"We will?"

"We will." Tyler takes my hands, hauls me to my feet. "Now show me some hustle, Lightsey!"

Instead, I put my arms around his neck, say, "Tyler Bronco Moldenhauer, I love you."

Tyler puts his hands on either side of my face. "Aubrey Jade Lightsey, I love you."

"You know my name."

"I knew your name before you were born."

It is cheesy. But sometimes cheesy can be true.

Without taking his eyes off Aubrey, Martin tells me, "She moves like you. Graceful and determined. Knows exactly what she's doing."

Though I can't conjure up any such moments of certainty, I have accepted that, somehow, Martin and Aubrey believe that I always knew what I wanted and was implacable in getting it. "She has your eyes."

"I thought she might. From the Facebook photos. Everything else is you, though. Thank God."

"She'd love to meet you." I point to the trailer. "There's no one there."

"No. This isn't the right time for that. This is her time. Can we stay here for a while longer? Just watch her?"

"Sure, Martin. Of course."

We spy on them from our hidden spot for a long time until Martin says, "Be right back," and ducks into the clothing store behind us. I assume he's going to search out a restroom, but through the store window I watch him charm the owner into letting him use her computer.

On the square, the businesses all around close. One by one, the lights in the card store, the tile store, the coffee shop go out; the owners emerge and stroll down the block to line up and buy dinner from the newcomers to Parkhaven Square. They're obviously a tight group. They chat amiably, joke with one another as they carry their food to the tables chained to the tall oaks, then eat and visit as the sun sets and the day starts to cool.

Martin is back by my side when Aubrey opens the trailer's door. As she stoops through the low doorway and puts her foot onto the metal step, her new neighbors, the other business owners, hold up their cups and the paper trays of the food Aubrey made, and cheer her. Tyler hangs back at the open doorway, letting Aubrey have her moment.

Martin whispers to me as if Aubrey were near enough to hear, "This area, very good location. Very underserved. Ripe for exactly what she's doing."

All I can think is that I'm watching a thirty-thousand-dollar party.

"Can you believe she did this all by herself? She's so intrepid, isn't she?"

"I still haven't gotten past the lying and fraud."

"We'll deal with that."

I don't know how I feel about him saying "we," but I don't comment, and Martin never stops gazing at his daughter.

A pair of young men, one wearing a fedora, both in short-sleeved Western shirts, hurries past us, heading toward the trailer. They stare into iPhones as if they were holding Geiger counters that will lead them to the places that are hot.

"I knew it," Martin says. "I knew that the foodies would be all over this."

One of the young men pauses to read the name off a street sign, then works his thumbs, checking the spelling of the street as he enters that information.

Martin nods gleefully at the busy thumbs. "Let the Tweets begin."

I point a finger behind me at the clothing store computer he had borrowed earlier. "Did you . . . ?"

"Yep. Got the word out. The kids' complete lack of business savvy actually works in their favor with the cognoscenti. Foodies live for a discovery like this."

The kids. He called them "the kids."

He was right. More clumps arrive. They're mostly young with interesting haircuts, all of them eager, filled with purpose. Like shoppers on Black Friday, rushing to get a cut-rate laptop, they hurry to the order window, eat their food, discuss, trade bites, begin texting. A little while later, more clumps arrive.

We keep up our stakeout as it grows dark and the twinkle lights really do seem festive shining down on tables full of customers. After each new surge, Tyler comes out and wipes some menu item off the dry-erase board that we are too far away to read.

"Oh, that is fantastic," Martin says. "They're running out of food."

"That's good? Seems like poor planning to me."

"No, it's really good. Foodies love scarce and hard-to-get only slightly more than they love exotic. Hey, look, they're taking menus with them."

It's true; almost everyone grabs a menu from the rack outside the order window. When a couple hustles past us—both of them in thick, black, dorky-chic glasses—Martin asks if he could have one of the menus they've taken.

"It's my daughter's place," he explains. "But we don't want to intrude on her big night."

The young woman hands him a menu, tells him that the food is "surprisingly imaginative" and that they're coming back. "Soon."

Martin and I read the menu together. At the top of the sheet is the name "FalaFellows."

"FalaFellows?" I say out loud.

I read and reread the menu my daughter has created. In addition to daily specials like coffee-braised brisket and chicken and dumplings, their mainstay is falafel, a salad with blood oranges, and mint tea.

"What a hodgepodge," I conclude. "They might get a few first-night curiosity seekers, but all the people around here really want is burgers."

"Cam, don't you see?" Martin stares at me both amazed and exasperated. "Don't you get it?"

"Get what?"

"Those are the foods we ate in North Africa."

"Well, yeah. North African food and then a random assortment of other things."

Flabbergasted, he says, "Camille, our daughter is making the foods we ate when we fell in love."

The aromas of cumin, garlic, onion, cilantro, and chickpeas overtake me, overtake my anger and disappointment. For a long time I watch Aubrey moving inside the trailer, lit up like an actress onstage, and I experiment with this feeling of being offstage, of not having the leading role in her life. It hurts. College must have been invented to ease parents' pain, an institution devoted to helping everyone separate at the same time.

Martin betrays no mixed emotions; he is openly smitten. He beams the sort of paternal pride I wanted so badly to see on the face beside me at every Christmas pageant and band concert I ever attended by myself. It is so clear that he loves her the way I do—insanely—that I say, "I miss her."

"Of course you do."

"She'll never be little again."

"No, she never will."

"She'll never grow up with a father."

"She won't."

"This part is over."

"But a new part is starting."

"I'm not ready for the old one to end. I never taught her to change a tire."

"Cell phones."

"She has no idea how to check for a tripped switch in the fuse box."

"Google."

"God, look at her." Like so much else that seems to be happening without my permission, tears start running down my face. I squeegee them away. "I didn't even think she was listening. I thought she hated my stories. Shit, I thought she hated cooking. What else don't I know about the person I love the most in the whole world?"

"You know all the important stuff."

"But this?" I hold my hand out to indicate the entire world that my daughter has created without my knowledge.

Martin asks, "Do the roots know the tree that grows above them?"

I wrinkle my eyebrows in warning and he hurries to add, "That's not from Next."

"In that case, it's not a bad metaphor."

"Okay, it *is* from Next."

"You, Martin Lightsey, you are such a jackass!"

"Oh, we have firmly established my jackassnificence already, haven't we?"

I laugh. Martin could always make me laugh.

I want him to hold me. I want for us to have raised the daughter we're watching over now. I want for us to have raised her together amid a happy bounty of friends and families.

But laughing . . . laughing transports me to a place that is neither before nor after sixteen years ago but only right now, watching our beautiful girl dancing in the spotlight, doing what makes her happy.

Laughing is good. For right now, this one, singular moment, laughing is enough.

My biceps quiver from carrying a thirty-pound box of produce. I crunch across the frozen earth and pause, momentarily blinded by both the cloud of my breath, frozen in the early-morning air, and by the long, shaggy bangs that I forgot to pin back hanging down over my eyes. I rest the heavy box of exotic lettuces, hothouse heritage tomatoes, and high-dollar oranges on the tops of my thighs, catch my breath, and try to flip the damn bangs out of my eyes.

Up ahead is the back of the trailer. The door at the end is open and I can hear the clack of a metal spoon against a metal bowl, the thump of the big cutting board being lowered onto the counter, the murmur of requests, the morning chitchat of a business waking up.

All the trash cans behind the trailer are full, which means that business was booming yesterday. There are more red-and-white Coke cups strewn about than the Styrofoam cups they use for the hot mint tea: a clue that high school customers must have outnumbered the galloping gourmets, those intrepid Tweeters willing to travel for the hot new thing who have continued to create a following for FalaFellows since the opening five months ago.

Aubrey and Tyler also added "Ty-Mo's" to the business's name which, somehow, made the strange terrorist food more acceptable, so that all the fans of the biggest football hero Parkhaven ever produced, along with jocks and princesses, past and present, started coming. They joined the emo kids and alternative crowd who are drawn to sample delights from the land of hookahs and hashish. And for the first time in Parkhaven history, those two elements are sitting down and eating mashed chickpeas together.

Aubrey called this morning in a panic because her produce order wasn't ready when she went to pick it up, and time to get the lunch prep done was running out. It is MLK Day, and that means that a lot of the food bloggers have the day off and have already written that they are making the trek out to "the 'burbs." So, Aubrey had pleaded, could I please, please, please, please, please bring the order by on my way to work?

Every month that Aubrey has been in business seems to add another "please" to her requests. I had initially been stunned by just one. Five in a row seems like a minor miracle. At Christmas she'd come over and we'd made cookies. Six kinds. The Snicker Doodles had sold surprisingly well. I suggested that we sell chocolate-dipped strawberries at Valentine's. She loved the idea.

Every week, Tyler drops by and gives me 10 percent of what they made. He and Aubrey rent a garage apartment and spend almost nothing. Tyler has surprised me in many ways. He seems to have no material needs. And he's able to fix anything. I've been tempted to ask them to move in with me but have resisted. I've come to look on this as Aubrey's gap year. One that, it appears, I'm not going to have to pay for.

I heft the box of produce up again, lug it as far as the closest table, and drop it. Tyler can take it from here.

I start to yell for Tyler when the pleasant hum from the trailer stops and Tyler, his voice bristling with sudden anger, explodes, "No! You're kidding! You think we'd even be in business if I hadn't put my name out there? You think half of Parkhaven High is coming because of refried bean balls?"

"Wow, that is such a shitty thing to say," Aubrey snaps back. "What happened to building a dream together? Doing this the way we wanted to do it?"

I consider leaving the box and sneaking away, but the edges of the lettuce are already starting to turn black.

"The way *we* want? Try the way your father wants."

"What does my father have to do with this?"

"Pretty much everything. You have let him, a guy who ditched you when you were two years old, totally change you."

"I am not letting my father change me."

"Okay, whatever you say, but every time you have one of your little meetings with him, you come back with some new grand plan."

"Tyler, he knows how to start businesses. How to build a customer base. He helped one of the people he counseled start a *chain* of food trailers in L.A. Plus, P.S., he's my father. We're catching up on sixteen years."

I've seen how much Martin loves helping his daughter. And, it's true: All of his advice has been good. He really does know how to build and run a business.

"And that's fine, Aubs, it really is."

I try to recall when Aubrey stopped being A.J.

"I totally respect that. He's a cool guy and all. Getting the foodies to come out. Writing about us. That is cool. I mean, a shitload of work for, I'm not sure, a lot of payoff, but it's cool."

"Tyler, every idea he's given us has worked. It was his idea to put your name out there. Can we talk about this later?"

" 'Later'? There is no 'later' anymore, now that you're taking classes three nights a week. Then either doing homework or with your dad the rest of the time."

"Where is this coming from? You always said you supported me taking classes. One of us has to get some business skills if we ever want to grow this business."

"Right, and the *biology class* you're taking is going to help us how?"

"I'm getting prerequisites out of the way. You can't just waltz into the business courses."

"What was wrong with us just going out to the sites? We had guaranteed customers. A set menu. A set food order. Easy. Breezy."

"You're kidding. Tell me you are not seriously saying that we should be out on some construction site nuking crap food for the tool belts?"

"So this is better? Making bean burritos for hipsters?"

"You said you loved my falafel."

" 'Love'? How is it possible to 'love' refried beans?"

"God, condescend much? Tyler, this is what I want to do. I like this. I'm good at it, and people—people who know—recognize that I'm good at it. We're getting a buzz going. Look, we have got to get back to work. We are never going to be ready for lunch rush."

Tyler mutters something I can't hear and, for a second, the breath sticks in my chest.

"No, Tyler, seriously, I mean it, we have got to get back to work. Now!"

"Mmm, I like it when you get all boss-lady on me. You are definitely getting *my* buzz going."

"Tyler, no! Stop it!"

Aubrey laughs and the tension pressing in on me disappears.

"Ty, no, we can't."

"Oh, you know that we can."

"We're behind already."

"Did you just say you want it from behind? Because we can definitely go there."

"We're not off in the middle of nowhere anymore at some construction site. Someone might hear us."

"Then you're going to have to not scream so much."

"We'll have to bleach the counters again."

"Call me Mr. Clean."

The trailer door slams shut. I leave the box of produce on a table. The lettuce will survive. I hurry now. I'm late for work.

D riving to the hospital, I stop at the four-way sign beside Parkhaven High. The marching band was picked to compete in the Grand National Marching Band competition to be held next month in Sarasota. Consequently, Shupe has them all out trooping up and down the frozen field. The white plumes on their tricornered hats bounce and sparkle in the chilly sunshine and, instead of wishing I hadn't teased Aubrey about the hat, I just remember how happy she was swinging along behind her clarinet, part of that jolly feathered beast.

I drive away slowly, angling my side-view mirror so that I can watch the band. Captured within the silver frame of the mirror, the marchers shrink and motion blurs as I leave them behind. Soon the bright plumes become an indistinct fuzz, like the down of all baby birds. Like the soft, vulnerable fluff of the young that is bound to be shed even if the mama bird frets over the loss of every single gossamer puff.

At Parkhaven Medical Center the tall glass doors slide open and a cloud of warmth whooshes out as I step inside. The vast expanse of travertine flooring between the two banks of elevators is congested, and I have to navigate around a middle-aged woman crimping her step to match her mother's, who is struggling with an aluminum walker. Once free of the crush at the door, I hurry past the information desk, the gift shop, the waiting area. The smell of enchiladas coming from the cafeteria makes me consider ditching the bagel smeared with peanut butter I brought for lunch.

I pass the public areas and veer off onto a hallway that opens into the old part of the hospital. The travertine gives way to beige linoleum. Fluorescent fixtures buzz overhead. I dig for the key to my office. My *new* office. It took two months to talk admin into setting aside what used to be a supply closet so Janis, the other LC, and I could have an office, but in the end we won.

I hang up the big, pillowy jacket that Aubrey rejected and I've adopted, delighted to finally have a truly warm jacket, lock my purse in an empty file drawer, and log in on the hospital's system. I am hunting for the day's census sheet when Janis bursts in gripping a bakery bag in one hand and holding out a clipboard with the other. "This what you're looking for?" She is wearing, of course, animal-print scrubs. Cheetah, I think.

I take the clipboard, nod at the bag in her hand. "That looks dangerous."

"It's from the short fren in twenty-four twelve." Janis uses our shorthand for "frenulum," the bit of skin tethering the tongue to the floor of the mouth. When it's too short, it can hobble the tongue, making nursing hard.

Janis extracts a chocolate-chip cookie the size of a minipizza from the white bag and breaks it in two. I take half, hold it up, and wonder, "Why do our patients never express gratitude through a nice bowl of edamame? Maybe a perfect cantaloupe?" After the first bite, I answer my own question, "Okay, that's why. Because love runs on sugar and butter. What have we got?"

We review the census sheets together. Everyone that Janis has already seen that morning is highlighted in blue. Those who still need attention are highlighted in yellow.

Janis rushes through them in her haste to ask, "So?"

"So what?" I echo, knowing exactly what she's referring to.

"So, last night? Martin? Details?"

Before I have to dodge her question, Janis's cell rings. She checks the number and groans. "If that boy forgot his homework or lunch or head again, I will scream." She slides the phone open and murmurs to her nine-year-old son, "Hey, punkin, what's up?"

I wave the cookie in the general direction of the hospital's Mother/Baby Unit upstairs, signaling that I'm heading to work. Janis nods, covers the phone, orders me, "Details. Tomorrow. You have to tell me *everything*."

I nod, pretending that I will, and leave Janis asking her son, "Okay, so if you're 'three thousand percent' certain that put your book report in your backpack, is there a chance you left it on the bus?"

The morning after Aubrey's grand opening five months ago, I woke up refreshed from the first really good night's sleep I'd gotten since she met Tyler. I walked into the great room and wondered why I had stopped allowing myself to appreciate the glorious light streaming in. I brewed a cup of Earl Grey tea, returned to the room that I now found, indeed, great, sat on the sofa, and watched a Milky Way of dust motes float through the radiance. Each particle was so precise and perfect, it was as if I'd had the prescription in my glasses strengthened.

The celestial stream whirled past and I thought about how I'd stopped drinking coffee. Bobbi Mac had gotten me hooked when I was ten. Just a few tablespoons in the morning with lots of milk and sugar, "to get the heart started." In Europe, Martin and I had bonded over coffee, me proving to him how inherently sophisticated I was by learning to drink it the way he did, without the three spoons of sugar and half a pitcher of cream that I liked. In Sycamore Heights, coffee became a fetish—arabica, robusta, Jamaican Blue Mountain. I could not have imagined life without coffee any more than I could have imagined life without Martin.

And then, from the instant his sperm seduced my egg, coffee sickened me. One morning I craved it; the very next the smell nauseated me. Coffee became one more thing that Martin and I no longer had in common. In my fifth month, I tried to reclaim that bond and drank a cup of Kona Peaberry. I threw up longer and harder than I had during the morning-sickness months and never repeated the experiment.

Sipping Earl Grey in the great room that morning last August, I thought about Martin, about the life he had denied me, and I waited to be kneecapped by the rage and the sense of betrayal that usually skulked along with the topic. As with coffee, though, my craving for such a dark brew had vanished overnight.

Late that afternoon, Martin took a cab from the Candlewood Suites where he'd taken a long-term rental, stood on my porch, and very solemnly asked me out to dinner.

"How about a walk?" I suggested. "Maybe we can work up to dinner."

Martin had let out the smallest exhalation. Just enough that I could see that he was sufficiently nervous to be relieved. "A walk would be good."

We ambled around the Parkhaven reservoir and Martin asked, "Remember coming here? Pushing Aubrey in her stroller? How she used to say 'dug' for 'duck'?"

The answer I would have given him on any day of the past sixteen years would have been a dark, rich house blend of rage, grievance, and sarcasm. *No, there are just so many happy family memories to draw on that I lose track.* Or, wounded and accusing, I would have demanded, *What about all the times I was out here alone and she held her arms out to every male over ten and under seventy and said, "Daddy"?* And the walk would have been ruined.

But that day, on what turned out to be the first of many walks, I just said yes, I did remember, and was happy to have someone by my side who also remembered that our daughter used to say "dugs" for "ducks."

I step out of the elevator on the fifth floor, the Mother/Baby Unit. Beneath the odors of cleansers and sanitizers, machines and humans, I always catch a whiff of caramel. Though no one else I've ever pointed it out to can discern the sweet fragrance, I smell the caramel scent I first noticed on Aubrey's breath, exhaled on the milky breath of all the nursing infants on this floor.

One of my favorite maternity nurses, Celeste, a stocky Latina with the biceps of a Rumanian weight lifter, is at the nurses' station. "Cute top," Celeste trills. "You got a hot date after work?"

"If you consider Martin coming over to replace the hot-water heater a date, then yes, I have a date."

"I do!"

Like Janis, like the rest of my coworkers, like Dori, Celeste wants more "details" about Martin and me. They want to know what it means that I am "dating" my ex-husband, the father of my child, a man who once palled around with movie stars and who now spends his evenings repairing my hot-water heater and his days counseling a growing list of ex-Nextarians who, like Martin, hate the organization but still believe in "the tech." He makes a living working with some of them in person, many more around the country by phone, on Skype. Apparently in this underground railroad of "neXters," Martin has become Sojourner Truth.

I don't pry. I accept his life the way I've learned to accept Aubrey's. The way I accept the walks we take around the reservoir; the dinners we make together and eat in the great room at the long dining table; the trip he's planning because he wants to show me Sanibel Island in Florida; the sex—I accept it all. I can't recall consciously deciding to trick time, but that is what has happened. Somehow Martin and I, instead of being leashed for all eternity to what happened sixteen years ago, instead of that being the huge Before and After defining my life, have been set free. Sometimes he's the boy I met on the train. Mostly, though, he's a man I like being with who took a different route than I did to arrive back at us together.

None of this can be boiled down into a coworker-ready sound bite. Celeste's eagerness to move me from the perplexing limbo of a friend who may or may not be sleeping with her ex-husband into a known state of couplehood makes me understand how Aubrey felt when I grilled her about Tyler: It's too soon. I don't know. I might never know. And since I can't *not* be with him, it doesn't matter.

Dori, meanwhile, acts like she predicted the whole thing. "I told you," she reminds me regularly. "Didn't I tell you about the rekindled romance? Plus, remember: They're incredibly successful, these reunited relationships."

"Yeah, the mutual-delusion thing," I tell her, not adding what a big fan of delusion I've become.

Celeste, seeing that no "details" will be forthcoming, chirps, "Cute top. I love flutter sleeves. My shoulders are too broad for tops like that."

"Not true. Look at Michelle Obama. Show off the big guns."

"Well, some of us have to wear scrubs."

I gauge how much of a barbed edge there is in Celeste's comment. When I stopped wearing scrubs to work some of the nurses became grumpy about my defection from the ranks. I was called in to human resources and "counseled" that street clothes were "unprofessional." I had responded that "professional" was the last thing that a brand-new mom oozing colostrum and amniotic fluid and tears needed. If they were unhappy about my performance, I'd talk about that; otherwise, I had patients to see.

I guess I was feeling sassy because Martin was doing the same kinds of magical things on the Web for me and my practice that he had done for Aubrey and FalaFellows and I had more new patients than I could handle. If the hospital wanted to fire me, fine. But I was through wearing scrubs.

As I leave the nurses' station, I flap my arms so that my sleeves become tiny wings, rising and falling against my shoulders, carrying me away. Celeste can laugh or not, as she chooses. She laughs.

The first patient on my list is Ruth Lange. Outside Ruth's room, I study the notes left by the labor-and-delivery nurse. Ruth, twenty-six years old, had a baby boy, Levi, her first child, last night at 9:23. Levi was forty-one weeks at delivery and a brawny nine pounds, six ounces. I check Ruth's height and weight, five-four, 118 pounds, and wince: big baby, little mom. I note the number of poops, pees, minutes spent nursing, drop what's left of the cookie in the trash, hit the hand sanitizer, and shoulder the door open.

"I love that positioning," I announce the instant I step in the room and see Ruth holding Levi in a nice, comfy cross-cradle. Ruth is propped up in bed, her surgical gown open, exposing both breasts, a paperback copy of the New Testament open beside her. For a pale blond, Ruth's nipples are large and dark, with mud-puppy speckling at the edges. The deep blue veins running beneath her skin please me; good vascularization means a good milk supply. I'm not happy that Ruth is in bed, but we'll get to that in a second.

I introduce myself, ask, "May I?" and slip a finger in where Levi's toothless gums meet Ruth's nipple. "Oh, that is a good, deep latch."

Dad is seated at a small table on the other side of the room, playing a video game on his laptop. He's hunched over, keeping the volume low, but the sound of his feverish clicking combined with mechanized beeps and explosions and a voice commanding, "Bring it on, alien scumwad!" still echoes through the room.

It always baffles me when anyone around a newborn, barely dry after their swim from the other side, is not entranced by the only miracle they will ever be part of, yet I have witnessed more celestial voyagers welcomed into this world with Nelly ringtones and *WWE SmackDown* than I can count. Trying to ignore the destruction of a distant galaxy, I concentrate on Levi working steadily at Ruth's breast and hear the happy pattern I always want to hear—*suck, suck, gasp, swallow. Suck, suck, gasp, swallow.*

"Oh, this boy knows what to do." I lift the well-upholstered arm Levi rests lightly on Ruth's breast and let it droop back down. "See that? See how floppy it is? A hungry baby won't do that. A hungry baby keeps his fist balled up tight next to his face."

Ruth beams at her extraordinary son. Never has there been a baby like this.

"Are you feeling some good cramping?"

Ruth pulls her gaze from her baby and looks up at me. She has the sweet, besotted expression of a new mother insanely in love with her baby. "What?"

"Do you need to change your pad after you nurse?"

She nods.

"Good, your uterus is contracting. That's good."

Ruth dips her head, smiles at Levi as he grips her index finger. "He was turned around. They had to do a third-degree episiotomy."

"Oh, no. Baby."

Ruth gives a glum nod. "The doctor stuck the forceps in there and pulled him out."

"In that case, we have to get you into a better feeding position. Dad. Dad!" The father glances up from the computer screen, looks around the room, wondering why someone is calling for his father; then there is the stunned, scared look when he remembers.

"What's your name, hon?" I ask him.

"Eric."

"Eric . . ." A series of explosions burst from his video game. "Do you mind?" I waggle a finger toward the laptop. Eric snaps it shut, and the otherworldly calm a room with an infant in it can take on settles over us. "Let's get Ruth into a more comfortable position."

I wedge my finger between Levi's mouth and Ruth's breast. The suction breaks with a slurpy pop. I lift Levi away and, no matter how many hundreds of newborns I hold each year, this baby becomes Aubrey, with her furze of golden down like a halo around her head, and I am holding her again for the first time.

The father, his eyes skittering about, stands by and watches as his wife tries to lower herself into the chair.

"Eric, lend Ruth some of that upper-body strength."

Eric snaps to and helps Ruth. Awkwardly, he pokes pillows into all the wrong spots. I throw out a problem I know he can solve: "We need to get the weight off that incision. The higher you can get those knees, the better."

He rushes to haul over the chair he'd been sitting on to play video games and gently raises Ruth's feet onto it.

I nod. "Eric, that looks good." I make serious eye contact with him and give him his assignment: "No bed feeds at home, okay?"

"Not a problem. We've got this really great recliner."

"Good." I tell Eric to wash his hands. When he finishes, I place his son in his arms. Eric tenses, holds his breath, but the stunned, disengaged look has vanished, along with my fears about the newest of my fathers. Like all of them, he just needs to know what to do. Once it was saving the world from invading aliens and now it will be raising a fine son. Levi starts fussing and Eric glances up, panicked.

"Put your pinkie in Levi's mouth."

Eric looks to Ruth. Nestled onto her pillows, regal as a queen, she nods her permission.

Eric slips the end of his little finger into Levi's mouth, and his eyes pop when he feels his son apply himself to his pinkie.

"That is intense, isn't it?"

The new father nods, surrendering completely to the terrifying power of the life he created.

"There's your low-tech pacifier. You'll need that. Ruth won't want to hear Levi screaming when she goes to the bathroom. Number two is the dread of every small mom who has had a giant baby. All right, Ruth, are you ready?"

Again the queen-mother nod and Eric, careful as a bomb squad, lowers the baby into his wife's arms.

When Levi is snuggled in, I coach, "Ruth, bring his chin in deep. Make sure his lower lip is out."

I watch for a few minutes, jot down some notes, tell the new father, "Eric, set up the perfect spot for chair feedings. Keep the weight off that incision. See to it that Ruth has plenty to drink. Mostly water. Be there to take over when Ruth needs to rest."

I head for the door. "I'm not worried about you three," I say, pushing the door open with my back, but they are too engrossed in the new family they are creating to notice my benediction.

Out in the hall, Celeste calls to me, "Mom in twenty thirty-four asked for a consult."

I check my list. "I don't have her down. Did she take a class or something?"

"Didn't mention it. I think she's just another Cam fan. She demanded in no uncertain terms that she had to see you and only you. Very 'empowered,' " Celeste adds, hooking quote marks around the word. "Certainly fits your fan-club profile."

"Get out," I protest, but it's true. For the past few months, I've been even more passionate than I already was about all mothers getting what they want. My students, in turn, seem to have become equally passionate that I be part of that. The recent appearance of this "fan club" has helped me do my job the way I truly want to do it. "What 'profile'?" I ask Celeste.

"You know, tattoos, had to remove a piercing from a *very* tender place for delivery. And, uh, incidentally, ow. Anyway, you know, one of yours."

One of mine.

"Sorry, haven't even finished charting her yet. Basics are prima gravida. Five, fourteen. Not eating."

"Thanks." I hurry off, knowing that 2034 is a first-time mom who had a scrawny five-pound, fourteen-ounce baby that doesn't want to nurse. Outside her room, I rub in sanitizer, shove the door open with my hip, and meet my next patient.

The new mother—young, painfully young; lovely copper-colored hair twisted into dreadlocks that droop from her head like a jester's cap; plump arms sleeved with tattoos of anime princesses and a wizard trailing stardust—has her head down and doesn't notice me enter. Her breasts, rosy as Pink Lady apples, are exposed, offered to the infant in her arms. She lifts her head. Fairy wings beat in my memory and a little girl with a voice like Ethel Merman, as dreamy as she was brassy, looks up at me. My head fills with the smell of cinnamon, sugar, and butter from the endless pieces of cinnamon toast with the crusts cut off that I made for her and Aubrey to eat.

"Twyla, you came home."

Twyla nods, holds her free arm out to me, and I hug Dori's daughter and Dori's granddaughter. Twyla smells of labor, the hard, painful work of dragging a new soul onto this earth. Her baby smells like the reward. Running beneath both those scents is a fragrance as essential as newly cut wood that defined Twyla for me from the instant I first put my nose into her auburn curls a dozen years ago.

"You have a baby."

"Yeah, you pretty much have to have one to get in here." Twyla has grown into her husky voice; it fits her now. "I remembered that this is where you worked. I waited until my baby was already coming, so they had to admit me. I wanted to get her started right."

"Can I have a look?"

She nods, and, gently, I peel the soft flannel of the receiving blanket away from Twyla's daughter's face. She has given birth to a fairy baby as enchanted as the ones she and Aubrey once pretended to be. Her tiny lips are a perfect Gummi Bear pucker of cherry. Her squinted eyes twitch as she follows the dreams of a newborn waking to an unimaginably alien life.

"Oh, Twyla," I whisper. "She's beautiful."

A princess released momentarily from an evil spell, Twyla sheds the jittery rage she had once been armored in and glows with a simple serene radiance.

"What's her name?"

Tenderly as if she were stroking a soap bubble, Twyla runs the backs of her fingernails against her baby's cheek. "Aubrey. I always liked that name."

"Yeah, me too."

"Doesn't she remind you of Aubrey? The way she used to be? All shy and delicate."

"She does."

"I know she'll change, but who she is, right now, that's never really going to change, right?"

I think how whole and entire every newborn I've ever seen has been. The ones who enter the world, mouths open, howling, ready to devour whatever life brings their way. The ones who question and hold back. Aubrey showed me everything I needed to know about her from the first instant we met. Though it will take me what is left of my life to fully understand what that was, Aubrey was Aubrey from her first breath.

I tell Twyla, "No, that's never really going to change. Does your mom know you're here?"

"Uh-uh. I can't deal with her energy right now. She's so hectic. Does Aubrey still say 'hectic' all the time?"

Before I can answer, Twyla announces, "I'm going to be the kind of mom you were."

"What kind of mom was I?"

"Calm. You were always calm. Calm Cam."

"Cammando"? Now this? Calm Cam? I can't recall one moment of calmness while Aubrey was growing up that I didn't fake.

"You probably want to know what happened with my dad," Twyla goes on. "I left there months ago. He's an asshole. My mom got that much right."

"So you've . . ."

"Pretty much been on the street."

"Oh, Twyla."

"Then there was this little niblet." She lowers her nose to baby Aubrey's head, closes her eyes, and breathes. "So I went to Snowflakes, this Christian adoption agency. I had to tell them that if they didn't take me, I'd get an abortion. They still wouldn't let me in, though, until I signed a paper promising that I'd give my baby up to a 'fit Christian family.' That was fair. Seven months ago? I shouldn't have been raising an iguana. In fact, I *tried* to raise an iguana."

"So what happened?"

"He died."

"Not the iguana. The adoption."

"Oh, right, like I was ever going to let *that* happen." Twyla is her old, brash self as she gives a snort of derision. "No, they thought they had this ultratight security system. All high-tech James Bond and everything. Locked us in at night. But it was a joke. I stayed until I was ready. Until my baby was ready. Had all the extra dairy and folic acid and prenatal care you could dream of. Read every book they had. Just soaked it all up, then left when it was time to come back here."

Aubrey mewls weakly. Twyla tenses and places the newborn's mouth over her nipple. The scrawny infant simply lies quietly in Twyla's arms, her lovely goldfish lips barely resting on her mother's breast. I help Twyla express a drop of the first milk, so thick that I always think of it as nectar.

"That's colostrum, right?"

"Yes, it is," I answer, tucking Aubrey's head down to encourage her to latch. "Come on, baby girl. The umbilical cord is gone; this is how we eat now."

"You need this," Twyla coos to her child. "This will give you all my very best antibodies and immunoglobulins and help you get rid of that nasty meconium."

I remember what a smart girl Twyla was, able to sing entire songs after hearing them once.

Aubrey shows no interest in nursing. Twyla glances up, a spike of panic bringing back the familiar jitteriness, and asks, "Colostrum is the best thing to prevent jaundice, isn't it? If she doesn't nurse, her bilirubin levels are going to get dangerously high and the nurses will make me give her formula."

"You've been doing your homework. Sweetie, don't worry. Your nipples are just a little inverted is all."

"I know," Twyla moans. "I've got innie nips. I knew this wasn't going to work. The nurse told me they'd put her on formula if she didn't start. I'm going to have to feed her out of a can. Dori didn't nurse me and look what happened. It's ruined. It's all ruined."

"Twyla, nothing is ruined. This baby is going to nurse. Come on. The bed is a hard place to start. You're both healthy. Let's sit up in a chair and feel healthy and strong."

When Twyla is comfortably roosted on a chair, I settle Aubrey into her arms and notice how worryingly dry her lips are. Infants become dehydrated in such a short amount of time. Aubrey's whimpers begin to take on a shrill, dire edge as hunger sharpens.

Though nothing ever flusters me at work, this is different. This is Twyla. And a baby named Aubrey. So, though I make a show of sauntering out in a way that I hope projects calm assurance, once outside Twyla's door, I race to the supply closet and paw madly through the small plastic bins until I find a feeding pack. I grab a pumping machine and push it in front of me back to the room. Aubrey is blubbering by the time I return.

"Look, she's given up," Twyla wails. Aubrey is huddled against her; her hands with their matching bracelets of flaking skin are fisted up next to her face.

I hold up a nipple shield. "You are about to become an outie, Mama." I poke the cone inward, press it against Twyla's breast, then pop it out. Her nipple, sucked into the shield, comes with it.

"All right, now we'll just get you hooked up here." In less than a minute, I've pumped out ten ccs of colostrum.

"Now, I don't do this very often, but for Aubrey's namesake . . ." I peel the rubber band off the feeding pack, tear into the plastic wrap, fit a small, curved plastic tip onto a syringe, and use it to suck up some of Twyla's milk. Then, like feeding a baby bird, I squirt a few drops into Aubrey's mouth.

The milk dribbles untasted over her lips and I start to worry. I imagine the doctors, nurses, teachers, counselors, every authority that Twyla will encounter from here on out. How they will take one look at her and see nothing but young, unmarried, tattooed, and they will dismiss her. They aren't going to realize that Twyla knows about folic acid and meconium. That she can sing the entire sound track from *Moulin Rouge*. They'll automatically assume she's not up to the challenge. They'll peg her as a mom who'd use formula. And their beginning—mother and daughter—will be marred.

"No." I say the word out loud. Twyla, who did not have so many of the things that a dreamy, fairy-winged little girl like her should have had, must have this.

I pluck the cap off Aubrey's head and beating there is the part left unarmored, the fontanel. "Wake up, little one." I chafe my knuckles against the rose petal of her ear.

Twyla stops my hand. "What are you doing?"

"She has to wake up and eat."

I worry her ear some more and Aubrey scrunches her face up.

"You're hurting her."

I squirt two more drops of colostrum into Aubrey's mouth. She retreats farther from the assault of light and noise and liquid. I jiggle her diaper, the tiny body within a rustle of motion. "Sorry, schnooks, it's time to go to work. Life begins now. It's hard, I know; it's hard."

"Don't." Twyla grabs my hand. "Call the nurse. She doesn't know what to do. Don't ask her to do something she doesn't know how to do."

"She knows," I coo to Aubrey. "You know what to do, don't you?"

I tickle Aubrey's armpit. "Hey, boo-boo. I know you want to go home, back to where it was dark and warm and safe and you didn't have to work for a living. I wish that was a choice, but it's not."

I make Twyla shift to a football hold, take Aubrey's shirt off, tickle her back, but she only squinches up more tightly against this assault. There will be so many hard things in this child's life and I haven't been able to hold the first one off. Out of pure stubbornness, I give Aubrey one last hummingbird sip of milk.

Her lower lip trembles. The fragile hinging of her jaw shifts.

"Twyla, look, she's swallowing."

I rush to snug Aubrey tight up against Twyla's breast and let the next squirt trickle down over her nipple and into the baby's mouth. Her lips contract into the tiniest of smacks.

"She likes it." Twyla is tremulous.

As she swallows a few more drops, I whisper to my child's namesake, "The first of untold numbers of sweet things you will taste in this life." It is my blessing. Laying out a trail of milk drops, I lure Aubrey to Twyla's nipple.

"Line her up. Skin to skin," I coach, snuggling the whisper of a body against her mother's. "Wait for what looks like a yawn. There. There it is." Aubrey opens her mouth and I nudge her between the shoulder blades, pushing her open mouth onto Twyla's nipple.

"Oh, lovely. That is a picture-perfect latch. Your daughter is a genius."

The baby sucks. Aubrey's chin bobs rhythmically against Twyla's breast.

"Is it working?" Twyla asks. "Is anything coming out?"

"Listen."

The only sound in the universe for the next few seconds is the satisfied *suck-suck-gasp-swallow* of Twyla's daughter.

"I'm feeding her," Twyla marvels. "I'm feeding my baby."

"Yes, you are."

A strangled yip of a sob escapes Twyla. "I thought she hated me. She doesn't hate me." Twyla finally relaxes and strokes her daughter's face, the top of her head where the beat of life remains visible, and I remember the first time I held Aubrey and touched that emblem of her vulnerability. I made a pact in that instant. The same one that my mother, Rose, with all her heart and as best she knew how, had made when she first held me. The same one that Bobbi Mac made more than six decades ago and that Aubrey will one day make: You will be mine forever and I will never let anything hurt you.

Twyla strokes her child's hair and declares fiercely, "I am going to be the best fucking mother there ever was."

I tell the little girl who sang answers to questions about waffles, "You'll be the best mother you know how to be. Just like your mother was the best mother she knew how to be and wasn't always. Just like you won't always be. So forgive her, Twyla, okay? Forgive your mother, forgive everyone, but most of all, forgive yourself. Okay, sweetie?"

Twyla doesn't answer. She will do everything right; she is certain of it. Everything her mother did, she will do the opposite and it will all be right. We watch in silence as her daughter sips her first meal.

Without lifting her eyes from her daughter's face, Twyla asks, "How is Aubrey?"

As I consider the answer to that question, the conversation I'd overheard outside the trailer plays and replays in my mind. Tyler's voice. Aubrey's. Tyler's. Aubrey's. Gradually, the words blur away. In their place, I hear the language of tones and tenors, pitches and accents that Aubrey and I taught each other. Translated into that language I hear a young woman gathering strength to burst from the silver chrysalis that contains her now.

I tell Twyla all about what her old friend is doing.

"Wow," she says. "I was certain that Aubrey would be all, 'Go, college'!"

"Certain and humans," I muse. "Such a hard mix."

"Oh, look," Twyla exclaims. Aubrey has started sucking ferociously. "She's really going for it now!" With food in her minuscule stomach, Aubrey becomes a different baby, a baby who applies herself to the job at hand with exactly the sort of determined energy she will need to be One Shot's Never Enough's granddaughter.

When Aubrey's walnut of a fist finally unclenches, then droops to the side and her head lolls back, I put a full, fed, contented baby in the bassinet beside Twyla's bed and they both sleep.

Out in the hall, I call Dori and tell her that Twyla is back. I tell her that her daughter is safe and that she is a grandmother.

"They're sleeping now, so you have time to collect yourself. Be calm when you come."

Dori is sobbing too hard to answer. I tell her I'll wait for her outside.

Later, as I watch for Dori in the pickup/dropoff zone, the cold wind blows my hair around my head. I dig in my pocket, find the rubber band I pulled off Twyla's feeding kit, and use it to slick the tangling hair into a ponytail. For the first time since I cut the ill-advised bangs, they smooth back neatly with all the rest of my hair.

It feels great to have those damn Mamie Eisenhower bangs out of my eyes.

ACKNOWLEDGMENTS

I am indebted to the Dobie-Paisano Fellowship at the University of Texas, the Johnston Foundation, and the Texas Institute of Letters for giving me the support and sanctuary I needed to finish *The Gap Year*. In particular, I must thank Michael Adams, the Saint Francis of writers, for allowing me to light awhile on his shoulder.

Kristine Kovach inspired me with her humor, empathy, and vast expertise as a lactation consultant. She was extraordinarily generous in allowing me to shadow her on her hospital rounds, audit her classes, and steal juicy chunks of her great material.

Thank you, Gabriel Bird-Jones, for understanding that the only child going off to college in this book isn't you.

Tiffany Yates, super copy editor, supermodel, it was a happy day for me when you stepped into the Hyde Park Theater.

The book benefited immeasurably from the insights of early readers Kristine Kovach, Robin Chotzinoff (no relation to Dori), Carol Dawson, Caroline Zancan, Mary Helen Specht, Cora Walters, Gabriel Bird-Jones, Kathleen Orillion, Mary Lengel, Sarah Farr, Christy Krames, and *mis hermanitas,* Martha and Kay Bird.

Knopf is the best there is. I am grateful that Patricia Johnson and Christine Gillespie connected with the book; that Caroline Zancan kept it on schedule; that Kathleen Fridella guaranteed that all the infelicities were corrected; that Iris Weinstein created an elegant design; that Barbara de Wilde captured the book's essence in a lyrical jacket; that Kim Thornton will help readers find it.

There would be no novel, no career, without Ann Close and Kristine Dahl, editor, agent, true friends. Ann, you always find the narrative fulcrum where even a minor shifting of the load brings it all into balance. Kris, thank you for getting me through this summer. No writer has ever been luckier.

And always, always, always to my sweet G-Men, George and Gabriel.

A NOTE ABOUT THE AUTHOR

Sarah Bird is the author of seven previous novels: *How Perfect Is That*, *The Flamenco Academy*, *The Yokota Officers Club*, *Virgin of the Rodeo*, *The Mommy Club*, *The Boyfriend School*, and *Alamo House*. She lives in Austin, Texas.

A NOTE ON THE TYPE

Part of this book was set in Caledonia, a Linotype face
designed by W. A. Dwiggins (1880–1956). It belongs to the
family of printing types called "modern face" by printers—
a term used to mark the change in style of the type letters
that occurred around 1800.

Part of this book was set in Myriad, a humanist sans-serif
typeface designed by Robert Slimbach and Carol Twombly for
Adobe Systems. The typeface is best known for its usage by
Apple Inc., replacing Apple Garamond as Apple's corporate font
since 2002. Myriad is easily distinguished from other sans-serif
fonts due to its special "y" descender (tail) and slanting "e" cut.

COMPOSED BY *Creative Graphics, Allentown, Pennsylvania*
PRINTED AND BOUND BY *Berryville Graphics, Berryville, Virginia*
DESIGNED BY *Iris Weinstein*